Praise for the no

"All of the elements that [....] romantic suspense nove[....] eye-popping read manifest th[.... th]ere—a feverish romance, a pervasive sense of danger, and an exhilarating chase full of adrenaline-fueled encounters ... few romantic suspense authors know how to write a chase sequence as thrillingly as Squires."

—*Publishers Weekly* on *No More Lies*

"Squires' fast-paced conspiracy novel gives readers a run for their money, and then some."

—*Booklist* on *No More Lies*

"Readers of such historical titles as Claudia Dain's *To Burn* will enjoy Squires' epic style and unforgettable characters."

—*Booklist* on *Danelaw*

"Electrifying and sensual sci-fi romance ... Squires' deft plotting and full-bodied characters make this whirlwind adventure worthwhile."

—*Publishers Weekly* on *Body Electric*

"Wow! Susan Squires gives her readers a breathless hardcore ride in her latest, *Body Electric*."

—*Romantic Times* Top Pick on *Body Electric*

"*Body Electric* is dynamite. It keeps you on the edge of your seat even while it makes you think—and it does it with great characters and a zing of sensuality. This book is a ripping good read. I couldn't put it down."

—Catherine Asaro, on *Body Electric*

MORE...

The COMPANION

Susan Squires

St. Martin's Paperbacks

THE COMPANION

Copyright © 2004 by Susan Squires.

All rights reserved. No part of this book may be used or reproduced in any manner whatsoever without written permission except in the case of brief quotations embodied in critical articles or reviews. For information address St. Martin's Press, 175 Fifth Avenue, New York, NY 10010.

ISBN: 0-312-99853-8
EAN: 80312-99853-0

Printed in the United States of America

St. Martin's Paperbacks edition / May 2005

St. Martin's Paperbacks are published by St. Martin's Press, 175 Fifth Avenue, New York, NY 10010.

10 9 8 7 6 5 4 3 2 1

To my editor, Jennifer Enderlin, for taking a chance on me; to the staff of St. Martin's Press for their hard work, especially Barbara Wild, my copy editor; and to Harry, a writer in his own right, for getting me into this in the first place and for his continuing support, my sincere gratitude.

The COMPANION

One

Fear drained away as he watched her from underneath his lashes. One long gold-painted nail beckoned to him. She lay draped across the chaise. The blood-red silks that hung from her shoulders were fastened only with a girdle of twined gold at her waist. Outside, the wind began to wail. Sand shushed against the walls of the tent. The scent of cinnamon and something else he could not name suffused the hot, dry air inside. In the dim light her skin glowed with perspiration and the very air vibrated with her vitality. Under the almost transparent fabric her nipples were clearly visible. He did not want to respond to her. But his swelling need surged over him.

"Come," she said. He could lose himself in those black eyes, lined with kohl.

He staggered to his feet. His naked body was still damp from bathing in the muddy pool of the oasis. His shoulder bled, as well as his thigh. She would like that.

She pointed to a place at her side. He dropped to his knees again. He knew what she wanted, and suddenly he wanted to give it to her more than he had ever wanted anything in his life. He lifted his mouth as she bent her head. Her breasts hung forward, tantalizing. Her lips were soft against his. He kissed her hungrily. Some part of him knew his danger, but the throbbing in his loins cycled up until he was lost.

As she reached for him her eyes began to glow red, blood-red like her silks.

Whispering and low moaning woke him from the nightmare. His veins and arteries carried pain to every fiber of his body. The moaning was his own. "Do it now," someone whispered in Arabic. He cracked one eye. Light stabbed him. A cluster of men in burnooses hovered over him. The open door silhouetted them in excruciating radiance. Light gleamed on a raised sword. He was too weak, too dispirited, to resist death. He could only clench his eyes shut.

Chaos! Shouting! "What are you doing, man?" someone yelled. "Jenks! Kiley!"

He cowered away from the light, trembling.

"Let him finish it," an Arab hissed, in English now. "This one is bad. He has the scars."

"No one will be killed here. This soil is England!" the Englishman roared.

Boot heels clattered. He chanced opening his eyelids a crack. The light was cut by a crowd of bodies in the door. They wore uniforms.

"Escort these men from the compound." The sword clattered to the ground. The Arabs were hustled out. The Englishman came to stand over him as the door swung mercifully shut. "Why do they bother? He'll die soon anyway."

"Pray to your God he does die, Excellency," the single remaining Arab whispered. The voices were growing indistinct. "And I will pray to Allah."

The room wavered. *Death,* he thought. *Is that even possible for one such as I?*

The Englishman reached forward. "What's this?"

The leather pouch at his neck jerked. The thong gave way. Darkness ate at the edges of his vision. He heard the gasp as they saw the contents of the pouch.

"Who *are* you, my friend?"

He could not answer. The darkness was winning. The room dimmed.

"Post a guard. Make sure he's English." He heard it from a distance.

Then nothing.

SAHARA DESERT, BI'ER TAGHIERI, SEPTEMBER 1818

Elizabeth Rochewell gazed around the tiny room: white-washed walls, a dark wood dresser carved in the native style she found clumsy and dear at once, the bed covered with her own counterpane. How many rooms in how many towns strewn across the Levant and North Africa just like this had she seen since she joined her father on his expeditions? Fifty? Blended together, they represented the only home she had known, the only place she felt comfortable.

She leaned over to draw the black lace mantilla off the bed by one corner. She had never thought to use this souvenir of Barcelona in such a manner. Indeed, she had expected none of this. The pillar that had crumbled after forty-five hundred years, give or take, tore her father from her so suddenly, so unfairly, she was stunned. It could not be an act of God, for what God could be cruel enough to kill a man at forty-eight, still a very healthy specimen?

The spotted mirror above the dresser showed eyes bloodshot from lack of sleep as she placed the mantilla. That she couldn't help. She had not slept for more than a few minutes at a time since the awful event. She couldn't help the face, either. She got it from her Egyptian mother. Her wide-set eyes were neither gold nor green but something in between. Her mouth was too wide for beauty, and her complexion could only be considered brown. Her dark hair was braided and coiled around her head, the only way she could manage it without crimping irons to tame its curls. Even so, escaping tendrils frothed about her face. Then there was her figure. She might be well formed enough, but she was short. There were just no two ways about it. Her father said her mother

was the most beautiful woman he had ever met and that Beth
looked very like her. He must have been blinded by love. She
would never be attractive to anyone in England or Africa.
There she was too Egyptian; here she was too British.

At least she was useful. Beth had spent all her adult life
helping her father catalog the history of mankind in the
physical traces of ancient times left behind. After a disastrous experience at Crofts School for Girls, she had escaped
to join her father. It was she who organized her father's expeditions, she who translated from the ancient texts the clues
that guided them on their quest for the lost sister city of Petra. She studied the aging of stones to date their finds. She
had found a place at her father's side. In Africa, people
thought of her as some strange creature, not quite woman.
She existed beyond conventions.

But that existence might have disappeared with her father's death. She pulled the mantilla over her braids. She did
not own a black dress, but a round-necked gray cambric
gown with a single black ribbon at the throat would do. She
could hardly believe she was getting ready for her father's
funeral. He may have been an unconventional parent, but he
had loved her as much as she loved him. He was her best
friend, her confidant, her professional mentor, and the sole
support of a life she loved. What would she do without him?

A bluff knock sounded downstairs. She heard the door
open quietly on leather hinges, the small man who owned
this apartment salute the guest.

"Monsieur L'Bareaux," she greeted him in the tiny parlor
next to her sleeping quarters.

He was a large man, her father's partner on the last three
expeditions. Monsieur L'Bareaux's mustache was black and
expressive, his kindly eyes an indeterminate gray that could
go hard when bargaining. That he was French might surprise, since France and England were incessantly at war. But
out here, wars were subordinate to the lure of antiquities. It
was the French who, initially armed with money from
Napoleon, had swept across the Mediterranean looking for
traces of human dynasties long dead. It was a Frenchman,

Monsieur Broussard, who had discovered the city of Petra in Palestine six years ago.

Monsieur L'Bareaux was more interested in salability than historical significance. But Monsieur L'Bareaux's way coincided with her father's dream. As Edwin Rochewell and his daughter trekked about North Africa looking for the lost city of Kivala, they cataloged one wonderful repository of antiquities after another, leaving Monsieur L'Bareaux plenty of opportunity to send back treasures to his dealers in Paris and provide enough money to help fund the next expedition.

"Do you bear up, Mademoiselle Beth?" His grave gaze roved over her.

"Yes." Was that true? Beth had not yet been able to cry for her father. She could not yet even comprehend his death. Did that mean she was "bearing up"?

"That's a good girl." Monsieur L'Bareaux patted her shoulder. "You are *tres fortissant.*"

"You really want to know whether I'm ready," Beth returned in the forthright way that disconcerted so many people in England. "I am."

Monsieur L'Bareaux opened the door and she plodded down the stairs. She mustn't think about the fact that she was burying her father today. She must think about how to get what she needed from Monsieur L'Bareaux. It was the only way to carry on her father's dream. It was the only way to preserve the only existence she knew.

The nightmares receded. He was awake, but he didn't open his eyes. Something had changed. The burning pain in his veins was gone. In fact, he felt . . . strong, stronger than he had ever been. Blood pulsed through his arteries. His heart thumped a rhythm in his chest. His senses assaulted him. Linen rasped over his bare skin from a light coverlet. The aroma of beef and onions cooking in olive oil was obvious, as was the jasmine. But dust, the faintest of scented oils, perhaps used long ago, and the smell of leather lurked just under the cooking. How could he smell those things? There was a joyful quality to the surging of his blood. He thrust it away. *She* told him she felt that way when she fed, just to torment him.

Despair fought with the joy thrumming inside him. He wasn't going to die. Now he might truly be damned—or worse, he might be Satan himself. Had he become like *her*?

A doctor. He needed an English doctor. A frightened Arab goatherd had said there were Englishmen at El Golea. Had he made it to his goal? He remembered English voices.

He opened his eyes. It was the room he remembered from his delirium. Slats of sunlight coming through the shutters burned him. He dragged himself from his bed, stumbling to the window. He held himself up by the sill and scraped his fist along the slats to shut them. The wood broke with a crack. Light stabbed through the shattered shutters. He cried out and groped for the curtains hanging to each side of the embrasure. The room was cast into dimness. Even in the darkness he could see every detail of cracked plaster, every dart of a cockroach. Slowly, he sank to the floor, his back pressed against the plaster. How had he broken those shutters?

Booted feet thudded outside. The wooden door set in a border of blue-figured tiles creaked open. He was grateful for the huge form that blocked most of the light. He shielded his eyes. "Light," he croaked in a voice he did not recognize. "No light."

"Sorry," the figure said in English with a soft reminder of Yorkshire at the edges. It was the voice from his fever. The door closed. "You must have had enough of sun."

Now that the room was dim, he could see the figure for what it was. The face was English through and through, with slightly protuberant pale blue eyes, a prominent nose, and a chin that could have used a bit more strength. Still the man would be considered handsome. He wore the uniform of the Seventh Cavalry. How long since he had seen boots? The man had eaten eggs and dates and toast with orange marmalade for breakfast. Once he would never have known that. Now the fact that he could smell it frightened him. He could not let this Englishman know what he was, or the man would never help him to an English doctor.

"Yes," he croaked, because the man expected something. The pale blue eyes examined him. He looked down. He was naked. What did the officer stare at? The scars. Did they reveal him? The marks of the whip said he had been a slave. But the twin circles all over his body? He hoped to God no one knew what those meant. Of course, God had nothing to do with him now.

The officer leaned down and helped him to his bed. He collapsed against the slatted headboard. "Major Vernon Ware," the man said as he sat on the side of the bed. "Attached to the English legation at El Golea. We found you in the streets about a week ago. And you are?"

There might be a thousand answers to that, none of them good. But this Major wanted something simple . . . a name. "Ian George Angleston Rufford." He hadn't thought of himself by that name in more than two years.

"Rufford?" The Major peered at him. "I knocked about London with Rufford Primus. You must be his younger brother." He held out a long-fingered hand.

Ian did not take it. He was not sure he dared. "Third son," he said. "My brother is Lord Stanbridge now." His brother a Viscount. It sounded so . . . normal. Even if you were poor, your estates encumbered, and your wife a bore . . . it didn't matter. You knew who you were.

The Major's eyes lit with memory. "Your brother said you stripped to advantage at Jackson's. Won a pony on you."

Had he ever been the careless rake who boxed at Jackson's? That man was gone now.

"I'll have one of the lads bring you some broth," the Major said. "You'll be back to beef and claret soon, but you'd better take it slow. We didn't think you were going to make it. You . . . you must have had a hard time of it."

Ian nodded. If he knew how hard, the Major would despise him. His feeling of euphoric strength faded. He was tired. But the goal that had burned in him as he dragged himself over uncounted miles of sand pushed him to speak. "I need an English doctor."

The Major stood, looming over him, and pulled up the linen sheet. "No English doctor within six hundred miles of here. Rest now. We'll find you clothes. I kept your belongings."

Ian was puzzled. Belongings? Nothing had belonged to him for a long time.

"I threw the water skin away. Something had rotted inside it." Ian started. The water skin held damnation. "But the little pouch you had hanging around your neck is safe with me."

Ahhh. The diamonds. The diamonds were his way back to England. After a doctor cured him he would wager at White's and be fitted for a hat at Locke's and canter about Hyde Park at five of the clock like everyone else with nothing better to occupy them.

The room swam. The Major saw his weakness and withdrew. Ian did not have to be like *her.* And he would not submit himself to a woman again, ever. Someday the horror in the desert would be only an occasional nightmare. As his eyes closed, images of London filled him.

The patch of ragged grass was a tattered camouflage for the sand beneath. The hiss of sand being shoveled in on top of the coffin whispered that this was a foreign grave in a foreign place. With his dirty collar and slurring words, the priest was still the best the Christian God had in these climes. There was only a wooden cross to place at her father's grave. The stone would come in three weeks, if the stonemason did not get distracted by another job or go to stay with his cousins unexpectedly. That was the way of the world in these parts.

She turned away from the grave, still dry-eyed and empty, along with Monsieur L'Bareaux, several Arabs who had been with her father for years in one capacity or another, and the disheveled Italian who traded with them for supplies. It was a small enough group that dispersed into the rising heat of the late morning.

Monsieur handed her back up into the cart and sat heavily beside her. He snapped the reins over the donkey's back. They plodded toward the blockish outline of the village. The heat, settling over her mantilla and her cambric dress, was stifling.

She was alone in the world. Her father was gone. Her mother had died giving her life. She was an only child, just as her mother was—unusual in her mother's native land. There was only her father's sister, Lady Cecelia Rangle in London. Beth had met her only half a dozen times. She could not go back to England. She did not belong there. She belonged here, in Africa, carrying on her father's dream. Monsieur L'Bareaux held the key, she knew. She had resolved only this morning to accost him, and yet now she could not speak.

It was Monsieur L'Bareaux who finally cleared his throat. "Mademoiselle Beth," he began, not looking at her. "It is perhaps time we talked of you."

She took a breath and recruited her resources. He had made the first sally. It was now or never. The only tactic likely to prevail was a hit direct. "I could not agree more, monsieur. Once we have seen that Imam in Tunis, I will be able to map our course for Kivala."

Monsieur L'Bareaux pulled at his collar. It wasn't because of the heat. "I signed the contract with Revelle, *petite*. He will pay well for excavating the ancient kasbah at Qued Zem."

"But we have caught the scent of the Lost City now; I know it!" Her voice rose with her anxiety. She couldn't lose Monsieur L'Bareaux's support at the outset. "The old man's directions corroborate the text on that stylus outside Cairo, if one revises Robard's clumsy translation."

Monsieur L'Bareaux glanced down at her. His bushy brows, now drawn together, had long since stopped seeming fierce. His sympathy made her shrivel. "I have not the doubts that you are right, *petite*. But the francs say I must excavate Qued Zem."

Beth stared straight ahead. She must not let the fear into her voice. "Well, if it must be Qued Zem, it must. We can be ready in a fortnight." Perhaps the bluff Frenchman would not hear that little quaver. If she had to make the final sacrifice, he could not know that she was afraid.

There was a long pause. She dared not look at him. Perhaps he would just acquiesce. Or maybe he was only thinking how to break the bad news.

"You cannot stay here, *petite*." He said it softly but with finality. "It is not proper."

"Did my father care for propriety?" She shook her head. "If it comes to that, I took more care of him than he of me."

"I know."

"Who will organize everything, *and* who will translate texts for you? You know you read the Coptic very badly and you have no hieroglyphs at all."

He rubbed his mustaches with one hand. "I have engaged a foreman. We shall do without a scholar. We are just digging trinkets, you know.

"But why must you do without? What has changed?"

"Before, you had him. Whether he was watchful or no, the men knew that you were to be treated with respect. It would be different now." She could see he was sorry to have to explain this to her. The donkey plodded on under the blue dome of sky toward the village wall. They joined the main road, clogged with the commerce of the desert. Men hunched under lumpy nets of cheese and baskets of dates. Women carried fowl in crates.

"Even if I engaged a chaperone?"

"What woman would trek across the desert for months at a time?" He shook his head.

"A Bedouin woman or a Berber," she answered promptly.

"That would bring neither propriety nor protection."

"You could give me protection, Monsieur L'Bareaux." Her voice was small, but it was steady.

"*Assez*," he continued, "I have made the arrangements for you to have full escort on the next caravan to Tripoli. Lord Metherton, he knew your father. Already I have written that he should have a kindness for you, and see that you get back to England safely."

"What difference if I am alone on a caravan or on trek with you?" One last protest.

"You will go with an Arab family I know, as their daughter." He spoke slowly, as if she had suddenly become a child. "The caravan master will see that you are safe."

Well, she wasn't a child. She was a fully grown woman who should be able to stay in Africa if she wished. Night sky and total quiet echoed in her memory. How could one not feel close to God in the desert? She could feel the Sphinx towering above her in the unforgiving sun as she ran her hands over the pitted stone of its paws and had a revelation about it. She had seen many things in the desert that could not be explained by the rational mind: the old woman who healed others' wounds before her very eyes, the amulet that burned when you lied—she had seen more than most women in England saw in a lifetime. How could she give up the freedom, the excitement, for English drawing rooms? And if she could not even stay in Africa, she would never see her father's dream realized. She let that thought give her courage.

"There is one answer to both our problems," she heard herself say. "You get someone to organize and translate, and I stay in North Africa."

He glanced at her with wariness in his eyes as a herd of goats flowed around their cart. "What are you saying, *petite*?" She could tell he did not really want to know.

"I'm asking you to marry me, Monsieur L'Bareaux." She had known that it would come to this, a final sacrifice needed to do what she wished, be whom she wished.

The silence stretched. She must let him consider it. He couldn't be more than forty-two or forty-three. She was full twenty-four. Did he hesitate because he thought she would be demanding? "I shouldn't be a charge upon you," she blurted. "It would be a marriage of your convenience, sir, not mine. I could be as much or as little of a wife as you like." The arch of Bi'er Taghieri's west wall passed overhead. They plunged into the stifling village once more, its narrow streets constricting her hopes. Monsieur L'Bareaux's Adam's apple trekked up and down.

Then his shoulders sagged. "Mademoiselle Beth, I have sense of the honor you do me." He did not use the familiar *ma petite.* "But you would regret this thing and so would I."

"The difference in age cannot matter." She could not keep desperation out of her voice.

"No. But I do not look for a wife, even one so talented as you are." He cleared his throat. "I have no liking for . . . for the ladies."

Oh. Well, that made no difference. It simply meant the marriage would be truly only convenient. She was about to protest, but he held up a hand. "Call halt, Mademoiselle Beth." He patted her hand in a fatherly way. "It is for the best. You belong among your people." He went on with determined cheerfulness. "You have your father's share of the funerary pieces. They'll bring enough to get you home. He left your portion in Drummond's bank."

Beth stared ahead, not at the crowded narrow streets of Bi'er Taghieri, but at the prospect of long dreary years in drawing rooms, clapping politely when the young misses played on the pianoforte. Her sentence was handed down by the falling pillar in that wretched tomb. She was for Tripoli and an England in which she could not possibly belong. Her father's dream was dead, just as he was. All that was left was to walk through her days, missing him and longing for piercing sunshine and black nights and the smell of jasmine in the morning air.

It was late in the English compound. Ian sat with Major Ware in the courtyard under a pergola covered with vines of star jasmine. The red ends of their cigarillos glowed in the dark. It had been almost a month since Ian first waked to new life. The fever was gone, but so were his illusions. He had been eating like the starved man he was, but no amount of beef and bread could satisfy his cravings. The despair of knowing exactly what his body wanted beat at him until he couldn't sleep in his darkened room during daylight hours. The hunger had been growing for weeks now, until tonight as he sat at dinner with the ambassador, Lord Wembertin, and his staff, Ian could hear the thrumming of blood in veins, the pump of hearts around him. He'd startled everyone by knocking over a chair in his haste to be gone. But he might have done something they'd find far more horrible if he'd stayed.

He couldn't go on like this. Even now he could feel the throb of Ware's blood in the man's throat. He could see it pulse, even in the dark. In the pocket of his coat he fingered the small knife they'd given him to pare his nails. The knife was his hope. He had a plan.

"You must have put on three stone, Rufford," Ware remarked in the darkness. "Lord, but you were a scarecrow when you first got here! How long had you been out there?"

Ian wanted no questions. "I'm not sure," he said in a damping tone.

"Well, perhaps not. That new coat fits snug enough, in spite of the foreign tailoring. Sorry none of us had one to accommodate those shoulders of yours."

"You have been very kind." And he had. Ware had seen to it that he was cared for until he was strong again. Only Ware's constant vigilance had kept the Arabs at bay. Ian had to keep the Major from knowing just how strong he was. His fellow Englishmen would be frightened if they guessed Ian's abilities. Ian was still guessing and they frightened him.

"Feeling fit enough to be off for England soon, I daresay. Catching a ship in Algiers?"

"I go through Tripoli." He kept his voice flat. "You said there is an English doctor there."

"Yes. But have you still a need of one?"

Ian changed the subject. "I was bound for Tripoli on the way out, you know."

"In the diplomatic service?" The Major sat forward.

"Under Rockhampton." It was the first information he had volunteered.

"Capital fellow. I would love to serve under him." Ware's cheroot glowed brighter.

"At one point I thought it just the thing for me. Younger

son, family estates mortgaged to the hilt, you know the way of it. I inherited the family instability." Ware would understand he meant gambling and horses and women. "Don't know how I made it through Cambridge. Ran through what my mother had provided for me raking about town." He gave a bitter laugh.

"Don't try to tip me the double, Rufford. Rockhampton only takes the best."

Ian felt the Major's blood pumping in his arteries. He achieved a shrug. He must keep talking to stave off the pain crawling along his veins. "M'father's death stopped the rake's progress. Henry was pretty well brought to a stand when he inherited. Hadn't the sense to marry for money. I couldn't be a charge on him. He managed to buy Charlie a commission. I convinced Rockhampton I'd settled down. I write a fair hand and my dancing is well enough. All you need to succeed in the diplomatic corps."

Ware raised his brows. "Under Rockhampton? I hardly think . . ." But he apparently thought better of pressing Ian. After a moment he said, "But you never served."

"Barbary pirates off Algiers. Took the ship." Ian's voice was tight.

Ware nodded, his expression full of surmise. "How did you escape?"

"A story for another time." Ian's voice was harsher than he intended.

Ware stubbed out his cigar. "Well, money won't be a problem, not with the contents of that little leather bag. You need not serve Whitehall and the diplomats if you dislike it."

"No." He would know better what to do after he put the knife to use tonight.

"I'll leave you. It grows late. Or early. The night has become your time."

Ian's brows drew together. "Not by choice."

"Oh, you'll be riding to hounds with the Quorn before you know it. A touch of sun poisoning, that's all." Ware rose. "By the by, you'd best travel with a well-armed party. Nasty doings in the desert. A whole caravan was left for the vultures a hundred miles to the northwest."

Ian stopped breathing for a moment. "A whole caravan?" he asked stupidly.

"And there's worse. The animals were dead, sure, but not desecrated. The men . . ."

"The men what?" Ian found himself almost whispering.

"Well . . ." Ware hesitated. "No blood in their bodies. White as your shirt."

"The sand. It could have sunk into the sand."

"Not without it left some stain. Natives say they were killed by a demon."

Ian knew who had done it. No stopping her now. "When is your term of service here up?"

"Mere months." Ware grinned in deprecation. "They're closing El Golea, sending Wembertin home."

Wembertin was a fool. Who else would be assigned a delegation in so remote a desert outpost in the Sahara? Ian nodded. "Good."

"Why?" Ware asked.

"Just stay out of the desert, man, until you can get home to England."

Ware looked at him strangely and nodded. Touching his forehead in salute, he ducked out under the jasmine-laden pergola toward his room.

Ian sat without moving. The hunger gnawed at him, whispering what was needed to assuage it. At last shutters around the courtyard no longer seeped light. The compound would seem silent to another. Ian heard snoring and rats scurrying in the storeroom, the cat stalking them, the drip of precious water somewhere. The night was alive and only he could hear it.

He rose, aware of the supple grace his new strength gave him. Time to try assuaging his dreadful hunger with a substitute Major Ware would find distasteful but not a certain sign of evil. It was a slim hope but possible. He shed his very English coat and returned to a burnoose. Then he slipped out of the compound into the night, clutching the little knife.

The need surged inside him, bringing a sound from his throat that might be a growl. He had not much time.

Ian sat in his room with every crack sealed against the desert light. The feeling of life coursing through his veins had driven him to drink the blood in the water sack and kept him alive across the burning deserts of the Sahara even as fever raged in his body. Now it surged inside him with unbelievable strength.

His plan had failed. He thought that drinking the blood of a cow would appease his hunger. He'd cut its artery with the little knife, sucked the blood. When the cow had fallen on him he'd thrust its two thousand pounds off with no more concern than if it had been a lapdog.

But it was not his new strength that tore at his mind. He'd vomited up the cow's blood. And the hunger had surged up in seeming revenge, engulfing him, until he had done a thing unthinkable. He had sucked the blood of the young cowherd. Worse, he had not needed the little knife to open the artery in the young man's throat. Ian almost wailed his guilt, his dread of what he had become. He clapped a hand over his mouth to prevent the sound, grimacing his revulsion. He had not killed the boy, it was true. But he might have.

Was he mad? No. That was the worst of all. This was who he was now. This drive to life was part of the beast *she* had made him. He would drink blood to satisfy it. When the hunger was on him, he would do anything to keep alive. Dear God! He had inherited her evil!

There was only one answer. His resolve warred with the singing life in his veins.

So he sat in the dark while he battled the urge to life and gathered his strength. It was afternoon before he could place the chair. Every fiber of his body fought what he wanted to do. He had to rest before he could cut the rope net that supported the mattress on his cot. What he was about to do was wrong. But it was without doubt the lesser of two evils. He hoped that once he had done it God would forgive him, since he sought only to redeem the greater sin.

Now, in the heat of the afternoon when all were resting—
now was the time to do it.

He climbed the chair.

"He's dead, poor bastard." Ian heard the Major's voice
dimly. Someone held his wrist. He opened his eyes. Several
gasps were quite distinguishable. The room was at an angle.
He straightened his head. Jenks and Evans jerked back. Even
in the dim room he saw them go pale.

Major Ware hung over him. "Rufford?" he whispered.
His voice was uncertain.

Ian's neck felt . . . odd. He turned his head. No, that was
better.

Around the circle, the whispering grew frantic. At the
door Arabs made the sign against evil and scurried away,
gabbling.

Ian swallowed twice. "Why do you look like that?" he
asked the circle. His voice came out a croak.

"You . . . you had a near thing," the Major said. He
looked as though he'd seen a ghost.

Ian's gaze darted about the room. He was lying on a mattress on the floor. There was the chair, overturned. A shred of
rope still hung from the beam where they must have cut him
down. "I remember." His voice was clearer now. The sore-
ness in his throat dissolved. Sadness pushed on his chest and
made breathing difficult. "Even the last solace is denied me."

Sadness boiled over into rage without notice. He sat bolt
upright. The men leaped back as though he had attacked
them. "Go!" he yelled. "Get out of here! What are you looking at?"

They disappeared as fog evaporates under the blast of the
sun. Only Ware stayed. Ian could see the questions burning
inside him, questions so outrageous they could not be asked.
"You, too, Ware," he growled, sinking back onto the mattress. "You can do no good here."

Ware rose, uncertainty mirrored clearly in his face. He
was considering whether he should leave a man who had just

tried to commit suicide to his own devices or whether he was
a fool for not running from the room screaming. Personally,
Ian recommended the latter.

"What happened to you out there, man?" Ware asked
hoarsely.

Rufford stared at him for a long moment. He had never
asked about the slavery, about the marks on Ian's body, even
about what was in the water skin, though speculation on all
those topics was rampant throughout the delegation. Ian
could always hear the whispers. As payment for that forbear-
ance, the man deserved an answer. "I became my worst enemy, friend, my very own nightmare." He closed his eyes.
"Now go, for your own good, go."

Ware turned to the door. "The men will tell Wembertin,"
he said, not looking back.

"He won't believe them. And he won't want the scandal.
I'll be gone tomorrow."

Ware nodded. "I'll tell him," he said as he closed the
door.

Two

The late-afternoon sun was sinking behind the black spiky forest of masts in the harbor of Tripoli as Beth and Mrs. Pargutter and Mrs. Pargutter's maid, Jenny Fellows, rocked in a small boat pulling for the merchantman frigate *Beltrane,* bound for Port Mahon, Gibraltar, Brest, and Portsmouth. Their convoy was to be escorted by one of His Majesty's sloops as far as Lisbon, to protect them from being taken by Barbary pirates or illicit privateers.

The boat pulled up to the rocking ship and the scruffy man who stood in the prow called up to the deck in Arabic for a bo'sun's chair. Beth hoped someone on board the English ship spoke the native tongue. Soon a kind of a swing was lowered over the side from a boom and Beth helped strap a protesting Mrs. Pargutter into it. That good lady was somewhat stout, with rouged cheeks that contrasted sharply with the overly brassy color of her hair. She swung up over the ship's side, wailing, to the deck above. Beth took her place and soared aloft herself, pressing her skirts around her. Callused hands helped her onto the gently rocking deck, and as she looked around, the boom swung out again for their trunks.

Sailors scurried everywhere both on the deck and in the

rigging above. Orders Beth found incomprehensible echoed and were answered. The slight roll of the deck beneath them, even though the *Beltrane* stood at anchor, whispered of less conformable seas to come. The scents of the ocean and tar and hemp made a heady combination announcing some new world as she left behind forever Lady Metherton's drawing rooms at the British delegation in Tripoli. Her small single trunk and the valise that contained her scrolls, Mrs. Pargutter's two huge trunks, and Jenny's carpetbag were deposited on the deck inside a net of rope. The sailors dressed in red-striped shirts and nankeens, most sporting hair greased back into long braids and earrings, largely ignored them.

"Well," Mrs. Pargutter declared, her vast breasts heaving in her widow's weeds. "None of these rude men seems to know the least about how to treat a lady." Mrs. Pargutter had been left in much the same situation as Beth by the most inconsiderate passing of her late husband, a trader of olives and oils between the ports of the Mediterranean, before the couple could get home to Nottingham. Lady Metherton had most kindly paired the two ladies, ill sorted as they might be, to make the journey back to Portsmouth together.

"I should think they are very busy just now, preparing to cast off or some such," Beth said soothingly. "I'm sure they will take notice of us soon, because our trunks are in the way."

Indeed, Lady Metherton had been so kind, the last several weeks had been all but unbearable to Beth. She took Beth entirely under her expensively dressed maternal wing and tut-tutted about the kind of father who would bring a gently bred girl into the wilds of North Africa. Even Tripoli, a thriving metropolis, was hardly civilized enough for a refined British woman, let alone the desert, with all that nasty sand and sun. No wonder Beth's manners were less than refined. Why (Beth could hear her cultured voice, particularly well modulated as a lady's should be), Beth could not help her brown complexion, and no doubt traipsing about on those dirty camels had stunted her growth. A sigh. It could not be helped, and England was the only remedy for her condition.

Beth was fairly sure that England would not be the remedy or that it would, at the very least, be a very nasty draught if Lady Metherton's reaction to her was any indication of the reception she would receive in the drawing rooms of London.

"Well, well, ladies," a bluff voice echoed behind them. Beth and Mrs. Pargutter turned to see a large man with a rolling gait dressed in a dark blue coat of superfine with huge metallic buttons across his chest in civilian imitation of a naval officer. "Welcome to the *Beltrane*, the finest merchant ship in the Med and your home for a few weeks if the breeze blows well. I'm Captain Tindly." He bowed.

"Captain," Beth said, extending her hand. "I am Miss Rochewell, and may I present Mrs. Pargutter and her companion Miss Fellows?" Beth naturally took the lead, though Mrs. Pargutter was nominally her protector.

"Your servant, madam," the Captain said in a voice born to bellow orders at sea. "We cast off at sunset." He called to the nearest seamen, "Mr. Severn, Mr. Cobb, see these trunks to the forward cabins. Shake a leg, there." He turned to bawl orders about fo'c'sles and hammocks and grates, then surveyed the shore and muttered, "Damn all passengers. Where is he?"

A man scurried into the rigging and scrambled up it rather like a rat. Beth was used to such behavior, but Mrs. Pargutter gave out a little shriek and grasped Beth's arm. "Did you see that, my dear? Why, he looked hardly human!"

"Be easy, ma'am." Beth patted her hand. "Surely you saw sailors on your voyage out."

"Never like that!" she cried. "Positively bestial! Besides, I spent the whole voyage in my cabin, for I have never been a good traveler, and the sea quite oversets me."

Beth sighed. The trip stretched dismally ahead of her, though what she had expected from Mrs. Pargutter under the best of circumstances she could not say. Beth was suddenly very glad that Jenny would have the tending of what she suspected would be a determined invalid. The seamen hefted their trunks. "Perhaps you would like to go to your cabin?"

"Yes, yes. I am in need of a little restorative. I have a supply of laudanum." Mrs. Pargutter bustled after the seamen, Jenny Fellows in her wake. Beth did not follow.

"Blast! I swear I'll leave him," the Captain said behind her. "I'll not miss the tide."

A ship some way down the quay drifted away from its moorings, one sail flapping down and then another. A breath of offshore breeze kissed the neighbor's canvas. "Captain, if I stand against the wall of the quarterdeck, will I be out of your way? I'd like to see us sail."

"By the door there." The Captain smiled, pleased that she bothered to be out of the way.

"Ahoy the passenger's boat!" a sailor yelled.

Out of the growing gloom a boat thumped against the side. A large form swung a leg up over the rail and stepped on board.

"About time, Rufford!" the Captain called. "We was about to leave you."

The easy grace of the figure spoke of power. Even from here, with little more than a silhouette to guide her, Beth could sense it emanating from him. He had a pair of shoulders on him, a thick, blunt form with powerful thighs. And he was tall—a big man altogether. As he approached the Captain and bowed briefly, Beth saw his face. In some ways it was also blunt: unruly brows, a nose straight but slightly prominent, likewise chin, strong and cleft. She could not tell the color of his eyes, only that their expression was intense. It was his mouth that startled—full lips, so sensuous they did not seem to fit so masculine a figure. His hair was light brown and thick, long, pulled back into a queue old-fashioned even when Beth had last been in England.

"What kept you, man?" the Captain challenged, puffed up with his inconvenience.

"I stayed to dine." The passenger's voice was a grim rumble in that massive chest. "It will make a more comfortable voyage for everyone."

A trunk swung up over the side and thunked on the deck. The Captain harrumphed and began shouting orders to cast off. The passenger, Mr. Rufford he was called, went below with his trunks. As he passed, Beth saw that his eyes were blue. But that was not the startling thing about them. The pain they held was terrible to behold. His gaze raked her, but she was fairly certain he didn't truly see her. What man registered a girl as unattractive as she was?

Lines were cast off. Sailors' calls and responses echoed over the deck. The ship rocked slowly away from its moorings. Several sails flapped into place. They were away into the harbor, threading their way between moored behemoths Beth guessed were ships of the line—Royal Navy. Yes—there were the gun ports. She counted. A seventy-four. The mouth of the harbor opened before her. She turned. The lights of Tripoli blinked in the growing blackness, receding.

This was the last of Africa, the last of freedom, the dying dream that had been her father's and, therefore, hers. Strange that people should think her life had been uncertain here. It was far more certain in its principles, its qualities, than any she was like to find in England.

The wind whipped at her hair and took its wisps. The lights of Tripoli faded as the merchantman drifted into the current. She had never felt so alone. She grabbed for the rail to make her way back to the cabin.

The other passenger, Mr. Rufford, leaned against the rail, looking out to sea. She could not mistake his brawny form. Strands of hair escaped the small ribbon at his neck, whipping backward in the wind. He was directly in her way. She dared not start across the open deck. The sea had grown a little rough and the ship's roll was more pronounced. She squared her shoulders. Avoiding him was impossible, since they were to spend weeks as two of four passengers on a cargo ship. She decided to acknowledge him. A civil nod would be enough.

He rolled quite easily with the ship. His coat was dark blue like the indigo of sky behind him and the dark sea ruffled with white. As she drew near, she saw something gleam around his wrists. How odd! Were they bracelets? No. Scars. His wrists were scarred. She felt like an intruder, as though she were spying. Quite close now, she prepared to dash for the rope hold on the quarterdeck wall.

He looked up at her. At first he didn't seem to see her. His thoughts clearly dwelt on something unpleasant. The combination and the intensity of emotions roiling in those eyes were something she had never seen in a man's countenance: revulsion, longing, perhaps even fear. But he didn't look a coward. No, there was something of resolution about him. This was confirmed when he registered her presence and the eyes went flat, bottling up those emotions in a most determined way. He stood upright, pulling his cuffs down self-consciously, and nodded to her. They might have been in Lady Metherton's drawing room except for the roll of the deck and the wind whipping at their hair.

"Ian Rufford," he almost growled. "Your servant, madam." He actually turned away, not even waiting for her reciprocal introduction.

She should simply race across to the stairs below. It would be most improper to stay and speak to any man without an introduction other than his own. She might have been in Africa and the Levant for these ten years, but even she knew that. Still, she did not like being snubbed.

Beth grabbed the rail to steady herself. "Elizabeth Rochewell."

He turned back, surprised at her boldness. His eyes raked her as though he knew something about her she might not want anyone to know. She was acutely conscious of her short stature. Could he see her brown complexion in this light? Probably not. He could see her black pelisse and her kid half boots, fashionable, if moderate in style. She was glad Lady Metherton had talked her into buying them as part of her mourning clothes, even if this man was not the kind to care for fashion.

"What brings someone like you to Tripoli, Miss Rochewell?" His voice was indifferent.

"Someone like me," she mused as she turned out to the sea, determined not to let her anger show. He didn't think much of women or at least women who looked like her. "Someone like me was on an archaeological expedition with my father in the desert."

Behind them, a man's voice called out, "Luff up handsomely, there!" A sail flapped.

"Treasure hunting, like Lord Elgin?"

She didn't look at him. She didn't trust her eyes not to betray her outrage. "Searching for knowledge, Mr. Rufford, about who we are, and where our kind has been."

"And you thought you would find that in the barren deserts of North Africa. . . ."

He made it sound childish. "The desert holds many secrets. Look at the lost city of Petra—it gives us two thousand years of history and more."

"Petra, what is that?" She had piqued his curiosity.

"You don't get about much, Mr. Rufford, if you haven't heard of Petra. Discovered seven years ago in Palestine—a treasure trove of knowledge. A paper was read just last year at Somerset House before the Royal Society."

"Yes. Well. I have been otherwise engaged for the last two years. No time for announcements of obscure archaeological discoveries."

She shot a stealthy glance at him, remembering the scars. He was leaning out over the rail again, watching the ships of the convoy, now closing in around them. Had he been in prison? Why? His aura of danger took on a more palpable form. She let her words race on. "It was not obscure. It was a very important discovery."

He looked her over once again. Those full lips curled in a tiny smile that might have been a sneer. "So now all the bored aristocrats are wandering about the desert looking for meaning to their lives, even women. Did *you* discover anything important?"

She repressed a gasp. His rudeness deserved that she just

walk away, or rather lurch away toward the quarterdeck ropes. But she could not resist a setdown of a more telling nature. "I discovered that all the guesses about the age of the Sphinx in Egypt were only that—learned guesses, but very wrong." She paused. "You *have* heard of the Sphinx, have you not?"

He did not answer her sally. But he examined her once again. "Wrong." He let his disbelief hang in the air, just short of derision.

Beth turned to him, leaning against the rail for balance. "Yes. Wrong. I became interested in the patterns of erosion, Mr. Rufford, when I was looking into the geological phenomena around Petra and how those ravines came to be there waiting for a city to be carved out of them. I thought one might use erosion to date things. And I did, in a way."

"What way?" He was reserving judgment now.

"Erosion comes in several varieties: the kind made by wind and the kind made by dripping water, for instance, and they leave very different patterns on the objects they erode. Everyone thought the Sphinx was three or four thousand years old, eroded by the desert winds."

"But it wasn't."

"It was eroded by water, Mr. Rufford. The pattern is quite clear."

"Water, in the middle of the desert?" He thought briefly. "And we would not be talking floods, as of the Nile. You mean it *rained* on the Sphinx? Impossible."

Beth smiled slowly. He had caught the thing at once. He was brighter than most men, at any rate. "Ah, you are thinking of Egypt as we know it now. But think in terms of geological time, Mr. Rufford. The earth changes; mountains come and go; seas rise and fall. Once, the desert must have been wet. A *very* long time ago. It rained on the Sphinx for many centuries."

"How long ago?" He cocked his head.

"Ten thousand years, at least. I don't think the head is even original. You must have noted how small it is, and much better preserved than the lower parts. It was re-carved."

His brow wrinkled. "Ten thousand. But then who could have . . . ?" He trailed off.

"Could have made it?" Beth finished his question. "Ah, the mysteries of the Dark Continent, Mr. Rufford. It contains more than you and I have ever contemplated in our world."

His head sagged between his shoulders almost imperceptibly. "You are right about that." She had hurt him. She did not know how. He squared his shoulders. That was the courage again. "I should like to meet your father. He sounds an interesting sort."

Beth swallowed. Her loss washed over her so suddenly it must have been lying in wait. Rufford should have guessed from her mourning clothes that his remark was tactless. After she could breathe, she said, "Too late for that, sir. He is dead a month and more."

There was an awkward silence. "I'm sorry." The low rumble sounded sincere. What an odd creature he was, sneering and sincere in turns.

"So am I." She had said too much, flaunting knowledge like a bluestocking, determined to impress, and so taken unawares by lurking grief. "And what of you? Why are you in Tripoli?"

He hesitated. It was not such a hard question, unless of course he was a prison escapee. "I was staying at the British delegation at El Golea."

He said it as though that explained why he was in the middle of the Sahara and so far from England. "My father and I were organizing an expedition in Bi'er Tegheri to look for Petra's sister city, Kivala, sleeping somewhere under the sands of the desert."

He looked up sharply at her. "Did you find it?" Fear, even horror, flashed in his eyes.

"No. My father died before we could fairly start."

He caught his expression and carefully shut down. "Then you are lucky."

"What do you mean?" He couldn't mean she was lucky her father had died.

"You said yourself there are more things in the desert than we can comprehend. That particular section of desert is dangerous." He said it lightly, but he was hiding something.

"Oh." She wanted to ask him more, but just then Captain Tindly stepped on deck.

"Look sharp, boy, for a signal from the sloop!" he bellowed. "Prepare to back tops'ls."

Shouts and activity exploded. Beth turned to find her fellow passenger had disappeared.

The *Beltrane* was almost quiet now. Ian felt freer. Only a few hands were above decks, since she was "hove to," as they said, for the night with sails furled, waiting for the rest of the convoy to arrive. Those sailors awake smoked or huddled over their mugs of grog. Ships were close quarters. Hardly a word was exchanged but what four people did not witness it. He could not afford shipboard curiosity.

He'd taken careful sips of the dread substance he now craved for four nights running before he boarded, hoping to forestall his need. It had been almost more than he could manage to take only a pint from each of his victims, for the hunger was bestial in its demands. The need rose about two weeks after he fed. He'd taken passage on a vessel that had several ports of call. He must do what must be done onshore, not in the narrow and too-public confines of the ship.

He leaned over the rail, one boot on the hammock netting, staring out to sea. His thoughts strayed to the strange girl who'd been so incensed when he had not believed her wild theory about the Sphinx. Such a bluestocking—no address, odd-looking. He was surprised she was English with her outlandish looks. He was not surprised she'd tried to assert that dominance females always craved. She'd been determined to prove his ignorance. He admitted grudgingly he might have given her provocation with his derision. She was direct; he'd give her that.

His mind contracted. There were even more direct ways of gaining dominance than that poor girl could comprehend

in her small world. He straightened and took in a breath of
the salt air. He would not think of that or of *her*. He would
think of the brown bird of a girl. He'd seen the carapace that
covered her uncertainty about herself as she struck out at
him over her precious theories. Whatever would she do in
England? They valued everything she did not possess and
nothing of what she did. He couldn't help noticing how wistfully she gazed after Tripoli. She was right. She would be
better off there. Impossible, of course, without husband, father, brother.

The sea was quiet. The wind had died. That boded ill for
a quick journey west down the Med. It had been just such
weather when his ship was taken off the Barbary Coast two
years ago.

He wouldn't think about that. He skipped over the roar of
the guns blasting away at the fragile wooden sides of the
ships at close range, the smoke, the smell of blood, the roar
of the barbarous bastards as they came over the side. The
damned Captain hadn't even put up a good fight. He'd asked
for quarter as soon as it got down to hand combat.

He stared at the scars around his wrists. He didn't bother
to pull down his cuffs—no one was about to see them. They
were the beginning. And then he couldn't skip over it anymore. Shame suffused him as he remembered the foul creatures stripping him of everything—boots, belt, coat,
waistcoat, shirt, watch and fob, seal ring, even his stockings.
Then had come the first of many bindings, cruel hemp
around his wrists. Wearing only his breeches, he was thrown
into the hold with the other able-bodied. A saber cut or two
still qualified him as healthy.

The foul water in the belly of the ship was a foot deep.
Those who could stand, did so. Those who couldn't . . .

A rat swam by. He could not suppress a shudder.

"You'll thank God for the rats soon enough." The voice
came from about the point of Ian's thigh. The man must be
sitting in the water. They were almost touching in the pitch

dark of the hold. "We'll end eating them. These Barbary bastards won't waste rations on slaves."

"Slaves?"

"We're for market sure, maybe Algiers."

"I thought the Navy cleared the Med of pirates," Ian protested, half-dazed by the quickness of the whole action and the throb of his wounds.

"Mostly. But mostly don't appear to be good enough." The man coughed.

"Hope they don't try to convert us," an old salt rasped. "I cain't take torture at my age."

Ian shrank inside. He'd heard of the hot irons and knives that compelled a man to renounce Christ. The damned infidels thought they were saving souls. The stench of tar and fetid water was overwhelming. He breathed through his mouth, but that only made his throat close.

"I heard they cut your bollocks off," a young voice trembled.

"Sometimes. But the black ones, they cuts their balls and dicks clean off, too, so they dribble all over themselves. Bring 'em up from beyond the desert, in great long caravans. Arabs has always kept slaves. In droves, they keeps them." The fount of information sputtered to a stop.

"I read some firsthand accounts of Christian slaves." Ian recognized the master, one of the few officers not slain or heaved overboard and therefore one of the few men who could read. "They're employed as agents of business if they know the language, or to sail a rich man's ships if they are sailors."

Ian wished he'd learned more Arabic or knew how to sail a ship.

He lost all feeling in his hands before he located a splinter of wood he could grate against his ropes. It took long hours to free them, and the pain of the returning blood almost made him regret his effort. He passed his splinter to the next man, and the old salt pried off another. Soon they all had their hands free. He realized he had a fever when he started shaking uncontrollably. The saber cut on his upper arm must be infected. The odor of death was added to the reek of tar and fetid water when a sailor named Young who had renounced Christ on the deck above died soon after he returned to their purgatory. The nightmare of the dark and the stink, the hunger, and fear made the ship's boy set to shrieking until they knocked him senseless. They could hear the pumps working, yet the water rose until they were thigh deep and could not sit if they would. They slept fitfully, braced against the curve of the hull or leaning on another, in shifts. It was miserable to the point of unreality. Time lingered in a haze.

A great thump against the ship's side and muffled shouting, answered more faintly from afar, told them the ship had docked. It was not long before the hatch above opened, leaking a square of unbearable light. They did not have to understand the language to know that they were being bid up into the sun to a future more fearful even than their wretchedness in the hold.

The ship's boy was a gibbering idiot by now. The scurvy piratical lot cut him from the others and brought a club down upon his head once, twice, with a dull thud. No use for him. Ian squinted in horror against the stabbing light as they cast the lifeless body into the harbor. He hardly noticed the rope they used to fasten the remaining cargo together at the ankles until they were jerked down the gangplank. They stumbled into a town, thriving with the shout of commerce. Twenty-four survived out of the five-score sailors and passengers that set sail from Bristol. Famished, half-naked, they looked a poor bargain for whoever bought them.

The slave market was even more frenetic than the bazaar at large. Groups of young men gleaming ebon in the sun, their male areas smooth enough to make the English shudder, crouched in the dust. Women, some with faces as covered as their bodies, huddled together. Others sprawled naked and displayed. Traders called out the virtues of their human wares. And through all, the merciless sun beat on their heads, burning their pale and waterlogged bodies. Everywhere, the scent of human sweat and fear mingled with that

*of aromatic spices, overripe fruit, and meat hanging days
too long among the flies.*

*Their keeper cut the gaggle into individual lots. Ian found
himself pushed, stumbling, into a dusty ring surrounded by
shouting and whirling colors. It was over so quickly he
hardly had time to feel the shame. A stocky bearded man,
gabbling at him, cast a rope about his neck. In the background a tall figure swathed totally in a hooded burnoose,
his hands concealed in its sleeves, nodded. The burly man
said something to him and then tugged on Ian's rope, jerking
him through the hooting crowd. The tall specter strode in
their wake.*

Ian ripped his thoughts back to the cool Mediterranean
breeze that soothed his hot cheeks in the darkness. He had
been bought as a beast of burden for a caravan. Jenkins's
comforting accounts of slavery as a sailor or an agent of business were not for him. He probably had his beefy frame to
thank for that. He looked an admirable brawny pack animal.

He must not dwell upon that time. The flash of a raised
whip in the sun swept over him, the feel of skin rubbed
bloody raw under the ropes that held his giant pack as he
stumbled after the camels, equally laden, the unrelenting,
torturous sun.

No. He breathed in the cool sea air. He wouldn't think of
what followed, either.

He would think of an England that boasted the finest
medical minds, of Henry and his hopeful family and the
Stanbridge of his youth, of frivolous activities you could fill
your days with: rout parties and cockfights and turn-ups,
Jackson's and Tattersall's and White's. Thanks to the diamonds, he had enough money to enjoy London as he never
had before.

His breathing calmed. He listened to the creak of wood,
the squeal of rope, the slapping water at the hull. What use
all this memory? For better or for worse he was beyond that
time.

If only he could get beyond despair. The English doctor at Tripoli had been no help. Fool that he was, Ian had revealed all his symptoms. The doctor, horrified, ordered him from the room. Later Ian had received a note advising him to consult a doctor who specialized in hysteria. Ian was hurt and angry. *Hysteria* was a euphemism for conditions better confined in a madhouse. The doctor apparently took refuge in supposing Ian must be making up his symptoms. If only that were true . . .

After his visit with the doctor he tried a second time to end it. His naked body was blistered and cracked when a simple boy had dragged him out of the sun. The pain was so bad he'd made the boy gag him to muffle his groans. But he didn't die. He healed in three days. He had thought for sure that the sun . . .

He *must* not despair. He might yet escape what he had become. There were better doctors in England. Who was the chap who studied blood? Blundell? He might serve. And if there was no way back? Ian shuddered with a revulsion that shook his soul.

If there was no way back, then he must somehow accede to his needs without sacrificing his immortal soul and becoming like *her*. He would concentrate on his future in the radiant normalcy of England. No one need know his shameful secret. The chaos of London was his best opportunity for obscurity and normal life. He would take a bit of what he needed from the seething tide of humanity in the great sinful city. He could avoid women, lose himself in trivial occupations. He could still carve out a normal existence, but for that one not-so-small aberration.

Above all, he could escape from Africa and all it held. He would never set foot on those shores again. Already he was beyond her reach. He blinked, eyes suddenly full, and despised his weakness. He could not afford weakness if he was to keep that which grew inside him in check.

As he passed beyond that dreadful time when he was counted among the livestock of the caravan and the far more devastating months that followed, he had perhaps passed out of all human experience into some realm not quite tethered to the earth. That was his danger.

He must not let go. He must engage with the world lest the force that lurked inside him, strong and rejoicing, grow powerful enough to claim his soul.

Three

Beth wakened the next morning and realized that the ship was under way. She raised herself from her narrow cot to peer out her little window and saw several other ships of the convoy, their spread of sail magnificently white under the blue of the Mediterranean sky. She should want to leap up and be about. Often enough on other journeys the invigorating climate of the sea coupled with the promise of adventure had infused her with an energy that made her father wince. But neither the lure of Mrs. Pargutter's company nor the prospect of England was enough to draw her out of her cot this morning.

The loss of her father weighed on her. Since his death, she had seemed . . . distant from herself and from the world. It was sometimes too much effort to engage with those around her, and indeed, since she was going back to a society that would not welcome her, estrangement might be the less painful policy. Lady Metherton's drawing rooms had been a daunting precursor to a life Beth had no wish to master. Her refusal to attempt attaching any of a dozen eligible young men had driven her benefactor to distraction. They had all seemed so dull. . . .

With the rock of the swell under her, she lay back into her

bedding. Her thoughts turned again to the strange passenger,
Mr. Rufford, even as they had for long hours in the night. He
was the opposite of eligible: taciturn, gruff, the pain in his
eyes keeping everyone at a distance. What was it about him
that drew her? She could hardly deny that curiosity had
turned almost instantly to fascination. It must have to do
with the scars about his wrists. He had been a prisoner. But
he was certainly a gentleman. Had he escaped from a trans-
port on its way to Botany Bay? For what had he been im-
prisoned, and by whom? The British? The French? That
country still schemed abroad even though the war was over.
Was it one of the innumerable Pashas and Deys who set
themselves against the Turkish Sultan in this most treacher-
ous part of the world? And for what crime was he incarcer-
ated, or for what purpose if not punishment of a crime?

That was one part of the mystery of Ian Rufford. But it
was more than his scars or the fact that someone had held
him prisoner. It was the contained horror, the determination
that opposed it, and his starts of cynicism and sincerity that
provoked thought. She wanted to know more. Indeed, her
outburst of pique at his dismissal of her had been her most
spirited engagement with another since Monsieur L'Bareaux
had refused her.

It had been unseemly to converse with this stranger so
freely. She skipped ahead to considering what possible excuse she could invent to engage him. Hmmmm. He seemed
to have knowledge of Kivala and the desert. Perhaps he
could confirm her theory that the city her father had
dreamed of finding was indeed there. She and her father
thought it lay south of the mountains of the Rif. It would be
a hollow victory, since she would never see the city herself,
but just to know . . .

He might be on deck even now. She threw back her quilt,
shrugged off her night shift, and rinsed herself from her
basin, then dressed with more care than she had in some
time. The smell of grilled kidneys and greasy eggs filled her
nostrils. Nothing had ever smelled so good.

The passengers were berthed in the refurbished quarters

used by the midshipmen and minor officers when the frigate had sailed for His Majesty's Navy. There was a small common room onto which the cabins opened. The whole was forward of the foremast, as opposed to the Captain's quarters under the quarterdeck aft and the merchantman's current officers' quarters on the deck below that. On her way through the common room she was caught up short by the sound of low moaning. Guiltily she remembered her other fellow traveler. "Mrs. Pargutter?" she called, rapping gently at the cabin door. "Are you well?"

"My dear, I am wretched," came the fainting reply.

Beth stuck her head in to see her erstwhile companion holding a handkerchief reeking of vinaigrette to her mouth, the little silver-chased holder box clasped to her breast.

"Can I do anything for you, ma'am?" Beth inquired. "Call Jenny perhaps?"

"Only make them stop cooking. The smell will be the death of me!"

"Oh, dear. Well, I can certainly try." Beth doubted she could stop the crew from eating.

She swung open the door to the outer deck, a strange expectancy lodging in her throat. *You are excited about being at sea; that is all,* she told herself severely. At any rate, he had been most provoking, rude and self-involved. Arrogant. It was not he who excited her by any means.

The merchantman was under sail, many sails in fact, with an air of exhilaration about her. Beth had felt it on other ships. It came from a sailor's joy in fair weather and a rising wind. They came alive with the animation of their ship, reveling in the almost animal grace of the frigate. Steel blue swells laced with white pushed their charge along the sea. Out beyond the tangle of tarred rigging, five others of their convoy and the graceful naval sloop sailed. Even from here she could see the sloop's gun ports, her sides checkered black and white in imitation of Nelson's colors. Beth's gaze swept the deck around her in vain for the figure she sought. Bales and common crates littered the deck. Three sheep and a goat were tethered aft. Crated fowl emitted periodic squawks. The hope she refused to acknowledge died in her breast. Sailors scurried about in answer to shouts from the master on the quarterdeck and the bo'sun in the waist.

These were working men, including the officers who were no doubt eating the eggs and bacon, kidneys, and mutton she could smell. She could no more ask them to forgo the hearty breakfast of their occupation than she could return to Tripoli. It was the passengers' lot to adjust, rather than the sailors', even if that lot included smelling mutton chops and greasy eggs when you were not quite well. Mrs. Pargutter would have to deal with her problem on her own. What Beth *could* do was procure a draught from the ship's surgeon to comfort that lady's stomach.

In the bowels of the lower deck, called the orlop, she found Dr. Granger. She had not counted on the pickled state that characterized both the man and the anatomical specimens sloshing in jars around his cabin. The surgeon was bleary and leering, quite distasteful as well as ineffectual, and this at only one bell past the change of watch in the morning. One must hope the ship's crew did not require anything that might tax their medical man. Still a draught was not beyond his powers. Escaping into the light and wind of the upper decks, she delivered the paregoric to Mrs. Pargutter and refreshed that lady's vinaigrette while the patient moaned her misery. Beth wondered if it was possible for her escort to be seasick all the way to London.

The day was long. Books in her tiny, tidy cabin lined with wood and brass, and her own thoughts, were her only companions. Busy as the ship was, she did not belong to it. She was an outsider here, her role a precursor of the life that was like to await her in England and an echo of her estrangement years ago in the Crofts School for Girls.

How she longed for life in the busy, purposeful present of her father's expeditions, always the hope of the next discovery to indulge her curiosity for things strange and rare. Her conversation had been with men who had ideas and opinions and who listened to hers in return. What use, what purpose, would she have now? Her mind darted across the possibility that she would simply drift into . . . into what? Madness? Or would she become some useless female curiosity, pointed out as a hopeless antidote if she dared to walk in the park?

She took tea alone in the great stern cabin volunteered by the Captain for her comfort. The view out the great sloping windows slowly shaded as she stared at two barques from the convoy riding lightly ahead. The sea turned almost amethyst. The sun must have set.

She still had choices. She vowed to engage with the world at every turn, though she was sure she would not fit that world. Better an antidote despised for her boring talk of archaeology and geology than a madwoman locked in some asylum. Rising purposefully, she strode onto the deck, determined to sit with Mrs. Pargutter, whether that lady would or no.

But there, just coming up into the short Mediterranean twilight, was the most intriguing of her fellow passengers. The breadth of him filled the doorway. He seemed to exude power, energy . . . what should she call it? He was very, very male. Even the busy sailors felt his presence, though he was behind them, and gave way.

He looked about himself. She saw him place the position of the other vessels in the fading light and the sloop that guarded them. Then he cast his eyes about the deck. After they moved over her, they came back and rested on her in speculation. Beth was used to the eyes of personable men moving over her. She was not used to them returning. She felt her color rise. Would that her brown complexion did not show her confusion.

He moved purposefully in her direction and bowed, most correctly. He wore a black coat and buff breeches. His boots shone, though he must have tended them himself, since he had come on board without even a servant. He was clean shaven, his hair tied back neatly, no fobs or seals or rings. "Miss . . . Rochewell." He had to search for her name. Not surprising.

"Mr. . . . Mr. Rufford." Her own hesitancy was not because she did not recall his name.

He glanced to the sea again. "All is well, I hope? The convoy skims along prosperously?"

"Why, yes. How not?"

"Oh, I expect we shall hit calm seas sooner or later and wallow in our own filth for a week. Or . . ." here his deep voice grew harder, "we might even see an enemy sail."

"What enemy? Napoléon is vanquished these three years, the American war long ended."

His smile was not humorous. "We might always catch sight of a local corsair."

Beth chuckled, dismissing his fears. "We have a sloop of the Royal Navy for protection. No pirate would dare to come within a league of us."

"True, if the sloop's Captain fights true. I have known them to run shy when there were only merchantmen involved." The bitterness in his voice was back.

"Who is more competent than the King's Navy? They rule the water."

He did not contradict her. He simply looked at the merchantmen shushing through the sea around them, silent with their distance, the placement of HMS the sloop, then cast his eyes to the rigging and swept the deck and its occupants. Sailors were putting out lanterns in the rigging. Lamps flickered on the boats around them as well, a small, warm constellation.

He seemed disinclined to continue conversation. Beth racked her brain for a way to engage him. "You have been in your cabin all the day, sir. Does the voyage not agree with you?"

He fixed her with his steady gaze. "Night is more congenial to one of my temperament."

"Ahh." The silence stretched. The crew moved about on tasks unknowable, oblivious. "Do you dine with the Captain? I am afraid you must be famished, having missed your dinner."

He nodded and picked out his watch. It was two hours to supper. "We have some time before we eat," he remarked, looking conscious, as if he considered making a proposal.

Beth mustered her courage. "I saw a chessboard in the stern cabin."

"Do you play?" he asked, curious.

"A little."

"Why do I think you are a Trojan horse, Miss Rochewell?"

"Because no one who really plays chess only 'a little' would admit it?"

A tiny smile played about his lips. "Just so. Let us repair to the stern cabin. I wonder if you can give me a brisk game."

She could, for she had played with her father for all those long equatorial evenings. But she began with a conservative opening. Boldness was for later. She could not help but notice that he wore some spicy scent, cinnamon and something more elusive. It did not fit with his austerity.

They played in silence. Beth wondered how she would broach any subject at all with her mysterious partner. Her eyes were drawn to the way his coat bulged over his biceps as he put his elbows on the table. He laid his cleft chin on his clasped hands, eyes on the board. Finally he glanced to her face. "You know the classic game. Are you capable of more?"

He moved his knight in a rogue attack, too early by far, on her queen, three—no, four moves out. She stared, sorting through the sequences engendered by each possible counter-attack. Conservative play said she should block with her knight. But if she attacked with her rook she not only blocked but also set up a sequence that, if he complied, might weigh the balance in her favor. The flurry of taken pieces might distract him. She reached for the crenellated ivory.

Play accelerated. Both collected their downed opponents. The rush of play unfolded as each pursued a strategy that must collide, Beth knew.

There! He had allowed her queen the avenue required.

She moved.

He sucked in a breath, stopped. Seconds stretched. The climax loomed. One possibility . . .

He moved his king.

"Stalemate," she said, letting go her pent-up breath. "You have robbed me."

"But I could not win."

"No," she agreed, letting it be known she had expected that.

"So . . ." He pushed back from the table, glancing one final time at the board as if to retrieve some other outcome. "This voyage will allow scope for a rematch?"

"If you like." She let her tone say, "If you dare."

Behind him, Redding, the loblolly boy who had served her tea, looked in on them. "Miss Rochewell, Mr. Rufford, may I get you some lemon scrub, perhaps, before dinner?"

"Wine for me, I think, and Madeira for the lady," Mr. Rufford responded.

Redding ducked his head and disappeared.

"I am surprised you did not order ratafia for me," Beth observed, too sweetly.

He looked surprised. "You wanted wine? Madeira survives shipping in far better countenance than any claret."

"Perhaps I wanted to choose for myself." She scooped the pieces into their box.

He lounged back in his chair. "You are a strange creature, Miss Rochewell."

"I have no doubt of that." She was very well aware that she was not attractive. Was that what he meant by *strange*? She felt herself flushing as she put the box away. Behind her there was silence. But she could feel the physical presence of him. She glanced behind her and saw him flushing in return.

"My apologies," he said in that sensuous baritone of his as he looked away. "I, of all people, have no right to call another strange."

What could he mean? "Well," she managed. "Perhaps we have our strangeness in common as well as our humanity."

He looked up at her with a longing she found painful. "Perhaps not," he whispered. He rose, as though he might flee.

Luckily or unluckily, Redding returned with the wine.

"Sorry, miss, Mr. Rufford, these particul'r bottles wa'n't easy to come by, if you get my meaning."

Rufford's scruples apparently would not allow him to abandon her publicly. He sat on the edge of his chair while Redding poured. By the time Redding bowed out, Rufford had recovered his composure and Beth had decided that the mystery of Mr. Rufford was deeper than she had supposed.

He raised his glass. "To England, Miss Rochewell, and a quick voyage."

"To England," she returned, with rather less enthusiasm. She sat opposite him.

"Where do you call home in England?"

Beth watched his valiant effort at nonchalance, fascinated. Light from the swinging lamp moved across his form. What was it about him that was so . . . attractive? It was the way his body moved inside his clothes, perhaps. Or the thick column of his throat. The cleft chin? Maybe. The eyes, of course, the curling hair. She felt his presence almost viscerally, somewhere deep inside her. He seemed more physical than anyone she had ever known and . . . male, as Monsieur L'Bareaux or the camel drivers never had.

He raised his brows and she realized that he was waiting for some answer. What had he asked? Oh yes. "I . . . I don't call anywhere in England home. I am bound for my aunt's house in London. And that will surprise her immensely, so I can only hope my letter arrives before I do, so she may pretend a welcome."

He did not press her but looked out on the dark sea through the great stern windows to where the lanterns of other ships bobbed on the swell.

"And you, sir? Where do you go?" Suddenly she wanted to keep him talking.

"Perhaps to Suffolk. My brother will be surprised as well. Henry inherited a couple of years ago. He will no doubt have set things to rights. He was always very practical."

His tone said he denigrated practicality. She decided being practical had its deficits. "Then you also must have lost your father," she said, hesitating. "My condolences."

"Unnecessary, believe me." He tossed off a glug of wine. "The old autocrat terrorized his family and brought the estate to wrack with his gambling and his . . . other habits." He shook his head to shake off any effect his father had on him. Ludicrous, of course, but natural.

"Fathers can be complicated. My own father loved me but was so distracted he sometimes quite forgot to provide for me. His payments to my school were irregular to say the least. The silver lining was that I was forced to insist he take me with him at fifteen. The independence I learned arranging his expeditions would be useful anywhere but England."

"How do you mean?" He put his hand out to toy with his wineglass. It was inches from her clasped hands. She felt it like a magnet. If she was not careful, she would take it in her own.

"Only . . . only that in England no one seems to allow females to provide for themselves."

"Females provide for themselves in quite a determined manner on the Marriage Mart." His expression darkened.

"By getting a man to do so by proxy," she protested. "A husband controls his wife's fortune, her property. A woman is lucky if her father can negotiate settlements to provide for her widowhood. No, I was thinking of something more direct."

His smile was very small. It changed his face. "You mean setting up as a governess?"

She sighed. "I hope I do not have to resort to employment. Almost no one wants their children to learn archaeology and geology and Arabic."

His brows drew together. "Perhaps your aunt will help you to a suitable match."

"Unlikely. I will never marry a man I cannot respect, or even . . ." Should she say it? What was this man to her that she should refrain? "Love."

"I hope you have choices which suit you, then." He dismissed her as naïve.

"I have a fair portion which should let me live independently." She did not relish being thought naïve, whether that was true or not. She rushed on. "Father put money in the Consuls in my name. I was considering whether to offer up my portion to support his next expedition when he was struck on the head by that perfectly arbitrary bit of masonry." She sighed. "I can't help feeling his death was a judgment on my selfishness."

"Selfishness?" Rufford snorted. "Because you *considered* keeping the provision he had made for your future in just such a case? And don't tell me you believe in divine retribution for your thoughts, because anyone who plays chess as you do would be lying."

All the tears she had not yet shed tangled in her chest and made breath difficult. "You don't understand how important his dream was to him. A significant discovery would mean he had mattered. He wanted to find that lost city more than he wanted anything." She smiled wistfully. "Including me." She came to herself. "My portion would have been a small sacrifice."

She sipped her Madeira, conscious of his gaze.

He said in a tight voice, "You would not want to find that city. It is evil."

"So the folklore says," she agreed eagerly. "I collected maps, testimonials, even all those tales of bloodsucking and ancient evil. I found one Imam, very old, in Tunis, who I think has actually been to Kivala. I know we could have found it. We were on our way to consult him when my father . . ." Her companion's face contorted in horror. "Whatever is the matter?"

Mr. Rufford was saved by the pipe to dinner from answering. He sprang up as though released and knocked his head upon a beam, swearing under his breath. When he raised it, he was master once again. "Shall we?" he asked, only a slight hoarseness conveying the distress she had witnessed.

She nodded, her brow knotted. Why that severe reaction? What had she said?

She preceded Mr. Rufford across the deck to the Captain's cabin, his bulk and his emotion a dark force almost palpable behind her, his cinnamon scent dissipated by the ocean air. The mystery of the man was not lessened by her conversation. She doubted that a dinner in the very public company of the ship's officers was likely to shed any light on that mystery. But the voyage was long and suddenly very much more interesting than she had thought it would be.

Four

Damn her eyes! Why did he have to be confined on a ship with one of the few English people who knew anything at all about the legends of an evil in the desert?

Ian stood at the rail again watching the lights on the merchantmen, now drifting farther away, now nearing in the wee hours as the convoy cruised slowly on at the speed of the most sluggish of her members. The boys heaving the log sang out four knots at most.

Supper with the officers stopped any prying questions. And it had allowed him to take his gauge of her more fully. She spoke fluent Turkish. He had not let on that he understood her as she complimented the Turkish sailing master on the science of navigation his ancestors had defined. Only the Captain or the passengers could initiate conversation, and Tindly was a blockish man who indulged in avaricious anecdotes. So she made it her job to knit conversation together across the table of officers with practical questions. She dealt with the crew's attention good-naturedly, not mistaking it for real regard. She *did* have social graces. They were simply different from those practiced in London drawing rooms.

She was not conventionally pretty and she definitely thought she had no beauty. She might be wrong. Her tawny

green eyes were certainly a shock in the light. They made
her look exotic. And there was something about her . . . Just
what it was eluded him. Was it that she was an original?
What woman did he know who could give him a game of
chess and spoke Turkish? Or was it the way she moved, with
unconscious . . . freedom? Whatever it was, her particular
charms would not be valued in parochial England. He gazed
out over the waters. The fact that she was intelligent and
even knew Kivala by name meant his secrets were not safe.
She was a woman, too, and therefore untrustworthy. An image darted into his brain of lithe white limbs, billowing silk
curtains, compulsion overwhelming even pain with lust. . . .

"Jib and topsails!" Bare feet hurried unseen and a triangular sheet flapped into place.

He jerked himself from the rail and lurched across the waist
to climb the forward stairs to the bow. Let the wind wash his
thoughts clean. White water coursed out from the ship's side.

He would never allow a woman to overcome him again.

He thought of his brother Henry and his Mary. If only
you could keep that first tenuous promise of happiness and
interlocking sympathies throughout the years. How many
marriages had he seen where the woman strove in subtle
ways to make her husband feel smaller, more mean-spirited,
than he was and in consequence behave that way? Would his
father have been the absent wastrel if his mother had not
been the oppressive saint? They lived only to torment each
other and gain the upper hand. No, women were not for him.

He steeled his emotions. When he got to Stanbridge
Court he would find Mary grown into a fat shrew and Henry
looking for more temporary and convenient comforts else-
where while taking solace in the fact that he was immortal
through his children.

Immortality . . .

*The caravan gathered at the edge of the desert. Braying
camels settled in the sand, their packs piled beside them,
their brightly colored rope halters fitted with dangling tas-*

sels to keep the flies from their eyes. Still their ears twitched almost constantly. Flies were everywhere. Men in striped burnooses and plain walked among the beasts. Others bargained with merchant victualers in loud voices. Boys hopped among the camel drivers, hawking figs and dates.

Ian stumbled into camp, urged on by shouting in a language he did not understand and by the crack of the whip across his bare back. He was linked by rough hemp rope at the neck to five others, all half-naked as he was. They had fitted him with rough sandals to protect his feet. His breeches had been replaced by a scrap of cloth tied around his loins. How he had survived the march from the slave market in Algiers to this remote stretch of godforsaken desert he could hardly tell. His back was raw with lashes. The rope at his neck, rubbing the sweaty skin, had worn a necklace of blood. He was burnt by the sun. For days he had stumbled on, delirious with sun and the infection in his shoulder. But slowly he had regained his senses. The slaves were given water at intervals and allowed to sleep, a rough canvas slung over them when their small party stopped in the worst heat of the day. The six slaves were all fine male specimens, big, with powerful muscles and comely features. Only one other European, a Frenchman, was tied in their train. The rest were Arabs and a huge black man. Ian spoke excellent French, enough to communicate with the Black and the Frenchman, but the slaves were beaten for speaking to one another, so it came to nothing.

Tents dotted the perimeter of the caravan, the inner ones fine, the outer ones shabby and ragged. And one tent, much richer than the others, stood at a distance from the bustle under some waving palms. The awning had worked borders in blue and gold. Nearby, a litter sat in the sand, colorful silk pillows just visible inside the thick draperies.

The slaves were whipped toward several large posts driven deep in the sand and set with heavy metal rings. Another half-dozen well-made males were already shackled there. At some distance a rabble of other slaves, ranging from old to young and including some women, huddled in a rope pen. A fat bearded man took charge of the newcomers

*and shouted at them, gesturing toward an anvil. They shuf-
fled forward, and the hemp at their necks was replaced by a
heavy metal wristband, closed by a bolt pounded home with
a great hammer on the anvil. Each shackle carried a length
of chain. Thus separated, they were chained to the posts.
There was no awning for the slaves. They sat in the heat,
drooping. A boy came over with a bucket from the nearby oasis. The water was hot and brackish, but each gulped their
share from the ewer.*

*Ian dozed, fevered dreams of England tumbling in his
head. As the sun dropped below the horizon, the caravan began to murmur. Lamps flickered in the beautiful tent. Ian could
see a form moving inside, a particularly lithe female form.*

*As the twilight deepened, the flap of the tent opened and a
woman emerged. Immediately stares from every part of the
caravan camp converged upon her. And what was more natural? She walked with hips thrust out, long legs creamy white
emerging from an almost translucent skirt in dusky orange,
slit to her hip. Ian had never seen a more shapely leg. Her
torso was both covered and revealed by an X of cloth that
covered her breasts and bared her belly. Around her neck
was a collar six inches wide made of long cylindrical beads
of crystal, jet, and lapis lazuli that matched the earrings
that dripped from her ears.*

*It was her face that hypnotized. Her nose was long,
straight, her lips full in a small mouth. She had a delicate,
pointed chin. But her most striking features were her eyes.
They were black, as far as he could tell in the dim light, and
outlined in kohl so that each streaked out to a point on her
temples, making her look Eastern and exotic, as though she
were not the embodiment of the exotic already. Her cosmet-
ics and her dress were Egyptian, yet the white of her flesh
contradicted them. The air around her seemed to vibrate
with vitality. The thrust of her hips proclaimed that she knew
men; the cold insolence of her eyes said that she was mistress of them.*

*And so she was. Men bent low before her and pushed their
foreheads into the sand. She must certainly be the owner of*

*the caravan and all its contents. The tall, thin figure who had
bought Ian walked behind her, his hood now thrown back.
He was no slave, for his look was proud. Behind him ran
young boys, perhaps fourteen, slaves by the chains on their
thin wrists.*

*She looked about her at the quiescent caravan and issued
some peremptory orders Ian did not understand. The tall
Arab gestured toward the stakes where the new slaves were
tethered and whispered in her ear. Their keeper beat the
slaves into appropriate prostration. Raising his eyes, Ian
could see her feet, toenails painted with delicate opales-
cence so that they gleamed even in the twilight, silver rings
upon two or three of her toes. An anklet thick with tiny bells
tinkled. The scent of cinnamon and something else wafted
over him. He had never felt so wretched as when the finely
worked leather of her sandals stopped before him. She spoke
to the keeper. Her voice was musical, throaty. The keeper
poked Ian's shoulder with his whip, his rough voice humble.
Ian struggled to his feet and the keeper urged the others up
as well. Then a boy went along the line, jerking their loin-
cloths from them until they were naked before her.*

*Ian wondered that he could yet flush with all he had en-
dured in the last weeks. The boy stepped up in response to
her instruction and squeezed Ian's testicles. Ian bellowed
and slapped him away. The keeper struck Ian about his head
with a truncheon and knocked him to his knees, where he
crouched in defense. Swearing, the keeper kicked him in the
ribs. Ian's head cleared only slowly. The queenly woman
asked the boy a question. The boy responded in the affirma-
tive, then went down the line, apparently testing each man
for evidence that he was not a eunuch. The others learned
from the results of Ian's outburst and did not protest. The
woman conversed with the tall Arab. She pointed to six of
the slaves, including one of the Arabs from his party, the
Black, and Ian. Then she drifted away on the slight breeze
that breathed hot on Ian's neck. The tall Arab stalked silently
behind her.*

As the moon rose, the caravan wakened. Camels were

loaded. So were the slaves. Ian was fitted with an enormous
pack: a wooden frame tied on with rough hemp straps over
his shoulders. His iron bracelet, chafing at his wrist, dangled
the chain that could be used to bind him to any handy post.
He was just another naked pack animal for the caravan.

The black man was sent to the litter. Ian watched as the mis-
tress of the caravan stepped delicately into the silken interior.
The slaves hefted its poles to their shoulders. Camels rose to
their feet. The slave keeper whipped his charges into line. Ian
staggered under the weight of his pack. He was positioned just
in front of the litter by his bearded keeper, while the men not
chosen joined the rabble of other slaves at the back of the long
line. The caravan started south across a rocky wash toward
the open desert, plodding over the sand into the night.

Not a dream but memories filtered into Ian's consciousness
as he woke to daylight leaking under the door of the cabin
and the ship making way across the sea again. There had
been many months of cruel treatment as the caravan wandered in the desert without a seeming destination. What kind
of a caravan did not trade but packed its goods merely as
supplies for some circuitous journey? He should have known
something was wrong. The fact that they traveled by night,
and bandits ran from them, and the strange wounds that always marked the one slave who walked beside the litter—all
should have made Ian tremble in fear. And there was the horrible disease that seemed to be killing the poorer stock of
slaves. One died every few days of some condition that left
them like dried husks in the sand.

A despairing chuckle gurgled in Ian's throat. How innocent he had been! But even had he realized the import of
what he saw, what could he have done? There was no escape
so deep in the desert, as he had learned to his cost. Slowly,
he had become a beast himself, raw from the leather and
rope of the pack, cringing from the blows of his keeper, always thirsty, always seeking relief from the glaring eye of
the sun. Perhaps the only sign that he was yet a man had

been that he learned rudimentary Arabic from the rough men around him. There was no other choice if he was to avoid a beating. Again the memories assaulted him.

The slave beside the litter was drawn inside the curtains sometimes several times a night. After some weeks, he died one night in his tracks of the strange wounds he bore.

She alighted, her black hair shining silver in the moonlight. Without a glance at the slave's crumpled body she ordered him dragged away, left in the desert for the vultures and jackals. A camel driver approached and accosted her about the water rations. She growled, low in her throat, and hit him a backhanded blow. It took his head off. Blood spattered. Ian blinked, unbelieving. Was she that strong? Ian struggled for breath. The tall Arab deposited the second body with the first, its head separate, as all others gaped, stunned.

She walked around the palanquin, looking the bearers up and down. She motioned the big Arab away from his pole. The keeper unlocked his chain. Fear made the Arab's eyes roll white. She glanced ahead to where Ian and the Frenchman and two more Arabs shouldered their packs. Ian stared resolutely at the ground, trying to look unworthy of her attention.

But the keeper cuffed him and commanded him to kneel. The pack was loosened. As in a nightmare he shrugged it off. The keeper spoke sharply and whipped him over to the rear pole vacated by the Arab. His chain was fastened to the ring. Ian and the other three bearers hefted the litter, and the caravan moved off once again. Before they had gone a mile, the hangings opened and a slender arm beckoned to the Arab. The slave shook his head, a low wail growing in his throat. Suddenly all his resistance, all his fear, ceased. The slave crawled up through the hangings. Ian felt his weight descend upon the litter. For many miles, the shifting weights, the movement inside, made it an even more wearisome burden.

• • •

A huge crash brought Beth up from her cabin in the late afternoon, clutching her cloak around her. The day had been filled with confused shouting and Mrs. Pargutter's moans, punctuated by the flapping rain and thunder of a very persistent storm. Water sluiced on deck everywhere. Wood chips cascaded as a great pole was planed smooth to form a makeshift spar. Men spliced broken rope and hauled bales and crates back to their places. The Captain shouted orders for more sail. Beyond the frantic activity the sun set in some splendor, the ominous black now scudding away to the north. Not a single ship of the convoy was visible.

A cry from aloft made Beth crane her head upward. "Sail-ho, east-sou'east!"

Beth looked around, but she could see nothing from the level of the deck. Tension filled the air, each man turning anxiously to the quarterdeck. The Captain heaved his bulk up the quarterdeck stairs, calling for his glass. They should feel relieved that the convoy converged, yet relief was nowhere evident. Slowly, Beth realized that if they had fallen behind the convoy because of the broken mast, a sail astern might not be welcome news.

The Captain stood braced on the rail, glass to his eye. "Heave the log!" he shouted.

Off to her right a young man sent a small round log over the side attached to a knotted rope. He let the knots slip through his hands as another boy held an hourglass. The second boy shouted, "Stop!" The other pinched the rope. "Five knots, two fathoms."

Beth watched the Captain search the rigging, then the sky, still filled with wind. "Stud' s'ls upper and lower!" he shouted. His words were echoed by at least two others, and men scurried up the rigging. Out to the sides like wings, sails flapped into place. The ship lurched ahead.

Beth staggered to the rail as the sail behind them held its distance or even gained.

" 'E got the weather gauge," a fearsome-looking man with a scarred cheek and a great long pigtail muttered.

"Cain't come up afore nightfall," another, stouter, reassured him. "We'll crack on."

"This bucket won't make eight knots, and he don't keep her rigged taut, neither."

This brought only a glum grunt from his partner. Beth searched the horizon again in the gloom to the east. The following ship was definitely closer. What kind of ship could it be? England was at peace with Spain and France. A privateer?

"No doubt those buggers in the sloop will start lookin' fer stragglers," the first muttered.

"Better hope."

The Captain gave incessant orders. Beth stood now on the starboard deck in the waist as discreetly as she could and tried to be small enough to be out of everyone's way. She did not want to be stifled below deck in this hour of the ship's need, though there was nothing she could do to help. She concentrated on the dark shape in the gathering gloom so hard she yelped when Mr. Rufford's bass rumble sounded almost in her ear.

"What's toward?" he asked.

"Oh my!" Beth held her palm to her breast. "It's you."

He stared into the darkness astern. The chasing ship was hardly visible.

"That boat appeared about an hour ago. The crew seemed quite concerned." He glanced at her and lifted one brow. She chuffed in annoyance. "Very well. We lost a spar in the storm. Which you must have known, because who could ever sleep through such a din? We fell behind. And the convoy is scattered, so we're entirely without protection at the moment."

"I can see," he said, again peering aft.

He couldn't possibly see, since it was quite dark. "Well, you may not have noticed the confusion. Things are, as seamen say, all ahoo. No one seems to catch the Captain's orders, and they don't respect them, either. And the other ship quite clearly has the . . . the weather gauge."

"Our chaser *is* more organized." He pointed at the shadow against the dark of the east.

No one could make out anything there now, Beth thought.

"Have they said what she is?"

"No," Beth said. "How could they?"

"The Captain knows, for he has a glass and he is cracking on as best he can even after dark." He looked up. "The damn fool hasn't doused his running lights. Maybe he is waiting until right before he wears the ship."

"Wears?" Beth asked.

"Turns it by setting it into the wind. It backs around instead of tacking. He'll wait until after it is true dark, then set out in a new direction to see if he can lose our chaser."

"Could it not be a friendly boat?" Beth asked in a small voice.

The tension in his body as he gripped the rail answered her even before he said, "She's a xebec by the set of her sails, likely a Barbary ship, or a Turk."

Beth lost her assurance that he couldn't see the vessel. "A pirate, then?"

"Yes." The words were torn from tight lips. He glanced up at the sails of their own frigate. "No foretopgallant, no royals. He could make more sail."

"Perhaps he thinks he'll break another mast. . . ."

"No time for caution." Rufford whirled and stalked up the ladder right into the Captain's sacred domain. Rough words ensued, ending in Rufford being escorted off the quarterdeck.

"Keep yourself to yourself, sir," the first mate muttered, "or you'll be locked in irons."

"Fool!"

"Aye, but 'e's Captain nonetheless," the first mate said, low, and retreated.

"He means to try to outrun her, but he sets his sails timidly," Rufford said in a flat voice. "He thinks he can make the protection of the sloop before she carries us. He's sure it is on its way back to collect us. That is why he leaves his lights on, and plans no evasive maneuver."

Beth caught her breath. "You don't think it is possible?"

He glanced at her and hardened. "Perhaps."

"A pleasant lie but probably not useful," she remarked. "In case you don't think I know what that might mean, I do. And since I am nowhere near pretty enough to grace a first-rate seraglio, it might be relatively unpleasant."

Her bluntness must have startled him, for he looked sharply at her.

"What are we to do, then?" she asked, prompting.

He straightened. "They will not sink us. They do not mean to see our cargo at the bottom of the sea. They'll try to board. Our guns are not near those of our sloop-protector—carronades fit only for close range and even then hardly accurate. We'll have to let them close with us to fire them. If they manage to board, we might repel them, if these bastards will fight." He looked his apology for the profanity.

"Then let us hope these bastards will fight," she returned. "They seem hardened enough, but they are only merchant seamen. One can never tell what is in a man's heart. Will he fight if he is not led?" She looked pointedly up at him.

"You already know my opinion of Tindly."

"There must be a remedy for that. . . ." Let him make of it what he would.

He peered around. "They have seen action. Look at them. Eager. Thank God pirates are willing to fight at night. There may still be hope."

What did he mean? Their chances must surely be much better if the pirates did not engage them at night. He turned again to her. "We will put you females into the hold. You may escape the second-rate seraglio yet, ma'am." He smiled, tightly. That was his resolution again.

"Poor Mrs. Pargutter! Surely we do not have to take such measures yet."

"Battles at sea are damnably slow, Miss Rochewell. They will not catch us for hours."

Beth vowed she would not be clapped into the hold to await her fate. There must be some more active role she could play to be of use.

Something else occurred to her. She looked up at Rufford. He might be killed in the battle that was coming. She might be killed or worse. To have all the possibilities of life twisted off at the root so suddenly seemed . . . unfair. Mr. Rufford might never live to see the sorrow in his eyes quenched by a renewed love of life. And she . . . she would never even have been kissed.

Five

For the next hours Ian watched the pirate corsair close on them with the girl at his side. Their Captain's orders were timid and contrary, causing havoc on deck. That damned incompetent would be the death of them. Ian swore he would not be taken slave again. Since suicide was denied him, he must fight to the last drop of his blood.

"Does he *want* them to board us?" he muttered to Miss Rochewell as they leaned over the railing, craning to see. "If he will not crack on, why does he not wear and give them a broadside? We are in range, surely." The crews were ready at their guns. Carronades required only two men to fight them, unlike the longer cannons, which took eight. Merchant ships carried far fewer men than a Navy vessel or a pirate.

The girl started as the hands brought up a clanking batch of sabers and pikes. "The Captain certainly thinks we will be boarded," she observed with a creditable imitation of calm.

No weapon was offered to Ian, but he could rectify that lapse once the fighting started. The hands hoisted a net of ropes above the frigate's waist.

"What thing is this?" Miss Rochewell cried.

"It protects the deck from splinters." It was no good to

minimize the danger, and she did not seem to be a female who wanted lies. "The pirates will try to take out our rigging with their cannon instead of sinking the ship."

She gulped and nodded. "I suppose you mean very great splinters."

"I have seen them two-foot-long and more."

"So you have experience of battle at sea?"

He tried to keep his voice flat. "And of the unhappy issue of losing such a battle."

At last the order came: "Wear ship! Prepare the starboard guns."

"You must go below." He hallooed the first mate and explained his plan for the women.

"I'll see to Mrs. Pargutter and Jenny. You are needed here." But she did not turn to go. She looked up at him for a long moment with those luminous eyes. She was afraid, and yet she wanted something.

"What is it?" he asked, not sure he wanted to know.

She cleared her throat. "I have never been kissed, you know."

He almost smiled. She had obviously never been in mortal danger, either. Not so much to ask. He leaned down. She looked up, wide-eyed with expectation. The burden of that expectation could not be fulfilled. Still, he brushed her lips with his. A shock went through him, straight to his unruly member. Her mouth was soft, yielding. He did not intend to linger, and yet . . .

He pulled away. She stared up at him, unblinking.

She came to herself. "Thank you," she said simply. She turned with almost a shiver and rushed away. Looking back over her shoulder, she called anxiously, "Be careful of splinters!"

He watched her hurry into the cabin. Why had he done that? Had he not forsworn women? What right had she to ask him for a kiss? It had seemed a simple request. But it was not. He rubbed his mouth, the feel of her lips still lingering there.

"Good job, mate." A sailor winked.

"Aye, maybe she'll need another!" A young man with a dirty face leered.

"She won't," Ian said roughly. Damn the chit!

The ship came slowly round. Men leaned over their guns. The sulfurous smell of powder and lit match drifted across the deck in trails of smoke.

"On my signal, fore to aft!" called the Captain. "Fire!" He missed the roll of the swell. Still, the squat guns fired off in a ragged, sequential bark that left the deck covered in smoke and Ian's hearing deadened. The stout brass cannons jerked back against their housings. Crews heaved them up to their ports, rammed home a swab on a stick, and stuffed down more powder and ball. Ian heard answering booms from the pirate. Above him, sails shrieked as they split.

Their own guns spoke again in an irregular order. The xebec answered quickly. The pirates fired faster and they fired clean. Rigging fell across the splinter net. Sails flapped free and drooped over the waist. The *Beltrane*'s bowsprit was carried away in the third volley. She could not steer against the wind. A gunner screamed as his carronade broke its housing and crushed him against the opposite rail. The mast shuddered as it was hit. Their only hope was to sink their enemy before she closed. The xebec must be taking punishment, even with the inaccuracy of the carronades and the difficulty of aiming through the smoke.

They heard her before they saw her. The wash of water from her bow was clear in the silence between the speaking guns. Ian lurched for the pile of cutlasses. Above him, the mast finally fell across the deck, pinning several hands. There was no time to answer their screams, for the xebec appeared like a ghost ship out of the smoke. Was she going to ram them?

The master on the enemy deck could be seen spinning the wheel madly. Sails flapped down, and suddenly the ship backed and turned in her own length. The pirates, whatever their origins, were capital sailors. The ship coasted in, side to side.

"Prepare to repel boarders!" the Captain shouted. The call was repeated along the deck.

Across scant feet of water, the waist of the pirate ship was filled to overflowing with eager swarthy faces, many scarred, their hair wound in bandanas or hanging down in braids, their beards full and flowing. Ian was struck to the heart. Just such as these had taken him before.

And he would be damned if they were going to take him again! He hefted the cutlass, meant for brutal combat at close quarters. So be it. Wild life throbbed in his veins.

Ian glanced to the quarterdeck. The Captain whispered orders. The damned coward was going to strike his colors! Boarding lines were cast from the enemy to anchor the ships together. Around him men were confused, uncertain.

"If they take us," Ian shouted, his voice booming over the din, "they'll put to slavery any they don't torture into conversion!" Men around him turned. "I'll not be a slave again in this life or the next!" The ships were almost kissing sides. Several seasoned hands gripped their cutlasses. More picked up weapons. "There's no surrender, here, even if the colors come down!" Pirates came pouring over the side. "For God and country if you like, or for yourselves and freedom!"

He lunged into the cascade of bodies, slashing madly. The first man to feel his cutlass's bite lost an arm and fell shrieking. The second was cut half-through. Behind him, the *Beltranes* gave a shout. Several stepped up beside him, hacking. Something inside him wakened. Power surged up through his veins. He should have felt afraid; whether of the horrible odds or of the terrible gush of strength and joy that surged inside him, he could not tell. But he was not afraid.

In moments the deck was awash in blood. Ian shoved and cut about him with abandon. He felt a slash along his thigh from a fallen pirate and kicked him away. The pirates forged ahead with wicked recklessness, shouting in foreign tongues. Bodies piled. Ian's shoulder took a pike whose owner spouted a fountain of red in the next instant. A small circle gave way and Ian whirled his heavy sword in a deadly swathe. Two heads toppled to the deck. Three. *Beltranes* screamed in triumph and filled the gap he'd made. The tide of battle changed.

A shout rang out. The pirates were falling back. Would they be able to regroup? He looked around wildly. The ships were side to side. Carronades might win the day! Ian sprang into action. The cannons were all askew. Several rolled about the deck, creating havoc, maiming men. Ian put a shoulder into a great gun as it careered by him. He rolled its fifteen hundredweight up to an empty gun port. A seaman with a grisly scalp wound bound it in place with rope strands from a ruined halyard. Ian swabbed and put the powder down. There was no match. He searched the deck.

He saw her, pressed against the quarterdeck wall, not safe in the hold below. She held a capstan bar like a club. Two pirates lay at her feet with bloody pates. He swore to himself. She saw him. Her eyes lit in recognition of his need. She plucked a lit match from the dead hand of a boy not old enough to shave and lunged forward. Ian heaved up the back end of the gun so it pointed down as far as the port allowed. Miss Rochewell handed him the match.

"On the downward roll!" Ian yelled. A pause for the swell; match to powder. The gun roared. The ball plowed into the xebec below the waterline. Ian took the brunt of the recoil in his shoulder as the damaged cat's paw breeching broke. His shoulder buckled. The gun creaked to a stop.

"Get below!" he yelled to the girl. "Are your brains to let?"

Sporadic fighting ranged over the deck. He pushed her toward the companionway and turned back to the xebec. The pirates were regrouping for another assault. The merchant crew was hopelessly outnumbered. Their only chance was to sink the pirate ship. Sailors ran two guns up to their ports but could not lift their rear ends high enough to get their shot below the enemy's waterline. Ian put his shoulder under the first and heaved, yelling, "Fire the damn thing!" The sailors protested that the recoil would kill him, but they fired anyway.

It did not. He could feel another crack in his shoulder, but the pain was distant. The second gun was served the same. The pirates still leaped from the waist to the merchantman. Motion to the left caught his eye and he swung round to see

the damned girl with a lantern. She swung it back and forth
for momentum and heaved it over the side to the pirate vessel. It broke across a gun. The powder sack exploded. Flame
leaped up the tarred ropes to the canvas above.

"Stand away, girl!" Ian bellowed. One of the pirates
lunged for her and caught her about the throat. Ian strode
across the heaving deck to jerk him away and run him
through. Several *Beltranes* caught the girl's idea and lanterns
now hailed onto the pirate ship. Ian slashed and tossed bodies overboard, his cutlass running red. Bodies littered the
deck, some groaning, others past all sound. Fire engulfed the
xebec. The *Beltrane*'s Captain shouted to the crew to make
what sail they could. Men scrambled up the rigging. The
Beltrane began to pull away.

The pirates must board or die. Their vessel was wallow-
ing ominously. The rigging was alight. A rain of grappling
hooks caught the merchant's railing and pulled the ships together once again. A crowd of desperate men prepared to
leap across and fight for their lives.

Ian picked up the giant spar and waded through the fighting. He braced it against the corsair and heaved. The ropes
of the grappling hooks narrowed and stretched with a clear
creak behind the shouts and grunts of fighting. Ian felt a
thump against his back, as though a horse had kicked him. A
rope burst with a twang, and then another. He pushed himself against the spar. Other *Beltranes* joined him. The ropes
gave a sproinging sound as they snapped, and the xebec
drifted beyond the reach of the spar.

As the distance grew, a dozen pirates leaped into the water, a hail of bodies, rather than stay on their burning ship.
The few remaining enemies on board the *Beltrane* begged
quarter. Ian watched the flaming torch of a ship recede, even
as his joy and strength ebbed. The *Beltrane* slowly pulled
away again. At two hundred yards, the xebec exploded in a
travesty of celebration fireworks as her powder stores
caught.

The *Beltranes* roared amid the raining debris.

"Let that serve them for attacking free English vessels."

Though Ian did not think he said it loudly, yet cries of "Hear him!" and "As the gentleman says!" rose around him.

They watched in silence as pieces of the corsair burned on the water. All hands left on that ship were lost.

"Get the wounded below!" the Captain bellowed. "Bo'-sun, rig the spare as mainmast!"

Ian took a breath. There would be no slavery this time. A strange lassitude came over him and with it, pain in a hundred parts of his body. He looked down and saw his coat, his breeches, both soaked with blood. His boots squelched with it. His hand on his sword hilt was red-black in the dim light where blood had dripped down his sleeve.

"You'd best get to the surgeon." Resentment choked the Captain's sentiment.

But with his returning senses, Ian knew he could do no such thing.

"It's mostly pirate blood. I shall retire, with your permission." He turned carefully, head spinning. He was hardly in command of himself by the time he reached the girl. He could do no more than nod to her before plunging into the common room and groping his way to his cabin. He shut the door, held out a shaky hand toward his cot, and collapsed.

Beth watched Mr. Rufford stumble past her, her senses overwhelmed. Small pieces of burning wood and ash hailed on the deck from the exploding pirate ship amid a pervasive scent of gunpowder. Sailors picked themselves up and began to loot the bodies of their enemies. Splashes sounded as some were heaved overboard. The ship's officers were barking orders. Men who were able strode to the pumps. Others carried their fellows to the sick bay. *I hope the surgeon is not drunk*, she thought.

Wait! She turned to where Mr. Rufford had disappeared. Realization struck her. He had been covered in blood, with unseeing eyes and stumbling step. She pushed into the passengers' common room. The lantern swung in lazy arcs above, casting wild shadows. Mrs. Pargutter's cabin was empty, Beth having bundled her and Jenny below an eternity ago.

Mr. Rufford's door was closed. "Mr. Rufford?" There was no answer. She rapped hesitantly on the door. "Are you well, sir?"

Only silence was returned.

Biting her lip, Beth opened the door. It would swing but part way. Her heart beginning to race, she stuck her head round through the opening and saw what she had feared. Mr. Rufford lay slumped on his side across the bottom of his cot. His boots stopped the door from opening. She pushed the door in with her shoulder until she could squeeze through.

One look told her it was useless to try to revive him. Blood pooled on the floor, soaked the quilt, and covered his breeches and his coat in gore. She must get help! Yet while she ran for help he might bleed to death. What to do? At least she could get a tourniquet around that dreadful gash in his leg that welled so ominously. Glancing around, she saw a small kit that held a razor. She grabbed the ivory handle and used the blade to cut away his clothing, down to his boots. How had he held that massive spar with a shoulder so obviously dislocated? She stripped off his neck cloth, twisting it. She had never been squeamish and this was no time for thoughts of propriety. She pressed down her acute awareness of his masculinity, suffused with shame. She had seen naked humanity in a hundred hot lands. This man was no different.

She surveyed him resolutely. He had a bullet wound in his lower back. Nothing she could do there. The wound in his thigh seemed most pressing. Some artery was nicked. She pulled him onto his back and put her hands between his bloody thighs to thread the twisted neck cloth under his leg, just where it joined his loins. She pulled the cloth, already soaked red, tight, then put her knee where it crossed and tied it, the knot just above the wound to press against the artery.

What now? Surely his shoulder. The hole left by a pike was bleeding copiously, too. She ripped his shirt, made a pad of the sleeve, then embraced him as she slid a knotted strip under him and tied the pad in place. Pressing on the wound, she felt the bones in his shoulder give, sickeningly. They were all broken, sure. She surveyed the rest through the smeared blood. Left chest wall was crushed, his forearm gouged, and his chest was slashed across. His scalp bled into his sandy hair. How could a man lose so much blood and live?

She had done what she could. She ran for the open deck, pushing her way among the seamen to the forward stairway and so down to the orlop where the surgeon held sway.

She found that gentleman, red-eyed but seemingly sober, awash in wounded. They packed every cranny of the triangular space open to the deck above and into the companionway. There were some grievous belly wounds, slashes, obvious broken bones. Some men might not see daylight. The loblolly boy was hauling a man up onto two lockers covered with bloody canvas. "We'll have that leg off," the doctor muttered, looking around distractedly.

"Dr. Granger, if you please!" she called over the groans and panting breath.

He looked up in surprise. "Are you wounded, miss?" He gave directions for tying his patient down with leather padded chains.

"No, but Mr. Rufford is badly hurt. He needs you." The request seemed lame even to her.

"Get some men to bring him down." Granger selected a saw from instruments laid out across a locker. "Gag that man!" he barked.

The surgeon was right. He could not be spared in the midst of such waves of agony. She had to get Mr. Rufford to the surgery. She dashed back up the stairs.

The deck was a mass of confusion as every able-bodied man pumped, spliced rigging, heaved at spars, or scurried up the masts. She clutched at several arms and begged for help to carry Mr. Rufford, but though they might touch their forelocks deferentially, all swore the bo'sun would flog them were they to leave their present task. "Not a moment to be lost," was their common refrain. The Captain on the quarter-

deck finally yelled, "Passengers below!" at her and she knew
she would have no help from the deck.

Panic surged. She hurried back to the cabin, dreading that
she would find him already dead. The door opened easily. To
her surprise, she found Mr. Rufford had dragged himself up
to lie more securely in his cot. His stare roamed across the
ceiling, swimming and insensible. Then his eyes closed.

What could she do? Well, she could bind up the sundry
cuts at least, if she could come at them. She was certain she
was unequal to removing the bullet. It had looked as though
it was lodged perilously close to his spine. Perhaps the first
step was to clean him up enough to survey the secondary
damage. She soaked the towel hanging by his washstand and
began to mop his chest and arms. She could not but be sensible of his massive shoulders and the muscle across his chest.
He must weigh fifteen or sixteen stone, distributed most
agreeably across a frame of more than six feet. His skin was
tanned evenly across his body, even his loins, as though he
had spent a long time naked in the sun. She glanced away
from his private parts, though she could not help but note
that he was well endowed. *Concentrate, you silly goose!*

Some part of her noted the scars, white against tanned
skin. As she wrung out the towel, now soaked with blood,
her gaze moved over the fine, massive body. He had been
whipped. The lace of scars on shoulders, ribs, and hips said
as much. A necklace of scars matched his bracelets, and cal-
luses and scars across his collarbone and under his arms
made her think he had carried some kind of pack at one time
with straps that galled him most grievously. There were
jagged scars across his breast, others across biceps and
thighs, even at his groin. Most curious of all, there were
many pairs of small circular scars. What could have made
those?

She jerked her attention to his gashes. They were her
business now.

What? What was this? Her glance ranged over his body,
even as her heart beat faster. God's breath! These wounds
could not have bled so! A pike thrust that gouged his side

looked days old, its edges puckering. The wound in his shoulder closed perceptibly as she watched. He was healing before her eyes! Panic surged inside her. What was happening here?

She brought a hand to her mouth and swallowed convulsively. What was this man that he could heal horrible wounds at such a rate? She sat, transfixed by fear, afraid to rise and turn her back on something so outside human experience but yet afraid to stay. The wounds closed together. The half-crushed chest wall swelled and rounded; the shattered shoulder straightened.

"My God," she whispered.

"I'm afraid God has nothing to do with it."

The hoarse whisper made her jump half out of her skin. Her gaze rose to his face. He was haggard, sure. There was a strange almost reddish cast to his pupils. But he wasn't dead, and color was coming back into his cheeks. How could . . . how could this *be*?

Suddenly his red eyes widened and he lurched up from his pillow and jerked her hand away from her mouth, where she still clasped it, perhaps to keep from screaming. "Don't touch your mouth! You are covered with my blood."

She shrank and backed away from him.

He held out a hand; whether to touch her or in supplication she couldn't tell. "I mean you no harm." He swallowed once, as though deciding. "One of the few things I know about my . . . condition is that it is spread through blood."

She looked at her hand, the blood on it half-congealed. Her glance darted back to him. Several of his wounds had healed to the extent that they were only jagged, seeping marks upon his body. If anything, she now looked more like the one wounded in battle. His life's fluid smeared her hands, her dress, and probably her cheeks as well.

"Go wash at my basin," he said softly, in that rumbling voice.

She had no intention of staying a moment more in that room. She resolved to lurch out onto the deck amid the press of humanity and the racket of sailors shouting. But somehow, looking into those eyes, the red in them now fading, she did not. She turned and went slowly to the basin. "There is a fresh cloth, just under it," she heard him say. Mechanically she watched herself take the towel, pour the water from the pitcher into the basin, take up the soap. "Wash carefully now, your mouth first. Get every bit from beneath your nails. . . ." The murmured instructions were comforting, human, real. Was that why she obeyed? For obey she did.

Her mind, a comforting blank, began to engage as she dried her face. Here was a mystery, lying on the cot not three feet away. She stole a glance at him. He was still naked, the proof of his manhood lying in a nest of hair a shade darker than his sandy curls. He was a particularly fine physical specimen, and he looked strong and healthy. Now that the fear that he might be dying had subsided—oh, God . . . why was he not dying?—the awareness of his nakedness doubled and trebled within her. She felt her face grow warm. That was not the only place that felt the heat. It seemed to streak downward from her pounding heart. He saw her discomfiture and realized his state. He grabbed a bloodied quilt and clutched it to his chest. The wounds she could still see ceased their seeping and drew together into red angry weals, the skin shining pink. She had no doubt they would leave no scars. If he could heal thus, why did he bear any scars at all?

Fear cycled in her belly. Yet why? Was it because if he could heal himself he represented the unknown? Was he evil? What would the poor wretches in Dr. Granger's surgery not give to heal as this man had? Her thoughts danced about the battle tonight. Healing was not his only strangeness. She had seen him fight with incredible strength, cleaving multiple enemies, lifting a great spar it might take half a dozen men to wield. Who *was* this man, or what?

She cleared her throat and gathered her courage, her curiosity now piqued. "You said you have a condition. . . . What is it, sir?"

"That I cannot explain, since I do not know myself," he said, pushing himself up. The quilt covered his thighs and loins but left his torso bare. She was only too aware of the soft nipples, the brush of light hair across his chest, the throbbing of a pulse under the damp skin of his throat. He was wary of her. "I hope a good English physician will be able to tell me. But seamen are a superstitious lot. If they were to find out I am not like them . . . well, at the least it would make for a most unhappy ship. Or the results might be more violent."

It seemed doubtful that any confrontation would end in his death. Was he really concerned for theirs? "I have no intention of telling anyone what I saw, if that is what you mean," Beth said stiffly. "No one would believe me, in any case."

"They will already be uneasy. They saw me lift the spar."

"Men can sometimes perform extraordinary feats of strength in times of great stress. And you were very anxious not to be taken as a slave. Again." That was the explanation for the whip scars, of course, and the fact that he had gone naked in the desert. Why was she giving him a way out of his dilemma? Should she not be shouting his alien nature from the mizzenmast?

"As you say." He inclined his head, wary. "You have overcome your initial abhorrence."

Beth was about to protest but could not. It was true. She was intensely curious, but whether it was his prosaic speech in this most seamanlike cabin, or the simple human action of washing herself, she was not quite so frightened of him. "I regret my tactless reaction, sir. It was the natural human response to the unfamiliar," she said, hesitating. "We all fear the unknown. But I know that someone built the Sphinx before men knew how to put two blocks together. I have seen men walk on coals with no burns or scars." She drew herself up. "In short, I have seen the mysteries of the world, and know enough to realize that not everything can be explained."

He nodded, still speculating. His sandy curls had escaped their ribbon in the heat of battle, and his hair waved about his scarred shoulders. He might have been a warrior on the steppes of Russia or a hunter on the plains of Catalonia a thousand years ago.

"What do you know of your . . . condition, even if you

cannot name it?" she stuttered, looking for some conversational ground that did not move beneath her feet.

His eyes, so intensely blue now that all trace of red was gone, blinked once and a veil descended upon them. "I heal when none should heal, and fast. I have great strength at my command. It was a careless drop of blood on my lips that started it all. I know no more."

"But would it not be something great to convey these powers to others? I wonder how long a man could heal himself. Would life itself be extended?" The possibilities lit up inside her.

"You run too fast, Miss Rochewell. It would be a sin to pass the malady to others without full knowledge of the effect." His tone was damping.

"And you do not like the sun, do you?" she mused. "Is that a part of it?"

"My eyes and skin are particularly sensitive." He looked alarmed at her surmises.

"So to choose the ability to heal would be to deny the daylight forever." A heavy price.

"In Tripoli I found if I used colored lenses and covered myself from head to toe I could survive, but it is inconvenient." His expression was dark. "Enough about this foolish condition." He looked at her pointedly. "I wish merely to live as much like everyone else as I can."

"But surely you want to study the ramifications, that we might know as much as possible about it? That is the way of science, and the progress of mankind."

"The way of science will have to plod along without me, Miss Rochewell. All I ask is to be left alone." He looked so drained after his ordeal she could not in conscience press him now. Who knew what resources a body claimed in order to affect that miraculous recovery?

"Very well, Mr. Rufford. I shall leave you to your rest. We can talk another time."

He looked far from resigned to that event. But as she turned to go, he called out, "Miss Rochewell . . . I am indebted to you for your efforts on my behalf."

She felt herself blushing again. "They were nothing and not needed, in any case."

She closed the door softly behind her. But she could not close the door on her thoughts. How had he been infected by a drop of blood? What were the full effects of his condition? What was he hiding? He knew something he was not telling her.

She peeked in on Mrs. Pargutter. Jenny had resorted to laudanum to calm her. The older woman was now sleeping heavily. Beth retired to her own cabin, knowing sleep was far away in spite of the quite pronounced letdown after so much excitement. There was a full-fledged mystery aboard the *Beltrane*. And she wanted to know more about it—about him.

Six

Exhausted as he was, sleep did not overtake Ian easily. For the first time, a human being had mastered the natural abhorrence for his state, and she was only a woman. Even a man who had been a soldier and a diplomat like Ware had not done as much. She would not be so sanguine if she knew he sucked blood, and he was glad she didn't realize he had compelled her to wash.

Her acceptance was most strange. Perhaps it was rooted in her experience divining rational explanations for things others could not explain, gotten from her father's archaeology. She might be the one woman capable of accepting as much of him as he would allow her to see. Not that she was much of a woman. She was far from those flowers of white heaving bosoms and sensibility he had known in London or . . . or the other female who so dominated his body and his soul. But all women were driven to control a man, if not straightforwardly, then with caressing ways meant to assert superiority. They must make up for their weaker physical being by using a man, directly or indirectly. The females of the species were all the same, even this one.

Still, her blunt straightforwardness was unlike the coy manipulation he had known or the direct cruelty he'd experienced in the desert. Her impulse had been to help him. That spoke of underlying goodness and competence. She was almost more like a man. Her father had certainly treated her like a son, traipsing about Africa. He already knew she was intelligent. Tonight she'd guessed that he'd been a slave, though she could not know the depth of his servitude. No one could imagine that. He would not think of it. He would think of England and the normal life that lay ahead of him, if he could only reach it. . . .

An oasis. The caravan stopped. The slaves were allowed to put down the litter. Her tent was erected as the sun rose. She stepped out of the litter and into the dark reaches of her tent. The chosen slaves, the sturdy males just around her litter, were given wooden cups of water. One of the rabble of slaves from the back of the caravan was sent into her tent, a woman. She would be dragged out again shortly, Ian knew, dead and deathly pale, her flesh collapsed against her bones. The beautiful owner had been going through the horde of slaves at the rate of one a week, or even two.

Ian's keeper used a great metal pair of pliers to crimp the slaves' chains to several posts. Naked, he crouched next to his post, alone there, since several of the other slaves had died. Ian glanced over at the Frenchman. Red marks, twin circles, as well as longer slashing cuts adorned his body. The twin circles were at his neck, his wrists, the crooks of his arms, his upper thighs. The slashes were everywhere. He had lasted longer than most, maybe a month. He was tough, that Frenchman. Now he crouched, rocking and murmuring. Perhaps his mind was gone at last.

"Go with God," Ian murmured to the Frenchman, though he was not sure the man could hear and was certain God was not listening to this particular part of his creation, since their many prayers for delivery had gone unnoticed. Or perhaps God did not hold sway here.

He peeked up to see the tall Arab who followed the mistress of the caravan look sharply at him. The man was

*clothed from head to foot in a burnoose with a hood. Ian
wondered if he would be whipped for whispering. But the
keeper was busy throwing jerked meat and dried dates into a
bowl to feed the mistress's specially chosen slaves. They were
fed better than the rabble at the rear, at least. Ian ate his portion greedily and dozed in the growing heat.*

*The date palms gave a little shade, but that was reserved
for the camels and their drivers. He could hear the drivers
saying that this was the last oasis for many days. They would
stay for two days to let the camels drink their fill. That meant
rest.*

*Sunset. Someone kicked him. He scrambled to his knees
with lowered head, hoping to avoid the lash. The others still
dozed. The sandaled foot did not belong to the keeper.*

*"You," said a voice in heavily accented English. "You are
Briton?"*

*The sound was sweet. He had heard no English for six
months. "Yes, Master. English."*

*"Where do you come from?" The air vibrated around
him, but to a lesser extent than around the woman who
owned the caravan.*

*"Suffolk." It was the Arab. He had heard Ian speak to the
Frenchman in English.*

*"Keeper!" the man called in Arabic. "Release this slave.
I will take his chain." The heavy keeper hurried over and un-
bent the iron link, handing Ian's chain to the Arab.*

*"Come, English." The chain was jerked up. Ian heaved
himself to his feet and staggered stiffly after his new custo-
dian. The man took him to the far side of the pool of precious water, away from the caravan encampment, and bade
him drink. Ian knelt and slurped long and noisily. "Now,
face." Ian glanced up and then cupped his hands and rinsed
the dust and grit from his face and neck, splashing water
even into his hair. He had never felt such luxury. His chain
was jerked again and he crept to the side of the man, who sat
upon the trunk of a fallen date palm.*

*"Tell me of Briton . . . no, England," he corrected him-
self. "It is long since I was there."*

"What . . . what would the master like to know?" he croaked, his voice hardly human after not being used for so many months.

"Is it still green? So green, it was." The man smelled a little like her, like cinnamon.

"Yes. Green. When I was last there." The ache of an English May, so verdant and alive, swept over him until he thought he might waste his body's water in tears.

"And Londinium? No, London now. Is it grown even larger?"

"They say almost a million souls."

"A million?" the Arab marveled. "It must be squalid, with so many."

"In the poor neighborhoods yes. On the west side, there are the parks and squares, with flowers." Ian grew a little braver. Yet still he was puzzled. Londinium?

"Did they ever buy back Richard?"

Now Ian was truly at sea. "Richard?"

"Of the heart of the lion. I came away, and then . . . there were other things to occupy me."

Ian stole a glance upward, expecting a cuff for his boldness, but he had to see if he was being made game of. The Arab's face was only expectant. Ian ducked his head. "He was ransomed. He came home from the Crusades and took his rightful crown from his brother John."

"Good. Never did I like this John. He was not like some others of your countrymen. They were good to me. One Walter of Ghent helped me in the prison of the Moors when they had cut my bollocks off. We fought each other in Jerusalem, but when you are in a prison, what matters a city a thousand miles away? We broke from the prison of the Moors and sailed for England."

Ian shot a look up and saw fond memory pass over the Arab's face. "I passed some years there. I liked Walter's people." He rose suddenly. "But it was too green. I came home to the sand and Asharti found me, and I found my destiny." He jerked the chain at Ian's wrist. "Mayhap we will talk English again if you are still alive tomorrow."

Ian stumbled back to his fellows behind the Arab. His owner's name was Asharti. The Frenchman was being carried away. He had made his escape at last, though it had taken death to set him free. An imperious command came from the tent, and the Arab hurried ahead in the black night with the stars wheeling against the sky in mute disregard of human suffering. Ian could hear the Arab's voice, soothing; then Asharti burst from her tent. Ian was being chained nearest to her of all the slaves. She did not hesitate in choosing among them this time. Even before he could be refastened to his post, she gestured at his keeper. Ian could understand enough to know she was giving orders for him to be washed.

Ian's heart leaped into his mouth. If only the Arab had not singled him out he would not have been standing where he could catch her attention. She might have chosen the Nubian she had picked up at the last village, or the Turk. She turned back to her tent. His keeper jerked his chain and suddenly, regardless of the consequence, he jerked back. His hands were free, and a lethal chain clanked at his wrist. He swung it at the keeper, hitting him across the cheek and nose. The man went down like a horse at the knacker's and Ian stumbled around the pool. The keeper raised a cry. Ian saw the camel drivers just ahead of him jolt upright from where they smoked their tobacco. But he was by them, stumbling naked into the deep sand beyond the pool. Ahead were only the black night lit by stars and the white sand pulling at his feet. His breath heaved in his lungs—the freedom of it! He pounded on, expecting the crack of guns at his back from the camel drivers, waiting for the sear of pain that said he was hit, welcoming it, if only his death would come while he was running free in the desert night. But no shot came. Instead he heard the honking cry of a camel, the rhythmic beat of its great splayed feet, so much more suitable than his for sand. He turned just as it galloped past him. There was the sear of pain but it was from a truncheon wielded by a man leaning from the camel's back. Light flashed in Ian's head like a thousand stars and he dropped to the sand, dazed.

Hands pulled at him, shouting. Blows fell about his shoulders. He stumbled, was dragged up, back to the pool. Hands shoved him into the water. He fell to his knees. The water was only to his chest. Two of the camel boys scrubbed him with a rough cloth until he was raw. They held him down and took a razor to his beard, pulled him out, and dusted him with lime to kill lice. His senses began to return, along with a mighty ache in his head. Then it was into the water again, strong lye soap, dried roughly and delivered naked to the flap of the embroidered tent. The angry keeper, a weal across his face, unbolted Ian's shackle and replaced it with a hemp rope. He was about to deliver a fisted blow when the tall Arab raised his voice.

"Do not damage him!" The keeper fell back reluctantly and the tall Arab gestured Ian through the flap. "English, it is your time." He looked sorry. "Your rebellion will please her."

Ian straightened. What could one woman who probably didn't weigh nine stone possibly do to a man who even still weighed fourteen? What indeed? Something inside him shuddered so deeply he thought he might faint.

Inside the tent, lamps burned in a soft glow, their flames flickering on the red fabric of the tent walls. There were the carpets that were rolled every day and put across a camel's back, unfurled now in sumptuous luxury, and soft cushions, fabric that hung from the tent pole in shades of orange and magenta and burgundy. In the center of the room a low carved table was set with plates of dates and sweetmeats.

She lay across a low couch, her body draped insouciantly over cushions embroidered in gold. She wore a diaphanous gown that hid nothing, clipped at the shoulders with gold brooches and held at the waist by a girdle of worked gold. Her lips were painted gold, and her toenails. She was barefoot, her leg up to her thigh bared by the slit in that transparent fabric. He could smell her scent. Ambergris. That was what it was. She smelled like cinnamon and ambergris.

"If you think I'm going to service you like some bullock at a town fair services the local heifers, you're damned well mistaken," he said through clenched teeth. Let her have him beaten to death. He didn't give a damn. He expected shouting, a call to someone to punish him. Even if she knew no English, she could not mistake the tone.

She smiled. A cobra might smile like that when it saw a rat that thought it could avoid the inevitable. The smile grew, showing even white teeth. She was so beautiful and so sure of it in that flickering lamplight; the black eyes, the skin that never saw the sun, creamy and soft looking. She raised a hand and beckoned to him. He sealed his lips and stood where he was.

A low chuckle escaped her, as though she enjoyed his resistance, his battle with his fear. She beckoned again, only this time her eyes seemed to glow in the lamplight. It was the strangest thing he had ever seen, like cats' eyes in the glow of a lantern, only red. He found himself taking a step toward her. He tried to stop, tried to look away, and he could do neither. He felt strangely distant from himself as he took step after step toward her. Then he was kneeling beside her. He could feel what she demanded of him regardless of the difference in language, and there was no refusing. He did not even want to refuse her. He wanted her, lusted after her as he had never lusted after any woman in his life. He saw his hand reach out and run his palm up the smooth skin of her calf, up the back of her knee, and so on up to her thigh. If only she would allow him to pleasure her . . . He felt the throb in his loins and knew that he was hard and ready for her. She leaned over him. He raised his face to hers that he might gaze deeply into those red, shining eyes. Her breasts hung almost within reach. She wanted him to touch them, so he did, feeling the heft, thumbing her nipple. She put one hand, with those incredibly long nails, at the back of his neck under the fall of his newly washed hair and lifted his lips to hers while her other hand raked across his back, the nails scratching lightly over his most recent welts, threatening. Her mouth was soft, supple. She opened his lips with her *tongue and caressed his mouth from the inside. She wanted his tongue as well, and he slipped it inside her mouth and drew it across her teeth. Her canines were sharp. She moved her lips over his face. His eyes closed briefly. She lapped at his temple where a trickle of blood from the truncheon blow wound down toward his cheek. This seemed to excite her and she grew more urgent.*

Somewhere he knew that he was not his own man in this moment. Even his cock was not his own. She pressed herself against him and wrapped her fingers, with those long golden nails, around his shaft. He was hard as he had ever been. Lava pooled in his balls, ready to spurt. He gave a moan as she pulled on his cock, lightly and then with more force. He thought he would burst. But she would not let him burst. She bade him look into her eyes, and with that one look she bottled his lust up inside him. She controlled him, mind and body. The horror of that realization began to work on him. She pulled aside the diaphanous red cloth and bared her breast to him. He bent to suckle it. He tried to pull away, tried with all his soul. She chuckled, low in her throat, and bared her other breast. He bent over it in answer to her demand. Her palms cupped his buttocks, her thumbs feeling the raised welts of the whip across them.

At last she lay back against the back of her low chaise and pushed his head down to where her gown was split to the waist. She wanted her pleasure from his tongue and not his cock. He gave a groan and found her nub of pleasure. She tasted salty and warm. He was sweating lightly in the heat of the tent. He knew what she wanted, exactly. He did not know how he knew. He lapped in long strokes and then flicked lightly, back and forth, on and on, easing her by stages toward her climax. When it came, she pressed him against her with surprising strength and bucked against him, moaning. Her image seemed to waver for a moment, soft around the edges; then she popped back into hard-edged focus and went limp.

She released him and wriggled into her cushions like a kitten. Ian sat back, his own need unsatisfied, an ache deep in his loins. Her eyes opened and began to glow red again. She gestured to the table. He fed her dates and offered her honeyed mead from a chased goblet. He was still erect. She ran her hand through his hair as she might pet a dog. She lifted his chin to look at his face, opened his eyelids wider to see the blue. She fingered his nipples and rubbed his throat. Then her caresses grew rougher. He felt the compulsion in his mind grow until she held him tight in mind and body once again and began her demanding.

This time she opened her knees to him. In spite of his need, he entered slowly, as she allowed him to do. She held his testicles approvingly as he pushed inside her. Ian's breath was already coming short and shallowly. His body sweated as he thrust inside her, his cock filling her as she wanted to be filled. He would go on as long as she wished to go on, because he had no choice and because it was her choice if he was to have a release. She would choose the time and the strength and the means. Or she might choose no release at all and keep him hard and needing forever. She arched into him and pressed her breasts against his heaving chest. Then she drew him down on top of her and began licking at his throat. He thrust on as she clamped her legs about his hips and banged in counterpoint. A sharp stab of pain at his neck that was not pain but something akin to ecstasy almost put him over the top, but she had him firmly, and they rocked together as she suckled at his neck. Ian gasped for air as she sucked on, and then he felt her release for the second time, a grunting throb that threatened his consciousness. It rocked on and on. Then she allowed his own release as hers ebbed. He came in a shrieking burst as she stopped the sucking at his throat and he collapsed against her, almost unconscious.

She pushed him away. He lay there on the carpets, strangely weak. He could barely lift his head. The scent of cinnamon and ambergris made him want to gag. She told him to go, and he had to crawl to the flap of the tent. He looked back to see her rearranging her garment into some sort of order. Then hands took him and tied his rope to a post driven into the sand just outside the door of the tent. He lay there, sand clinging to his sweating body until he was dried by the warm sirocco. He fingered the place where she had pierced his throat and suckled. There were two round, raised wounds. The memory of the other slaves, covered in those round marks, made him wail inside. Now that it was over, the full horror of what had happened overwhelmed him. She could make him do anything. He would service her like her own private stud. He was no stronger than the others had been. There was no escape. The memory of the red eyes tormented him. She was not human. And he was wholly in her power, at least until he went mad, like the Frenchman, or died of his wounds. He prayed for an early death, without hope that his prayers would be answered.

Ian shut his eyes as despair washed over him. It lurked in him still, ready to submerge him under its dark waves. Pray as he might, death was denied him now. He could heal a broken neck. The burns from going naked into the sun had left no trace. If he had needed any more proof of his invincibility, tonight had certainly provided it. His only recourse was to put as much distance between him and the desert as he could and try to forget the monster he had escaped. He could only hope to resist becoming a monster, too. He would not think of her. He would not let her poison who he was with her foul practices, her despicable . . . And yet had he escaped? Was he not fouled as surely, as insidiously, as if he still knelt in chains at her side?

Ian swallowed, tried to breathe, and huddled into his bloody quilts. He squeezed his stinging eyes shut. If he could not pray for death, at least he might pray for sleep. Who would answer prayers from such as he? What God would allow this to happen to one of his creatures?

Beth woke from uneasy sleep before dawn, raised from her dreams of red eyes by the noise of sailors holystoning the deck and singing some chantey. At first she wondered

whether she had dreamed the whole battle with the pirates
and the confrontation with a man who might not be quite human as she knew it. She raised her hand. There was the nail
she had broken grabbing up the capstan bar. The black dress
hanging on the door was stiff with dried blood.

It was real. A kiss she had asked for, pirates attacking, furious battle, Mr. Rufford's extraordinary feats of heroism,
the awful price he paid in wounds, frantic fear for his life, the
shock of his healing, and her strange acceptance of his un-
natural qualities. *Had* she accepted them? Why? She gave a
shudder as she remembered the red glow that had suffused
his eyes.

Now, as she lay in her cot, the sensations of last night
poured over her. What stood out was an overwhelming sensation of the . . . maleness of him. As she lay in her gently
swinging cot, remembering the feel of his lips on hers and
the silk of his skin against her fingers made her breath hiss
in the back of her throat. She thought herself immune to the
naked male body, yet his had an intrinsically different effect
on her from the many natives she had seen. It made her flush
even in memory. Her eyes swam and she seemed to drift
away to a place where she could remember perfectly the hip
bone beneath his flesh, the hollow of his belly dusted with an
arrow of light brown hair that pointed to his sex. His nipples
had been soft over the swell of pectorals. His neck was a pillar of strength with that pulse beating in the most vulnerable
hollow of his throat. The muscles in arms and shoulders had
been heavy. He was not lean or rangy like so many men.
Then his face—handsome, surely, but very particular in its
character. His waving hair, thick and soft as a girl's, only
made him seem more intensely masculine.

The heat that suffused her seemed to gather in her loins,
producing a strangely satisfying throb. Was it her mother's
Egyptian blood in her veins that pulsed inside her? Her mother
had bequeathed to her the heat of the desert. That blood was
not something she was proud of, but perhaps she could not
avoid its effects. All she knew now was that she wanted to find
out more about Ian Rufford and that he called to her in some

elemental way that her blood understood, if she did not.

He would not be on deck. It was daylight. But, after last night, could she not use her concern as an excuse to look in on him?

That got her up and dressed in a fresh black kerseymere dress. Two bells struck on deck. It was only seven in the morning. She could not go calling this early.

Beth went out on a deck just drying from its morning scrub. The blood from the night was washed away. The wind was fresh. The ship bore a cloud of sail in the pale, clear light. Carpenters mounted a new main topgallant spar and men mended canvas ripped by shot. Several sailors touched their forelocks with a knuckle or smiled and nodded. She smiled in return. They must be feeling the general gladness at escape that filled her breast. A young boy heaved the log, let the knots run past his fingers. A grizzled man beside him held a glass with pouring sand close to his face. "Hold!" he called.

"Four and one fathom," the boy piped.

In the distance she could see another ship. Her heart skipped. A pirate? She looked up to the quarterdeck. The Captain was not there, but Mr. Rait, the first mate, stood just behind the master at the wheel. He noticed her and came forward, tripping lightly down the ladder.

"The convoy, miss," he reassured her. He pointed behind her.

She turned to see two more ships, sporting hardly any canvas. "What a relief." Then she saw the twelve long canvas sacks lying just under the rail. "Oh, dear."

"The butcher's bill was steep," Mr. Rait said gravely. "And there will be some additions. We'll bury them in the forenoon watch."

"Shouldn't we take them home for burial?"

"Carrying of dead men is the worst luck a ship can have, miss." Then seeing her look, he continued. "At least it was quick and in battle. We have a fear of drowning. That's why so few sailors learn to swim. Better to go fast than slow if we go overboard."

She nodded. "It seems a hard life, only sleeping four hours at a time, and all the work they have, with only salt pork and biscuit to eat."

"Not as bad as being poor at home, miss." He smiled. "Mostly there is salt beef, too, and the ship has banyan days, with peas or beans, and we catch fish and turtles. Sometimes the flying fish and the squids fairly throw themselves on board by the hundreds. Nothing like fried flying fish for breakfast. And of course, there's the grog."

He seemed kindly and forthcoming this morning. Still, she could not ask him why he chose such a life, where pleasures still seemed few in spite of all he said and pirates could descend at any moment and create a "butcher's bill."

Mr. Rait cleared his throat. "The hands and the officers have expressed the greatest admiration for your courage and your . . . your invention last night during the boarding, miss. You showed the way, slinging that lantern like you did."

Beth blushed in confusion. So that was the reason for the smiles and nods. The sailors were doing so even now, around the deck, as they listened to the conversation. "Your other passenger was of far more aid than I."

Mr. Rait's features darkened. "None of us quite knows what to make of that, miss."

She raised her brows. "As far as I can tell, he 'saved your bacon,' as they say."

"But the manner of it . . ." Mr. Rait grew pensive. "I mean, he lifted a whole mainmast spar, not just a tops'l spar or a studs'l boom. And the punishment he took shouldering them guns . . . the wounds . . ."

"Men do extraordinary things under pressure," she said smoothly. "I got the impression that Mr. Rufford was most anxious to avoid being captured by pirates. Do you think he has had some experience with that before?"

Mr. Rait nodded slowly. All hands around listened to the exchange. "What he said, about not being made slave . . ."

"The scars on his wrists," Beth added. "Surely you remarked them."

"No. I hadn't." But that gave him something to think

about. "I hope he was not too much wounded. Dr. Granger never saw him."

"I checked in on him," she said. "Just to see how he did. He was a bit knocked about, but the blood belonged to our attackers."

"I can sure believe that," the young man said fervently. "I ain't never seen anything like the way he got after them." He gestured to Redding, just coming out from the galley. "Mr. Redding, hop along and get Miss Rochewell a spot of early toast and coffee."

Beth drank her coffee strong and black from a tin cup on the deck, rather than from the Captain's china in the stern cabin, and munched on a slice of buttered toast. No sustenance had been so welcome in some time. Had she been unable to taste since her father's death? The pain struck home and she put it away for another time. It was the first time she had been able to do that. The hands all gave her room with nary a complaint that she was in the way. One fierce-looking fellow with a long braid and a ring in his ear gestured to a canvas bag and invited her to sit "comfortable-like on the cheese of wads." When she ventured to ask him what that was, he explained seriously and slowly, as though she were deaf or simple, that the wads they used for stuffing powder and shot in their guns came in round bags that looked like a wheel of cheese.

The watch had changed and the morning watch was two bells in, which made it nine o'clock, when she felt it might be respectable to inquire after her fellow passenger. She was on her way to Mr. Rufford's cabin door when she remembered with extreme guilt that she had another fellow passenger who should demand the courtesy of a call.

"Mrs. Pargutter!" she called, knocking on that lady's door.

"Come in!" a weak voice called.

"How do you this morning, ma'am?"

Mrs. Pargutter was in her dressing gown and cap, sitting in her cot with a lace handkerchief pressed to her mouth. "Why did I leave Tripoli?" she wailed. "Pirates! And being stuffed down in the bowels of the ship when I am so very ill—what would have happened had they captured us? My virtue soiled, relegated to rule over the Sultan's harem, a slave to his insatiable physical needs . . ."

Beth blushed to think of her own fears. At least she had not aspired to preeminence. "I think we should have been ransomed for gold," she said in a damping tone.

"I shall not take a step outside this cabin for the rest of the voyage, no matter how many pirates attack. Do you know that dreadful place below smelled like tar?"

"I'm sure it did," Beth soothed. Then, not proud of her cowardice, she added, "Should I just send Jenny to you?"

"Oh yes," Mrs. Pargutter sighed gratefully. "And do ask her to bring my tatting. She had more room in her cabin for some of my things than I had in mine, you know."

"Of course," Beth murmured, privately thinking that Jenny would be named a saint at any moment if ever she would turn Papist.

When Jenny was summoned and Beth's excuses made, she again turned toward Mr. Rufford's silent cabin. Her heartbeat fluttered. "Mr. Rufford?" she called softly, knocking. Would he be asleep, in line with his peculiar habits?

"Come in, Miss Rochewell."

The deep voice never failed to thrill her. Was she more enamored of him now she knew he held even more secrets than she had suspected? She opened the cabin door.

He was sitting, his cravat neatly tied, his coat of blue superfine smooth across his shoulders, his buff breeches tight across his thighs, his boots gleaming, in front of his basin, putting up his shaving gear. His sandy curls were tied back neatly once more in a black ribbon. His face was smooth and slightly pink with shaving. It was as though last night had never been. But in the mirror she saw painful emotion in his eyes that startled her. A shaving cut showed on his cleft chin. As he mustered himself and turned to her, it disappeared. Her stomach sank. The phenomenon was even more disconcerting in the daytime, though here the room was lit by a lamp since the tiny window was covered with a black cloth. A bullet lay on his dressing table. It must have come from his back. She tried to imagine his body simply thrusting it out as he healed.

Nerves twanged inside her. The enormity of his strangeness came thumping back. She had accepted his explanation of an infection of his blood with complete naïveté. What if he was some kind of monster? She had been misled by her body's response to him. It had all started with the kiss she asked for. What had she been thinking? She had not considered . . . What could she say to excuse her presence here? In the end, words came without her permission. "I'm afraid I ruined the edge of your razor by cutting off your clothing. I am sorry, sir."

The pain in his eyes seeped away. He sighed, not quite in amusement. "I have never heard a prettier apology, or a more unusual one."

Beth felt her color rise. It was an idiotic thing to have said.

"I should not have ruined your apology by calling you to account," he murmured. "I am grateful for your most practical attitude."

She had to say something about having asked him for a kiss. "I owe you another apology, I'm afraid. You must think me forward, with . . . with my strange request yesterday."

He seemed at a loss, and then his face softened in recognition. "Another practical approach to your problem. I did not object, you will recall."

She turned the subject, flushing. "The hands are most thankful for your prowess in battle."

He lifted his brows, his gaze penetrating now.

At least she had done him a service. If he was worried that the men would hold his efforts on the ship's behalf against him, she could allay those fears. "I told them men were capable of great feats when in the throes of fear or battle."

"So cowardice is now widely regarded to have induced my strength?"

Beth shrugged. "Better that . . ."

"I suppose I should be thankful you did not go shrieking to Captain Tindly."

"You misjudge me," she reproached. He turned a speculating gaze on her. To escape it, she looked around his tidy cabin, and saw a pile of books. "You are reading novels, sir?"

He cleared his throat, also eager for escape. "I find Mr. Fielding's vision of England most comforting. The legation had something by a Miss Austen, though no one had apparently read it. A sympathetic denizen, Colonel Ware, said I might take it. I find her view of society most acute, in spite of its domestic tendencies. I . . . I wonder, have you read it? It is quite new."

Beth smiled at this torrent of exculpatory remarks. "I am reading *Sense and Sensibility* even as we speak. And I agree with your analysis. It is an acute, and most satisfying, even humorous book I . . . I quite identify with the practical sister. But I had quite figured you for philosophers, or perhaps poetry."

He grimaced. "You are severe with me. You no doubt think me a devotee of Mr. Byron?"

"No," she said slowly. "Lord Byron has a certain freedom about his lines, of course, and an activity which would suit you. But you would not like his assumption of the romantic hero. You might even consider it coy. No, I think you like your tales of courage and adventure with less self-consciousness. Upon the whole I would have said you might be reading the classic Greeks. *The Iliad* perhaps?"

His eyes widened slightly. He picked up a volume that was hidden under the pillow of his cot. *The Iliad.* "You quite amaze me, Miss Rochewell, or unnerve me. I cannot yet say which."

"Then we are even, Mr. Rufford." She hesitated. She had revealed her fear.

A step sounded in the common room outside. She was in a single man's cabin. If the ship knew it, as they seemed to know everything, her reputation would not be worth a shilling. She was not in North Africa now but on a British merchantman that subscribed to stolid British values. "You need your rest. I only wished to know that you were quite recovered." But the nature of that recovery was still so strange that she flushed again. She turned to go.

"Perhaps a game of chess, at sunset?"

She did not look over her shoulder. "Perhaps." She pushed out into the corridor, smiling. She would like another game of chess.

Seven

Ian's eyes closed over his book and he sank into a dreamless sleep, commanded by his body. No bells or sailors' shouts could rouse him. He had spent the previous night deep in unconsciousness, too. When he woke, he felt the sun sinking below the horizon, although its light did not penetrate his cabin. Would he always know the position of the sun now?

As consciousness took full hold, the hunger woke within him, a gnawing at his gut. He sat bolt upright. He had fed not four days ago! He had counted on two weeks of respite from his need, that he might reach a port of call to quench it. The healing must have weakened him. He bit his lip. The hunger was manageable now. But for how long? How long until they made landfall?

He jumped from his cot, straightened his coat and his cravat, and strode out onto the deck. The girl was there, just ducking into the stern cabin. He must make sure somehow that she kept his secret. Best to reassure her that he was not a monster, lie though that might be. He must engage her in the most innocuous way to ensure her continued sanguine reaction to his nature.

But that was for later. He glanced around. The guardian sloop and no fewer than seven sails from the convoy were visible in the choppy sea around them. The Captain paced the quarterdeck. He might not take kindly to the fact that Ian led the defense last night when the Captain wanted to surrender. No matter. He had an urgent need for information. Collaring one of the youngsters, he asked the lad to give his respects and might he approach for a word?

The Captain nodded. Ian ran up the stairs. "Captain, do we make progress?"

"We jury-rigged a main topmast and shipped a bowsprit. The barky is making six knots."

"What is our next landfall?"

"Port Mahon if the winds will carry us there."

"Is there a doubt?"

"Aye. The glass is dropping." A bank of green-black clouds scudded to the larboard. "Can't get into Port Mahon with the wind in the southwest. The harbor entrance is uncommon narrow. Could blow for days or weeks, the ship beating up, never making no progress. The sloop might decide to leave those that must dock there under protection of the battery, and make for Gibraltar with the rest of us."

Ian's disappointment must have shown in his face.

"Sailors is slave to the weather, sir, and nothing to be done." Captain Tindly cleared his throat. "I have written a dispatch outlining the . . . astonishing role you played in saving the ship and its cargo from the pirates. I'll send a copy, writ out fair, to the Captain of the sloop and to the Company. I have no doubt they will reward you handsomely."

Ian turned from scanning the blackening horizon to the Captain. "I need no reward," he said shortly. "How long to Gibraltar if the wind won't let us in to Port Mahon?"

"No knowing," the Captain began, then glancing to Ian, "if weather plays fair, four days."

Four days. He hoped to God he could last four days.

Beth pored over the maps she had spread across her writing desk. They showed the eastern Sahara, with small marks for oases and several Xs where ruins of some sixth-century tombs had been found. But there was no mark for the finest ruin she knew was somewhere in that desert. The lost city had not been found. The old Imam in Tunis would have told her for certain where it lay, she was sure. Then her father died and everything changed. The ancient texts might hold a clue, though she had been over them a thousand times.

She carefully unrolled a scroll whose papyrus was crumbling. These scrolls were her most precious possessions. In some ways, she'd been preparing to analyze them for years, studying hieroglyphics with the French scholar Champollion as he decoded the stone found twenty years ago by French soldiers in Rashīd (called Rosetta in English), learning Coptic, Demotic, Greek. The gold that once outlined each capital was mostly rubbed away. She could just discern the author's name. Hamarabi. She pressed the scroll out flat on the little desk and scanned the figures until she found the passage she wanted.

"And in the desert," she translated to herself, moving her lips silently, "there is a great evil, born of the sky, laid in the earth, sustained by the blood of men. It is manifest in the Temple of Waiting that is carved into the city of Kivala, poison to man's soul as well as to his body. For he who mingles his blood with the blood of the Powerful One shall eat that power at the cost of his soul. He will banish death and age and slashes." Was that right? No. "Death and age, nor wounds nor blood, will not worry him." That was better. "Yet his needs will become unclean."

The words made her shudder every time she read them. She skipped ahead. "And when the moon shall touch the tallest peaks of the spine of the earth, then shall its light reveal the city living in the rock six thumbs from the most north peak, waiting for the return of the ones who abandoned their brother. By the half solstice shall the city be known and only righteous men shall enter, at the peril of their souls."

What a strange mixture of Hebrew syntax, like righteous men, and the phrases of the Koran, like spine of the earth, all written in a language far older than either. It was as if the text was the basis of the other religions, either that or a later text that used ecumenical language to obscure its origin. Yet this passage was the closest to a direction for Kivala she had found.

She sat up and sighed. What chance did she now have to follow her father's dream? She was for England and a staid propriety that stifled women. She was reading the texts to take her mind off Mr. Rufford. She knew that. She tried to think about him as her father would have. The explanation for his healing must lie in some advanced form of coagulation, adhesion taken to extremes. If only she knew more about medicine! But her experience was limited to splinting and stitching simple wounds—superfluous where Mr. Rufford was concerned. What could have happened to him that he was given the ability to heal wounds other men would die of? It was not something he was born with, for he spoke of an infection, passed by blood.

Her gaze descended to the passage once again. "He who mingles his blood . . . nor wounds . . . will not worry him. . . ."

She sucked in a breath sharply.

Was this passage talking about Mr. Rufford and his strange ability to heal himself being passed through blood? Or was she putting an explanation upon the text because it comforted her to have things tied neatly in a package?

She gazed up out of the hatch window. It was nearly sunset. She had an engagement to play chess with a mystery. She would not tell him about her discovery of a text that seemed to mention his condition, not until she knew more about him.

Three days. It had been three days since they had vanquished the pirates, and in those three days they had been delayed, then denied a call at Port Mahon by the vagaries of the wind, and finally, most cursed of all, the winds had almost died out altogether. They made two knots at best, keeping to the pace of the slowest tub in the convoy. Ian paced in the stern cabin as the great sweep of curved windows went purple and the clouds gave back the pink glow of the sun.

The Captain now said he had no idea how long until they

made Gibraltar. Ian's fate was controlled by the weather, and no one could tell how long the sullen, breezeless state would last.

Ian could not last much longer. His mouth was dry in some strange manner that neither water nor wine could wet. His thirst boiled up from his veins and made him irritable and distracted. But it did not stop his hearing, now preternaturally acute, which could detect the throb of blood in hearts around him. He *must* not feed on the ship, where the results would be obvious.

Where was she? She knew he waited for her every evening at this time right here. He had begun to enjoy her company. He had to admit that. He liked the fact that she seemed to enjoy his company in return without any of the missish airs he had known in England. He threw himself into the elbow chair at the great table and pushed the pieces of the chessboard about fiercely. Did she keep him waiting just to show her power over him? No chess partner was worth that.

The door opened and she swung lightly in, sucking on her finger. "Forgive me," she said, removing her finger from her mouth, her large hazel eyes luminous in the light of the lamp swinging over the table. "I had some scrolls out, and the time got away from me. See?" she asked, holding out the finger. "One snapped at me and gave me a nasty paper cut."

Ian did not have to examine the finger. He could smell the fulsome scent, almost sweet, but ripe, too. He could almost taste the copper tang, the thick richness on his tongue. His agitation swung up a notch, like sound of the ship's rigging in a rising wind. He hardly spared a glance for the welling drop upon her finger but rose, whipped out his handkerchief, and tossed it on the table. He turned away, saying in a gruff voice he hardly recognized, "You had better bind it up before you bleed on your frock. You're good at bandaging."

She glanced to him. "Are you all right, sir?" she asked, her voice constrained.

"Perfectly," he lied. "Only somewhat put out. I must have caught the seaman's disease of punctuality. I am a very impatient waiter." Then he realized how uncivil that was and simply sat again. He cleared his throat. "Black or white?"

"Oh, black, I think." She bound up her paper cut. The white linen grew a red flower.

"You always choose black. I thought women wanted white."

"And how many women have you played chess with?"

He grabbed for breath and shook his head. "You are the first. Except for . . . well, except for a girl I knew in London, and then I always let her win."

"Why?" She moved a pawn out. "Why did you let her win?"

"I . . . I wanted something else from her than winning a game of chess." He knocked over his knight as he brought it out, and righted it.

"Then why didn't she call you on it? It's quite easy to see when someone is letting you win, I find." Her bishop swooped out diagonally.

He spoke without thinking as he brought out a pawn to protect the knight. "She was too busy being coy, I suppose. She, too, wanted more than winning. Or maybe she liked winning very well and wanted to win on every scale, no matter how small. Women do, you know."

"I like winning," Miss Rochewell said emphatically. "But not if you are going to play in so scattered a fashion. It hardly does me credit." Her own knight came out.

"Don't think I will let you win." He took a pawn with his knight.

"I think nothing of the kind," she said, taking his knight. "But something has you in a bother. Will you tell me about it?"

"Oh, it's all this idling about. I had hoped to be in Gibraltar by now." He moved as if by rote another pawn. At this rate he *would* lose.

"I see. And you think perhaps that by failing to shave and setting your neck cloth all ahoo, as the sailors say, you might push the ship along faster?"

His hand darted to his chin and rubbed it. He *had* forgotten to shave. He took a breath. He must look a sight. She was certainly looking at him strangely. "Forgive me," he mumbled.

"At least you remembered your scent. Cinnamon and what? I cannot place it."

Ian felt the world drop away. "I smell like cinnamon and ambergris?"

"That's it," she returned. "Not overwhelming. Certainly not unpleasant. Shouldn't you?"

He sagged. "Yes. I should." Another way he was like *her*. He had never noticed because you couldn't smell your own scent. The hunger raking his flesh seemed ever more sinister.

She sat back in her chair, uninterested in the board. "Perhaps your thoughts need some distraction. You spend many hours alone. Shall I tell you about my own problem?"

He swallowed. "Yes, do," he managed. Did she know that he could see the pulse beating in her throat? His veins were scratchy with pain.

"Perhaps you can help me. I have been studying scrolls that hint at the location of Kivala." He raised his eyes, hoping his dread did not show there. She went on. "I never got to see the old Imam who had been there, but perhaps the scrolls will tell me."

"Knowing the location now will do you no good in London," he said repressively.

"We all like to feel vindicated," she said, shrugging. "I almost have it. The texts are quite specific as to the position of the moon over the spine of the world and the time of year. But where is this 'spine'? One thinks of the mountains just south of Addis Ababa, yet there are no sandstone washes like those at Petra. Perhaps the Atlas, but they stretch for hundreds of miles."

God, she really did know where it was! If the text was so specific, perhaps others would find it east of the Atlas Mountains and south of the Rif, too. But what did he care, as long as he was far away in England?

"You seemed to know something of the city," she continued. "You said when I first came on board that it was evil. And so the texts seem to confirm."

"Do they?" He thought he might choke.

" 'And in the desert,' " she quoted, " 'there is a great evil, born of the sky, laid in the earth, sustained by the blood of men. It is manifest in the Temple of Waiting that is carved into the rock of Kivala, poison to man's soul as well as to his body. For he who mingles blood with the blood of the Powerful One shall eat that power at the cost of his soul. Death and age, nor wounds nor blood, will not worry him.' And so I thought of you, with that last part, you know, and I remembered what you said about the city, damping my pretensions, I expect." She looked at him with a prosaic expression. "So I thought you might have been to Kivala, and could tell me exactly how to locate the 'spine of the earth.' "

He stood. The chair tipped backward with a crash. "I can tell you nothing," he rasped. He staggered against the table, unseeing. The chess pieces crashed to the ground. Then he was out the door. Blindly he wondered where on this small ship he was proof against her prying questions. He glanced aloft. She could not follow there. He swung himself into the ratlines and scrambled up to the maintop, bending backward to grab the futtock shrouds. A ship's boy sat on the folded studding sails. Ian growled a command to run up to the crosstrees or choose another mast. But then he realized that this boy was the answer to his most urgent dilemma.

"Come here, boy," he whispered, and drew on the strength that flowed in his veins. He let it shine out through his eyes to quiet the boy. He would take just enough to make it to Gibraltar. No, perhaps that would be too much for a single boy to provide in Ian's depleted state. He would send this one below when he had taken only a little and will another aloft. Just a sip, if a sip he could manage, and perhaps the evidence of his activities would go unnoticed.

The wind has picked up. Thank the gods of sky and sea, Beth thought as the day died. They might make Gibraltar tomorrow, and that might soothe Mr. Rufford's strangled nerves. He had been nowhere in evidence all evening—not an easy feat in a ship not two hundred feet long. His cabin had been dark. No one had seen him. It was most strange. Perhaps it was her talk of Kivala. But no, he had been upset even before she raised that topic.

Beth went down to the surgeon's cabin. "Dr. Granger?" The surgeon had one of the ship's boys under the skylight and was peering at his neck.

The man glanced up at her. He seemed to be better once out of sight of land, for she had not seen him drunk for days. "Here for Mrs. Pargutter's draught?" he asked.

She shrugged agreement and smiled. "I don't mean to interrupt."

"Not at all. Callow here is not in danger of dying. He has two insect bites, rather inflamed. I bled him, and he will answer now." He turned to the cabinet that held the dried herbs and drugs that made up his cure for seasickness.

Beth nodded to the young man. "I hope you are not in distress, sir?"

The boy straightened and puffed out his narrow chest. "No, ma'am. I only came because the bo'sun said they wasn't natural, like, and I was havin' dreams—like a fever, maybe."

Beth's eyes opened involuntarily. Two round wounds, slightly swollen, pricked Callow's neck right over the main artery. She saw them as from a distance, heard the grinding of herbs in Granger's mortar, the creaking of the wooden walls. The surgeon asked whether the tincture of laudanum was sufficient to assure Mrs. Pargutter rest. She managed some answer.

Two round wounds—she could not help but recognize them. Would they leave two round white scars? She had seen such scars, repeated many times, on another body in the ship.

"I would think he had been bitten by a bat," Granger said conversationally, breaking all his patients' confidences without compunction, "or perhaps a rat if there were any large enough. But the *Beltrane* is not producing rats of that size yet," he laughed, "and we are far from Brazil."

"Why Brazil?" she asked, transfixed by those two round wounds.

"Because there is a bat there that drinks blood, and the wound here is right over the carotid artery." Granger turned to mixing the draught.

Drinks blood? "How. . . . how dreadful."

"Not according to the bat. Some bats like fruit, and some, by nature, like blood. It isn't fatal to their victims, and the poor beasts can't help it, certain. Vampire bats, they call them."

"I hope you recover fully," she murmured to Callow as she took the draught. A thousand thoughts raced through her mind. Was Mr. Rufford's nemesis here upon the boat? How could that be and he did not know it? Perhaps he did know it—that was why he was so distracted. She knew his condition was catching. But Callow could not have shared his blood. . . . In any case, the scars on his body related to his servitude, not his disease, did they not?

She almost stumbled into Mr. Rufford. She looked up and saw in his countenance questions, concern, but none of the distracted distress of last night.

"Miss Rochewell, are you well?" The rumble of the voice in his chest was always disturbing, all the more so tonight.

"Yes. Yes, sir, I am." She pushed a wisp of hair behind her ear, searching his face. What would he say about Callow? She must know. "But young Callow is not."

His brows drew together. "The ship's boy? Is he ill?" He stared beyond her to the hatchway. His expression was nothing less than horrified. "I should perhaps look in on him. You will excuse me, Miss Rochewell," he said, not looking at her but focused entirely on the stairs to the orlop, "if I postpone our game."

He hurried down the ladder with a grace he could not have achieved last night. Indeed, as she watched him go, she thought she had never seen a clearer embodiment of power. Surmises swirled in her mind, half-fearful theories forming and melting. What was her mystery doing now? Did she truly want to know?

She did. But she could not follow him without revealing herself. Instead, she waited on the deck where he must reappear.

Appear he did. Before he saw her standing in the shadows where he had left her, his face was illuminated by the light from below. Sadness. An incredible regret. Shame? Loathing? He sucked in the sea air and lifted his face to the stars, unseeing.

"The surgeon says he will recover," she whispered. "A passing weakness, no more."

Her low voice yanked him away from his thoughts. She watched him try to mold his expression into one of bland civility. He was not successful. "Miss Rochewell, you're still here," he said in a choked voice. "Yes. Yes, I'm sure. The young are resilient." A crooked smile strained for nonchalance, but he could not hold it and looked away.

She did not have the heart to ask him what had caused the marks. He knew. That was evident. But he would never tell her the truth when he was so clearly devastated by his knowledge. She began to suspect that there was someone or something hiding on the ship. What was Mr. Rufford so afraid of?

The night sea heaved under the keel. Wind sang in the rigging. The all-pervasive fecund scent of the sea drifted just below the smell of tar and wood, hemp and paint, and, faintly, cinnamon. She stood just behind his shoulder and felt the incredible distance between them. His hair escaped its confinement and wisps swirled around his face as he stared into the night, one hand on the shrouds. At last he clenched his eyes shut, then opened them slowly.

"My apologies. I am no fit company tonight." Still he did not look at her. "Please excuse me from my obligation." He bowed briefly and stalked forward into his cabin.

Beth stared after him for some time, her back against the wall of the quarterdeck. Whatever had happened to this man had happened in North Africa. He had disappeared, for something like two years. He was held prisoner and treated badly. His scars said that. He had acquired a "condition," which gave him strange abilities. And one of her scrolls might just mention what had become of him. What had it said? "Death and age, nor wounds nor blood, will not worry him. Yet his needs will become unclean." Ahhh! And what did that last part mean? She chewed her lip. Perhaps she would just spend this night studying the scrolls with new eyes.

She had not quite left the mysteries of the land she loved behind her. That might be a relief or a burden. She did not yet know. But was she not exactly suited to sort out those mysteries? It was what she had spent her life doing. The Dark Continent had followed her on board the *Beltrane*. She would force it to yield up one last of its secrets. And she would be careful. Something had Mr. Rufford afraid. Suddenly so was she.

Ian sat on his rocking cot with his head in his hands. It had not gotten easier. Each time he must feed, the disgust he felt for himself was as powerful as that first time. What if young Callow had died? He thought he had been careful to take only enough to weaken, but in the first moment the girl had told him that Callow was in sick bay, he had been sure the boy was dead. And Watkins had not even declared his injury yet. Perhaps he would not, if Ian's suggestion to him that it was a pleasant dream of childhood lasted. If the boy wore his stock, no one would be the wiser. Ian leaned against the cupboard. Already he could feel the faint glow of hunger in his veins. But it was only two days now until Gibraltar with luck and wind.

Revulsion overcame him once again. He might dream of England, but he would be taking the nature *she* had thrust upon him back into the bosom of his homeland. How could he expect a normal life when he must suck human blood to sustain himself? No choice, alas. He could not kill himself. He had not the strength to deny the hunger when it burned through his veins. He could only try to moderate his parasitic nature.

God! Why had he been afflicted thus? There must be no God, not as men supposed him to be. The universe was cold and random, and evil grew up unchecked, with no one to regret it except its victims. He shook himself. What use these thoughts? Long hours locked in his cabin with his regret were not healthy for his sanity. But he could not be trusted at large. He would stay confined here until they reached Gibraltar.

And the girl . . . she had looked at him so strangely as she reported that Callow was in sick bay. How much did she know or guess? She had read him a description of the temple. She recognized the depiction of his condition. What else did her texts say about him?

He raised his head. Actually, what they said might be useful to him as well. Perhaps there existed some arcane formula for getting back his humanity. He must press her upon the subject. And yet . . . he must not let her know what he was. She might accept the healing, even the strength, but she would not accept him sucking blood, and she had no idea about his ability to compel others. That she would never countenance. Ahh, the compulsion. Perhaps that was the greatest evil. It was certainly his greatest temptation. His breath came shallowly as the desert night reached out for him. He knew firsthand the evil of compulsion.

Fedeyah, for that was the tall Arab's name, leaned into the silk curtains to talk to Asharti and then called the caravan to a halt. Ian fell to his knees in the sand as the litter was lowered carefully to the ground by the four bearers. He knew what stopping often meant for him. The hot, dry air made the stars pulse in the night sky. Or maybe it was the blackness pulsing at the edge of Ian's vision. He shook his head to clear it. It had been . . . how long since he had first been called to Asharti's tent? He did not know. Months. But he was weakening. His body bore the marks of her teeth on both sides of his neck and on the inside of his elbows, the large vessels between groin and thighs. Recently she had begun to rip his flesh, too, so she could lick his blood as well as suck. He was torn in a half a dozen places. She never took enough to drain him. He ran his dry tongue over cracked lips. Water rations to the slaves had been cut, what few slaves were left. The caravan had shrunk as they used supplies.

Fedeyah returned to the palanquin as the camels up and down the line sank to the sand and settled themselves. "How much farther, Worshipped One? Shall I take a sextant reading?"

"Yes," came the throaty voice in Arabic. She spoke a dozen languages and used whichever she pleased at any time. "We must be near."

"Allah let it be so," Fedeyah acknowledged. "Will you want your favorite?"

"Water him with the rest. Then wash him, inside and out." The silk dropped into place.

A reprieve! But she would want him later. And he would serve her. What did she mean, wash him inside? He felt the rope at his wrist jerked and he stumbled to his feet. He was not allowed a chain after he had used it against his keeper. The smell of water from the barrel being opened flooded over him. Fedeyah pulled him away from the caravan, now busy with watering the slaves, toward an outcropping of tumbled rock up a little sandy incline. Fedeyah wanted to talk of England. The Arab found some time to talk to Ian almost every night. Ian glanced behind him. Was he not to be watered? She had given permission for him to be watered. If Fedeyah took him away he would miss his chance. He sagged as he stumbled after the Arab. He should welcome death from thirst. But his body was cowardly. It longed for water.

Fedeyah sat on the outcropping and grunted for him to kneel in the sand at his feet. The Arab sighted along his brass sextant and took a very fine watch from underneath his burnoose. He grunted and sighted again to check himself. Apparently satisfied, he wrapped the sextant in its embroidered cloth bag and eased a basket lined with leather from its strap about his neck. Ahhh, water. Ian could smell it as Fedeyah opened the basket and lifted it to his bearded chin. Ian's tongue was thick in his mouth. When Fedeyah had wiped his lips, he offered the basket to Ian.

Ian took it with trembling hands and upended it over his mouth. The water, tasting of leather, flowed down his throat in sweet relief. He sputtered and gulped again.

"Enough, slave," Fedeyah said roughly, and pulled the basket away. "You are careless. Anyone would know you were born on an island surrounded by water."

Ian wiped his mouth and licked his hand to get the last. "Yet you will wash me in it."

Fedeyah shrugged. "She spends the water as she wishes." He peered at Ian's body. "You have lasted longer than any favorite in a hundred years. She savors you."

"Why?" All he wanted was for her to drain him one night and let his suffering cease.

"Because you care." Fedeyah looked out over the caravan. "When her dominance is a torment, it gives her greater satisfaction. Some do not care, you know. Some grow to like it. Or they go mad and are past caring." He turned his flat black eyes on Ian. "She says she can feel your will fluttering against her. She tries to break you. But she likes it that she cannot."

Ian wondered that he could still flush with shame. "So the way to escape is to enjoy it?"

Fedeyah looked out across the desert to the caravan below. "Not even that will save you now. She has other plans for you. Still, your servitude will last but a single lifetime."

Maybe he could get Fedeyah to do the job instead. "You are like her, Arab. I have seen you suck the blood from the slaves." He let his tone hold insolence not tolerated in a slave.

The Arab's voice was hollow. "Would I was more like her."

"She is stronger than you are?"

A strange look came over his face, as though he were far away, beyond Ian's taunts. "Oh yes. She made me, after all. Soon she will be stronger yet."

Ian tried to think of some other challenge that would anger the Arab. But something puzzled him. "Is she so much stronger that she can make you serve her?"

He looked slowly back at Ian, and his eyes were old. "I do not serve her as you do. The Moors had my manhood. No, she wanted a procurer, an arranger. Why find a mortal who would become useless in fifty years? So she made a permanent servant."

"Why do you stay?" Ian asked softly. How could this man choose to serve pure evil?

"My bonds are stronger than yours, English. They are of my own making. Do you know what it is to love against your will, in spite of what she is, because of what she is, with a love that does not die, even over centuries?" His voice grew hoarse. *"She takes an endless series of slaves to fill a need I will never quench."* He turned eyes now lit with twisted emotion. *"Yet you come and go. I am always here. She needs me, too."*

"You are as evil as she is." He expected the light in the eunuch's eyes to glow red.

Instead it died. "Yes," he said. *"May Allah forgive me."*

The keeper of slaves hurried as quickly up the hill as his great bulk would take him. "She calls for the slave, Fedeyah. He must be washed."

Fedeyah rose and started down the hill. Ian staggered to his feet, yanked forward, dread filling him. His reprieve was ended. Fedeyah and the keeper took Ian to the barrel of water. The keeper dipped a rag in the precious liquid and scrubbed at Ian with the lye soap. It stung in his wounds. The rough handling opened some of the fresher cuts. But he was used to that. Fedeyah rummaged in a pack on one of the camels and came up with a leather bag attached to a very long wooden nipple, not unlike a water skin. Ian stared, uncomprehending, while Fedeyah calmly filled it with water.

"Kneel!" the keeper barked. *Fedeyah handed him the bag. "On all fours."*

Ian obeyed, his forehead creasing in premonition. He had not long to wait until his dread was made certain. The keeper spread his buttocks and inserted the wooden nipple, squeezing the cool water up into him. "Hold it," he commanded, *"or you will feel the lash."*

Ian scrunched his face in shame. What new humiliation was in store? Was he to be given to the keeper? He had seen the keeper at the other slaves, but never with one of Asharti's chosen and never bothering with preparation. Fedeyah rummaged in the pack again and brought out two phalluses, one shaped like a man's cock, made out of some kind of polished wood, and one of intricately carved stone that looked horribly inhuman.

Ian stared at Fedeyah in horror. The Arab wore no expression. He simply turned, strode the few paces to the palanquin, and handed the two rods in through the silks. Breath rasped in Ian's throat. Asharti had found a new way to break his spirit. He vowed to let her.

Ian's stomach clenched. Apparently he had not tried hard enough to let his spirit be broken. Use of the phalluses had become one of her favorite games with him. As he looked back, it was probably the fact that he hated what she did that made his will "flutter" against hers. His only comfort was that no one here knew his shame. Let her do what she would in Africa. She could kill them all for all he cared. He had escaped. Except for that part of her he carried inside. No one else need ever know what he had become in the desert.

He was not sure himself. He knew about drinking blood, of course, and the long life, from Fedeyah. And he had discovered the healing. He knew the sun burned him, but that seemed to be getting infinitesimally better. He used compulsion to get blood. But surely there was more.

That brought him back to the girl. Her scrolls might be able to tell him. He rose and let himself into the common cabin. Light showed under her door only. The bell outside struck softly. It was two in the morning. As he stood hesitating, the light blinked out. He could not accost her in her cabin this late. He would merely frighten her. And that he could not afford to do.

Beth nodded over her scroll and the careful transcription she was making. It was no good to continue. She rolled the scroll carefully and replaced it in her satchel, then doused her lamp and crawled into her cot. Now that she was in her bed, sleep fled.

There had been no more references she could make out either to Mr. Rufford's condition or to Kivala. But she was determined to know more about her strange fellow passenger. Why had his agitation disappeared? Why had he been in such distress about Callow? Why did Callow's wounds echo Rufford's own? He was so eager to reach Gibraltar. She had heard him ask the Captain repeatedly about it. Why? What was there for him? She had to know.

A bold plan began to take shape. He would go ashore in Gibraltar. She wanted to know what he did there. A British woman in a dress would attract too much attention. She smiled in the dark. She could fix that. She was about to do something that Lady Rangle would despise.

Eight

The convoy put in to the harbor at Gibraltar on the late-afternoon tide. Mrs. Pargutter had recovered miraculously and now stood with Beth and Jenny at the rail as the *Beltrane* found her place among the crowded shipping fleet rocking on the water in the translucent light.

"How long are we to have in port?" Mrs. Pargutter asked Beth. "I must see all the shops." Her voice was eager, her plump cheeks pink.

"The Captain says we sail on tomorrow evening's ebb. We stay to acquire some five new members of our convoy." Beth hoped Mr. Rufford would have time to carry out whatever it was he was planning, for she meant to discover what that was.

Mrs. Pargutter gasped in dismay. "A single day? Well! I shall bespeak a room ashore tonight, for a prompt start in the morning." She turned to Beth. "You will come with us, dear Miss Rochewell? Will it not be heaven to feel solid land beneath our feet?"

Beth gazed out at the immense Rock that rose above the little harbor town. The stark stone rising sharply into the sky loomed over the waterfront. Lush gardens by the shore lined a broad avenue Beth remembered as the Grand Parade. It was filled to overflowing with a cross section of the world. She could pick out the red coats of the lobsters and the blue of naval officers of course, though not as many as during the war, before the Rock had been ceded back to Spain. Even from here she spied white turbans, the rich colors of Turks and Greeks, the pale blue robes of Tangier Coptic Christians, the black of Barbary Jews. Whitewashed walls, terracotta roof tiles, and bright shutters marched up the shoulders of the Rock. "I hope you are not disappointed of dress shops," she said to Mrs. Pargutter. "This has always been a military town."

"Nonsense, my dear," Mrs. Pargutter tutted, her brassy curls shivering. "Wherever there are military men, you find the women who follow them and mantua makers aplenty. I am only sorry we are to be whisked away so cruelly."

"Not a moment to be lost." Beth smiled, quoting the naval phrase heard most often on any ship, even a Company Indiaman.

"Captain!" Mrs. Pargutter called, interrupting the Captain's discussion of the state of the ship's best bower anchor with his first mate. "How soon may we have a boat to go ashore?"

"Another glass." The Captain frowned. "I will send my barge with you."

Mrs. Pargutter turned to Beth. "Is he making me wait while he drinks?" she asked, outrage pulling down the corners of her mouth.

"No, no," Beth soothed. "He means in half an hour. You have remarked that the sand runs in the glass, there by the bell, in half-hour increments? They toll their bell on the half hour."

"The infernal bell!" Mrs. Pargutter exclaimed. "It has been giving me the headache for two weeks and more."

Beth noted with satisfaction that the barge would be shipping across at sunset. True to her surmise, Mr. Rufford appeared just as the boat was launching, and ran down the side into the barge with a small valise.

"You, too, sleep ashore, sir?" Beth asked as the coxswain directed him to a seat facing her.

He glanced at her and carefully away. "One must take one's opportunity as it presents."

"Pull out, there!" the coxswain bellowed. The boat swung away from the side of the frigate and made for the quays, wending its way between the high walls of the moored ships.

"I do hope we may find lodging," Mrs. Pargutter worried. She had burdened Jenny, sitting on her other side, with the huge valise she required for one night ashore.

"My father and I lodged at an inn called Fruit of the Vine on several trips into the Med," Beth remarked. "It is most conveniently located, but quiet. We can try there first if you like." She shot a glance to Mr. Rufford. She did not want to be looking all over town for where he had lodged. "Do you have a place bespoke, sir?"

"Not yet." His answer was short, to discourage her.

"Single gentlemen prefer The Bells, I believe. The staff speaks English, and French as well as Spanish and Catalan."

He raised his brows at her.

She refused to blush. "My father's partner, Monsieur L'Bareaux, always stayed there."

He said nothing. She could only hope that he would be found later at The Bells.

It was after midnight. Beth pulled the rough cloth of her jacket around her and huddled farther into the doorway. The breeze off the harbor carried a bite that said the warmth of autumn waned. Overhead moon and stars were obscured by clouds, and the air held the threat of rain. Rufford had chosen The Bells after all. The boy from whom she'd bought her clothing knew exactly where the English gentleman with the broad shoulders had lodged. These homeless scamps knew everything, and luckily this one spoke only partially broken French, for her own Spanish extended hardly beyond commonplace courtesies. Her pieces of silver had been exchanged for coarse flaxen trousers held up by a rope, a ragged knit shirt, and the all-concealing jacket, as well as some sturdy sandals. Trousers came naturally to her, since she had often worn them when digging with her father, and they were far more practical than a dress for straddling a camel. She had concealed her hair under a bright kerchief bought from the market. With her brown complexion and small stature, she was sure she could pass for a street urchin.

The streets cleared of drunken soldiers and sailors, some *Beltranes* among them, and lights dimmed. Beth sank into a heap in her doorway, so anyone passing would think she was another orphan. Off-key voices howled closer until a last wheelbarrow trundled by with two souls dead to the world piled in it, pushed by two more scarcely better off. Beth began to wonder if she had mistaken her man, or whether he would creep out some back door and avoid her entirely. Her backside was numb. Just as she despaired, a shadow eased out of the door across the street. She would know those burly shoulders anywhere.

He glanced around, but his gaze passed over her still form and he strode off toward the corner. She waited until he turned uphill, and followed silently. He made no attempt to conceal himself as he walked up into the poorer sections of town. It was she who melted from doorway to doorway in pursuit. Cobblestones gave way to packed earth. The houses grew smaller, crouched behind stone walls that faced the street. Once he stopped at a house where an open window gave directly onto the roadway. It was half-open to catch the breeze off the water. But a dog began to bark and he moved on.

At last a door opened just as he passed, and light leaked full onto his countenance from what looked to be a small tavern. "Estancia, where are you going?" a voice yelled in Spanish. The slamming door was the only answer. A woman stepped into the street, swearing under her breath, almost into Rufford's arms. He stepped back in surprise. Beth sheltered behind a morning glory vine draped over a wall, blossoms sleeping in the darkness.

"Ehh, hombre," the woman challenged, sizing up Rufford with a practiced gaze. Her blouse, white in the dark Gibraltar night, had slipped from one shoulder. "Soy yo. ¿Tu quieros hacer con una mujer a muy habilidos esta noche?"

Rufford hesitated.

"Francais?" she asked. "Bon. C'est une nuit parfait pour l'amour, n'est pas? C'est un jardin tout près."

Still he hesitated, so she reached out slowly and took his hand, as she would a wild animal's. He let her draw him through an arch covered with the same vine that sheltered Beth. She gave them a moment, then tiptoed after them. Peering around the arch, she saw the woman lead Rufford to a stone bench in a circle of flagstones, surrounded by a black jungle of tropical plants. The woman lounged across the bench, breasts swelling beneath her low-cut blouse. Rufford loomed above her, uncertain, as though he might turn and run at any moment. Then Beth saw his shoulders sag. He sank to the bench.

Beth slid through the dark leaves, some smooth and shiny, perhaps schefflera, and some light and prickly, Pride of Madeira, their purple flower cones now indigo in the night. Had Rufford come ashore for a common liaison with a Spanish harlot? But there was something in his defeated attitude that said this was more important, more costly, than a carnal need. The moon broke through the clouds and lit the flagstone circle as though it were a stage. Beth found a place where she could crouch among the riot of the garden unseen and yet see Rufford's face.

The woman urged him on, her full-throated murmurs unintelligible. Perhaps she quoted prices; perhaps she promised ecstasy—Beth couldn't hear. She ran her fingers through his hair until his ribbon came loose and it tumbled forward. Beth could almost feel its lush curls. The whore pressed her breasts against his chest as he hung above her, and Beth held her breath.

Rufford himself inhaled and turned his head up, as if in supplication.

When his gaze dropped, Beth was shocked to see that his eyes had gone red. They glowed in the night with their own inner light, crimson instead of blue. His eyes had betrayed a faintly red cast that night she saw him heal, but nothing like this inhuman fire. He gazed at the whore, who went suddenly limp. She would have fallen, but he caught her. She lay draped across his arm, her breast heaving, her head lolling so that her throat was bared. Rufford panted over her for a long moment, then opened his mouth. By the light of the moon, Beth saw canines gleam, impossibly long. Then he bent over the harlot's throat. Beth saw her jerk once, then lift herself to Rufford in a sensual pull as he stayed there, kissing. Kissing? Sucking?

Revulsion showered Beth. Of course, sucking! Like a bat. One of those vampire bats Granger mentioned. He was a *vampire*? Her heart wrenched in anger, in grief or horror. She wanted to run from the garden, but she dared not move lest he see her and she, too, fall victim to him. Her heart trembled and her stomach heaved. This was no "condition." She tried to remember vague legends: garlic, wolfbane, sun, blood, dead but undead, immortal, evil.

With a grunt of effort, Rufford tore his lips from the woman's throat, and sagged over her body. With effort, he raised himself and resettled his victim against his shoulder. Beth watched in morbid fascination as the woman's eyes fluttered open. "You will remember only that someone thought you were beautiful, valuable, that you were loved," he growled as his eyes began to fade through burgundy to blue again.

The woman woke, as from a trance. She sat up and looked around, confused. Rufford stood. Beth could see him flushing, even in the moonlight that washed the color from the world. "For your trouble," he muttered, and laid a golden coin upon the bench.

"Estancia!" a male voice called from the tavern. Light flickered in a window that gave onto the garden. "Dónde estás, Estancia?"

Rufford looked around to the voice, then back at his victim. "Comó estás? Bueno?"

She looked up at him, dazed, and nodded. "Bien, assez bien."

He turned, striding out through the arch as the call within the tavern rose again.

Beth pushed after him, freed from her spell. In the arch-way, he looked both ways, hesitated, and then headed uphill again, away from his inn and the wharf.

She should scurry back to the Fruit of the Vine and safety. She knew what Rufford wanted with Gibraltar now. She knew why Callow bore the same marks that Rufford did. She wondered that she hadn't realized it long before. She, too, paused in the archway, undecided. Behind her, a door opened. Light cascaded over her. "Estancia, venga. Se está haciendo tarde."

Beth stepped out of the light to avoid discovery. Almost against her will she turned to follow Rufford's retreating shadow. She was following evil itself into the night. Why? Why would she do that? Her heart was still pounding, but her brain cleared enough to think.

Her brain did not like the words *evil* and *horror*. Those were superstitious words, words in which her father had never believed. Granger's words about bats came back to her: "Some, by nature, like blood. It isn't fatal to their vic-tims, and the poor beasts can't help it, certain." Was a drunken surgeon more liberal-minded than she was? The look of shame on his face, the sag of his shoulders, said that even Rufford didn't think it was a condition, but some evil. She remembered his wild concern for Callow, his guilty, al-most tender questioning of the whore.

Her thoughts collided all the while her feet followed Ruf-ford. Clouds closed over the moon, casting the street into darkness. Beth longed to move to the center of the dirt lane to avoid the filth at the edge, but though Rufford now seemed oblivious to his surroundings, she dared not risk discovery. Whatever he was, he would not like being followed by a fel-low passenger. Fellow passenger? How could she return to the confines of a ship with one such as Rufford? Yet she didn't have enough money to bespeak a coach in the morn-ing and abandon her voyage.

He turned into a narrow alley. Had she seen another shadow there? She stopped, then moved quietly to the corner where he had disappeared. She saw him gliding, almost preternaturally smooth and quiet, a blacker shadow on the darkness. Ahead of him flickered another shadow, or was it two?

The alley was filled with crates and rotting vegetables, molding rags and human filth. The stench was nauseating. Ahead, Rufford slid after his quarry. She picked her way through the maze of half-seen obstacles to another narrow lane. Rufford was moving faster now into an empty field with grasses growing up around half-burnt timbers and fallen stones. He was gaining on the other shadows—three? They sauntered, muttering, up to no good this late, surely. Could he manage to subdue three? But she had seen his strength. He had pushed off a pirate's corsair single-handed. He had not been violent with the woman, but with three to one, someone would get hurt. Should she shout? Should she warn them of their danger? But that would reveal her. And she could not let Rufford know he had been discovered.

It was all one in the end, for she tripped over a stone in the tall grass and went down with a gasp. The quarries glanced back and began running. Rufford hesitated and stalked back toward her. She struggled to her feet and turned to dash away, heart pounding.

A strong clasp gripped her arm. He turned her with a growl. She squirmed to escape, keeping her face turned away, her eyes downcast. He had her by both shoulders. But he did not shake her, hit her, do all the thousand things he might have done if he was angry. The heated power in his hands on her shoulders seared her.

"Don't be afraid," he murmured. "No tiene miedo." He dragged her to a crumbled stone fireplace, sheltered by a tree only singed by the fire that had destroyed the building.

And she was not afraid. His arm encircled her. She sagged against his strength. He pressed her to his chest while he fumbled with her shirt collar. She could see him perfectly clearly in the moonlight!: the cleft of his chin, the vulnerable lips that puckered too sweetly for evil, the curling hair, unbound. But more than these was the strength that emanated from him, the scent of cinnamon and ambergris. The sense of him penetrated to her core. Her head lay along his arm. He leaned over her. She could hear his panting breath, a low sound in his throat like a growl. She turned to him, baring her carotid artery, and looked up.

"You!" he exclaimed. But he was gasping. His eyes had gone full red. "Why have you done this?" She thought for a moment he would pull away, but then, with something like a snarl, he bent to her throat.

The twin pains, when they came, were not unexpected. She only thought they would be sharper. Perhaps it was the languor that overcame her, but the piercing of her skin did not seem important. What was important was his scent and the nearness of his body. His lips were soft against her skin. Now both arms embraced her and pressed her breasts into his chest. His mouth pulled at her throat, sucking, and she moved her body in some instinctive counterpoint, her hips pressing against his thigh, which had somehow gotten between hers and hers between his. She was burning, throbbing in her loins with the pulse of her blood, her mother's blood that ran within it, his blood. He held her tighter. She could hardly breathe, and now his hips were thrusting back, even as he pulled against her throat and pressed her against his body. She did not care. Let him take all the blood she had, just so she might stay here, in this almost ecstasy, forever with him.

With a cry, he withdrew. He wiped the blood from his mouth and shook his head, as if to clear it. "Too much. Too much." But still he held her close. She looked up into that countenance as if she had known it forever. She saw guilt suffuse him. He turned his gaze to her, still burgundy, but fading. "You will remember . . ."

"Everything, always," she whispered.

His eyes widened and snapped back to blue. He let her go as though she were a hot coal. Beth dropped to her knees, unable to stand on her own. She wavered.

He threw himself down on his knees in front of her and took her shoulders to steady her, examining her neck with horror. "God, what have I done?"

She smiled sleepily at him, unable to speak. He looked

wildly around, came to himself, shook her to get her attention, and muttered, "You will remember nothing."

But it was too late and he knew it.

From somewhere far away she could see the pain in his eyes, see him swallow and look about himself as though something would occur to change what had just happened. He examined her again, taking in the ragged urchin's clothing, no doubt. "I must get you back to your rooms." He stood and hauled her to her feet. Taking her arm, he pulled her through the burnt remains toward the lane beyond. She didn't care if she got back to her rooms. She wanted to stay here, in the ruins, with him. She stumbled a few steps and sank again.

Rufford turned and swept her up in his arms, carrying her lightly, as if she weighed nothing at all. "The Fruit of the Vine, did you say?"

"Um-hmm." She buried her face in his shoulder, feeling the warmth emanating from him, breathing in his scent. The muscles beneath the fabric rolled as he shifted her weight. She had never been this close to a man not her father. Were they all this powerful, this overwhelming? she wondered, from very far away. She had been missing something in her life.

He strode down the lane, across, into another, always downhill. Beth must have swooned, for the next thing she knew, he was shouting for the landlord in Spanish and kicking at the door of the inn. The door cracked open; a small man with mustachios protested that it was too late for a room, to no avail. Rufford pushed past him. Loud voices, a querulous inquiry from the top of the stairs—another guest. Threats from Rufford to wake the whole inn. The landlord sent them to a small room at the back of the house.

Rufford laid her on the bed, shut the door, took off his boots for some reason, and sat next to her on the bed. Noises outside petered out. Then quiet. She drifted.

"What is the number of your room?" he asked in a low rumble.

"What?" she murmured from somewhere near unconsciousness.

"Your room. I must get you back there if there is not to be a scandal."

She looked up. His brows were drawn together in anger. Was he angry at her? "Eight."

He nodded. "Rest. I must wait until the house has gone back to sleep."

She smiled and drifted away.

Ian watched her in the moonlight from the opened shutters as sleep took her, and felt for her pulse. Her wrist was so small. He could break the bones between a thumb and fore-finger. Why in God's name had she followed him? It was all her fault, putting herself in his way just as he was bent on feeding. Dressed like an urchin, no less! He would never have . . . but he had. Even when he saw her eyes, those un-mistakable green-gold eyes, he had been unable to restrain himself. He had fed from her. And it was more than feeding. The act had been totally unlike taking sustenance from Cal-low or the harlot earlier tonight.

He fingered her wrist again. He could feel no pulse. Panic surged. What had he done? He put his palm across her frag-ile throat and felt with thumb and middle finger for her carotid. The two round red circles accused him. There! Faint and fluttery, but a definite pulse. Ian breathed again. He had taken far too much blood for one so small. What had come over him? He had already assuaged his most urgent need. The feel of her slender body pressed against him made his body react even now. It had bordered on . . . ecstasy. That must be why he had so lost control. Who had begun to move their hips first? He could not control his caroming thoughts.

Why had she done it? He had to admit it had taken courage. She must have seen him with the woman in the garden, else she could not have followed him to the burnt ruins. She knew what he was, and even so, she continued. Perhaps she had known all along. She had seen the boy on the ship, the marks.

He put one shaking hand to his mouth, trying to quiet his mind. She might still die. She had been seriously weakened.

But if she survived she must be preserved from her folly. He could not let her be found in boy's clothes, having been carried in by a strange man last night. He would place her back in her own room in her own clothes. That would take care of the maids. Would the landlord connect the sick boy who must have a room at long past midnight with the sick girl to be found in number eight tomorrow? Gold would keep his silence.

The inn had dropped back into slumber. He could hear Mrs. Pargutter's distinctive sputtering snore. He gathered the girl in his arms and picking up his boots he crept silently down the hall. The door of number eight was locked. Well, he could cover the price of a new lock. He wrenched the knob and stepped in, grabbing his boots and shutting the door.

He laid her in her own bed and glanced around for her things. Her valise was still packed, but he rummaged through it and found a fine lawn night shift. Thank God it had not only long sleeves but also a high Oriental collar to hide the marks on her throat.

Feeling huge and ungainly, he sat next to her on the bed. Beneath her, what must be a brightly embroidered coverlet was only dark and light blotches in the night. First he took the kerchief from her head and unwound her hair. Women did not sleep with their hair tied up. He had much experience of women. It was heavy, a luxurious fall. He took the coarse sandals from her delicate feet and tossed them to the floor. He hesitated before he fumbled at the rough rope belt at her waist. What was the problem? Had he not undressed a score of women? But they were willing partners and far more experienced than this small figure. She was virgin to a man's eyes, he was almost sure, and would consider what he was doing a violation. The knot defied his fingers, so he simply grasped it with both hands and snapped it. Forcing his mind to a careful blank, he slid the ragged canvas trousers from her. He unbuttoned the shirt and shrugged first one shoulder and then the other from both shirt and jacket at once. Her skin was the color of coffee with too much cream in it. *Brown* could not describe a complexion such as hers.

Gathering the clothes and shoes, he put them in a heap by the door, so he would not forget them when he left. He turned back to the bed and stopped stock still.

She lay against the coverlet, limbs in disarray, dark, thick hair falling over the pillow, and the sight just . . . stopped him. She was tiny but well formed, and her breasts were rather heavy for her size. How had he never noticed that? Their dusky areoles framed delicate nipples. The angle of her collarbone made her seem even more fragile. She had a narrow waist and flaring hips, something the modern mode of dress would never reveal. The dark triangle between her hips seemed too small to welcome a man.

He felt a thrill in his loins, a desire to touch her so strong it made him hold his breath. She would never respond to such as he was. Willingly. A thought, fleeting, darted into his mind and said he could compel her.

Instantly revulsion drenched him. As he had been compelled? As *she* had compelled him? The horror of that brief thought made his stomach churn. What was he becoming, that he could think such things? In one stride, he grabbed up the girl's night shift. He gathered it from the bottom, shoved her hands through the sleeves, and dragged it over her head, pulling it down around her. He lifted her with one arm, pulled back the coverlet. Her warmth against his side tortured him. To his dismay, the dark lashes lifted and the green-gold cat's eyes looked up at him. Were they accusing? No . . . they were something else. She raised a hand to his neck and drew him down. His lips brushed hers. He held his breath.

"Are you a dream?" she murmured into his mouth. She pressed her body, free from restraint under her shift, against him. He groaned, his need rising in him, not for her blood this time but for other kinds of sharing. "I don't care," she murmured. "Love me."

There was no question of compulsion. She was a willing partner. In fact, the words had sounded like a command. He looked into her eyes and saw a kind of sureness there. A shudder of revulsion shook him. A woman commanded him? He had vowed never to let that happen again! He jerked away from her. She fell back against the pillow. Her eyes were swimming.

"Not a dream?" she said. Her eyelids fluttered even as he stared in horror at her and she seemed to faint. Ian stood, shuddering. He had escaped entanglement by the barest chance of her words. An overwhelming desire to escape came over him. An instant was all that was needed to cover her, gather up the urchin's clothes, and slide out the door with his boots. He flung a gold piece on the taproom bar and pushed out into the night where creatures such as he belonged.

Back in his room at The Bells he could not sleep but paced from shuttered windows to the door and back. Tortured by the prospect that he could not hold his new nature at bay, dismayed that she had offered herself to him, he yet found room to be appalled that the fear and revulsion at her offer were so overpowering. He seemed caught between evils.

On the one hand, he might be becoming what Asharti was. God knows, he was no angel. His early years at Cambridge and just after had been filled with women, gaming, every kind of sport, savory and unsavory. But he had always preserved some moral ground, however narrow. He never betrayed a confidence, he supported his friends even if it took courage, treated horses, dogs, and women well, even if he didn't love them. When Henry inherited, Ian settled down, managed to clear most of his debts, found a diplomatic post, and applied himself. He had put aside wickedness. But his thoughts about the girl tonight bordered on mad or evil.

He wanted this girl. But when she seemed to command him, the memory of his time with Asharti forbade responding to her, even with another kiss. Perhaps he had always been cut off from women. He lusted, but he had never loved one. And now Asharti intervened. He might be becoming like her, but even if he was not, she ruled his life.

He had been changed, not only by that single drop of blood, but also by the months preceding it. As the crack in the shutters showed a lightening day, memories descended on him.

. . .

All day the slaves had lain, covered with a tarpaulin, barely
able to breathe as the wind raged. The weight of sand made
the canvas a heavy blanket indeed. The sun was a small orange ball overlooking hell. It was not his first sandstorm.
This one offered no less death than the others. Two slaves
had suffocated. But now he did not care for death and was
disappointed when, as the blow decreased a bit, the caravan
had moved forward even through the howling wind and
stinging sand, driven by Asharti's will alone. He staggered
beside the palanquin, its silken hangings covered by canvas,
tied down tightly. The falling wind still flung sand against his
bare flesh and left it caked in his wounds. A voice called out,
croaking in triumph somewhere ahead. They had reached the
oasis, Haasi Fokra. The wind died, as if the oasis were immune to storm. The caravan seemed to sigh in relief. An expressive arm, ending in a long-nailed hand, gestured from
the palanquin. Ian flinched. She could not want him now in
all his dirt.

She did not. Fedeyah drifted up from the rear and un-
hitched the rope that held the canvas sides by grommets tight
against the wind. "Worshipped One?" he inquired.

"Water the caravan. This oasis will be the last," Ian
heard Asharti murmur. "Take our position as soon as the sky
has cleared."

Ian waited his turn at the tiny pool, almost drained by the
prodigious needs of the camels and the few remaining
slaves. The drivers filled the company's huge casks.

"We must turn back," one driver muttered. "With this water, we may get back alive. If we go farther . . ." He did not
need to complete his thought. The others muttered their assent.

Let them take their proposal to Asharti, Ian thought bitterly. But they would not. They were almost as afraid of her
as he was. They would go to their deaths rather than risk her
wrath.

His turn to drink came and he fell to his knees in the soft
mud at the edge of the depleted pool. A few frowsy palms

and some tattered bushes cloaked in dust ringed the sad puddle. He was the last to drink. He gulped the brown water churned up by the camels and the slaves before him, taking all he could before the keeper pulled him away. He was dimly aware that he was allowed more than the other slaves, no doubt due to his position as the favorite Asharti intended to "savor." He was growing a little weaker day by day, though. He would not last forever. That was a comforting thought. As he lurched away from the dirty pool, he saw Asharti, dressed in a chartreuse silk that glowed in the desert night, exchanging the sextant with Fedeyah not far away. The keeper pushed him to his knees with a cuff, muttering. He bowed his head, but not before he saw Asharti nod, glowing with an energy he had not seen in her before. She spoke, excited, in Arabic. He could almost make out all the words.

"Three days, if we hurry, servant. Three days! All I have sought is within my grasp. I will no longer have to work through a man to rule." *She whirled away from Fedeyah and paced beside him.* "Take your reading at noon tomorrow. We must be sure of our position."

Fedeyah bowed. "The chronometers make the difference. We will find it this time."

"You bear the light well," *Asharti remarked.* "I remember when your flesh would sizzle like fried fat even in the dawning rays of the sun."

"We grow tougher with age," *he replied. But Ian knew he didn't think that true.*

Asharti paced again. "Let the slaves be whipped forward briskly. The camels dawdle to match their pace. We must reach the exact spot at the full of the moon. It is not the half solstice, but with the proper calculations, we can make adjustments."

"The slaves dwindle, Goddess Mine. They may not assuage your need on the return."

Ian peered up through his lashes to see Asharti smile. It was a secret smile, assured. "I shall have no need of them. I will have more important blood than theirs to swell my veins."

"Shall you take blood tonight?" *Fedeyah asked.*

She surveyed the slaves, a score only, down from fifty and those replenished frequently during the first part of their wandering, then turned her gaze to Ian. He quickly bowed his head. "We need them as an offering. I will abstain from draining any tonight. But wash the favorite and send him to me. My blood runs high in anticipation of my triumph."

Fedeyah dragged Ian back through the mud to the pool. "Wash yourself, English."

Ian sank to his knees in the shallow, brackish water and laved it over his shoulders. "Why do my wounds not fester, Arab?" Once he had hoped infection would release him.

The eunuch threw him soap and sat in the sand above the muddy verge. "Her spittle prevents festering. When she licks the wounds they heal by first intent."

"Until she opens them again," Ian muttered, soaping his body.

"As you say. Her spittle also keeps them flowing while she feeds." The Arab's whole demeanor spoke of defeat. Ian wondered what kind of wounds she opened in her servant.

"Three days to the end of our endless journey?"

"Perhaps. It has been what? A year? No, nearly two. So short a time. So long."

"You think she will not need you after that." Ian stated it boldly as he soaped his genitals. What did the Arab think would happen tomorrow? What would change?

"The end of our journey will be far worse for you than me," the Arab returned, "and worse for the world. Or we may all be dead."

"What does she seek?" Ian whispered.

"Ultimate power," Fedeyah said, his voice dead. "And Allah help us if she finds it." He shook himself. "No more questions, slave. Your hair is gritty. That will not please her."

Ian submerged his head and scrubbed at his scalp. He surfaced, sputtering. The Arab tugged at his rope and Ian staggered up toward him. Fedeyah produced a jug filled with scented oil, with which Ian was only too familiar. Ian held out his cupped hands and Fedeyah filled them from the amphora. Ian rubbed the oil over his chest and belly. It smelled of myrrh. Asharti's imminent demands oppressed his spirit. His only consolation was that Fedeyah had not produced the hated leather skin used to clean his anal passage. Was he to be spared the rods?

Fedeyah led him, dripping, from the pool toward the palanquin, silvered by moonlight. The failing breeze behind the storm dried his body. Several of his wounds now drooled fresh blood. That would excite her, he knew. Fedeyah held the hangings aside and Ian crawled into the silk cocoon. Its floor was a well-stuffed mattress four feet wide and perhaps eight in length, strewn with pillows in deep green and the purple of grapes. Now the dim light showed only tones of gray and black. The silk swung shut behind him, shutting out even moonlight. Asharti lounged among the luxurious hangings, the pale chartreuse of her deep-cut gown gleaming faintly in the dark against her pale skin. Slowly, Ian's eyes adjusted to the shadows. A call to start the caravan echoed in the night outside. He knelt at the base of her bed, wavering as the palanquin was lifted by the slaves who bore it. His breath already came heavy in his chest in anticipation of the coming ordeal, repeated so often he could not remember a time when she had not commanded, he not served. Her scent suffused the palanquin. Its sweetness nauseated him. He waited for her eyes to go red and his body to respond to her in spite of his best efforts to suppress it. He closed his eyes once as she tapped the silks at her side, and crawled forward.

She tapped the bed again and he lay beside her. Her breasts, the nipples prominent under the liquid chartreuse silk, brushed against his chest. Her black hair cascaded over him as she leaned over. She whispered to him in French, "It is a special night, slave. Can you not feel it?" Her long nails trailed over his shoulder, touching the slashing wound she had made there, leaking once again. "Power trembles in the air." Her full lips touched his forehead, even as she pushed his chin up. "I will sip first." She drew back, surveying him. "Where shall I open you?"

He sighed, deep in his soul, and bared his throat, her fa-

vorite place to suck. But she did not bend to his suggestion. Instead she ran her fingers over the bloody furrows on his chest, his belly. She touched the twin marks of her sucking at the big veins in his groin, the cut on his thighs, then over his hips, around to his buttocks where she had made incisions. She cupped his elbow, presenting the vein she had opened on the tender inside. His chest rose convulsively with anxiety. Her lips brushed his cheekbone. He could feel her hot breath. He took her lip between his teeth and sucked. She always liked that. Her tongue ran under his lips, promising her own fulfillment, if not his. He felt the familiar tightness in his loins. She pressed her body against him, ran her hand around to the nape of his neck. His head lolled against her grip, baring his throat. Her lips strayed down over the stubble at his chin and she licked the twin wounds in the artery there. He could feel himself pulsing with it as it beat in his neck.

The piercing pain was expected. She molded her body to his as she pulled at his neck, suckling. Their bodies moved in time to the throb of his blood and the rhythm of her urgency. But she withdrew quickly with a little moan. He opened his eyes. She licked his blood from her fulsome lips and pressed herself rhythmically against him. Her hand moved to his cock, caressing its full length. "You obey, slave, to perfection," she murmured. She moved aside the chartreuse silk, baring her breasts. She did not command him to suck them but instead brushed them against his nipples, provoking a groan as she tugged more firmly at his cock. For some time, she did no more than stroke his cock, his buttocks, press her hips and her naked breasts against him, and occasionally lick at his neck and the wound on his shoulder he had opened at the pool. The need in his loins became a torment in itself.

"Finish with me," he muttered. He had not begged her, as she liked him to do.

"At your command," she whispered.

She pushed him to his back, hiked up her silks, and sat astride him, her hot slit greasing his cock with slick juices as it lay erect across his belly. He arched under her as she bent to·his right breast. She licked at the half-healed gash there and opened it with her canines, dragging the furrow down toward his nipple. Her tongue was soft, moist, amid the pain. She lapped the welling blood, making small sounds of satisfaction. Then, taking his hands above his head, she made a fresh gash in his right biceps, moving her body along his as she sucked at the wound.

Ian groaned his submission, unable to stop hating that he did it. Why could he not simply give in to her? She sat up, raised herself, and placed his erect member inside her, then rocked against him for several strokes before she bent to the other side of his throat. His hands stole to her waist as she moved faster. His own need rose inside him, and he wondered that she did not contain it by the force of will that had stoppered him so many times before. She usually did not allow him to ejaculate so early in the night, if she allowed it at all. He careened down a narrowing tunnel to the blinding light that always frightened and enticed him.

Still she did not prevent his rising urgency but increased her pace, grunting in her need as she sucked, first at his throat, then at his breast, and then again at the biceps torn by her teeth. His release overtook him in a shudder, the light engulfing him even as he felt her wrenching cry.

He almost swooned, he felt so empty. She hung above him, satisfaction in her eyes, still straddling his hips. "So, slave, is your submission complete?"

He took his hands from her waist. What did she mean? His submission was complete the first time her eyes went red. A nasty smile curved her lips. "You do not even know."

"Know what?" he growled. Should he even be able to speak to her so coarsely?

"You think I used my powers on you? Not tonight, my most submissive slave. I drew the power only to produce my teeth, the better to open you."

A feeling of sinking horror suffused him. "What? What do you mean?"

"You serviced me all on your own." Again the chortling satisfaction.

*Ian stared at her. It was not true! He would never pleasure
her willingly. He searched her face, its amusement and triumph a torment. Had he not felt her compulsion? He was not
sure. He had been able to tell her to finish it. That had never
happened before. And she had made no attempt to control
his release.*

Oh, God.

He pushed her off him. "Bitch," *he hissed, and struggled
to his knees.* "Bitch! I should . . ."

*Her eyes blinked crimson. He felt the compulsion shower
over him, beating him back against the cushions, almost preventing breath.* "Should what?" *she said, rising upon her elbows, her face furious.* "I should tear you limb from limb!"

Kill me, *he thought.* Kill me now. *He had submitted to
her willingly. The thought was almost soul-destroying. But
did that not mean that she would finally finish with him and
release him from his torment? Fedeyah thought so.*

*She mastered herself. Her eyes dimmed and he could
breathe again. Her fury dissolved into that throaty laughter.
When she could speak, it was in French.* "How delicious that
you still rebel! And how very, very satisfying that you hate
yourself for servicing me. There is much yet to savor about
you. And we have not yet progressed to an affection for the
phalluses, the submission, even the whip." *She chuckled, low
in her throat.*

*Ian could not speak. He gasped for breath, chest heaving.
He saw the whole. If he had mastered his anger, she might
have killed him and moved on to another. He might be free
even now. His shoulders sagged.*

*She sat up, in control again, and arranged her silks
around her.* "No, I would not have killed you," *she said, answering his unspoken thought.* "You are an important part of
my offering." *She studied him, head cocked for a moment.*
"But I might not find you so attractive, or need your services
so often." *Her eyes bored through to Ian's soul.* "Let me feel
your rebellion again." *She beckoned with one golden-nailed
finger.* "Kneel, slave, with your knees wide."

Ian's remaining spirit fluttered inside him. He tried to

suppress any struggle against the will that showered over him. He labored to his knees. But as he felt his cock swell again and his thin blood throb, it was against his will. Blackness trembled around the edges of his vision, but he knew from experience that she could rouse him even from a swoon.

"Knees wider. Now, rub your fine English cock. I wish its service yet this night."

He could not help but obey, but it raked his soul to do it. That was what pleased her most.

Nine

Beth swam up through layers of cotton that clogged her brain. She was warm. The sun was bright against her closed eyelids, but it seemed much too much effort to open them. She had been dreaming. The dream had been intense and . . . sensual. It dissipated like fog, even as she tried to make her way back into its world.

A pounding on the door shook her senses. That was what had wakened her.

"Miss Rochewell!" Jenny called. "Are you up yet?"

"Miss Rochewell!" Mrs. Pargutter's shrill voice called. "We are late. The shops await."

Beth opened her eyes and looked around, confused. Where was she? She pushed herself up to sit, but blackness at the edge of her vision threatened to overwhelm her. She hung her head to gather her senses. "Go . . . go on without me, Mrs. Pargutter. I have . . . the headache."

Much whispering outside the door. "Well, if you're sure, my dear. We shall return in time to take you up before we go out to the ship." More muttering between Mrs. Pargutter and Jenny and the sound of footsteps on the stairs.

Beth collapsed to her pillows. What was wrong with her? The night came back to her in a rush: following Mr. Rufford, seeing him drink the Spanish harlot's blood, the look of pain and shame on his face, the fear when he discovered her, the feel of his body against hers, the press of his lips at her throat.

Her hands felt under her collar for the wounds he had made. Yes, there were the twin bumps. Was it loss of blood that made her so weak? She remembered Rufford carrying her into the inn. How had she gotten into bed? Who had changed her clothes? Jenny? Mrs. Pargutter?

Rufford!

The little blood she had left went careening around her body. He must have seen her naked. He must have rifled through her things. And then, even more tenuous in her memory, was the feeling of him bending over her, a brush of lips that made her throb, and then . . . Had she offered herself to him? She felt her face flush, and then the dark, floating circles spread around her field of vision. This time they would not be denied.

Ian peered out between his shutters into the bright morning using the blue spectacles he had ordered made in Tripoli. His eyes had grown a little more tolerant of sunshine. Fedeyah said that, as the years passed, he had lost his sensitivity to the sun. The Arab had taken sextant readings in the daylight. Perhaps there was hope that Ian would not always be a creature of the night.

He surveyed the quay for the hundredth time this morning through slitted eyes, waiting for Miss Rochewell to make her way to the *Beltrane*. The docks were a veritable hive. Sailors from all lands loaded boats with cargo for the ships whose forest of spars rocked in the harbor. A woman's garb could not be missed in that sea of masculinity. He thought for certain that Mrs. Pargutter would support her in her trek back to the ship, but Mrs. Pargutter and her maid had sallied off into the town, chattering like jaybirds, several hours ago. That meant Miss Rochewell had not confided in them. That was good, in some ways.

But where was Miss Rochewell? True, the ship did not sail until the evening, but would she not want to go back, even if she wasn't feeling well, so the doctor could look to her?

Perhaps she was too ill to go by herself. Mrs. Pargutter had abandoned her, at least for the day. That woman had not a shred of common sense. Or Miss Rochewell was afraid to go back to the ship because she imagined he would be there. That thought was sobering. He would not inflict his presence on her. He would make the long overland trek through Spain, over the Alps, and across the Channel to England. But she did not know that.

With a growl of displeasure, he slung a cape about his shoulders and pulled its collar up around his ears. He had no wish to see the chit again. She might well ply her wiles on him. He was more than capable of resisting this morning. Lord knew what had come over him last night. But her condition was his responsibility. He shoved on a hat and settled his blue glasses on the bridge of his nose. He took an extra stock and muffled the bottom of his face and reached for his gloves. It was two blocks from The Bells to the Fruit of the Vine. The left side of the street would still be in shade. He'd have to dash across the square, of course. He would look a strange sight in the warmth of a Gibraltar October, muffled up like a bandit in colder climes, but he might just make it to her room.

It was the landlady who greeted him in the taproom as he unwound his stock. "Sit down, sir," she cried, in accented English, "and let me bring you some refreshment. You look flushed."

Ian panted as he took off his hat and gloves. "If you will show me to room eight . . ."

"I'm sorry, sir," she answered, bobbing. "That room is taken by a young lady."

"A young lady who, I have it on authority, is ill." He turned and took the stairs two at a time, not waiting for his hostess. A perfunctory knock, an infinitesimal pause for decency, and he pushed into the room, dreading what he would see.

She lay there, tiny in the bed, just where he had left her,

her hair a dark cloud against the white pillows and her dusky lashes brushing her cheeks. She did not move at his abrupt entrance or open her eyes. Her countenance was pale, the creamy coffee color having acquired a gray undertone. Under her eyes, bluish half circles hung. Guilt and panic warred in his breast. With two strides he was at her side. He checked the pulse at her neck and found it fluttering there, stronger than last night but hardly hearty. It throbbed against his fingers.

She opened her eyes. As they registered his identity a soft look came into them; then they widened in a fear that cut him deeply.

"Good morning, Miss Rochewell," he said, as prosaically as he could, pressing down his guilt. "I am sorry to find you out of trim." He half-turned his head and took in the gaggle of heads behind his hostess in the doorway. That lady was sputtering into protest at his unseemly behavior. "Send for a doctor," he commanded. When chaos ensued in the doorway, he only raised his brows and frowned. "Now?"

One of the maids at the rear squeaked, "I'll go, mum," in Spanish and disappeared.

"You may make yourself useful, good lady, by providing some sustaining broth and a glass of porter," he said to his hostess, as calmly as he could. "At your *earliest* convenience?" He spared a moment to see her depart indignantly and the maids scatter, and then turned to Miss Rochewell.

He hardly knew what to say. What was proper when one had sucked another's blood? How could he allay her fear? And then there was the fact that his thigh was laid along her hip with only the coverlet between them. The feelings that stirred inside him only reminded him of the shameful thoughts he had entertained last night. She was right to be afraid of him.

Beth looked up at the humiliation in the handsome face above her as he struggled for words. The blue eyes glanced away and down, his long lashes brushing his cheeks. Evil was never ashamed of itself, was it? Ah, but perhaps he could not control the evil, once it was loosed. He might be of two minds about what he did. But he did it, did he not? She shivered. And what of her? Was she to be trusted? What she thought might have happened last night was . . . but that was only a dream. Wasn't it?

He cleared his throat and raised his eyes to hers. "I . . . I should like to apologize for . . . for last night. I had not meant to . . ." He trailed off, then straightened and spoke more formally. "You have suffered at my hands in an extremely distasteful manner. I extend my abject apologies and assure you that I shall see that you receive proper care and are delivered to the ship in time for sailing if you should choose to do so. I myself shall be proceeding overland. Rest assured that you will not be burdened by my presence."

She nodded, wary, feeling weak and vulnerable. His thigh lay along her hip. She could feel its heat through the quilt. It made her shiver, but not in fear.

"If there is any way . . ." Here again he stumbled and recovered with difficulty. "If you can think of any manner in which I can give a more substantial sign of my extreme regret, I beg you will inform me."

"You are too good, sir," she mumbled, just to make him stop. The startled and hurt look he cast her said he thought she tried to wound him. "If you would leave me . . ."

A knock sounded at the door. A small man in a full-bottomed wig and a mouse-colored waistcoat with definite gravy stains upon it bustled into the room, smelling strongly of raw onions and human sweat. He was English by his look, but he also appeared to have been absent from England for some time. His clothes were not fashionable. Nor had he occasion to launder his shirt. Rufford rose hastily and ceded his place to the doctor. He did not leave, in spite of Miss Rochewell's request, nor did the doctor ask him to do so. The doctor must believe that she was under Mr. Rufford's "protection." That was the genteel phraseology, was it not?

She must get away from Mr. Rufford, but how, when she was so weak? If she made a scene now, they might both be ejected from the inn. She pinned her hopes on the doctor. If he could restore her strength she could get to the ship.

"Well, well, sit up, my dear," the doctor said. "So you are a passenger on the *Beltrane*?"

She nodded and struggled to sit. The telltale black globules began to form at the edge of her vision. Rufford moved to help her, then thought better of it and clasped his hands behind his back. Her vision cleared a bit. She stuck out her tongue, coughed, and generally obeyed the doctor's instructions.

"What are the symptoms?" the little man said in his most professional voice as he drew down her lower eyelids. "Look up."

She rolled her eyes to Rufford, who was looking anxious. "A general malaise," she said. "Weakness." The doctor would not believe her if she told him what had really happened. And if she tried, Rufford might well kill her or the doctor or both.

The little man gave over examining her eyes, felt under her jaw for swellings, and by accident found the two small wounds at her neck. Rufford pressed those vulnerable lips together into a thin, hard line and waited.

"Well, well," the doctor said. "Does your ship have rats? They are most uncommon bold these days, I swear. You are not febrile, and the wounds do not seem infected. They are not the cause of your symptoms." He sat up. "My dear, I think a cupping, twelve or fourteen ounces at the most, should set you up." From his pocket he drew out a lancet covered in rusty flakes.

"You will *not* bleed her." Rufford suddenly loomed over the doctor, looking very angry and very frightening. He grabbed the little doctor by the upper arm and lifted him bodily from the bed. "Charlatan!" he growled, propelling him toward the door. "You should be flogged."

"Unhand me!" the doctor squeaked. Rufford almost threw him out the door. "My fee . . ."

Rufford reached into his pocket and flipped a sovereign at the doctor with contempt. The little man caught it, examined it, and retreated, almost into the laden arms of the landlady. "I shall not be available when next called upon," he threatened, and scooted down the stairs.

When the landlady met Rufford's glowering countenance, any protest about his handling of the doctor died in her throat.

"Give me that." He took the tray and shut the door in her purpling face without ceremony. "Cupping, for the Lord's sake! It will not answer." The bass growl rolled over her.

Beth retreated into her pillows as he turned that angry face on her. He had just cut her off from any help, and with that look in his eyes she might need help at any moment. What was she to do locked in a room with a man who had turned into a monster last night? Then he softened, his face losing the expression that said he was capable of anything. She knew what "anything" in this case might entail.

"Forgive my outburst," he muttered, and she saw him consciously master himself.

"I beg you will leave me, sir," she said with all the strength she could muster.

He shook his head. "Not until you have consumed this broth and the porter in the tankard." He set the tray upon her lap and retreated to the fireplace, cold, since October in the Med was still quite warm, and leaned against the mantel with folded arms.

At least he gave her a little space. The inn's silver felt strangely weighty as she lifted spoonfuls of broth to her lips, conscious of his eyes upon her. Rufford paced to the window. After a half-dozen sips her hand began to shake. She managed two more before the spoon clattered to the tray. She sank back.

He pressed his body against the far wall as if he did not trust himself or her before he spoke. "Could you take more? I might be of assistance. . . ."

Beth shook her head, exhaustion setting in. How would she ever make it to the ship?

His assessment of her chances seemed much the same. "If you would like to remain in Gibraltar for some days, to recoup your strength, I could engage some local woman. . . ."

She did not want to be confined in Gibraltar, weak and incapacitated, a woman alone in a strange town with a vampire ashore. She wanted to leave this horrible place and him with it. If she could make it to the ship and know that he went overland, that there were hundreds of miles between them . . . "I shall do, I am sure," she said with all the firmness she could muster. "Mrs. Pargutter will see to me once I am aboard, and the surgeon, of course."

His brows drew together briefly. Then he glanced to the bedside table and took up the tankard. "Porter is said to be valuable in restoring strength. I have seen it used with men in an exsanguinary state from wounds." He hesitated, then sat beside her, raising his brows in inquiry.

He was too close. "No, no," she breathed. "You must go, sir. Go this instant."

Shame suffused his face. He handed her the tankard. "When you have drunk this."

She took the tankard in both hands, the metal cool and damp against her palms. It was all she could do to lift it, but if this was what it took to make him go, then she would drink. The porter was so thick you could almost chew it. The yeast and burnt grain taste was smothering. After a few gulps, she sputtered and lay back. "Now, see to your promise," she murmured.

A sharp rapping on the door behind them made them both start. "The room has got to be made up, which is to say there is a gentleman bespeaking it below, if free."

Rufford swung to the door and jerked it open to reveal a shocked young man, fingers dark from boot blacking. "Tell the gentleman to go to the devil," Rufford said. "Miss Rochewell is not to be disturbed this afternoon." He looked back at her. "Rest. I will let no one intrude."

Indeed, her eyes were heavy even now. She felt like she could sleep for days. Days? What if she slept through the ship's sailing? "Tell them to call me . . ." But now her exhaustion was such that she slurred her words. Or maybe it was the porter.

The last thing she heard was his apologetic mutter: "It is the least I can do."

. . .

Ian sat in the dim taproom with a bottle of claret, his second of the afternoon. Damn her! To be so frightened of him, so dependent upon others, at this awkward juncture! She had outlined his choices only too clearly in her artless conversation. She placed all her faith in Mrs. Pargutter and the surgeon of the *Beltrane*. That she did not want to stay alone in Gibraltar he could understand. She would certainly get no medical help here. But he had even less faith in the surgeon of the *Beltrane*. Would Granger not bleed her? He had bled Callow. Since Ian had not taken half so much blood from the ship's boy, there was no lasting harm.

Miss Rochewell could not sustain the same. As for Mrs. Pargutter . . . But it looked very like he would have to engage that lady to help Miss Rochewell. She and the maid were the only allies Miss Rochewell would have on the ship. He had his doubts. He was considering how much to tell Mrs. Pargutter when that lady sailed into the taproom like a frigate before the wind, with the maid, loaded above her head with parcels, trailing in the larger woman's lee.

"There is hardly time to pack before we must be at the quay." Mrs. Pargutter's black silks exhibited great dark half circles of sweat beneath her arms, and beads winked upon her forehead under her fat, unnaturally colored curls. "I have hardly a moment to refresh myself." She collapsed upon a bench and waved weakly at the barman. "A glass of negus, sir."

Jenny peered around the bandboxes for a place to set them down. "No, no!" Mrs. Pargutter exclaimed. "Take those upstairs and pack my things. There is not a moment to be lost." The urgency in her voice was almost comic. "And do check on dear Miss Rochewell."

That sounded promising. Ian rose and took the glass of negus from the barman. "Madam," he said politely as he set it down. "Allow me."

"Oh, you young men are always trying to ingratiate yourselves with a pretty woman," she simpered. "Do join me, Mr. Rufford, in a glass."

He sat across from Mrs. Pargutter.

"You should have seen the clever little reticules I found, made entirely from feathers. And lace as fine as any in Madrid or Barcelona. I purchased several ells, in black, of course."

"Miss Rochewell is ill, madam. A physician was summoned to her this morning."

"Oh, dear!" Mrs. Pargutter exclaimed. "Is it catching? I sat next to her in the boat."

"It is not contagious. And she has you to sustain her on the ship." Ian peered at her.

"Me?" Mrs. Pargutter's eyes widened in shock. "I am a very bad sailor, sir, as you must have noticed." She shook her head. "I could not possibly attend a sickbed."

"Perhaps Jenny?"

"But she will be busy attending to me." Mrs. Pargutter placed the tip of her forefinger in a dimple just under her mouth, considering. "Miss Rochewell had best stay in Gibraltar until she recovers. No one will have time to bother about her on board a ship."

"Staying in Gibraltar does not seem suitable for a young lady alone." Ian rose. It was much as he suspected. Still, the crew of the ship adored Miss Rochewell. They would care for her if the doctor could be kept at bay.

"Well, perhaps a good cupping would set her up in form," Mrs. Pargutter offered. "Landlord, another glass."

Ian turned away in exasperation. What was all this preoccupation with letting blood? Lord, they didn't even drink it. This woman was of no use. Miss Rochewell had no protector, no one who could even see her back to health. What was his obligation here?

But that was only too evident. He was the cause of Miss Rochewell's malaise, and he must protect her. It would mean breaking his promise. He set his lips. Well, that was for later. He strode out of the inn without a word to Mrs. Pargutter. Her indignant harrumph pursued him.

• • •

The streets down to the quay were crowded with soldiers, sailors, passengers, and merchants all engaged in seeing the convoy once more to sea in the late afternoon. Ian supported Miss Rochewell, half-fainting on his arm, toward the barge that flew the *Beltrane*'s number. Under his other arm he hefted a crate of porter. His neck cloth slipped and he almost cried out as the waning sun struck his face full on. He dared not stop to pull it up. He noted dimly that Mrs. Pargutter waited at the wrong dock.

"Ho there, are you for the *Beltrane*?" he called.

The Captain's cox'sun turned, took in the situation, and motioned several hands forward.

"Miss Rochewell is not feeling quite the thing," Ian muttered, through the searing pain.

But they had her already in hand. "Put a foot just here," one said as he lifted her in. Did she wish to sit there by the stern? This extra cloak might be welcome in the freshening breeze. It would be but a moment until they had her aboard, they said. They glared at Ian as though they knew that he had caused her malaise.

"A physician recommended porter," Ian lied. He handed over the crate he'd purchased from the landlord. It took two men to stow it. They looked at him with even more suspicion.

Behind him, Mrs. Pargutter bustled up, wailing. "Wait!" she called. "Wait for me!"

"Full up," the cox'sun barked. "Take that there skiff."

The boat pushed off. "Stretch out!" the cox'sun barked, and the men pulled at the oars. Miss Rochewell huddled in the huge woolen cloak, not even waving to him. He pulled up his neck cloth and stepped into the skiff with Mrs. Pargutter and Jenny. He had eyes only for the Captain's barge. He was relieved to see that the cox'sun called for a bo'sun's chair for Miss Rochewell before his boat ever kissed the ship's side. They bundled her into that contraption tenderly, then scrambled nimbly up the side to take her out on deck. She was already in her quarters by the time Ian had run up the side himself.

In the fading light Mrs. Pargutter was shrilling about the stowing of her parcels. Ian strode to the forward hatch and so down to the surgeon's domain below the waterline, stripping off his gloves, cravat, and hat. "Granger!" he barked. The surgeon smelled of spirits. A hanging lantern cast wild shadows as it swung with the roll of the ship. The air was close down here, stinking of alcohol and the vile concoctions he poured down the sailors' throats. Granger raised bloodshot eyes to his. "Miss Rochewell is ill," Ian said. "You will be called. You are not to bleed her. You will instead prescribe sustaining food five times daily, to include both meats and vegetables, and porter whenever she can take it. Am I understood?"

Granger managed to get to his feet. "You dare to dictate to me, sir?"

Ian's anger swelled. This man could harm Miss Rochewell, even cause her death, with his stupidity. With the anger, Ian felt a singing along his veins. The song buzzed in his ears, even blurred his vision. Granger shrank back and Ian knew his eyes had gone red. "You will not bleed her." The whisper would echo in Granger's mind. "You will consult me before any treatment."

Granger nodded blankly.

"And stop drinking." Ian whirled and climbed up to the deck. He would order some gruel and chopped boiled fowl to be taken to her cabin. Could she eat on her own? The ship's rigging groaned. He felt the pull of her sails. The convoy was under way. The next stop was Brest.

There were no secrets in a ship. The moon sank in a sky streaked with clouds. The steady creak of rigging and spars and the slip of water past the keel were the only sounds apart from the whispering crew. He stood at the bowsprit, the very apex of the ship, where he was most nearly alone. In the middle watch, Ian's newly sensitive hearing had picked up the mutterings. He was blamed for Miss Rochewell's condition. They remembered the strength he had shown against the pirates and speculated about the wounds some thought he had sustained. Callow's dreams were discussed, and the fact that Ian never came on deck in daylight. They would soon work themselves up to some paroxysm of superstitious madness.

His spirits sagged. They were right. He was a monster. He had drained her! But he had taken responsibility. He got her on board. He had come on board himself to ensure her care, a betrayal she would soon discover. But that was not the worst.

He realized too late that she held his fate in her hands. Once he had agreed that no one would believe her if she told what she knew. Now some might be more than ready to listen. If they attacked him, could he restrain himself from making a defense? If he could not, the death that would ensue would not be his.

But there was an even greater problem. She was going home to England. She could poison society there against him with her accusations. She could take away all hope of a normal life and send him into exile, roaming the world. How could he maintain his humanity then? Would he become like . . . like Asharti, killing humans without a care?

Asharti would simply kill the girl. Ian's stomach revolted at the thought. It was Asharti's influence that such a thing would even occur to him, just like the thought of compelling her to make love to him last night had been. But in the end, who wanted to compel whom? Had she not commanded him to make love to her? She was sick. She thought he was a dream. But she had asked him quite boldly to kiss him before the pirates attacked. It was all of a piece. He pushed his resentment away and shook himself. He dared not stray in either dark direction.

What could he do? He bowed his head into the wind. She had every right to be afraid. What had come over him that he fed even when he knew her and lingered long, sucking, feeling the thick copper-tanged liquid slide down his throat, their bodies twined in ecstasy?

He must convince her not to bear witness against him. Her goodwill could disarm the crew's suspicions. Her silence in England would allow his dream of home to blossom. But how? He racked his brain, every lie, every possible excuse, only sounding lame in his own ears. What fabrication would a woman like that believe?

He closed his eyes against the round of fruitless thoughts as the sky grayed. An image of her, frail against the quilts, gnawed at him. Her chess game, played to win, but thoughtfully, rose to mind, and her practical acceptance of his healing powers. He saw the flash of her eyes as she told him she had seen the mysteries of the Levant and explained her theory about the Sphinx.

The key to his dilemma lay in who she was . . . a searcher for truth, no matter how strange, a practical woman, more intelligent than most men he knew, who accepted no condescension. He sighed as the conclusion became inescapable. He would have to tell her at least part of the truth.

This was bad. It would be the hardest thing he had ever done. It would put him in a woman's power to an even greater degree—something he had vowed never to let happen. He turned and paced back toward the waist, the crew melting out of his way. The price to his pride was too great. He couldn't do it, no matter the consequence. The pipe called the morning watch up to clean the decks. It was his signal to retire for the coming day.

On the other hand, how badly did he want to go home to England?

Ten

Beth woke to painful light streaming through the window hatch. Tapping sounded at the door. The roll of the ship was a comfort. She must be a hundred miles away from Rufford now. She had escaped. She was *glad* to be away from him. Absolutely ecstatic. She felt a little better today. Redding had brought her a bit of roasted chicken last night and more of that vile porter. And she had slept the night through, with only a couple of disturbing dreams she would not think about. One had to be forgiven for one's dreams, did one not? In some ways, those dreams seemed to be her blood, her Egyptian blood, calling to her.

The tapping came again. "Yes?" she called, amazed at the smallness of her own voice.

"Redding, miss. The cook thought you might fancy a boiled egg and a bit of gruel. And the doctor is here to see you."

"Just leave the tray." She sat up and pulled the quilt to her chin. "I am not dressed."

But the door opened and the doctor brought in the tray. "I am a medical man, my dear. It makes no difference whether you are dressed." He filled the narrow stateroom, looking haggard this morning but not drunk. He set the tray on her lap. She had no desire for another examination. At least Rufford could not interrupt and throw the doctor bodily out the door.

But the surgeon showed no signs of wanting to examine her. "I thought you would require bleeding, but I find you much improved," he said, looking nervous somehow. "I think just a diet filled with red meat to stimulate your bodily functions, some good strong porter, and perhaps a tonic bolus of Peruvian bark should set you up."

She nodded warily. "I'm glad you decided against bleeding. . . ."

"As am I," a familiar bass voice rumbled. "Miss Rochewell, you seem improved."

The doctor started as badly as Beth. Rufford loomed behind him.

"I shall look in later with your bolus." The surgeon practically scurried from the room.

"What are you doing here?" Beth said, trembling, when left face-to-face with Rufford. "You promised you would go overland. . . ."

"I regret I had to break that promise." He slipped into the room and closed the door. Beth shrank away. "I could not trust the good doctor not to bleed you and there seemed no one to see to your needs."

"Mrs. Pargutter—"

"—could not be bothered even to see you to the launch," he cut her off brutally. His face was reddened and a little swollen, as though he had been in the sun. Which he had, she remembered. He had come to the inn in daylight to see how she did and walked her to the barge.

"Well, you had no need to worry. The doctor did not want to bleed me, and Redding brought a most sustaining supper from the cook last night. You might have kept your promise after all." She was almost sure she was frightened to death that her tormentor was on board the ship. Certainly her heart was pounding, and the telltale black circles floated in her vision.

"Calm yourself, madam." He squinted against the light

from the small window. Now he reached for the little curtain, drew it, and cast the cabin into twilight. He was planning to stay.

"Go now," she ordered.

"I must talk with you."

"Go this minute or I will scream." The black circles threatened to close in on her.

"If you would calm yourself and let me explain—"

"What can you explain?" He had sucked her blood, though she didn't like to say that where others could possibly hear. He loomed over her. "If you kill me they will know it was you," she whispered. "They will clap you in irons." An empty threat, with his strength.

He looked at his hands as though to gather courage. They were strong, square hands. She remembered the feel of his fingers on her throat. If he had wanted to kill her, it would have been easy then. He raised his eyes. They were filled with such dismay she was startled.

"You think I would kill you?" His mouth was mobile. "I would not harm you. I have sought only to remedy my . . . my indiscretion." He took a breath. "No. No excuses—my inexcusable sin." He continued when she could think of no reply. "You may call the Captain, of course. You have the marks on your neck and Callow's for corroboration. The sailors distrust me since the pirate attack. They might believe you." He seemed to gather courage. "I want to go to England—to get back some version of a normal life. I am guilty of my needs unless—no, until a doctor cures me of what I have become. If you desire it, I will confess."

Why? Why would he confess? All he could expect was incarceration, which for him would be death without blood to sustain him. Or being torn limb from limb by a mob here on the ship or when he was tried in England. Unless his healing powers could preserve him. But still—to expose himself to that risk, the physical pain . . . Her gaze darted over his face looking for an answer. She did not have far to look. It was in his shame, in the distress that had lurked in his eyes since the moment she first saw him. He said he wanted to justify himself, but underneath he believed he deserved the worst.

She blinked. "I shall consider your offer to confess." She should demand he leave.

He looked down again, awkward. "You have a scientific curiosity. Perhaps you will find my story . . . interesting," he murmured. "Listen, then do what you must." He grabbed the stool from beneath her basin and pulled it between his legs before she could say yes or no. His knees touched her cot. His thick lashes brushed his cheeks as he stared at the wood floor. "I did not choose to become what I am."

Beth said nothing.

His brows drew together. "I was taken out of a Navy sloop two years ago by Barbary pirates and sold as a slave. You have guessed as much." He stopped, unable to go on.

Beth realized that the mystery she had so wanted to unravel now wanted to explain himself. Suddenly she wanted to hear his story very much. How had she let fear stand in the way? "You have been cruelly treated." Would that make it easier for him to say what he wanted so much to tell her, yet obviously dreaded telling?

He took a breath, dared a glance at her. She nodded encouragement.

"I was sold as a pack animal to a caravan, or so I thought."

Beth checked a sharp intake of breath. "How horrible!"

He gave a chuckle he meant to be rueful. It cracked in the middle. "Oh, that was not the horrible part. The keepers beat me, of course, and the life was hard. No one spoke to me until Fedeyah wanted to practice his English. They treated me like a mule or an ox. But they fed me well and watered me so that I could bear the work. I grew used to the drudgery and the whip. One can grow used to almost anything, you know." He studied the hands he had clasped before him. "But this was a special kind of caravan. It traveled by night and did not carry goods to trade, but only supplies for an endless journey through the desert. The owner of the caravan rode in a strange litter. Slaves sent into the owner's tent came back dead, drained of blood." He swallowed. "One slave at a time was chosen to serve the owner . . . more . . . personally."

Rufford's knuckles were white on his clasped hands. Beth knew she had to help him if he was to get the story out. "Who was this owner?"

"Her name was . . . Asharti." The name came with difficulty to his lips.

Oh, dear. She had a good idea where the story was going. She waited.

"She circled the desert, searching for your lost city, Kivala."

Beth opened her eyes wide. Had he actually been there? She checked any excited questions. Now was definitely not the time for eager curiosity.

"She traded only to take on new slaves to fill her . . . needs." Again he stopped. His eyes flickered with memories so painful he looked like they might strangle him.

She must tell him that she knew. It might free him to let his story flow. "I saw the marks of her teeth on your body," Beth whispered, remembering the fine body as well as the marks.

He nodded, faked nonchalance with a shrug, not free at all. "I lived longer than most. She took only a little blood each time." There was more; Beth could feel it. He cleared his throat and shut his eyes. "She . . . could compel . . . with her eyes. . . ."

Just what could Asharti compel? Something that shamed Rufford. He must say it or it would eat him alive. "Did she make you kill for her?"

He rolled his head and stared at the ceiling. "No. She never thought of that, thank God." He gave that cracked half-chuckle. "She thought of other things, though."

Beth recalled the places on his body she had seen the round scars: loins and thighs and buttocks as well as his throat. A dreadful surety of what Asharti had compelled rose inside her.

"It was her blood that infected me. One thoroughly evil drop of blood." He took a breath and held it, then consciously released it as he unclenched his hands. "She left me

for dead. But I didn't die, more's the pity, and now even suicide seems to be denied me."

He had tried to kill himself? Beth bit her lip to keep from
protesting against the act of suicide or even comforting him.
He would never allow it.

"You will chastise me for not starving myself of blood. I
have tried. But when the craving becomes too strong, there
is some . . . discomfort. My mind grows unclear. I am in
danger of filling my need recklessly at the cost of lives." He
took a breath. "So," he said brusquely, putting his palms on
his knees and straightening, "I take a very little blood from
any one person. I . . . I lost myself with you; I don't know
why. I hope you can . . ." He choked and was silent. He had
been about to ask forgiveness but couldn't because at heart
he did not think he deserved it. He started again, without
conviction. "Not a happy situation. But I vow I will do no
lasting harm. I shall be like a banker who lives off the interest of others' invested funds, or a painter who captures the
spirit of a sitter and sells his paintings for a living. And I can
leave them something in return, a memory of being . . . valued by someone." He looked away.

Now that he had told his story, or all that he could tell, he
finally flushed. "I do not know exactly what I am. But I cling
to my humanity. The anchor of normal life in England, or at
least as normal as I can make it, among people I know and
love, may counterbalance the evil blood that taints me." He
sucked in air again. "Some things I am denied. Marriage and
children are out of the question, if I can even reproduce. I
have reason to believe I will outlive contemporaries, so
friends and connections will pass away. She . . . Asharti was
very old. But I want to reclaim what life I can." He looked up
at last, his eyes defiant, not realizing that even in his defiance
he exuded a vulnerability that belied his more-than-human
properties.

No words of hers could erase what had been done to him.
All she could do was the one thing he could not ask of her.
She looked inside and knew that whatever he was when the
madness of his need was on him, she could not hate him.

She knew what he was, if he did not. But how could she tell him he was a vampire? Would that not undermine his resolve to fight his condition? She forgave him what he was precisely because he would never forgive himself. And she could never tell him that without shaming him further.

"A normal life does not seem too much to ask," she whispered.

He swallowed. He licked his lips and she could swear his eyes filled. "It is."

Her own eyes filled and overflowed.

"Look, your food has grown cold," he said gruffly. "Let me procure you another plate."

She had forgotten the tray was there. "I'm not hungry."

"Nonsense," he said, standing. "You require food to restore your strength." He turned to the door, dashing the back of his hand across one cheek.

"Redding!" he called.

He had told her almost everything. He would never tell anyone about the final degradation. Only Asharti and Fedeyah knew, for the rest were dead. He would never see those two again once he was safe in England. He watched the girl sleep, weakened by his vile need for blood. She had revealed herself to him as well. Had she not tried to command him when in the grip of fever? Were all women like Asharti in some way? And yet, who had produced her fever? He had. Whose fault that she was weak and said she knew not what? His. He should be wary of her, but he dare not blame . . .

He was exhausted by the strain of reliving the nightmare in the desert. A day did not go by but he reproduced it in dreams, in memories. But to speak of it . . .

Ian closed the book he had been reading to her after she had eaten and drunk her dose of porter. *The Iliad.* How simple Homer's view of life's tribulations seemed. Ian had gotten only a few lines out before she drifted off. In some ways it was a touching signal that she trusted him. Or perhaps it was a sign of her debilitation. He pulled the quilt up around her and retired through the common cabin to his own chamber and shut the door carefully against the light. At least now there was some hope she would not put a spoke in his wheel by accusing him publicly. He knew she would never gossip about him privately to make herself seem important. She was not that kind of woman. The next days would tell if she regretted her decision today.

The Atlantic wind pushed the *Beltrane* toward Brest more reliably than the variable breezes of the Med. They coursed northward along the coast of Portugal and Spain. Time passed in a blur for Beth. Both she and Rufford acted as though his confession had never occurred. But he called on her daily in the late afternoon, draping her window, and in the evenings. Rufford's face recovered from its sunburn, and she noticed that his tan was fading, too, as he spent more and more time out of the light. He read to her or asked about her travels. He was most insistent about her drinking the porter and eating, until she was sure she would grow positively fat. For her part, she dozed, even in his presence, and took up the needlework that Lady Metherton had pressed upon her as the sole genteel occupation for a lady of quality. It was the only thing her mind could compass sometimes.

Mrs. Pargutter did not once come to see her, but Jenny stole minutes away from her mistress on several occasions and looked in to dress Beth's hair, winding the escaping frizz into curls beside her face and pinning her hair up into a thick knot high on her crown. At first she thought that her reputation would suffer from the visits of a single gentleman like Rufford, not that she cared at this point. But if Redding and Rait were any example, the crew turned an indulgent eye on his attentions, perhaps due to her condition. Jenny was most practical about it, noting that under the circumstances it was very nice to have such generous support.

The loblolly boys brought in the hip bath one day and carried hot water from the galley that Jenny poured over Beth. A bath had never felt so good. As Mrs. Pargutter wailed Jenny's name, she calmly helped Beth dress for the first time in one of her black morning gowns, then gave her over into Mr. Rufford's care while the seamen removed the bath and tidied her cabin—a task that required swabbing and drying and polishing.

Mr. Rufford handed her to an elbow chair in the common cabin. He had pulled canvas curtains across the small windows under the bow of the ship. "You look charming, Miss Rochewell. I hope you are feeling more the thing."

"The bath was wonderful," Beth sighed.

"I hoped it might be." He sat opposite her.

"*You* ordered a bath for me?" She flushed.

"Sailors would never think of it, and Jenny is preoccupied." His voice was matter-of-fact.

Beth blushed, remembering that he had undressed her in Gibraltar. "You shouldn't have troubled yourself," she said crossly. "I am quite capable of ordering my own bath."

He raised his brows and took a tray from Redding with a telltale tankard on it.

"And I am heartily sick of this dreadful brew." She pushed the proffered tankard away. "I should like a glass of Madeira, Redding, if you please."

Rufford had only to shake his head.

Redding bobbed. "Begging your pardon, miss, but Mr. Rufford said wine wasn't no good for your condition, miss. I dasn't serve you wine. None of us would."

Beth sent a furious glance to Rufford, who looked smug. "Mr. Rufford ordering for me?"

Redding bobbed again. "Takes quite the care of you. Orders special dinners from the cook and questions me to see that it was served just so at two. Orders suppers, too. We all put in our Parmesan for your toasted cheese last night. And hopes you liked it."

Beth sighed. "You are all taking most oppressive care of me. I thank you."

Redding beamed and bowed himself out.

"Your temper indicates you are recovering quite nicely," Rufford observed from a safe distance across the table.

"A few more days of everyone treating me like an invalid and I shall go stark, staring mad!" she exclaimed.

"Then it seems to me you might be recovered enough for a game of chess." Beth saw his blue eyes laughing at her behind their serious pretense.

"Only if you don't let me win to keep my invalid spirits up," she muttered.

"No danger of that," he said demurely.

"I rise to a challenge every time, sir," she said with asperity as he set out the pieces, automatically giving her the black.

"I shall strive to remember that." His voice was quite solemn, but she thought he might be making game of her. She sniffed. Did he mean to use her fractiousness against her?

"The crew seems to have lost their dread of you, at least if Redding is any example."

"I have redeemed myself by my care of you. They seem quite reconciled."

"They must believe monsters cannot have a softer side." She was immediately sorry she had said it. She glanced up quickly. He looked as though she had slapped him. She pushed hastily on. "I know I do." He glowered. "Oh, don't take umbrage, Rufford, pray. My brain is too fogged to mind my mouth. And, truth be told, choosing my words has never been my best point. Forgive me."

"Forgive you? Not necessary. Yours is not the fault for telling truth." He moved his knight out, brashly. He did not even offer her first move.

"I did say true. I don't think that goodness coexists with evil." She moved out her pawn.

"Then your view of life is too simple by far, child." Pawn.

"Oh, are you so much wiser than I?" She made a small moue and cleared her bishop.

"I have experience of evil. Evil can taint anything, anyone." He got a hard curve to his vulnerable mouth and slapped his pawn down. "And I am most afraid it slowly consumes all that remains of good, a bite at a time." He winced at his reference to teeth.

She laughed. "See, neither of us is safe with a subtext to everything we might say. We shall simply have to accustom ourselves to this reality."

He looked at her strangely. There was a puzzled smile just at one corner of his mouth. You might miss it if you weren't looking for it.

"What is more, you are not attending to your game." Her bishop took his knight.

He glanced to the board. "I will remedy that." He studied the board and moved his rook.

He did win, and in spite of her bold front, she was most happy to retire to her cabin for a nap afterward. In the following days she gained strength more rapidly. The Captain visited her for an awkward quarter hour after supper two days later under the watchful eyes of Rufford and hoped he might see her on deck soon. She vowed she would attempt it the next morning.

She was most surprised when Rufford appeared at about ten, dressed in a very well-fitted black coat, with gloves, hat, and blue spectacles in hand. He bowed when she opened the door.

"Miss Rochewell, do you take some air?"

She already had on her pelisse and was just drawing on her gloves. The air was colder as they headed north. "Why, yes. I was just about to go on deck."

He offered his arm.

"But surely you cannot go out on deck!"

"I am resolved to test my limits," he said. "If I keep to the shade of the quarterdeck—"

"You must not risk it!" she protested.

"Already I grow less sensitive to sunlight, else I could not have essayed the inn in Gibraltar. When first I woke to my new condition, my eyes could stand no crack of light; my skin blistered at the first ray. From something said by . . . Asharti once, I think it grows more tolerable with time." Beth noted that he still choked on her name. "Besides, how will I have a normal life if I cannot stand a stray beam of sunshine?" He held out his arm once more.

She sighed and took it. He wanted to be normal with an intensity that flamed in his eyes. The feel of his arm beneath her hand flashed through her. She shook herself. She felt the fabric of his coat, nothing more.

They walked through the common cabin. He opened the door, and though he flinched, he fixed his blue glasses more securely and ventured out into the shade cast by the quarter-deck walls. His muscles tightened as he braced himself against what must be for him intolerable glare. He staggered a bit and put his back against the wall. His breath was ragged.

"Let us go in," she whispered. "There is no point to suffering so."

"Nonsense," he said, through gritted teeth. "Do you care to take a turn or two?"

He made a fair appearance of calm as they paced out of the shade into the waist, to the forecastle wall, and back again. Only she could feel the iron in his arm, clenched in effort. Beth noticed that all hands looked at them kindly. Several touched their foreheads.

"Feeling more the thing, miss?" the purser asked. She thought his name was Gilman. Several others hovered to hear her answer.

"Yes, thank you, Mr. Gilman. Mr. Rufford is so kind as to support me." In truth she half-supported him. But the sailors nodded and looked at her companion with complacence.

Mr. Gilman peered at Rufford. "You seem a bit under the weather yourself, sir."

"A little sun poisoning I acquired in the Sahara." He smiled thinly. "Nothing to speak of."

They pressed on for several turns. Beth glanced at Rufford's reddening countenance. Knowing he would never relent, she sighed audibly. "That is all I can manage for today."

His sigh of relief was no less clear. "If you are sure . . ."

They made for the door to the wardroom with haste just this side of unseemly. Rufford sank into a chair, pulled off his gloves, and removed his spectacles, breathing as though he had run a mile. He smiled crookedly. "There, that wasn't so hard."

"Your face is reddened even by being out for so few minutes." She stepped into her cabin and came back with a blue glass jar. "Here, slather yourself with some of this complexion cream. It will ease the effect of the sun. If we had strawberries, it would be even better."

He took two fingers' full, rubbed his hands, spread it over his face. "The burn won't last. I tried, once, to . . ."

"Yes?"

But he would not go on. "Trust that I know that no matter the degree of sunburn, it is not fatal. I blister and crack, then fade. In truth, I grow paler every day. Have you not noticed?"

"Well, I am sure that does not make the burn less uncomfortable." She looked at him, her natural curiosity bubbling up again. She could not ask him about Kivala. But there were so many other things she wanted to know. "It must be so hard to have this condition thrust upon you without knowing anything about it."

"I would give my left arm to know how to go on," he said ruefully. "Or possibly my eyeteeth, since they seem to be so inconvenient anyway."

"But no, you need them now. How else would you feed?"

"You speak of it so matter-of-factly."

She shrugged. "For you it is like saying, 'A man requires meat.' She looked sharply at him. "By the by, do you think you can make it to Brest before you need to feed again?"

"The Captain says that, God willing and wind stays true, it is but another two days. The hunger has not yet grown upon me." He flushed directly as he remembered why.

She made as if she did not notice. Indeed, something had occurred to distract her. She might be able to help him. "I think I should like to return to my scrolls. They could shed some light upon your situation."

"I would be grateful," he said, quite humbly, and she knew he had had it in his mind for some time but would not ask. His humility was a function of great pride. "But only if you will not tire yourself."

She smiled at him. "Of course not."

So she began the tedious process of searching for particular information among her many scrolls. Some she knew quite well; others required wearying translation and transcription. The tiny table in the common room of the forecastle could not accommodate the scrolls. So they sat in the evenings in the Captain's great cabin as his guests at one corner of the long table that also held the Captain and his guests after supper, usually in some state of inebriation, telling stories. Most were old hands who had been in the Navy during the Napoléonic wars, and many were the heroic actions they had seen, both by sea against the French and by land against bastions of female virtue. With the wars resolved and the Navy reducing its force, they had taken merchant berths rather than be marooned on land at half pay with their wives. Their noise gave a backdrop to her labors that soon became much like the heaving of the sea or the creaking of the timbers. After a time they even gave over remarking on her bluestocking ways.

So she and Rufford, who apparently had little interest in either intricately described sea battles or bastions of virtue, kept their end of the table. It was her task to keep her attention on her work when he sat so near, across from her, a curl escaping his ribbon and the light playing across his features. Her strategy was to translate selections taken from different places in each scroll, like a survey to locate potentially profitable sections. Many times she was misled as the scrolls talked about ghouls or jinn who inhabited specific oases or ruins. Many times, too, Rufford, who sat reading her transcriptions, would guide her to her cabin like a despot, his hands on her elbows sending shivers through her, ignoring all protests that she was not tired at all. Several times, she heard him in the cabin into the wee hours and, peeking out, saw him comparing her transcriptions with the originals, though what he hoped to gain she could not tell.

This effort went on through their docking at Brest. It was she who had to tell him that he must go ashore, that there was nothing he could do for her.

"You must maintain your strength, sir," she whispered as the ship lay rocking in the harbor just before supper. "We don't want a repetition of the effects of excessive hunger."

That made him close his countenance and look away. She put a hand on his arm.

"It has been more than two weeks since Gibraltar. Are you not feeling the need?" She knew he had been easily distracted last night, and his nerves were on the jump all this evening.

He rolled his upper lip between his teeth. "We are in England soon."

"If we don't have to beat up against the wind in the Channel. That can take days or even weeks. I asked the Captain." He looked at her as though she had no business asking the Captain anything he might want to know. "Besides," she said, trying to mollify him, "you can't want to land in Portsmouth needing immediate sustenance. . . ."

He sucked in air and nodded. "But the Captain does not send the boats ashore until morning." He glanced to the hefty bulk at the far end of the table, roaring with laughter.

"I'm sure he will oblige you with a boat, if you would but ask."

Rufford looked mulish.

"You do not like to ask for anything, do you?" She stood. "Captain?"

The entire upper end of the table turned her way. She blushed and bowed her head. "Mr. Rufford has business in Brest. I know he wishes to be ashore but will not incommode you."

"What, at this time of night?" the Captain sputtered.

"What other time is there, since the sun is difficult for him?" she asked sweetly.

"Nonsense, Captain. There is no need . . ." Rufford stood, too, stooping under the beams and glaring daggers at her.

"Well, well, I can spare the jolly boat and a man," the

Captain chortled, amused at Rufford's discomfiture. "Get you up, Rait, and roust out a hand to pull Mr. Rufford in to shore. Make it Williams. He's reliable. Will you want to come back before dawn?"

"What time do you set sail tomorrow?" Rufford's voice was low.

"Four by the clock, with the ebb."

"Then yes, I would come back just before dawn."

"Make it so, Rait." The Captain grinned. He thought he knew what business Rufford had.

"Thank you, Captain," Rufford said stiffly, bowing. "You have my gratitude."

"You don't need to be grateful to me, Rufford," the Captain chortled. "Miss Rochewell did your negotiating for you."

Rufford nodded curtly and strode out on deck. Beth followed him, wondering at herself, that she should make possible what he was to do tonight. She stood behind him, unacknowledged, as the boat was lifted over the side with a boom. It splashed in the water.

"If you can minister to me for my own good, I can help you to yours," she said.

He made no response but stood looking out toward the lights of Brest. Williams scrambled over the rail and down the side. "Be careful," she added.

He sent her one reproachful look and went down the side into the boat.

That night was long for Beth. She wondered whether he would take his blood from a fulsome woman like the one in Gibraltar, or a boy like Callow, and which she preferred. Then she was so ashamed of preferring either that she knelt directly and said her prayers.

She was not a religious woman in the usual sense. She had a great sense of the force of the world, which she absolutely called God. But the Anglican church of her father seemed sadly small in its concept of the Almighty. It did not admit of things she had seen, and it would not admit of Mr. Rufford. Yet those things did exist. Mr. Rufford existed. If any of the many sects she had come across, Christian or otherwise, admitted of Mr. Rufford, they would call him the devil, pure and simple. But it was not so simple at all. Not for a man who strove with his internal demons. She had no idea what sins he had committed in his youth. And yet, what sin could justify what had happened to him? Was he not an innocent, comparatively, who had been struck down? Therefore, what religion could deny him pity? Alas, to that she knew the answer. Religion could well result in a smaller soul, not a larger one. And it would be large souls indeed who could know what Rufford was and yet open their hearts to him.

Not that she had a large soul. But others would not be able to see him as intimately as she had. They would only see his stiffness, his reserve, his pride, his fierceness. He would not let them see the doubt, the shame, the simple longing for a normal life. It was only in extremity that he had revealed those aspects of himself to her.

She realized with a start that she had opened her heart to him. Lord, she had also just helped him to sustenance others would find horrific. Would he keep to his resolve to take but a little?

She heard the jolly boat come back just before dawn. She had been dozing, on the fret for his return. His step sounded, in the cabin. The close of his cabin door was soft. She could feel his distress from here. How taking what he needed seemed to weigh on him, in spite of all his talk of bankers and artists! She fell into a deeper sleep, her fears at least aboard, if not resolved.

He did not appear until late afternoon. She had been the guest at a raucous dinner in the great cabin, with a fine spotted dog pudding, a favorite with the officers. She had labored all afternoon over a scroll whose translation was difficult, and now her eyes were tired. The grand cabin was empty. The sinking sun cast a red glow over the sea visible out the stern windows.

She looked up and rubbed her eyes as he appeared. She could tell immediately that he had fed. He was filled to bursting with energy, his eyes snapping and his countenance glowing with some inner light. He was right. His countenance grew increasingly pale. But life shone from him. He had drained that life from someone else.

"Well, you look revived," she said.

"And you look tired." He sat opposite her, pushing some fragile scrolls to the side.

"Did you find what you needed?" she asked, examining his face.

His mouth drew down. "Yes. And everyone survived." At least he had answered. Relief lurked in his eyes, beneath his disapproval of the question.

She nodded and returned to her scroll.

"Give me one of those." He pulled one in front of him and began to unfurl it.

"What can you do with it?" she asked, startled.

He pulled a paper from his pocket. "I do not know the finer points, of course, but I have made out a key to the figures, by comparing your transcriptions to the originals."

"You have?" she asked, astonished.

"Coding is a valuable skill in the diplomatic corps. I was considered rather good at it—one reason Rockhampton gave me a post." He laid out his paper, perused the scroll, and began comparing and transcribing, rather more laboriously than she did, but transcribing just the same.

"You speak the ancient language?" she asked, recovering enough of her wits to reply.

"Oh no, it is just a code to me. I can read the decoded words, but one must apply some license of interpretation, since the literal would be ridiculous. That is better your province than mine." He bent over the scroll, holding it out flat with his blunt hand and wielding the stub of a pencil on the paper beside it studiously. She could smell his cinnamon and ambergris scent. She had missed that smell when he was ashore.

She bent to her own work. "I will interpret when you finish the passage." They worked on. The Captain came in. He was not feeling well from his excesses at dinner and repaired to his own cabin on the starboard side, the width of two passengers' cabins. The officers, without their host, supped in the gun room below. The silence was companionable between Rufford and Beth. She dared not marvel at his trick of translating, lest she be condescending.

"Wait . . ." he said slowly about ten in the evening. Excitement fairly glowed in his eyes, a plain blue glow, yet powerful.

"What?"

He pushed the scroll over to her. Some fragments crumbled at the edges. "Will you work on this passage? You are far faster than I." He pointed.

Slowly she moved her finger over the text. " 'Before the first of us, before even our gods, they were here. Their blood holds the power.' " This much he had translated. She looked up at him, holding her breath. He pointed again, urging her on. She bowed her head to the text. " 'The strength of stone, of the earth, they have from their friend.' No, not 'friend,' exactly. More like 'companion.' 'Like bats . . . ' Bats?" She nodded to herself. " 'Like bats they move through the night, not seen.' I think it means invisible. 'Blood-power glows red in their eyes. No man can withstand it.' " She glanced up at Ian. He was sitting there, ramrod-straight, eyes unseeing. "We know about that part. It must be hypnotism of some kind." She returned to where her finger pointed. " 'They show us how to till. Some say they gave the fire. To thank them we have built their . . . monuments.' Tombs? No, definitely monuments, because here it acts as though they are not dead. And they don't seem all bad. The writer of this scroll is grateful." She bent her head again. " 'They have gone away now. The world is smaller. We are smaller, because we can no longer serve them.' It goes on about the monuments." She looked up at Ian. He swallowed as though his throat was full. Pain had crept into his eyes, replacing the blue excitement. "Perhaps it does mean they died. *Gone away* could be a euphemism for death."

"No," Rufford said, his throat full. "They went away. All except one. And he is in the Temple of Waiting at Kivala."

"Kivala?" she asked, breathless. "I *thought* you had been there."

For a long moment he said nothing. "I have been there. I have seen him."

Eleven

Eleven

Ian stepped over the body as the caravan moved out again. He had long ago come to recognize the sunken flesh that meant the capillaries beneath the skin had been drained of blood. The slave had been a stringy man in life and now his muscles stood out in sharp relief around his bones. The eyes of the corpse were wild in the last paroxysm of fear. Asharti had not opened Ian for three days, though that did not mean she had not used him in other ways. His wounds were closing. She was saving him for something. He did not like to think what.

Fedeyah's sighting at the noon zenith a week ago, coupled with the position of the moon between two mountains, had led the caravan to a maze of deep washes southeast of the primary range, cut by water from the snows in winter rushing through the red sandstone. The air was not so oppressively hot near the mountains, but now the wind seemed fraught with evil. He stumbled beside the four remaining litter bearers as the sirocco whipped out from the cliffs that loomed above the caravan. Their lanterns bobbed like fireflies against the immensity. What they were looking for he did not know. Ahead, a crevice gaped, a vertical slit in the stone like the mouth of some living creature ready to devour them.

Fedeyah called a halt and came to consult with Asharti.

"My Goddess," he called softly just in front of Ian. The silk hangings drew back. Ian knelt automatically as the startling countenance almost beyond beauty leaned out into the night. From the corner of his eye he saw the gleam of excitement in her eyes. Had he ever seen her excited? Lustful, yes, but not excited. She looked up at the stone wall rising some hundred feet above them and surveyed the dark slit.

"Yes," she breathed. "It is as it was foretold in the ancient texts."

"Shall we camp, Exalted One?" Fedeyah asked. "We have tomorrow night to search."

"No," she commanded. "Leave the camels. Bring the slaves. We can get close tonight."

"What of the bearers?"

"Leave the bearers. We will have need of them on the return." She stepped gracefully out of the litter, wrapped in a cloak of finest red wool, edged with writing worked in gold thread that Ian did not recognize. Her small sandaled feet with their golden nails stopped in front of Ian. She lifted his chin, so he was forced to look up at her. The excitement had grown into something terrible and wild. "Bring the favorite. He will be my most personal offering."

So Ian, with a rope about his raw neck held by Asharti, stumbled just behind Fedeyah into the black crevice, its edges smoothed by water. The camel drivers seemed relieved to be abandoned outside the maze with their animals, their lanterns almost proof against their fear. The remaining party included the score or so of ragged slaves bought in Grizim, joined together with ropes at the ankles, and two keepers to tend them. Asharti saw clearly in the dark, as Ian knew too well, and Fedeyah must be the same. Still they carried lanterns, unlit now, against some future need. Above Ian the stars disappeared except for a narrow strip directly overhead. Beneath their feet the sand was deep. Pebble scree occasionally fanned out beneath a crack in the walls made by dripping water on some softer layer of sandstone. At least they were out of the wind. The rock echoed back every ex-

hortation of the slave keepers to their charges, every crack of the whip, along with the scrabble of small falling stones. It was not long until the keepers were oppressed into silence. Even Asharti and Fedeyah only whispered.

Ian's eyes grew used to the dimness. A strange feeling of distance had been growing in him. He was not meant to return from this journey, any more than the slaves behind him. His end might indeed be grisly. But at least it was an end. Pain-filled or horrific, he would welcome it. In the darkness a stairway cut into the stone loomed to his left. It wound upward into a hole made by rushing water in the stone above. The stairs were very steep, each step higher than a man could easily take. Were those stairs meant for humans?

His mind began to skitter over the possibilities for his death. He might be a human sacrifice to some bloodthirsty God. He had heard of special tables in far-off South American jungles with gutters carved for draining blood. Rumor had it that the priest could keep his victim alive for a very long time. Or he might be torn limb from limb by some beast. Of course, it did not have to be a beast in the traditional sense. Asharti had torn that camel driver apart with no more than a casual use of her enormous strength. Perhaps she would kill Ian herself.

But no, she had said he was to be part of her gift. That was even more ominous. Actually, she had not said he would die. What if some monster as great as or greater than she was kept him for its own use? Ian's heart beat faster. He had thought he was beyond fear. He was wrong.

After much twisting and turning, the ravine was marked by two huge pillars on either side, carved out of the stone itself, rising into the night like an entrance.

"Kivala," Asharti proclaimed. Ian staggered after her as she hurried forward on light feet in her eagerness to reach whatever horror lay ahead. What could drive her to search the deserts for . . . ? How long had it been? Two years, perhaps, or a lifetime?

Signs of civilization increased. Ornately carved entrances to what looked like tombs were carved into the rock.

Stairways branched off the wide sand trail. At last the ravine opened into an immense square. A hideous cry echoed across the night. The gaggle of slaves collapsed, gibbering. Even Asharti and Fedeyah stopped. The howl slid into the hooting laugh of a hyena.

Asharti and Fedeyah relaxed, though the slaves still sobbed and gasped. The moon, invisible in the ravine, now shone a cold light over the broad swath of stone ahead. Ian surveyed the pillars fallen in a circle, the empty, stepped seating of an amphitheater, and ruined statues, all made of striated red stone. The very air was dead. The hyena must be waiting for one of their party to turn into carrion, for there was no other life here.

Asharti jerked his rope as she started off across the square. The hemp rasped against the raw skin at his neck and he tottered forward, his bare feet cut by shards of stone. Whatever they were looking for, Asharti and Fedeyah did not think it was to be found in this empty square. Eager whispering on Asharti's part, wary pointing by Fedeyah, and they headed across the square for another opening in the rock that loomed on all sides. Ian was forced into a ragged trot. The repeated cracking of the whip signaled the other slaves to scramble ahead as well.

Into the darkness they plunged, the sand a relief after the littered stone floor of the square. Ian's breath scratched harshly in his throat. His small store of strength was fast coming to an end. Sweat dripped into his eyes. His vision narrowed to the cloak swirling in front of him, muddy red in the darkness, and the flash of her sandals. His awareness shrank to the heave of his lungs, the pain in his feet, the rasp of hemp at his neck.

Around one last curve, he stumbled to his hands and knees even as she cried out in something like ecstasy, "There!"

She stood, Fedeyah with her, apparently awestruck. Ian raised his head, gasping, and saw something close to a miracle cut into the wall of the ravine. A temple, hundreds of feet high, its multitude of balconies and pediments intri-

cately carved with winged beasts and skulls, symbols, and gargoyles. Pillars stretched into the darkness. Shallow steps led into a dark maw. The sandstone swirled in red and gold and the whole seemed both anchored inexorably in the rock and alive with movement.

The slaves behind him sobbed or gasped. Asharti and Fedeyah had gone perfectly still. "The Temple of Waiting," Asharti whispered, her anticipation palpable. "I triumph or die here."

"Goddess," Fedeyah muttered, staring at the blackness through the doorway. "You need not take this risk. What more do you need? You are so far above mere mortals you may do what you will." His voice was bold with his fear for her.

She turned toward Fedeyah slowly and her eyes glowed, not with red but with a single-minded avarice. "Humans do not matter, except as they slake my thirst, acolyte. It is our kind who must be brought to heel." Her voice rose, a violation of the silent temple looming before them, thrown back by the stone walls of the ravine. "They have exiled me? Their souls are small for all their age. Rubius, Sincai, Khalenberg, even Beatrix Lisse—they dare to question how I live? They have been no better than I. I like killing. I like making others do my will. Why should I have to rule in secret, behind some puny human man without the will, without any of the knowledge, I have? Napoléon was the last straw." Her voice was running faster now. Ian could hardly follow her Arabic. "They said I endangered their society—that humans would hunt them if I was not more discreet. What does that matter, Fedeyah? Are we not more powerful by a hundred times than mere humans? Let the battle rage! I will own this world and humans will be the cattle they were meant to be." She ran out of breath and stood, looking up at the man who loved her in spite of what she was.

Slowly she turned her head to the open doorway. "Fools! They exiled me to the one place where I can acquire the strength to best them all. They will regret their treachery." This last was hissed almost under her breath.

Fedeyah bowed his head. Ian knew he would never chal-

lenge Asharti. Not only because he loved her but also because he had not her force of soul. Asharti would not have allowed him to serve her if his spirit was as great as hers. Fedeyah probably knew that.

Asharti stalked toward the massive stone facade, jerking Ian up to lurch behind her. "Bring the slaves." Ian did not want to go through that door. The feeling grew more pronounced with every step. But up the shallow stairs he stumbled. The feel of something so strange it could not be named seeped out from that pitch-black maw. Behind him, Fedeyah mustered the keepers and slaves. It would take red eyes to compel them into this unknown.

At the edge of the portal, Asharti paused and scraped one of her long nails against a flint. A fountain of sparks caught the wick of her lamp. The smell of burning oil mixed with the smell of Asharti's perfume, magnified, wafted from the dark temple. The scent got into Ian's brain along with the pain and exhaustion and muddled his thoughts.

As they passed the threshold, the lamp cast incredible shadows onto a chamber of great height. Two immense statues with ibis heads and dog bodies still covered with flakes of their gilt and lapis lazuli crust framed another doorway. Beyond, the floor could be seen to ramp distinctly downward. The slaves and keepers were absolutely silent in the face of those impressive guardians. These statues had watched for untold years. The lamps cast a multiplicity of cross-shadows that danced across the stone figures and were swallowed in the doorway.

Asharti turned, with an enigmatic smile. "Can you feel him?"

Ian stared at her in stupefaction. What did she mean? Then he felt it, a slight throb, as though the stone of the temple lived. He had mistaken it for his own body protesting against the cuts on his swollen feet. A murmur went up from the slaves. But what did she mean, "him"?

Asharti darted forward between the two great guardians and into the downward passage. Ian stumbled after her. The smell of dust and time was overcome by that of cinnamon

*and ambergris as they descended. The scent wasn't quite
Asharti's. There was a burnt smell to the cinnamon as well.
The slaves shuffled behind them, driven forward by the
whips. The walls revealed by their lamps were covered with
strange symbols. Some bore a resemblance to the strange
figured writing of Egypt. He thought he recognized some
Arabic symbols as well, but they flicked past too quickly to
be sure.*

*Downward and ever down, with no branching corridors
and no possibility of hiding, all the while the smell and the
slow throb in the stone became more pronounced. Asharti
never hesitated. Ian could feel that her emotions were strung
bow-tight. At last the corridor leveled off and opened again
into a larger room filled with the sound of water flowing. In
the center, a green pool was lined with ornate blue and gold
tiles. Out of the fountain rose a spiral column, tapered at the
tip, which pulsed with dim light in a dozen colors in time to
the throb in the stone. Asharti stopped, Ian just behind her.
Her lamp played upon the pillar. It was covered in a million
facets, winking through the water that cascaded down its
sides.*

*Dully, Ian realized he was seeing an untold fortune in
jewels twisted into some coherent heap that seemed to live.
The green were emeralds as big as your thumb; the red were
rubies; the blue, sapphires. The diamonds were so brilliant
they cast erratic stars over the walls and ceiling when the
lamplight struck them through the trickling water. The light
reflected on the pool and Ian could see that jewels had showered into the water and lay winking beneath the surface. The
drivers darted forward, laughing, the harsh echoes of their
triumph a sin against the weight of silent stone above. They
did not seem to mind the fact that the pillar was pulsing in
some silent song of light beyond human comprehension.
They capered about the fountain as they plucked blood-red
rubies and winking great emeralds from the pool.*

*Fedeyah glanced around him, fearful. Ian felt the throb
beneath his feet grow more pronounced. The water in the*

pool shuddered. Something was waking here. Or perhaps the temple itself was waking in reaction to this sacrilege.

Asharti barked, "Enough. The scintillation of those stones will drive you mad."

"But, Excellent One," a camel driver laughed, "we have found the treasure!"

Asharti smiled. "Do not look too long into their facets. There is greater treasure yet."

"Greater? What could be greater?" they murmured. "Allah be praised."

"We will come back through this chamber and you may take whatever you can carry." Ian could feel that she was lying or telling some half truth. But the drivers could not.

"Let us be after the greater treasure!" one exclaimed, and it was only with difficulty that they let Asharti lead the way, Ian in her wake. They hurried their frightened slaves along.

Down again through the mountain of stone they went. Its weight was suffocating. The air, suffused with burnt cinnamon, was cooler now, so that he shivered, whether from the cold or from the sense of impending evil, he could not tell.

Then the passage came to an abrupt end, the way ahead blocked by a blank stone wall, broken only by a square stone bearing undecipherable carved figures. The slave drivers wailed their disappointment. The tablet was lit in a green glow by two massive emeralds in niches on either side. Asharti raised her lamp, examining the writing. She exchanged glances with Fedeyah. Then her delicate long-nailed hands darted over the surface of the lettering, touching what looked like random symbols. One she could not reach easily. She stretched up to push the symbol with her right hand, pulling Ian's rope leash tight around his lacerated neck.

Asharti touched one final symbol and stood back. The wall of stone swung open.

A black, whirling abyss loomed beyond. The throb grew insistent enough to echo in Ian's chest, like a heartbeat answering his own. Something so unknown as to be evil whirled there, and behind the blackness was the thing that throbbed. A slave behind him shrieked: a wail that rose up the scale and then descended into insane sobs. Ian glanced back to see a tight mass of heaving human flesh.

Asharti passed through the doorway and into darkness as if she pressed through some invisible curtain, dragging Ian with her. He dreaded pushing through that barrier as he had never dreaded anything in his life. Something almost alive, half whirring air, half viscous liquid, bulged around him as she pulled him through. He popped into still air beyond and darkness their lamps did not penetrate. Ian trembled in the close, old air. The audible throbbing pervaded all, and heavy scent hung in the silent blackness. Ian could feel Asharti's electric energy, attuned to what he did not know. Behind him, the other slaves popped through, sobbing and wailing, a violation of the ancient stillness. Fedeyah came through last, herding the others ahead of him.

Independent of their lamps, the ambient light in the chamber slowly rose, blue from a thousand glowing sapphires. It was not the large chamber he expected. Nor was it dusty. In the slowly growing light he saw rich carpets and vibrant wall hangings stitched with scenes of figures not quite men hunting a large beast like an elephant, only with long hair and tusks that curved in giant swirls. The figure they saw hunched in a throne chair at the far end of the room, perhaps ten feet tall, wasn't human, either.

Ian gasped even as he heard the general intake of breath around him.

The being in front of him was rail-thin and too tall: seven feet, or eight. It was dressed in a close-fitting black garment. Man or woman, it was hard to tell. Its head was bent, its hands laid along the arms of the great throne. But what hands! The fingers were thin, each joint standing out clear, dead white and too long, with no sign of nails. At first, all he could see of the figure itself was that it was bald. Its pate was shining white, as though no hair had ever been. Slowly, it raised its head. Ian felt the stone walls recede as

*his stomach dropped. The unhuman nature of its counte-
nance washed over him. The eyes were large and oval, dead
black as human eyes can never be. The nose was so small as
to be almost invisible, the mouth a mere slit, the chin
pointed, all under a dome of forehead that dwarfed the
other features.*

*Behind him, he heard some kind of scuffle. He tore his
stare from the figure and glanced behind him. One of the
slaves had broken away and tried to dash back through the
doorway. He bounced back as though there were a thick oak
door across the portal, though Ian could see the passage beyond the blackness. Several slaves whimpered. Someone had
closed the door.*

*Ian turned back toward the being. Asharti stepped for-
ward to stand in front of it. Ian prayed she wouldn't take him
with her, but she had firm hold of the rope and he staggered
forward against his will. The revulsion he suddenly felt for
the throbbing and the overwhelming aroma of the place
made his stomach rebel.*

*"Ancient One," Asharti said in a voice that banged
against the walls and was returned. "I have sought you for
years." She spoke in Arabic.*

*The being said nothing. Its flat black eyes surveyed the in-
truders as from a great distance, slowly moving from one
side of the room to the other.*

*Asharti waited, then repeated her address in French. Still
the not-human did not respond. The great almond eyes came
back to rest on her.*

*"You . . . have . . . the . . . bloooooood compaaaaanion,"
it said, so slowly it was difficult to understand it. It spoke
Latin.*

*"Yes," Asharti said, relieved, in Latin. "I have the blood
companion."*

*"From . . . my . . . fountain?" Ian strained to piece to-
gether the sense of that immensely slow and sonorous voice.*

*"Yes. The fountain we call The Source. In the Carpathian
Mountains."*

It blinked once and its head moved from side to side

very slowly. "Why...do you...torture...me...with blood?"

"I have brought a gift of blood to He Who Waits."

The tiny nostrils flared. The narrow chest sucked in breath. "Bloooood." The voice sped up a trifle. "So looong since I had blood..."

Asharti motioned to Fedeyah. "Bring a slave."

Fedeyah took the nearest slave in an iron grip and dragged him forward, struggling.

"I want no blood," the being said without conviction. His eyes were fixed on the slave.

"Open him," Asharti hissed.

Fedeyah drew a pointed fingernail across the slave's carotid artery. A spurt of blood spattered the Arab's face. The Ancient One's gaze fixed itself on the gushing wound. The black eyes went burgundy red. Fedeyah brought the spurting, grunting slave forward, pushed the wailing man down, and then backed away to stand beside Asharti.

The Ancient One's burgundy gaze shone down upon the slave, who crawled, bleeding, to his feet. With infinite slowness, the right, impossibly attenuated hand left the arm of the throne and drew the whimpering slave up by his neck, nearer to the tiny slit of a mouth.

Ian watched in horror. Without warning, the Old One's mouth opened to reveal fanged canines, like Asharti's, only sharper, longer needles, like a cat's. The creature broke the slave's neck and held the artery in his throat to that tiny mouth. Three immense sucking sounds and an animal growl, and the slave was dry, his flesh collapsing around bones and muscle.

The Ancient One tossed the body into the corner of the room and raised his eyes to Asharti. Ian shuddered. Several slaves screamed. The eyes had come alive. They flickered with an animation not there before the blood. They were old, impossibly old. They had known places and experiences no human ever had. Was this evil? Surely, if ever evil there was. The Ancient One raised his hand and beckoned with a long bony finger. Fedeyah brought another slave. This time the

Ancient One did not wait for Fedeyah to open the carotid but took the screaming slave, buried fangs in his throat, and sucked. It was over in seconds.

Ian found himself trembling. The thrumming in the stone at their feet had grown more rapid. The finger beckoned. Again Fedeyah grabbed a slave and offered him. Again the man was slashed and drained. Ian could practically feel those needle teeth in his own throat, sharper than Asharti's, death quicker. He had longed for death, and this was certainly quick. Yet he wanted nothing more than to escape this den of horror. He stared wildly around, knowing the entrance had been sealed behind them. Slaves clung to one another, their wails echoing around the chamber. The throbbing in the stone floor notched up another point.

Then the slaves went silent. The Ancient One had fixed them with his glowing red-black eyes. He turned to Asharti. "Why do you come here, with this blood?" The voice was nearly normally paced, though it was much too sonorous to issue from such a narrow chest.

"A gift," Asharti said, "for one who has waited a long time for his kind to return and take him to his homeland." She, too, trembled.

"I can take this blood without your consent." The voice was devoid of emotion.

"And you can kill me. But then who will bring you more?" Asharti was using all her power just to answer those glowing, inhuman eyes. Some little part of Ian reveled in the fact that she had to fight to keep her will her own.

"You cannot leave this place," Asharti gasped, her breasts heaving. "What if you were not here when your fellows returned?"

The Ancient One considered this from whatever remote place he dwelt.

"But I will bring you blood to sate your Companion," Asharti promised.

"What do you want in return?" The red-black eyes flared, and the Ancient One waited.

"I want your blood," Asharti said, under the influence of

those eyes. "I will supply you with an endless stream of offerings, if you will but give me a drop of yours."

The eyes examined Asharti. "You over-reach."

"A single gulp each time I bring you blood to slake the thirst of deprivation."

Again no expression crossed the strange face, no emotion.

"As a mark of my intentions I bring you these score of slaves, full of blood, and I bring my own favorite, in return for your blood tonight." Asharti gestured to Ian.

The eyes wandered over Ian's body and came to rest on his face. Ian felt cold strike to his marrow. The gaze moved on, dismissing.

"Bring them. I will consider."

The keepers brought the slaves up one by one, and one by one they were drained and cast aside. The horror went on and on, slaves shrieking, the Old One growling as he sucked at them. The throbbing in Ian's chest had not so much disappeared as it had been transformed into a vibration just at the edges of his comprehension. It became a hum of energy, instead of the slow throb of a heartbeat. It was a more pronounced version of the vibrating energy that surrounded Asharti and, in lesser form, Fedeyah.

At the last there were only the two keepers, Fedeyah, Asharti, and Ian.

"I am still thirsty," the Old One rumbled. "Such a long fast." He looked at the keepers. Asharti shrugged. The keepers walked forward, under the compulsion of the Old One's eyes, and soon they were cast, drained, upon the heap. That left three.

"Now, Ancient One, for my share," Asharti whispered. "A drop of your blood, and I give you my favorite. I have starved myself that he might please you. His will is strong. His abasement to you will be satisfying. Drain him now, or keep him to sip at your leisure. In a month's time, I will bring you another score of spurting veins, and you will grant me your blood again."

The small head cocked. "You are more ambitious than others of this world."

Asharti nodded, unapologetic.

The Old One contemplated. "Who knows what is good? Perhaps it was written thus. I have drunk. I will need more." Then he used one of his needle canines to open his forefinger. He held it down and beckoned to Asharti. She knelt at his feet and opened her mouth. A single drop oozed from his finger. She focused on it with such a single purpose, time seemed to stop.

The drop fell. She caught it eagerly, swallowed. "More," she breathed.

"One drop is enough. Unless you relish pain, or even death."

"Very well." She wore a triumphant expression. "A bargain. You will not be sorry."

"Already I grieve."

"Slave!" Asharti jerked Ian's rope, her eyes glowing. "Kneel and offer yourself. This one's will is very strong, Ancient One. Consider enjoying him slowly for maximum satisfaction."

Ian walked forward under the compulsion of her eyes, all thought of escape gone. He knelt. He could not help himself but stared up at the inhuman countenance. The creature's gaze bored through him, as flat black as the garment the Old One wore. Yet something sparked behind those ancient eyes. Were they really so emotionless? Ian saw regret swimming in them; loss, yearning. The Old One had been separated from his kind for centuries, millennia even. Could he yet hope? Almost, no, and yet he waited. . . . He exuded the same breath of despair that had dogged Ian's steps across the desert. How did one hope when it was folly to continue and hope should long since have vanished? One hand snaked out to cup the nape of Ian's neck. Ian could feel the compulsion to tilt his head back and bare his throat, and yet he held the Old One's gaze for another moment, a final act of rebellion against inevitability.

Abruptly the Old One looked away. "You are right,

woman. He fights against yielding." He cast Ian aside. Ian
collapsed, sinking to all fours. "I do not want your leavings," he heard the Old One say. He could not tell whether
the words were spoken aloud or only echoed in his mind.
"You have sucked at this one. Take him away."

Asharti bowed and snapped, "To me, slave!"

Ian dragged himself to her side, unsure whether to regret
his rejection. Would the Old One have killed him immediately, or would he have tormented Ian in ways even more foul
than Asharti's? Asharti picked up Ian's rope, bowed once to
the figure on the throne, now vibrating with energy. She
backed from the room, Fedeyah behind her and Ian scrambling after them.

The vortex was open. They thrust through to the passage
beyond, their two remaining lanterns swinging wild shadows
on the wall, up the sloping corridor, into the treasure room.
Here Asharti stopped abruptly and motioned to Fedeyah.

"Take enough to fuel our war against men," she growled.
"But don't look at them. We can have them broken up in
Marrakech."

Fedeyah retrieved several small leather sacks from the
sleeves of his burnoose and quickly scooped handfuls of the
huge stones into each, pulling the strings tight. Asharti
pushed through the farther door with Ian in tow. They ran up
the next passage, Ian gasping, until they reached the an-
techamber with the two huge ibis-dog guardians.

In the echoing hall Asharti again halted. She bent double,
wheezing, laughing with reckless abandon. "Fedeyah, I have
done it! Ancient blood! Already I feel it burning in my
veins!" Straightening, she fairly shone.

Ian stared at her. She had taken but a single drop of the
Old One's blood, yet already he could detect a difference in
her. It was as if the angles of her face were smoothed. She
was made of alabaster, glowing from within. It was sheer
power that lit her eyes and her flesh.

"I am alive!" she hissed. "One drop and my power is
doubled. Where will this end?"

She flung aside her cloak. Ian saw her nipples beneath

her gossamer gown, tense with excitement or desire. She cast about the chamber, her gaze roving over the hieroglyphics and the guardian statues. Her eyes came to rest on Fedeyah, who studied her anxiously. "Life flows in me, Fedeyah," she whispered, stalking up to him. "I have never regretted the loss of your manhood more. You alone are of my kind. Yet you are useless as a consort."

Fedeyah contracted, though he kept his features almost as impassive as the Old One's. Asharti hurt him and his pain made no difference to her.

She turned, holding her arms out, mirth bubbling up through her chest and her throat into a rich laugh. Her gaze fell on Ian, moved on, paused, and returned. Their glow changed its character. "Life flows in me," she repeated slowly, "and must be released."

Ian shook his head in dumb resistance. "Must go . . ." he managed. Not here! Not now! Her eyes glowed more intensely than he had ever seen them. He fell to his knees on the stones.

"Goddess!" Fedeyah cried. "We must go from here. Suck him dry once we are away. . . ."

"The Old One's blood excites me, acolyte," she murmured, never taking her eyes from Ian's body. "I must have release. I am starved for several kinds of nourishment."

Ian felt his member rise at her unspoken command. He shook his head ever so slightly. It was a measure of his misery that he found the will at all.

She bore down upon him, dropping her lantern to the floor with a metallic clang. It lit her features from below, revealing the demon in her. Looming over him, her eyes pulsed red. He raised his face, his cock throbbing. She bent to kiss his forehead, trailing her lips to his temple even as he moaned his dismay. He swayed on his knees. She moved her lips down toward his. Her newly enhanced power washed over him, making the great stone statues spin. She touched his lips, taking his lower lip in her teeth. Ian, in his turn, took her full lower lip in his own mouth and sucked at her. Her instructions were there in his mind.

"*Worshipped One!*" Asharti jerked back, Fedeyah's hand at her shoulder. Ian's teeth cut Asharti's lip. The tang of blood blossomed in his mouth.

Asharti shrieked in fury as she rounded on Fedeyah. "*You dare to interrupt me?* She gave the Arab a backhanded swipe that sent him reeling. Then she froze and turned.

Ian licked his lips. Her blood was bitter copper.

Asharti's eyes went wide. She stood as still as one of the guardian statues for a long moment. Then anger suffused her. "*You have ruined everything!*" She raised a hand that could decapitate him. He did not cringe away. Let her kill him.

Slowly, she lowered her hand. She began to chuckle. The laugh crescendoed to a hysterical cry, reminiscent of the hyena. Ian felt her spell break. His will was his own.

"*Why bother?*" she managed around her fountain of laughter. "*The slow death of a new one will punish you more surely.*" She reached for his rope, casting a resentful glance at Fedeyah. "*We will go. And you will both be punished.*"

Twelve

Ian knelt, naked and shuddering, in the sand at the edge of the open desert with the rock of Kivala at his back. The sky was pink with coming sun. Fedeyah stood beside him, silent. The caravan prepared to depart. Asharti already reclined in her litter, the silk hangings tied tight against the dawn. Drivers whistled and clucked. Camels rose to their feet, ungainly packs of water and food swaying up. The four bearers shouldered the litter. The eastern horizon paled from pink to pearl.

Asharti had not called him to her litter, though she had been closeted there for the better part of an hour. She had overcome her desire. As they stumbled back through the wash, Ian had felt fever growing in him. He alternately sweated and shivered. By the time Asharti goaded the caravan into furious preparation, Ian wavered on his knees on the verge of collapse.

At the last minute, she had barked a single order to Fedeyah. "Leave him."

It meant his death, of course. No man could survive in this godforsaken land, naked and sick, without food or water. The only water besides the oasis three days ahead was probably the pool deep in that chamber of horrors. Ian would rather die than return there.

Death should be a relief. Had he not craved death for months? Still, he could not help but rail against the injustice of her anger. Whose fault was it that he was not virgin to bloodletting and the Old One had not wanted him? He had not bitten her lip intentionally, either. He watched the caravan recede. The moon still hung in the lightening sky, a ghost of itself.

Yet was that the real reason the Old One had rejected him as Asharti's gift? In the instant he had dared to look into those old eyes, he had felt some kind of connection to that incomprehensible being. Was it a mutual recognition of suffering? Some common railing of the spirit against the iniquity of the world? Something so alien, so powerful, could not connect to a human slave. He must have imagined it. The whole journey into the earth now seemed unreal.

What was real was his imminent suffering and death. Worse, both Fedeyah and Asharti believed his fate was to be even more horrible than dying from exposure and thirst. Asharti had promised him exceeding pain as punishment for his inadequacy and his transgression.

He looked up at Fedeyah, who stood beside him gazing after the object of his fruitless longing over centuries. Fedeyah carried his own punishment with him, as Asharti must know. The caravan moved off southwest along the cliffs. Fedeyah took a breath and turned to Ian. Ian saw that he had a bundle under his right arm.

"English," Fedeyah said, and then paused to gather himself. "Does a man deserve the death she has planned for you?" He asked himself, not Ian. "If we had not spoken of England, of her, you would be only another animal to me. I would not be tempted to defy her."

Ian waited, silent, for Fedeyah to say more.

Fedeyah threw down the bundle in front of Ian and stalked away. Over his shoulders drifted the words: "Protect your body from the sun. Drink sparingly. It may be enough to see you through the sickness. Don't look into the stones. We are for Marrakech."

Ian watched him break into a trot to catch up to the cara-

van, burnoose flapping. Ian surveyed the bundle with bleary
eyes and plucked at the fabric. It was a burnoose, a single
leather water bag, and a small leather pouch on a sling. He
opened the tiny sack, caught the glint of diamonds, and
jerked his gaze away. The honking cry of the camels faded.
The figures grew small, until they might be anyone. Ian's
heart sank. A burnoose, a single water sack, and some useless diamonds—if Fedeyah meant to give him a chance to
live he might have done better.

The red rim of the sun peeked over the horizon. Its first
rays stabbed Ian's naked body like a thousand needles. The
flash blinded him. He cried out and fell to the ground,
writhing. His lungs could not find air. His veins were on fire.
His skin seared. The sun! How could the first weak rays of
dawn cause so much pain? Shade! He needed shade. Groaning, he raised his head. The ravine! He dragged himself into
the deep shade of the ravine wall. The cool of the rock
against his back soothed his blistered flesh. He lay there
gasping, still unable to open his eyes more than a slit. Then
the shivering began again as fever racked his body. He
couldn't think. He could only lie in the sand, arm flung
across his eyes, teeth chattering.

Hours passed. Sometimes he was delirious. But he was
brought forcibly to his senses as fire stabbed his hand. He
jerked it into his body and chanced to crack his eyelids. The
shade of the wall was retreating as the sun rose higher. His
hand had been touched by sunlight. He shrank against the
stone. At noon he would be burned alive.

What to do? The burnoose! He raised his head. It lay
some ten feet away in the center of the ravine. It might as
well lie across a river of fire. Could it save his flesh? It must,
or why would Fedeyah leave it? He looked around through
slitted eyes. No stick, no miraculous shepherd's crook he
could use to reach the burnoose. He stared at the oat-colored
fabric and the burgundy threads that striped it. He had
wanted death but not death in such excruciating pain. He
imagined his skin cracking, cooking in the sun. He must be a
coward. If he was to avoid that death, there was one choice.

He must suffer the sun just long enough to lunge for the burnoose.

He could not take time to think. The shade shrank moment by moment. Sucking in his breath, he gathered himself. No matter how painful it was, he must keep moving. He must reach that burnoose. He lurched into the sun. Immediately the stabbing rays coated him with pain. He was blinded; his flesh seemed to bubble. His joints screamed. He scrambled across the sand, slowing with every second he was exposed to the toxic light. Cloth beneath his hands, he clenched and heaved himself backward, gasping. Each movement took an aeon as he struggled toward the narrow band of shade. He brought the fabric up over his shoulders and felt the searing flame subside. Weakly he scrabbled toward the rock wall.

Shade's cooling darkness touched first a hand and then, as he dragged himself against the wall, his head and shoulders. Moaning, he drew his body into a ball under the burnoose.

How he survived the noon he did not know. He huddled under the burnoose shivering with fever, his flesh seared from those moments in the sun. The very texture of the fabric against his tortured skin was hell. Sometime later, he realized the sun was creating shade on the far side of the ravine. He pulled himself, under the rasping burnoose, through sand that scraped him raw toward the other side, and collapsed, unconscious.

Night. The cool desert air crept under the fabric of the burnoose and roused him. He managed to throw off the fabric and lay there, semiconscious, staring up at the stars. The fever was worse. The sheen of sweat on his body left him victim to chills. The sky was cold and closed against him, the stars distant, the moon not yet risen.

Ian was thirsty, thirstier than he had ever been. His body screamed as though it had passed through fire. Asharti had condemned him to this suffering. Damn her to hell!

He breathed, riding the pain. His thoughts skittered to the water sack Fedeyah had left. The thought of water, flavor in-

describable, relief incalculable, filled him. If he could make it to the water . . . Impossible! He didn't have the strength to move. He'd die as Asharti meant him to die.

He rolled his head and saw the horn of the moon peek over the shoulder of the ravine. Let her win? Hatred stoked a fire in his belly. He had wanted to die to escape her. But she was gone. Was he so much a slave at heart that he would let her kill him in absentia? Fedeyah said the water sack might last him long enough to live. Fedeyah thought it was possible.

He rolled onto his side. His teeth began to chatter. He reached for the burnoose and pulled it over his head. Several strips of fabric tumbled from the folds. His tongue was a thick, dry lump in his mouth, like cloth. The water sack was . . . twenty feet away? It might as well be a mile. But not impossible, he told himself. Not impossible. Grunting, he rolled onto his belly. He shoved himself over the sand—one couldn't even call it crawling—sand and fabric torturing his burned skin. Slowly, with pain he did not think he could bear suffusing his body, he dragged himself forward. He had to reach that water skin.

He clutched the sueded leather like the prize it was. He jerked the cork from the mouthpiece, raised it to his trembling lips, and squeezed the sack. Instead of the cool purity of water, blood gushed into his mouth. He swallowed convulsively, coughing. Blood? Blood? He spat into the sand and retched, but he did not bring up the blood. It coursed into his gut.

His shaking stopped. Strength suffused him. He felt . . . whole. What was this? He rolled to his back. The pain of his burnt flesh receded a little. The stars were brighter now, or his sight had cleared. The moon rose over the ravine like an enigmatic smile. It was as if life ran in his veins.

Now, while he had the strength, he had to get back to the ravine wall. He struggled to his hands and knees. He glanced to the sack that held no water. Revulsion filled him. Yet it was the blood that banished the fever and pain. He knew that. Blood. Fedeyah had left him blood.

Realization enveloped him. He was as they were. He needed blood to live!

Ian scrambled back into the ravine as though he could escape the meaning of that water sack. It could not be! He would not let it be! His brain darted over all that had happened. Asharti wanted the Old One's blood to increase her power. Ian's teeth had torn her lip. The taste of her blood, her fury, her laugh when she said he would die the death of a new one all swirled before him in a kaleidoscope review.

It was true. He had gotten her nature through her blood. Despair flooded him. He clutched his knees and rocked. A keening sound issued from a throat newly moistened with blood. The evil had infected him. He was more her slave than ever. She had condemned him to death and left him. And he should die, if he was destined to be as she was. Let the sun come and burn him to a crisp! He'd rather die than be as they were. He sobbed and railed against the fate that let the Barbary pirates fall upon his ship, let Fedeyah buy him for Asharti, brought him to this lost city with its horror lurking underground. Self-pity tore at him.

The stars wheeled, uncaring, over his despair until dawn painted the promise of light over the eastern horizon. His tears were gone. Emotion had drained away. He was a dry husk, shaking with chills. The fever was returning, just as the sun would soon return. Then he would remove the burnoose, walk out into its deadly rays, and let it burn him to death. It was all that was left to him. But as he sat there, a small thorn niggled in his gut. What galled him was that she would have won. Just as she mastered Fedeyah, she would hold him in thrall until he did what she wanted—died a dreadful death. And he was going to apply her punishment himself. Some part of him rebelled one final time.

Fedeyah could make other choices. He didn't have to follow her. It was his weakness that he did follow. Then, too, Fedeyah was different from Asharti. He did not kill the slaves who fed him. Could Ian not be different, too? He had been thoughtless in his youth and profligate, but he had reformed, and joined the diplomatic corps to return some value for his life, to country or to his fellow men. He had not been an evil man. Could he not reform again?

But this infection, this disease he had of her, might change his essential nature. A thought struck him. If it was a disease, might it not be cured? Doctors were doing marvelous things these days for conditions that had long been mysteries. A draught of some herb and he could be stripped of the consequence of Asharti's blood. Perhaps it was the fever in his brain that made it seem possible, even likely, that a good English doctor could cure him. But he did not want to throw away the chance.

He did not want her to have won.

The sun would be up in another hour or two. Ian pulled up the hood of his burnoose.

He had to get to an English doctor.

He glanced to the water sack. Beside it lay the leather pouch that held diamonds. His resolve hardened inside him. To have any chance of thwarting Asharti's revenge or escaping what she had made him, he would need both sustenance and the means to get help. He must avail himself of both Fedeyah's parting gifts.

He needed blood to survive. So be it, for now. He looked around for the ragged strips of fabric that had fallen from the burnoose. They were half-buried in the sand. He shook them out and wrapped his feet and hands. Pulling the burnoose around him, he stalked out into the desert. He would do his walking at night and huddle under the burnoose in the daylight, his eyes wrapped with the remaining strip of cloth.

The fever was coming back, stronger now, and he was shaky on his feet, but he knew what would keep the fever at bay. He stooped to scoop up the two leather articles. He hung the tiny bag of diamonds around his neck. He squirted a small stream of the thickening blood far down his throat in the hope that he could prevent gagging. He couldn't. But he kept the blood down. Was it some slave's blood, or was it Fedeyah's? He bet on Fedeyah, as strength flowed through his body. Only the blood of one of them could confer such vibrant, frightening consequences. He slipped the water bag over his shoulder. He could follow the track of the caravan as far as the first oasis.

Then he would turn away from Marrakech.

• • •

Ian's eyes cleared as the memories drained away. The girl was speaking earnestly.

"Are you well?" she was asking.

He shook his head as if that could dispel the memory of that night when he had discovered what lived in Kivala and lost his humanity into the bargain. How long had he been staring at his hands, immobile? He cleared his throat before he dared to speak.

"As well as I can be these days."

Her eyes were round with concern. Concern? He did not deserve the concern of a virtuous woman. "Is the one you saw at Kivala so horrible?" she asked matter-of-factly.

"Horrible enough. It was also the night I became what I am today."

"Ahh. Was Asharti the one who waited? You said it was her blood that poisoned you."

"No. She wanted his blood. Apparently he is the ancestor of her kind. His ancient blood is very powerful. She thought his blood would make her invincible."

"To what purpose?"

"She wants to rule men. My guess is that she has plans for that corner of the world."

The girl pressed her lips together. "That would be bad."

He roused himself and rubbed the bridge of his nose as if to wipe away memories. "But we will be in England. She cannot reach that far. And neither can the One Who Waits at Kivala."

She was about to ask another question but apparently thought better of it. "Well, back to our original intent then. That is all the scroll tells us about the Old Ones. It moves on to talk about the monuments. What have we learned?" She glanced back at the scroll. "There is a 'blood companion,' whatever that means. It sounds like more than a disease. We see that they are very old. There is some power of compulsion that goes with the reddening of the eyes. And this reference to being 'invisible bats.' " She looked up. "Did you ever become a bat?"

"No." He made his voice as repressive as possible. But she would not be repressed.

"Well then, we must concentrate on what we do know. Tell me what happens when your eyes go red. Can you do it at will, or does it just come on you?"

He yielded to her matter-of-fact approach. "I suppose it comes on me."

"When?"

"When . . . I have the hunger and there is an opportunity to . . . feed."

"Could you call it?"

"I don't know."

"Did Asharti call it at will?"

He nodded. He did not trust himself to speak.

"Try it," she urged. "Try to make your eyes go red."

"No!" he exclaimed, his brows drawing together. "Are you mad?"

She cocked her head, exasperated. "It is an experiment. You said you wanted to know more about your condition. How else will we find out?"

He got up and paced the room, automatically compensating for the roll of the ship and bending under the beams of the low ceiling. "What if I unleash something I can't control?"

"How can you learn to control it if you don't try?" She lifted her chin in challenge.

He whirled away and took another turn, hands clasped behind his back. As he faced her again, she raised her brows and pointed to the chair. She was right, of course. If he said he wanted to know about his condition, he couldn't run from it. He sat.

"Try to go red." He could detect some quaver in her voice, but she nodded resolutely at him in encouragement.

He had no idea how to go about it. He sat there, blinking. Nothing. He shrugged helplessly. "What do I do?"

She bit her lip. "Hmmm. Try closing your eyes."

He closed his eyes. What difference would that make?

"Can you smell the tar that holds the ship together?" she asked, her voice soft.

He nodded slowly. He felt her rise and walk around behind him.

"Can you smell the wet of wood and seawater?"

"Yes," he breathed.

She rubbed his temples gently. Her touch was soft, revealing her tender nature. He began to be distracted by her touch until her voice brought him back. "Now, think about your body. Feel the weight of it in the chair, shifting with the sea beneath us." Her voice carried a curious lilt. His body had weight and substance he had never noticed. "Feel your muscles shift to brace yourself against the roll." Yes. He could feel that. "Now think about the air coming into your lungs. Breathe in, deeply." He filled his lungs. "Hold it there. Now breathe out. Bodies are quite marvelous, are they not?" *Yes, they are,* he thought. It was just her voice, in the night, and the roll of the sea beneath him.

"Now press your right hand across your breast and feel your heart pumping there." *Lub-dub, lub-dub.* Her fingers rubbed his temples in time with his heart. "It's pumping blood into your lungs and your belly and your legs and back again. Feel the blood coursing through your veins. The blood is the key, you see. Feel the blood."

Ian felt blood sliding along his veins. It pulsed in his carotids, down through his loins into his thighs, throbbing in his femoral arteries. Low, just above the throbbing of his heart, some song beat where he could not quite hear it. Behind him, she stepped back. The tender touch faded away, leaving only the rhythm of his heart. His strength, his feeling of well-being, was like a song. Something sang in his blood. To listen was dangerous. Yet he listened.

He heard rejoicing, reveling in strength. There was a sense of oneness, two as one. His gladness ramped up until life flowed along his veins, tingling, and Ian was more than he had ever been and what he was rejoiced, even as part of him was afraid of that giddy swirl of power.

From a distance, he heard Miss Rochewell whisper, "Do not cut the connection. Let yourself experience it or we will never know."

Ian opened his eyes. They would be red, he knew, red like his blood. He felt his core glowing, the song in his blood growing louder. Air could hardly fill his lungs full enough to fuel the fire that sang along his veins. The joy and the power were almost painful, and still they ramped up in some mad chorus of voices or instruments clashing in a music never heard by man. Ian thought he would scream. He was standing, though he had not felt himself rise, and he saw Miss Rochewell through some red haze of joy and power he knew must be wrong. But he couldn't stop it, didn't want to stop it. He wanted to feel it all. A blackness grew at the edges of that transparent pool of red. Already he could not quite see the doors to the cabins off the great room and the edges of the stern windows were melting into the dark night beyond the glass. The edges of his vision collapsed. The singing in his veins grew to a shriek and the pulsing blood now screamed, distributing pain throughout his body. All went black for a roaring moment. The pain was excruciating. His body felt as though it were turned inside out.

The shock of ice-cold seawater filling his lungs hammered his senses. He sank into the night-black ocean. For a long moment he was paralyzed, dazed by disconnection. Then he reached the ultimate darkness at the perigee of his descent. His senses shuddered into place. He kicked, lungs bursting, until he caught a glimmer above him that might be the moon. Groping upward, fear making him desperate, he clawed the insubstantial water toward the surface.

Bursting upward into moonlight and a choppy sea, he could see the ship receding, its stern lights glowing in the dark of the Atlantic.

"Beltrane!" he shouted. But a wave sloshed over him and converted his hail into no more than a gurgle. He looked around and saw nothing but dark night and cold black sea. He cursed the weight of boots that could not be removed. He

struck out for the ship, its sails taking it farther away at every moment.

Beth gasped as the figure before her with the red glowing eyes wavered at the edges and suddenly blinked out. He was there one moment, huge, menacing, a monster she had coaxed out of a man, and in the next moment he was gone.

For a moment she was so amazed she thought she had imagined it. She looked around the empty cabin. "Mr. Rufford?" Her voice was tentative in her own ears.

"Mr. Rufford!" She ran to the cabin doors, but each tiny room was empty, no possible place for him to hide. Did she not believe her eyes? He had disappeared, just as the scroll said he could, like a bat in the night. Panic rose inside her. Was he dead? Had he gone to some other world? Why had she encouraged him to draw the redness? What had she done?

She stumbled to the deck, thrown from side to side in the narrow passage by the roll of the ship. "Mr. Rait!" she called to the first officer she saw. "Have you seen Mr. Rufford?" She searched the deck wildly, but there was no familiar black coat.

"Miss Rochewell," Rait said, alarmed. "Are you well?" Sailors around her stopped what they were doing to gape at her.

"Where is he?" She looked up at the rigging as though he might have suddenly taken a fancy to climb the shrouds. The sails belled with the wind. The ship was moving fast.

"I couldn't hardly say, miss," Rait answered, obviously reserving judgment on her sanity.

At that moment they both heard a faint shout. *"Beltrane!"*

Beth ran to the rail on the leeward side, searched the black water, seeing nothing.

"Lookout!" Rait yelled. "What see you?"

A long moment passed. Beth clung to the railing. Rait came to stand behind her.

"Man overboard!" the lookout finally yelled. "Two points east of south."

"Back topsails!" Rait yelled. Sailors scurried up the yards. "Bring her off the bowline."

The ship gave way, sails shivering, and still Beth could not see him for the short-breaking, disorganized waves of the Bay of Biscay. There he was, a white face in a trough of the choppy seas. He was swimming strongly now, though the waves broke over him.

"Shall I send out a boat, Mr. Rait?" Mr. Gilman asked.

How could they not send out a boat?

Rait watched the figure a moment, then shook his head. "He'll be up with the ship before we could get anything launched." Sailors headed for the rail. Rait cocked a head up at the sails and then glanced out to the figure struggling in the heavy seas. "By the time we wore round to pick him up . . . No, we'll let Mr. Rufford display his swimming prowess."

Rufford came up the side by the leeward boarding stairs on the upward roll, holding to the rope they let down for him. Beth had been sure he was drowned a dozen times.

He came up heaving and sputtering. "Apologies, Mr. Rait, for checking your way," he gasped. He offered no explanation for how he had gone overboard. Beth felt it beyond herself to intervene with anything plausible. She was overcome with the image of a black whirling mist that disappeared from the Captain's great stern cabin. And she couldn't say that.

Rufford turned from the questioning glances and made his way, dripping, to his quarters.

Beth nodded to Rait and said she would retire herself after all the excitement. She knew she was leaving rampant speculation behind, but she could not face it alone.

In the light of the common room outside their cabins, Rufford stood, dripping. He looked up at her entrance. "So much for scientific experimentation." He tried to convey calm dismissal. He failed. Then he could not refrain from whispering a question. "What did you see?"

"Your eyes . . . your eyes went red," she said with as much

composure as she could manage. "Then a kind of black mist swirled around you and you . . . you disappeared."

"I reappeared about three feet above the water some forty yards astern. I should be glad it wasn't farther."

She swallowed. "I think you 'moved through the night like a bat, unseen.' "

He nodded, a puddle growing, unnoticed, at his feet. "Well, I hope I never do it again."

"What did you feel?" she could not help asking in her turn.

He searched her face, his blue-eyed gaze turned inward. "Life singing along my veins. Strength. I felt as though I was not alone." He blinked. "It felt . . . wonderful."

Neither of them thought that was necessarily a good sign. Beth nodded, trying to keep her face from betraying any astonishment, let alone disapproval. *He is just different,* she kept reminding herself. *Did you not want to know the mystery?*

"I intend to go to my cabin and try to stay there," Rufford growled. "I suggest you do the same, Miss Rochewell." He turned away and stalked toward his cabin door.

Beth watched him go. Their research into his nature had not proved a comfort to him. Rather the opposite. And for her? The mystery was greater than she had imagined.

Rufford discouraged further research into the scrolls as they beat up against the winds in the Channel, making for Portsmouth in the days that ensued. He did not mention again what had happened that night. He seemed to withdraw into some kind of austere acceptance of his condition that put up a barrier between them. Yet every night saw him leaning on the rail at the leeward side of the quarterdeck, willing the frigate on toward England with yearning in his eyes.

Beth pored over her scrolls in daylight, alone. But no more revelations came to light. As much as Rufford ached for England, so she dreaded its approach. Her father had been at her side whenever she returned to this strangest of lands since her school days. He had been her anchor, the source of her confidence, her friend. More than that, he was her protection against a society that disapproved of her life. Now she had no one. The emptiness was beguiled for a while by her fascination with the mystery of Rufford. But once the *Beltrane* anchored in Portsmouth, Rufford would vanish. That knowledge brought a stab of pain she had not expected. *It is only that his companionship beat back loneliness,* she told herself. The practical consequences of her father's death came home to her. She had still never cried for him. But her devastation was no less complete for being dry-eyed. The empty feeling of regret was echoed, though fainter, in the distance that Rufford now kept. He was afraid of what he had become and ashamed of all he had admitted to her. When she tried to discuss it, he simply shook his head.

"There is nothing for it but to see if a doctor can cure me," he had said when she asked him how he did. And he would say no more. Indeed, his expression was so closed and glowering she dared not question him or try to give him solace. The ability to disappear seemed to have horrified him all over again.

Still, the night before the *Beltrane* docked, he came out to where Beth played chess, black against white, a very sterile occupation. She heard his door open, felt him standing behind her.

"Well?" she asked, not turning to him, all the stiffness of his distance these last days and all her fear of the loneliness ahead in her voice.

"We dock tomorrow, or so the Captain seems to think."

"Yes." She moved the black rook.

"You will go ashore in the morning, no doubt."

"Yes."

"I . . . I wanted to thank you for your . . . understanding."

"There is nothing for which to thank me."

"I know of no one else who would overlook a deep wrong against her person and keep so objective an attitude about my . . . proclivities. I am fully sensible of my debt."

"You owe me nothing." She meant it as a kindness. Yet

that was not how it came out, somehow. She glanced behind her to see him bow his head and turn back into his cabin. That was all that was needed to sink whatever spirit remained to her. She had not meant it to end so.

This might be the last time she would ever see him. It was another loss, along with Africa, along with her father. She was surprised it hurt so badly.

Thirteen

The hackney coach stopped in front of number 27 Curzon Street. Beth looked up at the imposing stone front of the house, her emotions wound tight in her chest. Her nerves were still a-jangle from a day and a half on the Mail Coach with Mrs. Pargutter up from Portsmouth. She wondered how she would have supported the voyage had that lady not succumbed to seasickness. She'd been relieved to part company. Yet now that she had reached her destination, her mind was even more agitated. Had her letter arrived to inform Lady Celia Rangle of her coming? Would her aunt welcome her or view her as some sad trial? Was she even in London? Beth heaved a breath and let it out. The door to the coach opened. The driver handed her down. She stood uncertainly on the walk in front of the door as he unstrapped her trunks and piled them in a heap. The knocker was on the door, so her aunt was at home. Best get on with it. She could not stand forever in the street without attracting attention. Indeed, several people passing had looked at her with disapproval. She was already feeling out of place.

Paying the coachman, she stepped forward and raised the knocker. It sounded dreadfully importuning as it banged against the plate. The butler who answered it looked down at her from a height well above six feet, his mouth dour. He was an older man, his shoulders slightly stooped, one of those retainers who had been with Lady Rangle so long that he felt proprietary about her time and attention. Beth searched for a name. She had seen him several times.

"Edwards, is my aunt at home?" Did he remember her?

Recognition dawned in his eyes, followed close on by disapproval. He could hardly deny someone with a direct relationship, but he could frown his censure of luggage heaped in the street. "She is resting, Miss Elizabeth." He paused to emphasize his coming generosity. "However, I will have the underfootman take your things up to the blue bedroom." He stepped aside to let her in with great condescension. "You may wait in the drawing room."

She was expected, or taking her luggage to a bedroom would be out of the question. Beth stripped off her tan leather gloves and unbuttoned her russet pelisse as she looked about her. The town house was furnished in the latest style, always. Lady Rangle refurbished it continually to be slap up to the echo of fashion. Just now, with all the interest in the French exploration of Egyptian antiquities, that meant the entry hall and indeed what Beth could see of the front saloon were crowded with faux Egyptian pieces. Crouching cats held up the table upon which visiting cards were scattered. A most uncomfortable-looking pair of wooden chairs on U-shaped legs flanked a trio of ceremonial lances striped with lapis lazuli. She half-expected to see a mummy laid out upon the sofa in the large room where Edwards led her. She wandered about the room comparing the reproductions to her memories of the real treasures of Egypt. Lady Rangle could afford the best, but their very newness made them tawdry. She smiled to herself to think that what was lacking for verisimilitude must surely be the ever-present grit of the desert.

That humorous perspective was still floating about Beth when her aunt drifted into the room. Lady Rangle always seemed to drift. She was long past youth, yet her frame was willowy, her complexion pale and skin fragile. Her faded beauty (and she had been a great beauty in her day) was framed by ethereal curls helped to their palest shade of blonde by a much more delicate hand than Mrs. Pargutter used. There was not a hint of brass. Her morning dress was lustring faintly striped with lavender. Slippers of delicate lilac kid peeped from under her hem. Over her elbows, a shawl of Norwich silk draped negligently. A beaded reticule hung from one wrist even indoors, so her smelling salts were always close at hand in case her sensibilities were assaulted in any way. A magnifying glass hung around her neck by a ribbon, since she was very myopic and disdained the use of spectacles.

"Lizzy," she breathed. Her voice was always either languid or breathy. "How good it is to see you." Beth wondered if she meant it. She wafted forward and pecked Beth on each cheek.

"I hope my letter was not too inconvenient, Aunt—" Beth's anxiety banished her wry perspective. She did not even correct her aunt's use of a diminutive of Elizabeth she hated.

"Of course, dear Lizzy. And who should you come to in such shocking circumstances but your only relative?" She draped her figure on a pale satin chaise designed for comfort, not an Egyptian pedigree. "Do sit down, my dear. You always were such a dreadfully active child."

Beth perched on the edge of a sofa whose arms were inlaid with an ibis pattern.

"Now, let me look at you." Lady Rangle raised her glass. Her pale blue eye grew monstrous and distorted to Beth's view. It was all Beth could do not to squirm under that unblinking gaze. "Well," she said at last, letting the glass fall and looking world-weary. "It could be worse. You don't squint. And I detect no spots of any kind. I suppose your complexion can't be helped, or those eyes. Your mother gets the blame for them. You could hardly be shorter. But I don't despair of bringing you off creditably. We can't look too high, of course. You would never do for the fashionable set. But I'm sure there are some widowers of reasonable means who might not expect better. Old Marksby is in town just now to call in at Harley Street about his gout. Or there is always the City."

Beth's flush rose during this speech along with her indignation. She pressed her lips together against her first retort. After a moment she said with some constraint, "If you think I have cast myself upon you to arrange a marriage for me, Aunt, you do me no credit."

"But you must be married, child." Her aunt smiled kindly. "What else is there for you?"

"I am perfectly capable of independence, I assure you. And I might also say that it is my firm intention never to marry except where there may be love on both sides. In lieu of finding that, I shall do fine on my own." She saw her aunt's dubious look turn to amusement. "I shall call on my father's bankers at Drummond's tomorrow."

"A young female cannot simply set up house for herself," her aunt protested, chuckling. "Why, no one would receive you. I doubt the shops would sell you an ell of cloth. As for love, girls say they must have a love match as though that existed in real life. Many of us grow very fond of our husbands, however. Why, I positively doted on Rangle."

Doted? From what Beth remembered of her aunt's relationship with the stout and stern man who talked incessantly of sporting ventures, she was sure Lady Rangle confused "doted on" with "ignored." She schooled her countenance to polite reserve. "I would simply like to feel doting before I marry. I might seem distrustful, but I have no desire to buy a pig in a poke."

Lady Rangle reached out a hand and Beth came to stand in front of her. "My poor, dear Lizzy, raised in barbarian lands far from civilization. What was Edwin about? My foolish brother! It is no wonder you do not know how to go on. But you will be invited to the best houses, though town is thin of company until after the holidays. My name is not nothing. It opens many doors."

Lady Rangle meant to be kind. Beth knew that. And for

someone so languid to take upon herself the task of steering an ignorant girl through the shoals of London society was an act heroic in and of itself. Especially when the girl thrust upon her doorstep was nearly unknown to her and of questionable experience. So Beth did not say she had no desire to have doors opened or that she had no ambition to a knowledge of society. She did not reassert her determination to set up for herself even if it meant a lonely life. Instead, she cleared her throat. "You are very good, Aunt. And I am very sorry to put you to so much trouble, foisting myself upon you."

"I shall enjoy the dressing of you, my dear, and you must strive to do me credit. Of course, you will put off your blacks. No one would offer for a girl in mourning. Edwin has interfered quite enough in your life already."

Beth was about to protest, but instead managed a weak smile, feeling adrift in unfamiliar territory. Her father would not care if she wore black or not. She realized her aunt had never even asked her about her journey or commiserated on her father's death.

Ian waited in the comfortable drawing room outside Dr. James Blundell's consultation chamber in Harley Street, excitement and dread beating in his breast. All his hopes were pinned upon what would happen in the next hour. He had been in London three days, having posted up from Portsmouth with all haste. But Blundell was not easy to see, being so renowned a practitioner when it came to diseases of the blood, and Ian required an appointment in the evening, which occasioned several notes back and forth with the great doctor's secretary. However, that gave Ian time to read Blundell's treatise on transferring blood from one patient to another. The doctor had started as an obstetrician, perhaps not a sterling recommendation in the present case. His drive to perfect transfusion arose out of the terrible hemorrhages he had seen in childbirth, and he had since concentrated almost solely on researches in blood. The man was without doubt

on the edge of some new and fascinating discoveries. If anyone could help, he could.

Ian had struggled with how to describe his symptoms in
order to avoid being clapped up in Bedlam, chained in
dirty straw, and beaten twice a day. He must never talk
about compulsion or disappearing. Yet he had to interest
the great man in his case. He dared not talk about needing
to take human blood, did he? Yet was that not the crux of
the matter?

One by one, the patients who shared the drawing room
were called in. A frail man, supported by a servant, then a
portly gentleman with a florid face, all disappeared, not to
return. There must be another exit by which they were let
out. They had eyed him most strangely. Indeed, he had been
attracting attention everywhere he went in London. He had
only to walk into the lobby of the Clarendon Hotel and
everyone stopped what they were doing. They moved out of
his way as though he had the plague, which, in fact, he did.
But strangers could not know that, could they? There was no
trace of his change in the mirror that he could see, except
perhaps a certain vibrancy. And it was not quite fear he felt
in those around him. There seemed to be an air of awe about
them. Ian couldn't understand it. But the effect had been
growing.

Ian leaped up and paced the room when at last he was
alone, trying to calm his mind.

When finally the young secretary called him in, he found
himself bowing to an older man with an open countenance,
his grizzled hair worn long about a bald pate.

"Thank you for seeing me so late in the day," Ian began.

The doctor was dressed conservatively, his coat finely tailored but claret-colored, a shade from another age in these
days of black and dark blue coats. The room was lined from
floor to ceiling with bookshelves, bulging with leather vol-
umes, and to one side a long table was covered with glass
tubes and flasks that emitted strange odors. Ian recognized a
microscope fitted with several lenses. He had seen one at
Cambridge. Near the long windows that gave on to the

street, framed by burgundy velvet draperies, sat a huge desk. It was covered with a green blotter on which sat a book with blank pages, a pen, and an inkwell. The doctor motioned Ian to take a seat in the leather wing chair, while Blundell sat at his desk. His first cursory glance at his newest patient had turned into a rapt examination.

"It is not often that I see so fine a male specimen walk through my doors, Mr. Rufford." The doctor smiled. "You fairly glow with health. Pray, what can one of my specialty do for you?"

Ian cleared his throat. "I believe I have acquired an abnormality in my blood, sir, one for which I only hope you can prescribe a treatment."

Blundell smiled indulgently. "Now, now, young man, it is for me to make the diagnosis. What makes you think it is a disease of the blood?"

Ian was prepared for this. "I acquired it through blood from one similarly afflicted."

The doctor raised his eyebrows and nodded. He put on a pair of spectacles, picked up his quill, dipped it in the standish, and left it poised over the blank book. "Symptoms? Be detailed."

Ian swallowed once. "Extreme sensitivity to light, which is why I asked to see you in the evening. I cannot bear the sunlight."

The pen scratched. "Eyes or skin affected?"

"Both. My skin burns within moments, though it does not keep the color. I must wear blue or green spectacles of the darkest hue even to look through windows in daylight."

The pen scratched over the page. "Other symptoms?" Blundell peered over his spectacles.

Here it was. This was Ian's one chance and his biggest risk, well, almost his biggest risk. He removed a penknife from his coat pocket and pried open the blade. Then, pulling back his cuff, he slit the palm of his hand from the base of his thumb, across the pad of muscle, to his wrist in a clear, deep line that immediately welled blood.

"Mr. Rufford!" Blundell protested.

Ian held up the palm so the doctor could see it clearly. He felt the tingling along his veins that always felt so wonderful, the pricking pain in the wound as it stopped leaking blood. He knew what Blundell was seeing. The doctor's eyes went round.

When Ian thought enough time had elapsed he checked his palm: a red line only, then a white line of scar, then nothing—no evidence the cut had ever been.

Blundell scrambled from behind the desk. "Let me see. Is this some kind of a trick?"

"I wish it was, Doctor." He had the man's interest. The doctor took his hand, fingered his virgin palm. "Do you want to see it again, perhaps make the incision yourself? Feel free to use an instrument of your choosing."

The doctor peered up at him. "I shall. Take off your coat and roll up your sleeve."

The result was the same with the scalpel Blundell used, of course. As a doctor, he had no scruples about slicing flesh, and he cut a vigorous wound deep into the muscle on the inside of Ian's forearm. When the cut came together and left no trace, Blundell touched the skin in wonder. Then he turned his attention to Ian's wrist. "It seems you do scar," he observed.

"Before the infection," Ian said shortly.

"If we could harness this ability . . ." Blundell turned to his desk and pulled out several lancets, then scurried over to the glassware for some vials. "How were you infected? A wound?"

"A drop of blood on my lips which I touched with my tongue."

"Then I must have a sample of saliva as well." The doctor produced some tubing, fitted it to his lancets. The end of the tube he put into his vial. "But first the blood."

Ian rolled up his sleeve farther, baring the vein in the crook of his elbow, which he knew from experience would prove fruitful for lancing.

"What are these marks?" Blundell asked, peering at the twin scars left by Asharti's teeth directly over the vein.

Ian could not tell him about Asharti. "Old wounds."

Blundell glanced up at him. "Where were you when you were infected?"

"The desert of North Africa, northeast of Marrakech. I'm a little hazy about just where."

"This is, of course, an entirely new disease. But it might prove a valuable discovery. If we could increase the healing powers of our soldiers or sailors . . . the possibilities . . ." He pressed the lancet into the vein where Asharti had sipped so many times. "I will take sixteen or twenty ounces—a vigorous bleeding, no more." Blood flowed out the tube and into the glass vial. Blundell filled perhaps five of them. Then he asked Ian to expectorate into another vial.

"Do you have hope for a cure?" Ian asked. "I should like to be rid of this."

"How can I know before I know what happened to you?"

"A doctor in Tripoli spoke of humors of the blood, perhaps treating it with hellebore or a bark of some kind." That was before he knew all the symptoms and recommended a madhouse.

Blundell barked a short laugh. "Those are old ways. The answers lie in your blood."

"When might you have those answers?" Ian pressed as he rolled down his sleeve.

"Well, you have prevented me from sleeping tonight," Blundell said, excitement in his voice. He stoppered the little vials. "Several days, I should imagine. Call again Thursday."

Ian masked his disappointment. "Thursday it is." He strode to the door.

"Mr. Rufford . . ."

Ian turned to see the doctor peering over his glasses again. "Yes?"

"Is there anything else you would like to tell me about your condition?"

Ian hesitated. "No," he said finally and with what he hoped was firmness. "Nothing. I shall call at twilight on Thursday."

• • •

Beth came out of Drummond's into the late afternoon and stared around at the people passing in Cockspur Street without seeing them. The world succumbed to twilight. The gray permeating the city seemed to depress her breathing.

Gone. Her portion was gone, and with it all hope of independence.

Mr. Stevenson had been solicitous, but he had nevertheless been unable to meet her eyes as he told her that her father had closed out her account with a draft drawn to a bank in Cairo. He had not needed to say more. Her father had used her future security to finance his last expedition. And to think she had felt guilty about not offering it to him!

"Oh, Papa," she breathed. She could not be angry with him. It was so like him to be certain his next discovery would make all right and more. He had not done it to wound her. Indeed, as she thought about it, he could have done nothing else. It was his nature to be optimistic. And the search for treasures of the past was in his blood.

A man brushed by her, breaking her trance. She took a breath and looked around. A light rain began to fall. Her thoughts careened through the consequences of her discovery. No independent competence for her. She pushed through the shoppers on Regent Street and dreaded telling her aunt she was now an officially indigent relative. She could not trespass on her aunt's goodwill, however long that lasted. Perhaps not long.

She must look about her for a situation, if she wanted to avoid selling herself under her aunt's aegis to some elderly widower who could expect no better. But what could she do? Governess? Hardly. She spoke French well, but her Latin had the Continental accent rather than the strange English one and she had no Italian. No one wanted Arabic or ancient languages. She could draw. Had she not drawn figures of all the temples and tombs that came in their way? But what of needlework and singing and deportment? She had no skill at being a young lady, and that was what was truly valued in a governess these days. She was not fashionable enough to be a dresser or a milliner. Would anyone think that provisioning a caravan prepared one for a post as housekeeper? She might serve as a translator, or perhaps a tutor at Oxford or Cambridge. But would anyone there hire a woman? She bit her lip. Unlikely. The only thing she could be was a servant who specialized in drudgery. She knew how to work hard.

The prospect was hardly calculated to delight her. Her thoughts were dark as she turned off Piccadilly into Curzon Street. She went directly to her room to be sure of avoiding her aunt. But she could not do so forever. That evening before going out, her aunt looked in on her.

Lady Rangle was pulling on long white gloves to go with the gossamer primrose gown she wore. "I am promised to Lady Hildebrand tonight, my dear, but we shall go to the Countess Lieven's ball on Wednesday if we can procure anything decent for you to wear. I shall alert all my acquaintance tonight that I have a young person staying with me." She gave a self-satisfied, if languid, smile. "I trust you shall not find yourself wanting for occupation."

"You are too kind, Aunt."

Lady Rangle peered at her. "What is the matter, child?"

Beth looked up at her and hated the fact that tears welled in her eyes.

Lady Rangle heaved a sigh. "So, you had bad news from Drummond's, did you? I am not surprised. You might have known my reprehensible brother would have spent your portion."

Beth drew herself up. "His explorations were more important than any portion."

"The whole five thousand?"

Beth nodded dumbly.

"Well, then we shall have to get to work, won't we?" She suppressed the energy that had welled in her voice. "Lord, I am tired already." Then, looking at Beth kindly, she said, "Never fear, child. We shall bring you safely into the matrimonial harbor, even with no portion."

Beth did not say she did not want to be brought safely

into any harbor that did not include love. She did not speak
of her half-formed plans to find a position. She merely nodded as her aunt glided out of the door, wafting the scent of
lavender and trailing a fringed shawl.

The prospect of being dragged to a series of social engagements so her aunt might force her into a world to which
she could never belong daunted her. And yet . . . might she
not encounter someone with a country house far away from
London who needed a servant? It was not impossible. By
day she could put her name at placement agencies; by night
she could seek out information that gave her advance notice
of a position. At the least she might find someone who could
recommend her.

She must keep her activity secret from her aunt at all
costs. Imagine Lady Rangle's embarrassment if her niece
was known to be a servant! Nor would she be happy if, in the
unlikely event of a marriage offer, Beth refused.

How strange. She had been willing to marry Monsieur
L'Bareaux. He was older, and she did not love him. His proclivities would preclude the physical act of love. What was
so different now? Perhaps Monsieur L'Bareaux had something she valued to trade for marriage—an ability to stay in
North Africa and look for Kivala. But it was more than that.
What had changed in her that she would settle only for
love?

She shook herself. Such thoughts were fruitless. When
she had found a suitable position she would simply disappear and spare everyone the burden of her presence.

She closed the curtains around her bed that night feeling
absolutely alone. Her aunt would soon grow impatient with
an indigent relative who refused to help herself in the only
way Lady Rangle could approve. In some ways, her father
had abandoned her twice, once in death and once by spend-
ing her small portion, however well intentioned. Her
thoughts turned to Mr. Rufford, and she wondered where he
was this night, whether he had reconciled himself to feeding,
whether his experiences in the desert had so devastated him

as to make him sink into despair or depravity. His resolution to find some normal life and fight what he considered evil in himself she had found touching, even admirable. But he, too, had abandoned her. Not that she deserved more. She was an acquaintance of only a few weeks and one who knew enough of his secrets to be an uncomfortable companion. Yet in her mind's eye she saw expressive blue eyes, puckered lips, the shoulders . . . She remembered the hint of his smile when they were playing chess and the pain in his countenance when he grew afraid of what he was.

It was she who should be afraid. But she wasn't. Why was that? She hardly liked to think. No, she must not dwell on Mr. Rufford. She must not think about her father, either. They were gone. She must not even think too closely about her aunt, who would soon be lost to her as well.

But sleep would not come, and she could think of nothing else.

Beth sat holding a delicate teacup filled with punch and watched as couples twirled around the room. Slender Chippendale chairs lined a row of potted orange trees designed to screen off several corners of the giant room in Lord Winterly's town house in Grosvenor Square into smaller areas for taking refreshments. Lady Rangle sat to her immediate left, speculating with relish to the Countess Lieven about how long the old King could live and whether Prinny's debts would once again be paid by the new parliament. Beth could not be said to be enjoying herself, any more than she had enjoyed the endless series of calls all week, as her aunt introduced her to the women who could ensure her a place in society she would never claim.

Only this morning, Lady Rangle had been crowing, though always in her languid way, that Beth would be invited to whatever entertainments were to be had in London. Almack's would not begin until next month. But her aunt did not despair of them being given an invitation to several country houses, so that they might hardly call their time their own until Christmas.

The prospect chilled Beth. She could imagine nothing more deadly. She was a good rider, and she might enjoy careering over the countryside on a cold November morning very well. But the long stately dinners, the dances where she would no doubt drink punch and watch others dance just as she was doing now, or the circles of women plying their needles, the endless games of whist with indifferent players—she hardly knew how she would support it.

Behind her, Beth heard several young women chatter as they sat at one of the tiny tables. Rising over the whispering of her aunt and the Countess, she recognized the childish voice of Chlorinda Belchersand, not a child at all but a very self-assured young lady.

"I told them they must bring our ices here. We were too fagged to dance again."

"You are a harsh mistress, Miss Belchersand," another remarked. They all giggled.

"I suppose I am, but what more can men expect? If they want to dance with women of the first stare of fashion, they must do as they are bid."

"Yes," one of the others agreed, laughing. "If they don't do as they are told, they will end up dancing with that horrid brown girl Lady Rangle is trying to foist onto the *ton*."

"Have you seen her eyes? Like some kind of barbarian. They look diseased."

Beth flushed with anger and mortification. Crofts School for Girls hung in the air.

"Rangle will never bring her off. Who would have her?"

"A foreigner like that? No one, I'm sure. I haven't seen her dance all night."

"My mother invited them to a card party we are giving next week."

"Why would she do that? I can't imagine inviting them to my birthday ball." This from a Miss Campton.

"My mother and Lady Rangle were bosom bows as girls.

Rangle is received everywhere, and she is calling in her chits. We are like to trip over the Rochewell girl at every turn."

"That will soon grow tiresome."

More tiresome for me, Beth thought. The anger ebbed. It was no more than she'd expected. She thought of faking a headache and asking to go home. But how could she look like she did not appreciate her aunt's effort? It would be nothing short of ungrateful. No, until she could find a place somewhere, she must put up with all of this.

Her search had not been going well. The agency had been very short with her when she had said she could not supply a reference letter. It would humiliate her aunt to ask one of her friends. Making up a letter would suffice only until the reference was checked. She had been over all of it again and again to no avail.

She raised her cup mechanically. The punch was tasteless as paper in her mouth. An elbow in her ribs from her aunt brought her attention back from her melancholy thoughts. She found a man in his late fifties stalking toward them. He wore an old-fashioned bobbed wig and a bottle green coat that pegged him as unfashionable.

"Why, Admiral Anstey, what a delight!" her aunt breathed. "May I present my niece, Miss Elizabeth Rochewell?"

"Just what I was thinking to ask you to do, Lady Rangle. 'Go straight at 'em,' Nelson always said." He bent at the waist, emitting a distinct creak from his stays.

"Lizzy, Admiral Anstey is one of the Duke of Clarence's set."

Beth nodded. "The Duke is on the seafaring side of the royal family, I believe?"

The Admiral chuckled. "You could say that. Prinny don't like it much, though."

"I expect that is because it is quite a practical occupation," Beth agreed. "And the Regent doesn't seem the practical kind, himself."

"Oh, ho! You've the right of it there, Miss Rochewell."

He smiled on the Countess and Lady Rangle. "Though it might not be politic to say it out, just like that."

Beth smiled up at him. "What happened to 'Go straight at 'em'?"

The Admiral looked taken aback. Then he grinned. Beth realized he was wearing rouge. Why would a bluff seafaring man be wearing makeup? Because he was hanging out for a wife, of course. "Just the kind of female I like." He nodded again to the Countess and Lady Rangle. "I ain't much in the dancing line, or I would positively ask her to dance."

Beth was relieved. She couldn't imagine creaking around the floor with those stays.

"Perhaps my niece would like some refreshment," Lady Rangle suggested.

"Capital idea! I'll crowd sail over to the refreshment table and be back before you can get under way yourself." And, bowing, he turned and stalked away.

Beth let out her breath. Her aunt leaned in. "He's right. You mustn't talk about the Regent that way."

"You were just talking about him that way," Beth pointed out.

"To a bosom bow! A different thing entirely. He seemed to like you," she mused. "Rich as Croesus from taking prizes in the dreadful wars with Napoléon. He would do very nicely."

"He is near sixty, Aunt."

"One can't be choosy with your background. Don't talk about Africa or archaeology as you did with Clowe's second son. You quite put him off."

"But if I can't talk about current events, or my experience, or about anything scientific, whatever is left?" Beth whispered frantically as the Admiral set sail again across the busy room.

"The weather," her aunt declared.

The Countess nodded. "The weather is always safe."

Beth rolled her eyes. But she had no desire to embarrass her aunt.

The Admiral balanced a tiny plate of sweetmeats and a glass of ratafia as he bowed again.

She took a breath. "Fine fall weather we're having, isn't it?"

"Capital!" the Admiral said with real conviction. "Capital!"

Fourteen

Ian paced the deserted waiting room outside Blundell's office in the growing dark. Where was the damned quack? He had been to Stanbridge and found, to his shock, that all his preconceptions were wrong. Henry had not put the place to rights. On the contrary, his hopeful family had been forced to sell almost everything and let the servants go, just to hold on to the land. Henry hunted to supplement the family table. Curse his wastrel father! The debts had been much worse than anyone supposed. And Mary? Instead of the shrewish, domineering wife Ian expected, she was Henry's chief support and his redemption. The looks of love that passed between them had been . . . unnerving. They said Ian could be wrong about women, at least some women. Henry was saving to buy Mary a cow, so she could make cheese for the family, for God's sake. Ian rubbed his chin, irritated; whether with the doctor for being late or his brother for being in love, he did not know.

The one thing he did know, after seeing Stanbridge, was that he could never belong there again. His very presence was a danger to his brother and his family. Ian could not satisfy his cravings in a society so small. But it was more than that. A life composed of endless rounds of hunting, shooting, and small social engagements seemed . . . inconsequential. In Africa, Ian had thought that was what he wanted most. Now he understood that his experience in the desert and the new existence thrust upon him had shoved him beyond that simple life. The life that Stanbridge represented was lost to him. Even if Blundell could cure him, he was cut off forever from everything he had been. He could not go home again.

A parlor maid came in to light the fire, ducking her head apologetically.

Ian realized he had been glaring at her and consciously softened his expression. "Thank you, young woman," he said as she bowed herself hastily out of the room. She was as young as Miss Rochewell, though not as beautiful.

When had he realized Miss Rochewell was beautiful? In Gibraltar? Or even earlier when he saw her bent over a chessboard in swaying lamplight? How her exotic looks contrasted with her practical approach to living! He still marveled that she knew what he was and yet accepted him, had even tried to help him discover the principles governing his new nature.

Well, that was over now. She had moved on to her own life. He had been tempted to call upon her aunt. But Miss Rochewell would no doubt have decided long ago that she was well out of his acquaintance. After what he had done to her? He winced at the memory. Her acceptance, her friendship, was a result of the proximity forced on them by the voyage, the strange intimacy of those long nights of translating. It *was* friendship. A little island of friendship in what was likely to be a long and lonely existence brought on by his condition, if he could not cure it. He would treasure that friendship always.

He heaved in a breath and straightened. With any luck his condition would shortly be a thing of the past. The door to Blundell's inner sanctum opened and the doctor himself beckoned.

"Mr. Rufford . . . Will you not step this way?" He motioned to his study. As Ian brushed past him, Blundell's eyes were wary. "Please, sit."

"I shall stand to hear the verdict, Doctor. What have you found?" The harsh rasp of his voice surprised him. He thought he had better control.

Blundell pretended to study a sheaf of notes. "I hardly know how to begin."

Ian waited. The next seconds would decide his fate.

The doctor cleared his throat. "Well then. I examined your blood under my microscope."

"And . . . ?" Ian prompted. *Say it, man! Just say it out.*

"There is an . . . organism present throughout the sample, neither red blood cell nor white, and large enough to be seen plainly under the glass."

"I knew it! A disease!" A disease could be cured, couldn't it?

"Yes and no," Blundell temporized. "It seems to coexist harmoniously with your cells."

Hardly harmoniously. Ian cleared his throat. "Can it be destroyed? Some herb? A drug?"

Blundell chewed his lip. "The standard remedies—purging to release the humors, bleeding—would have no effect. It is pervasive. It subsists in the same environment that makes you healthy. Any herb or drug would affect it only along with your general physical state."

"What do you mean?"

"If I poison it, I poison you," Blundell said, his old eyes hard.

Ian nodded curtly. That was it, then. He should go. But Miss Rochewell's ancient texts came to mind. "Has anyone else come across this condition? Perhaps others . . ." It was an insult, but he had no choice but to ask.

"George Upcott's work on blood types may be related, but it hardly touches on the parasitic qualities I have seen here."

I have a parasite in my blood? It was dependent upon him. Worse, did he depend on it?

The doctor shuffled his notes, hesitating. "The saliva sample was less elusive."

"Saliva?" Ian stalked back to the desk. "I came to you for your expertise in blood."

"And it was my study of anticoagulants which was pertinent to the saliva sample." The doctor sat down abruptly. "Your saliva contains the same anticoagulant properties one finds in the saliva of a certain species of South American bats." He peered up at Ian over his spectacles. "They are called vampire bats. They get their nourishment from sucking the blood of their prey."

The room receded. *Vampire?* Was that what he was? It echoed with such force inside him he felt stunned. Who did not know the legend of the undead who suck the blood of the living? Why had he never realized that he was now one of those dread mythic creatures? Because it was too horrible to contemplate? Because he had never thought them real? Maybe one of those times he had attempted suicide he had really died. . . . He groped for the edge of the desk to steady himself. He must say something.

"What has that to do with their saliva?" he croaked to buy time for composure.

"The bat uses its saliva to keep the wounds made by its teeth open long enough to suck the victim's blood without clotting." Blundell kept his face deliberately neutral.

"My saliva could not . . ." But he remembered what Fedeyah had said of Asharti and her saliva.

"It could. As truly as there is an organism in your veins. I cannot tell all the properties of this organism, but it is early days. I may yet find the secret of its nature."

"I want to get back to the way I was," Ian almost hissed. "Find a way to kill it."

Blundell was taken aback. "I cannot remove the parasite without killing you."

Blundell could not kill him. But if he was impossible to destroy, the parasite must be equally hardy. Hope drained away. Blundell was the best the civilized world could offer. If he could not cure Ian, who could? "I understand, Doctor. Forgive me. I had such hopes."

Blundell relented. "It is early days. Science takes time." His eyes took on a glow. "I must understand how you healed so quickly. If I could isolate the positive properties . . ."

Ian hid behind a wry smile. "Then you might infect others with my disease?"

Horror infused the doctor's eyes. "Anyone who has a cut," Blundell whispered, "would be susceptible to even a drop of your blood. You must not . . . Not before we know more."

Ian held up a weary hand. So the doctor had guessed the less savory parts of his condition. "Never fear. I will keep my blood to myself." He peered at Blundell. He knew about Ian needing blood. Perhaps he would soon know the rest. Indeed, Blundell could be dangerous. "May I rely on your discretion?"

"I am a physician," Blundell muttered. "What would my practice be worth if my discretion could not be relied upon?"

Ian kept his face carefully closed. "You may find me at Albany House in Albany Court next to Burlington's great pile if you happen to find a way out of my dilemma." He spun on his heel and let himself out, leaving the doctor staring after him.

In the street, he turned at random through the night now grown chill with late November. A fine rain fell. He hunched his shoulders against it, brushing past the hurrying crowds. They split ahead of him, giving him unconscious precedence. *Vampire?* How had Miss Rochewell not called him that? Even if the ancient texts had not used that word, she must know. It was so obvious now. His soul trembled. He was the stuff of nightmares. Even now, hunger began to crawl down his veins. He could practically feel the unknown creature floating in his blood. He seethed with self-loathing. But he could not jump into the Thames or put a dueling pistol made by Joe Manton under his chin and pull the trigger. That would do no good. Even if he had actually died once, he could die no more.

He was trapped.

His steps slowed, dragged down by the wet and by despair. *Vampire.* He looked up and saw that he was in some square he did not know. Hunger tingled in him. He could resist it yet. But to what purpose? If he denied himself, it would only be more difficult to take only a little later. With despair eating at his gut, he saw two girls dressed in the height of fashion hurrying out of a carriage in front of a house with brightly lit windows.

One of the young things gasped and said, "Do go on, Clarissa; there is no sense in having both of us wet. I have left my muff in the carriage." She spun and hurried back through the darkness. The carriage had already begun to clatter away. She waved to no avail.

Ian looked around. The square was deserted, even at so early an hour. A park gleamed wetly black at the center. It was surrounded by wrought-iron palings, but they should not prove difficult for one as strong as he was. The girl sagged and turned back toward the house.

With a groan, he followed.

"There you are, Miss Rochewell. Where have you been hiding yourself?"

Beth's stomach sank. "Mr. Blakely," she greeted the pale young slip of a man who waved at her from across the main ballroom at Almack's Assembly Rooms in Kings Street. The room was bright with candlelight flickering from the giant chandeliers and sconces placed along the walls. Dancing couples swirled in the center. Around the outside, small groups formed and re-formed at tables laid out with orgeat punch and tiny insipid cakes. Beth glanced up at the Admiral. How could she bear both of them at once?

"I have written a new poem," the young man announced. "*'To Elizabeth, Whose Eyes Shine from Another World.'*" Beth noted with alarm that he held a tiny much-creased paper in his hand, which he unfolded. "Your eyes speak softly of a land beyond the seas—"

"Dear me, Mr. Blakely," she interrupted. She could hear the titters of several fashionable young women as they whispered behind their hands and glanced from the Admiral to Mr. Blakely. The Admiral himself tut-tutted disapprovingly. "I'm sure the poem deserves much more attention than we could give it in the middle of Almack's. Wouldn't you agree, Admiral?"

"Damned puppy is what I say! Poetry, of all things." The Admiral's long sideburns waggled along with his very bushy brows. He spoke loudly, since long experience of cannons on a ship of the line had made him deaf. "A girl wants a pretty compliment to be sure, lad, but no sad long bouts of poetry. Enough to make her go into a decline."

Mr. Blakely looked crestfallen. He refolded his paper carefully.

"I am not the kind to go into a decline, Admiral," Beth returned with some asperity. "And I like poetry very well. But not," she added as she saw Mr. Blakely's eyes light and his fingers begin to unfold the paper once again, "in the middle of Almack's."

"What you want is to come sailing," the Admiral declared roundly. "A good breeze just abaft the beam on my tight little yacht would set you up remarkably. Shall we say Wednesday?"

"She is promised to a reading by Mrs. Pierce-Northcott with me," Mr. Blakely returned.

"I am promised to neither of you," Beth replied. "And I am afraid, since I could not possibly choose between you, I must keep it that way." She looked imploringly between a disapproving face and a petulant one. "Neither of you happens to play chess, do you?"

"Chess?" they exclaimed in unison.

"Never mind," she sighed. She pretended to see one of the party of young women waving at her. Miss Fairfield was one of the few kind faces in the room, one Beth had met at her aunt's rout party last week. Beth had liked her at once. "Oh, there is Miss Fairfield motioning to me. You will excuse me, won't you?" She hurried over to the group of pastel flowers.

"Miss Fairfield," she whispered at that startled girl, "I throw myself upon your mercy. Do save me from the competitive attentions of the gentlemen behind me. I am about to go mad."

The other young women frowned, but Miss Fairfield glanced to Beth's suitors. "I should think you do need rescuing. Join us." She drew Beth into the circle.

Beth sighed in relief. "I feel positively persecuted."

"Poetry?"

Beth nodded. "From one and sailing terms from the other."

"Blakely was after Susan Wethersby last month."

"How did she rid herself of him?" Beth whispered.

"I believe she retired to Bath in the end." Miss Fairfield laughed at Beth's crestfallen expression. She had a very attractive laugh. "Your aunt should protect you from them."

In fact, Emma Fairfield was very attractive in general. *All the things I am not,* Beth thought. Fair skin, well-opened blue eyes, and hair the color of sovereigns. Beth was feeling decidedly unattractive in the pale pink dress her aunt had ordered. She knew very well that pink did not go with her coloring. Lady Rangle dismissed Beth's qualms about taking charity by saying that if she looked ragged, it would spoil her aunt's own reputation. But Beth could hardly think she did her aunt any credit. "My aunt has decided they are the only ones who might offer for me, so she encourages them shamelessly."

"What a strange girl you are," Chlorinda Belchersand's sandy brows drew together over a face one might say was rather pinched. "Still, if you are like to have no other offers . . ."

"You have been in town less than a month. It is early days," Miss Fairfield said.

The other two looked doubtfully at Beth.

"*My* mama has set her sights high," Jane Campton said, smoothing her unfortunate primrose half dress. Blondes with that ruddy complexion could rarely wear yellow. "Nothing but the best will do for me, Mama says."

"If she wants a Duke, only Cumberland is unattached, and he is nearly eighty." Miss Belchersand was most damping.

"It's not a title Mama wants." Miss Campton smiled slyly. "The younger Stanbridge, Rufford, is just come back to town. Have you seen him?"

Beth's heartbeat ratcheted up a notch. No one was paying her the least attention at the moment, which was excellent, since they would miss her blush.

"I heard he made his fortune in some odd foreign place." Miss Belchersand's tone was dismissive, but her eyes took on a most disconcerting glow.

"What a fortune! And the Stanbridges are ever so old a family." Miss Campton began fanning herself with the little painted ivory fan.

Miss Fairfield laughed again. "And what you are both *not* saying is that he is very pleasing in his person. What do you think of him, Miss Rochewell?"

The other girls' stares snapped to Beth, one reflecting disdain and one amazement that Miss Fairfield would even bother to ask Beth her opinion. "I . . . I have not encountered him at any parties I've attended," Beth said, her calm regained. It had the virtue of being truth.

Pitying looks were cast her way. "Well, you certainly could not miss him if you had."

"Now you can't say that his hair is fashionable." Miss Fairfield smiled. "It is much too long. And his neck cloths are only moderate in height. I thought you two always went in for fashionable fribbles like Sir Lucius Wentworth."

"One must make allowances," Miss Campton sniffed. "He has not yet been in London long. And you cannot fault the cut of his coat."

"No," said Miss Fairfield thoughtfully. "It fits most exactly. As do his riding breeches when one comes to think about it."

Miss Campton gasped at Miss Fairfield's bold language. Beth smiled. She liked the fact that Miss Fairfield said "breeches" and did not take refuge in calling them inexpressibles.

"Where did you see him?" Miss Belchersand queried sharply.

"He was going into Manton's Shooting Gallery just at sunset. He was up on that big chestnut mare." Miss Campton and Miss Belchersand scanned the crowded room across the field of dancing couples anxiously. "You cannot think to find him somewhere so insipid as Almack's!" Miss Fairfield exclaimed, amused. "He attends only the most dashing events."

"No wonder I have not encountered him." Only Miss Fairfield caught Beth's irony.

"I heard he won a fortune from old Beardsley," Miss Campton said confidentially. "Beardsley shot himself. And the Duchess of Devonshire introduced him as a special friend at her moonlight boat picnic on the Thames, though how he could have gotten cards when he is so new in town one cannot fathom."

"I heard he has a sponsor," Miss Fairfield said, lifting her brows, "or perhaps two."

"A sponsor? What do you mean?" Miss Campton tore her gaze from the doors.

"I mean Lady Mulgrave doted on him down at Oakhurst. Lady Sofingham invited him to Ashley to try his mare in the field, but he didn't hunt at all and only appeared at dinner."

"They are both married," Miss Belchersand said, dismissing two very powerful members of the *ton* at a single blow.

"You are so young sometimes, Chlorinda," Miss Fairfield remarked. They must have been at school together for Miss Fairfield to call her by her first name.

Sir Lucius Wentworth minced over from the table with the punch fountain and bowed in front of Miss Campton, who simpered as he led her to the floor.

Miss Belchersand was claimed a moment later by a grand figure in the uniform of the Seventh Hussars, but Miss Fairfield declined his friend, saying that she was still much too hot to continue dancing. She deftly rid herself of his company by pointing out an available partner.

"You quite amaze me, Miss Fairfield," Beth said as they turned to procure another glass of orgeat punch. She was absurdly grateful she had not been left alone. "You navigate the shoals of these social waters as though you were born to it."

"This will be my third season." But experience alone could not explain her proficiency.

"You must have had many offers," Beth observed.

"None tempting enough to give up my independence. My brother despairs of me."

Beth was wondering if she should ask if Miss Fairfield believed in love when her companion called out, "Oh, oh, Major!"

A handsome man with blond mustachios in a well-cut civilian coat glanced up and smiled. "Major Ware was walking home from Whitehall Lane this afternoon when my brother and I chanced upon him," Miss Fairfield murmured. "We have known him these many years. His father's hunting lodge is adjacent to our own." Major Ware's eyes rested on Miss Fairfield with an eagerness Beth could not mistake as he crossed the room and bowed over Miss Fairfield's hand. Now she would be left alone for certain.

"Major Ware, let me introduce you to Miss Elizabeth Rochewell. She is as much fixated on North Africa as you are. I think she has been quite everywhere in the Mediterranean."

"Not everywhere," Beth deprecated as he tore his gaze from Miss Fairfield and bowed punctiliously. "The Levant, Egypt, Tripoli, Marrakech . . ." She trailed off, remembering how dull people found references to places they did not know and did not care about.

"I was at El Golea with the British delegation. I am just back." His face grew serious. "I came with dispatches on the fastest sloop we could find. Marrakech has fallen."

"The Dey is deposed? Is he displaced by one of his brothers?" In Beth's long experience brothers and uncles constantly deposed one another in the complicated politics of the region.

The Major gave a nervous smile and glanced apologetically at Miss Fairfield. "I'm afraid it is worse than that." His eyes hardened. "An army follows a woman as though she were a goddess. They are sweeping across the desert, leaving destruction in their wake, and worse."

"What worse?" Miss Fairfield asked.

"That is not for a lady's ears." He managed a smile, but his eyes were troubled.

"Tell, Major. We shall not let him off so lightly, will we, Miss Fairfield?" A premonition of evil shivered down Beth's spine.

Before the Major could respond, the doors at the far side of the room opened. It was five to eleven and Almack's was about to close to newcomers. A woman entered, with several attendant satellites hovering behind her. All heads immediately turned. Conversation stopped.

She was the most beautiful woman Beth had ever seen. Her beauty did not lie in her pale, creamy skin, now faintly flushed, or her eyes, which seemed black at this distance, or her hair, which was dark yet laced with a red glow. Her figure was remarkable, and the décolleté of a dress that had been dampened showed a great deal of it. But it was the life that seemed to fairly blaze out of her that turned the room's attention. Beth had never seen a woman almost vibrate with energy. The fact that she wore deep rose satin when all other women dressed in pastels only made her burn with life the more.

"Who . . . who is that, Miss Fairfield?" Beth asked.

"The Countess of Lente," Miss Fairfield whispered, herself awed. "From Amsterdam. Took the town by storm when I was still in the schoolroom. She was not quite the thing, though all the men were at her feet, if you know what I mean. Especially an earl—what was his name? Black hair, green eyes—you know the one. Now she wanders about Europe with some fabulously wealthy French nobleman. Word has it she stays in London only to conclude some urgent business and is anxious to return to him. I thought perhaps time would dim her."

"I cannot imagine anyone being more full of life." The Countess made her way across the room to Lady Jersey and the Countess Lieven. Beth was sensible that the whole room now subtly revolved around the woman.

"Something in her has changed." Miss Fairfield paused. "There was once a sense of . . . boredom about her, as well as dissipation and a kind of recklessness."

Beth tore her eyes away. "Really? She hardly seems bored."

"No. My mother called her a dangerous woman. If anything, she looks more dangerous than ever. . . ." Miss Fairfield trailed away, then looked up with a guilty expression at the Major. "How unkind of me! I can't think what came over me to say such things."

They watched the magnetic woman greet her fellow lionesses of fashion and glance around the room. Her attention was riveted by a young woman standing just behind Beth. Suddenly the Countess of Lente had eyes for no one else. Beth's little group followed her gaze as one. The girl was nothing remarkable. Her dress was fashionable, a creamy satin whose tiny puff sleeves accentuated her plump arms. She wore a scarf twined around her neck and trailing out behind her and a pretty shawl of Norwich silk.

The Countess bore down on the girl. Beth stood fascinated, a silent witness.

"My dear, your scarf is charming," the beautiful woman said in a throaty contralto. She wore a tantalizing spicy perfume. "And so original. Whatever gave you the idea?"

The girl looked pale and fit to sink. "It was a necessity, my lady, no more."

The countess's eyes drilled into the girl. "Yes? But tell me."

The girl pulled at the scarf. "I don't know. These bites . . . I had a dream."

"So I see." The Countess straightened.

Beth, too, saw. All became clear. She blinked as the room flickered around her.

"A pleasant dream?"

The girl flushed deeply. "Yes."

"What does the man of your dreams look like?" At close range the Countess's eyes were only a deep brown and not precisely black. They locked onto the girl's gaze.

The girl swayed on her feet. She smiled a secret, inward smile. "Blue. His eyes were blue or red sometimes. His hair curled." Her hands circled vaguely at her shoulders. "Big. Strong-looking. Lips. I never saw lips like that."

Lady Lente turned without ceremony and cut through the

ballroom to the great doors. The crowd melted before her. Her entourage stared after her in astonishment.

Beth was sure that somehow this woman knew what had occurred here.

Mr. Rufford was indeed in town.

Ian folded the mortgages for Stanbridge and slipped them into the envelope. The herd of dairy cows was probably making its way up from Histon even now. He had paid enough so the cowherd didn't even blink at decking the leader out with ribbons just the blue of Mary's eyes. The furniture Henry had sold might already have arrived.

Candles flickered in his sitting room at the Albany House, quite the most stylish address for bachelors in London. He sat at a desk scattered with heavy paper, quill and standish, sealing wax, and a cut glass decanter half-filled with brandy beside his empty glass. He addressed the envelope to The Right Honorable Viscount Stanbridge. The diamonds had done some good. And he had no need of the few it would take to make Henry and Mary comfortable.

Now that he didn't care about money, it seemed to come to him effortlessly. The shipping company had sent a handsome reward for saving their cargo from pirates. He had won another fortune at cards. His mouth hardened. It was not his fault the fool committed suicide. He put a candle flame to his wax stick and dripped it onto the flap of the envelope.

He was about to snuff the candle when he saw a swirling blackness in the corner of the room. He blinked, wondering if it was an illusion brought on by fatigue. Before he could decide, the blackness resolved itself into a beautiful woman. The air fairly vibrated around her.

Ian stepped back as the woman came to herself and looked about. She was stunning-looking. Black eyes—they were black, weren't they?—deep auburn hair, fulsome figure. Her eyes snapped with energy. A delicate perfume he found only too familiar hung about her.

"She was right about the lips," the woman murmured. "And you should have cut your hair. You are quite unmistakable in the company of all these Brutus and Windswept styles."

"Who are you?" But he knew, at least in part. Miss Rochewell said that he had swirled with blackness just before he disappeared. And the scent was cinnamon and ambergris.

"Beatrix Lisse, Countess of Lente." She spoke with an accent—German perhaps? She stepped around the desk, unafraid. Her eyes bore into his. "Beatrix to those of my kind."

Fear tingled down Ian's spine. Beatrix Lisse had Asharti's glow of life. And she knew what he was. "What do you want here?" he barked.

She slipped out of her evening cape and draped it carelessly across a chair, revealing a deep rose satin dress. "Surely you know that, at least."

The only surmises he could make were based on his single other experience with a female of his new kind. He said nothing, for anything he said might further betray his ignorance, and ignorance was weakness in the face of one so obviously strong.

"You look uncomfortable. Perhaps we should sit?" She lounged into a wing chair set beside a fire that was hardly more than embers now. He loomed above her, caught himself chewing his lip, and tried to force himself to look as relaxed as she was.

"Well," she said, after a moment. "Perhaps you should tell me what you are doing here."

"Why should I do that?" he growled.

"Because only one of us is allowed to a city and London is mine again since Davinoff left, so, though I have been away, still you may not come here without my permission, which you should know." Her gaze flicked over him. "But you don't. Very well, then I shall tell you some things, and perhaps that will loosen your tongue." She stared him straight in the eyes, which made him glance away, afraid she would bend his will to hers. "So," she said. Then, "You are ignorant, which means you have been recently made and whoever made you abandoned you without telling you how to go on. They tell me you have come from North Africa. That means Asharti made you. You can't have had a good time of it with her. I know that because I have known Asharti and what she can do firsthand." Her countenance darkened in remembered anger before she mastered herself and went on. "And because I can see you expect the worst from me. How am I doing?"

Ian swallowed, trying to control the pounding of his heart. She knew everything. That was dangerous, but that also meant she had the knowledge about his condition he needed badly. How to proceed? Before he could muster any words, she spoke again.

"I thought so," she said calmly. "Your power is emerging as the Companion settles in. Yet already I feel it quite distinctly. That means you could be very strong, even for one of us. Rubius was right. You have not run mad, so you have a resilient mind." She put a finger to her full red lips. "Now we must determine the fell purpose for which Asharti sent one of her minions to London. Yet it is dangerous for her to leave you in ignorance," she mused. "Perhaps she told you just enough to accomplish whatever your mission is."

Ian's questions were banished in favor of outrage. "She did not send me here. She infected me accidentally with a drop of her blood and left me to burn in the desert sun. I crawled into El Golea on my own and came home to England to escape her."

"You lie," the woman said lightly, but power throbbed under her words. "No one survives infection without continued application of a vampire's blood to give their body immunity to the Companion. Conversion cannot be accidental where the victim lives."

"It . . . it was not her who saved me." He took a breath. "Fedeyah left me a skin of his own blood and a burnoose to cover me against the sun."

Lady Lente raised her brows, considering. "Poor Fedeyah!" she said at last. "He still follows her wherever she allows him. Why would he risk her wrath after all these centuries?"

Ian was startled at how easily she referred to extreme age. *Concentrate.* He needed this creature's goodwill. He wanted to know what perhaps only she could tell him. "Since he has not the will to escape, it might comfort him to know it was at least possible for someone."

The black eyes grew thoughtful. "It is easy to say she does not know you are here. You might have become her lover to gain the power of the Companion."

Ian could not swallow. "I never wanted what I have become."

Lady Lente tilted her head, speculating.

"I . . . I was her slave. She enjoys . . . compulsion." It was all he could admit.

"Yes. She does." The black eyes bored into his until he had to look away. "I am only too familiar with that. It is one reason she was exiled to the desert—that and the fact that she had no compunction about killing humans or making vampires. If a drop of her blood is so strong, no wonder she is bold enough to misbehave in Africa." Her eyes flickered as she thought.

A step sounded on the stair. Both Ian and the Countess went quiet. A rap on the door at five in the morning? "Rufford, I know you are awake. It's me: Ware."

Ware? Here from El Golea? He did not want the one person other than Miss Rochewell who knew something about him here in London. His position was precarious enough. He glanced at the Countess, willing her to disappear the way she had come. But she tapped her lips with one finger and slid silently instead into the bedchamber, leaving the door ajar.

"Rufford, answer, I say."

Ian opened the door. The Countess would hear all Ware's likely accusations. "Why are you here at this hour, raising the house?"

A voice yelled, "Quiet!" from across the stairwell.

"I have a message for you." Ware pushed past Ian into the candlelit room.

"From whom?" Ian shut the door and turned on his visitor.

Ware took a stiff envelope out of his breast pocket and looked at it with a fascination bordering on revulsion. "I believe her name is Asharti."

Ian felt the bottom drop out of his stomach. He could practically feel the flare of interest and threat behind the bedchamber door. But that was only a flicker compared to the dread that welled within his own breast as he stared at that letter. He thought he'd left the horror behind. Now it reached out for him, even here, in the staid respectability of Albany House in the middle of London in January 1819. He did not reach for the letter. "How does she know I am here?"

Major Ware let the hand holding the letter drop to his side. "I told her." His eyes dropped, too. "One does what she wants. If you know her, you understand."

Ian understood. He grabbed the decanter and poured a glass. Nodding toward a chair, he handed it to Ware. Then he filled his own. They might both need brandy tonight. Ware placed the envelope upon a side table, where it immediately became a vortex for all energy within reach.

They gulped brandy. "How did you meet Asharti?" Ian still said the name with difficulty.

"Marrakech fell to her hordes. Then she moved on Algiers. She came through El Golea."

Ian jerked his head around, started to speak, and thought better of it.

"I know," Ware continued. "It all happened so quickly, there has been little word of it in the capitals of Europe. One moment she had a ragtag band of Bedouins and Berbers in the desert, and the next they are storming Marrakech and . . . and performing horrible desecrations on the dead and dying." Ware tossed back more brandy and breathed in past its burn. "She killed the Dey, some say with her own hands, and his sons, uncles, brothers, too—all the males of his family. She set one of her own creatures on the throne."

"What do you mean, one of her creatures?" Ian did not want to know, yet he must.

"The ones who are like her . . . the ones who, who violate

before they kill. . . . Sometimes she orders them to let a man she selects take . . . their blood, and then . . ." He could not go on.

"Then the victims, too, suck human blood," Ian said, his voice harsh.

"There are more and more of them. They keep the troops in line and follow her like she was a goddess."

"If she is a goddess, then where she rules is hell." Ian strained to swallow.

"She killed the entire delegation in El Golea after asking each in turn where you were." Ware stared at his boots. "It was terrible."

"Except you."

The Major nodded slowly. "I was the only one who knew the name of your country seat. She spared me so I could bring this letter to you. Her army moved on to Algiers."

Ian's brows drew together. How did she know he was even alive to ask the British delegation where he was? Only Fedeyah . . . But of course! He wondered if Fedeyah threw his disobedience up to Asharti in some short-lived moment of defiance or whether he regretted his moment of compassion to Ian and sought to rectify it. Wait. . . . "Algiers?"

"The only question is whether, after Algiers, she presses on to Tripoli or skips across the Med to Rome." Ware looked up, his pale eyes horrified. "She means to have all Europe."

"Easy to say," Ian murmured, thinking quickly.

"I think she can," Ware almost whispered. "You haven't seen her Bedouins fight. Nothing seems to kill them."

Neither said anything for a moment but sipped their brandy. Did Ware know Ian was like the monsters Asharti created? He had seen the healing. Ian stared at the letter. There was no escaping it. The room seemed to shimmer as he reached for it. The heavy rag paper felt rich and oily against his fingers. There was no address on the outside. He turned it over. The seal was red wax, incised with two crossed flails like the symbol of the Pharaohs. It had been melted at the edges, opened, and resealed. Someone thought he would not notice, but his eyesight was very good these days. He broke the seal and ripped the envelope convulsively.

> *Dearest Ian,*
>
> *I have missed you terribly. You are now the only one with blood worthy of mine running in your veins. Meet me in Tripoli. My armies should be there by the time this reaches you, and you can return to Africa. You will be my consort when I am Queen of both the human and vampire world. I know where you are. Do not make me come to you.*
>
> *Asharti*

Ian's throat went dry. It all fell into place. He was the only one who had blood enriched by the power of the Old One, though he had it only once removed through her. It was Fedeyah who made her first minions, and after that they made one another. She did not allow them her blood direct. He had no illusions about the meaning of *consort*. She wanted a slave or a plaything, or she wanted him dead. Death would probably be quite creative, only slightly less horrible than being back in her power permanently. Most terrible of all, England wasn't far enough away. She could find him, bringing destruction and creating monsters as she came. And she knew about Stanbridge. Henry and Mary and the boys were in danger, too.

The world seemed to shudder. He looked around at the richly colored carpets, the flickering candles and dark woods of the sitting room. They appeared a sham, suddenly, as though they were a snakeskin that might be shed at any moment, covering desert sand and rock.

"What is it?" Ware asked. "What does she say?"

Ian glanced to the Major. The room shivered back into place. "You know very well. Did you take the letter to the Foreign Office in Whitehall? Or the Admiralty?" He watched

Ware try to dissemble and the anger drained away. "It doesn't matter. Patriots should not be despised."

"What will you do?" Ware studied his face. The letter confirmed exactly what Ian was. Ware knew Ian drank blood like Asharti's army. He thought him evil, like the bitch Queen herself. But then, why was he here? Only to obey Asharti? That was reason enough. Still . . .

"What do your betters want me to do?"

"I told them you . . . you might be able to stop her."

"Whatever made you think I would try?"

"I wasn't sure you would." Ware had eyes only for his glass. "But I thought it possible."

Ian tossed the letter on the writing desk and drained the brandy, pretending calm. "I don't know what I'll do." He shot a glance at Ware. "Can your contacts wait while I decide?"

Ware shrugged and rose. "I don't know." He looked curiously at Ian. "How long were you . . . with her?"

Ian kept his face impassive. "Until she discarded me. I won't submit to her power again."

Ware shuddered. "Of course." He picked up his hat and headed toward the door. "I am at the Hart and Hounds. I'll tell Whitehall to wait until Wednesday, that you're making plans."

He was gone. The Countess slipped back into the room. She went silently to the desk, read the letter while Ian poured himself another brandy. "So," she said at last.

"Indeed." His gut churned. If he did not go to Asharti, she would come to find him.

"She offers you a position at her side." Beatrix Lisse, Countess of Lente, still thought one who got letters from Asharti might be her minion.

"No. For her there is no relationship of equals. She offers a return to slavery, or she wants to kill me in case I pose a threat."

"And why exactly would you pose a threat?" The Countess's eyes were black metal.

Ian considered her for a moment, revulsion and fear plunging inside him for all his calm exterior. This woman knew things Ian must know. He must understand what he was and what he was up against, what tools and skills were at his disposal, if he was to have any chance to escape the fate Asharti planned for him. It might be clutching at straws, but he needed this woman. "Because I was infected with Asharti's blood *after* she got the blood of the Old One."

The Countess leaned over the desk. "You have the blood of the Old One in you?"

"Only once removed. Asharti drank a drop from his veins. She tore her lip on my teeth."

"That is why she is strong enough to best the champion Rubius sent against her," the vampire woman whispered. "Now she is making others. Her army drinks blood openly." She paced to the window, sprinkled with diamonds of raindrops against the blackness. After a moment she whirled. "If she is not stopped, there will be more vampires than humans on which to feed, to say nothing of drawing unwanted attention to our kind. It will mean war between the races. The delicate balance that sustains our society will be overturned forever."

"Then stop her," Ian snapped.

Lady Lente lifted her chin. "I am not sure we can. She killed Ivan Remstrev last month. He was second only to Rubius in strength."

"Muster your own army," Ian said, exasperated.

"Making vampires is forbidden. Rubius would never consent to spreading the Companion and later hunting down all we made to kill them before they could go mad or make others. We ourselves are strung out over the world. By the time we could gather, there might be too many of them to stop. And then, she has the blood of the Old One."

Revulsion filled Ian. If they could not stop her, Asharti would lay a swathe of destruction from Algiers, to Rome, to Paris, to London, and even to Stanbridge in order to eliminate him. He was the only other source, however diluted, of the power of the Old One.

Premonition filled Ian. As one, he and the Countess turned toward the rain-spattered window. It was almost dawn. With a start he remembered that he had a duel to fight this morning. As silly as that seemed at this point, he did not want it spread about that he had failed to appear.

She seemed about to speak and thought better of it. "I am sorry it took so long to find you tonight." She rose and took a card from her beaded reticule. "Call on me at sunset. Decisions must be made. There are things you must know. Do not fail." It was a threat, uttered in that musical contralto, but a threat nonetheless, the second against him tonight. She stepped toward the door, but she did not open it. Instead she paused. A whirling blackness overtook her that made Ian dizzy. When the shadows dissipated, she was gone.

Ian stood for a single moment, breathing hard, in the middle of the room. Then he strode down the hall and out the door to the waiting carriage. He must get to the dueling ground. The Mulgrave woman had bragged that they were lovers, false though it was, and her fool husband had challenged him in the middle of White's. Now he would be late. The sun might even have risen before the face-off could occur. Painful, but all he had to manage was a retreat to the drawn curtains of the carriage after letting himself be shot. The carriage pulled off at a brisk trot. Ian sank into the squabs, the enormity of what had happened this evening overwhelming him. Beatrix Lisse, Asharti, Major Ware, the letter, all whirled in his brain.

He was afraid of Beatrix Lisse. She was old and strong. But he was more afraid of Asharti. A sense of predestination filled him. What would Lady Lente want of him? Faustus selling his soul to the devil probably wouldn't touch it. Still, there must be some way she could help him escape Asharti, who would appear one day looking, literally, for blood. He glanced at the card.

Number 46 Berkeley Square.

Fifteen

"You refused Blakely?" Lady Rangle let her voice rise, all languor forgotten. She thrust up from the chaise longue in her boudoir and began to pace among the pale pink and lavender colors laid in swaths of fabric across windows, bed hangings, and upholstered furniture.

Beth did not relish the scene to come. "I cannot marry without love, or even respect."

"Respect!" Lady Rangle actually wrung her hands. Beth had never seen someone really do that. "I don't know whether you have looked in the mirror lately, my dear, but not all of us will have a variety of suitors from which to choose."

Beth knew she was not pretty. Still she had her pride. "He was at least four years my junior, Aunt, and he had little experience of the world. We should not have suited."

"Suited!" Lady Rangle cried. "He had a reasonable portion. He was not ill looking. He actually *offered* for you! And you refused him, after all the trouble I took to let you two be alone in Ranelagh Gardens. I can present them, but I cannot accept for you. You must do *something* on your own." She turned abruptly. "Still, if the Admiral can be brought to the mark . . ."

Beth repressed an urge to hang her head. "I shall refuse him as well, dear Aunt." She saw her aunt's eyes grow alarmingly protuberant. "Older than my father!" she said hastily. "And I hardly understand a word he says, his speech is so full of naval expressions."

"All you want to talk about is your precious North Africa, or some arcane study of something or other," her aunt accused. "For God's sake, what young lady plays *chess*?"

"I have been very careful not to talk about anything I was interested in, once I knew the effect," Beth said, her voice tight. "I have no wish to be a bore."

Lady Rangle was struck by a thought. "That nice young Major—he seemed to enjoy talking about foreign places with you last night. . . ."

"I would not hold out hope of the Major," Beth said severely, realizing that her aunt had eavesdropped on her conversations. "I believe he uses me as an excuse only to address Emma Fairfield. I expect an offer will be made, but not to me."

Lady Rangle sighed and collapsed upon an upholstered stool in front of her dressing table. "Ungrateful child!"

Beth's heart clenched. "I do not mean to be a charge upon you," she murmured. Perhaps her aunt was ready to hear that Beth was looking for a situation. After all, who else could provide her a recommendation? Beth was growing desperate. "I think I would prefer living retired in the country. If I could find a way to earn my bread, I would brush the soot of London from my shoulders in an instant."

Lady Rangle looked up, her eyes suddenly calculating. "Would you?" For the second time, Beth found herself examined like a commodity by her aunt. She saw the vague blue eyes sharpen as she rejected the possibility of governess, milliner, even lady's maid. "A companion," she said at last, "to an invalid. Though, to be sure, it would have to be a particularly snappish person who had run through several other attendants to resort to taking on someone with so little address." She nodded to herself. "I could make discreet inquiries."

Beth felt some door inside her close back emotions with a

clang, remembering Jenny's lot with Mrs. Pargutter. "I would be grateful, Aunt. The sooner I am settled, the better."

"Yes," her aunt murmured, already making mental lists as she gazed at her reflection in the mirror and pulled one indolent curl back into place. "Yes . . . I know just where to start."

Beth slid from the room.

Number 46 Berkeley Square was an exquisite example of a stepped-back town house built in slate-colored Portland stone in the last century, its tall arched windows lined in white, its doors painted a rebellious but elegant blue. Ian spent an hour in the morning recovering from the bullet wound in his shoulder. He had not allowed an examination by the doctor but ducked into his carriage, squinting in the painful sun. It would never do to let the gossiping physician let on that he'd been badly wounded. Mulgrave had been quite put out that he deloped. Perhaps now he would ask his stupid wife for the truth about the whole affair.

The servant answering the door at number 46 said the Countess of Lente was expecting him. Ian stepped into one of the loveliest drawing rooms he had seen. Shades of blue and taupe traveled from thick carpet to striped and flowered upholstery and through the draperies on the windows that looked into the street and the park beyond. A heavy rococo sideboard seemed born to accompany a tiny inlaid gaming table. Who would have thought to place them in the same room? Each balanced the other. A painting whose small gold plate said it was painted by J. M. W. Turner attracted his attention. A beautifully rendered cloudscape of a coming storm, all light and threatening air, loomed over a bucolic harvest scene still sunlit. It seemed prophetic somehow.

He stared at it, his thoughts whirling darkly in North Africa around the horror he thought he'd left behind. He had considered all through a sleepless day bolting from London to some backwater like America. But that would leave Henry and his family, Miss Rochewell, and all of England as fair game for Asharti. He told himself he did not care. In any case, he could not go without knowing more about what he was, what made Asharti different now that she had the Old One's blood, and what it might mean that he had an infinitesimal portion of that blood.

Ian felt his hostess's presence behind him. He turned to find her contemplating him with piercing eyes. He had felt that kind of evaluation before in a slave market. She wore a gown of deep peach silk that echoed the auburn in her hair and made her eyes look black indeed. "So, you came. Excellent choice. We have much to do." She pulled the bell rope. "Simington, bring the gentleman some brandy. Champagne for me. And cakes or some such."

The servant disappeared with a brief bow.

"I have come for knowledge, Lady Lente."

She draped herself on a chaise upholstered in taupe and cream stripes. "Have I not asked you to call me Beatrix?"

"I know nothing about you. Our connection hardly warrants familiarity."

"And you will not know anything about me. But Beatrix is the name my kind have called me for seven hundred years. Surely you, newly made though you are, can do no less."

He did not answer. He did not relish being admitted to "her kind's" inner circle.

The servant brought a tray with two cut glasses, a decanter, and a plate upon it. Ian waved away the nuts and *petit fours*, but as the servant retired the Countess poured him a brandy. "You will need this."

He did not doubt it. The first fiery gulp was most welcome.

"You are right," she observed. "You must be given information. We will start with questions and progress to practicum. I shall evaluate."

At least she was honest about the evaluation part. "First I would know what you will demand in return," Ian said stiffly. He had experience of demands by women such as this one.

She raised her brows at his temerity, then set her lips. "I will demand nothing if I do not find you capable. What I would ask I could not compel. So, you will choose."

Ian reddened. This woman knew Asharti. She knew compulsion. She might know what Asharti had done to him. Regardless of what she said, she might want to do the same.

"I shall determine your ability in the course of our studies. Sit." She pointed. "And ask."

He had been thinking all the hours of a sleepless day about what he must know. So he pushed down his rebellion and sat. "First, what is the Companion?"

"A parasite," she said simply. "A symbiotic partner, if you will, that shares our blood. It is not a disease, you know, but a new level of existence. If it gets into your veins you must acquire immunity from a vampire's blood to survive. But once you live, your Companion-partner shares power with you that mere humans cannot imagine." His face must have shown his repugnance. "You *are* still human, but now you are more, two beings in one."

"What can the power do?" He leaned forward, elbows on knees, hanging on her words.

"Our Companion rebuilds its host, for convenience' sake, indefinitely. That gives us what can be, for practical purposes, immortality."

He could not speak for some moments as that word rattled around in his head. *Immortality?* He had known Asharti and Fedeyah had lived for centuries, but . . . immortality? At last he cleared his throat and continued, because he could not think about that word. "You mentioned killing vampire minions, last night. How?" How he had wanted to know this!

"The damage must be too great for the Companion to repair. A completely severed head—separated, mind you, so it cannot connect—is effective. The heart carved out and removed entirely can work, though rarely. The Companion reconstructs quickly, including severed limbs and missing organs. We cannot bleed to death. We cannot be poisoned, or contract a disease the Companion cannot cure. We can kill each other if one is clearly stronger, though it is quite a brutal affair, but suicide is nearly impossible."

"I know."

"So it was truly not a welcome gift. How many times did you try?" she asked, curious.

He glanced away. He was not proud of his cowardice. Or perhaps he was just ashamed of failure. "Three, I suppose. I hanged myself and healed a broken neck. I went naked into the sun, but apparently that doesn't kill you. The burns healed. Then I fought a battle against such uneven odds that my wounds should have killed me. An indirect method but usually effective."

"You must have managed to last in the sun until you passed out from the pain."

He nodded.

"New ones always think the sun will kill them," she sighed. "Most don't have the courage to test the theory."

"What about the strength?" Ian swallowed.

"As I said, the Companion confers power; physical power, mental power. Thus our strength, and our ability to compel. You have felt compulsion, I think."

"I have used compulsion, too, to feed," he said, as evenly as he could.

"I would hope so. Do you induce them to forget what happened?"

"Yes." He did not admit he gave them joyful, affirming memories instead.

"Good. You did well. We can plant impressions, or induce a person to act in a certain way. We cannot read thoughts, however."

"I am familiar with those rules." His voice was almost under his command.

"Ahhh. From Asharti. But what else do you want to know?"

"Is there any way around needing . . . blood?" He held his breath.

She shook her head. "That is the hardest to accept when you are not born to the Companion. No, our partner needs human blood to live. When it hungers, you cannot resist."

"*I* cannot." He looked down and saw that his hands were clasped until his knuckles were white. "I try . . . I try to take only . . . enough. . . ." He faltered.

"None can resist. The trick is to feed frequently," she re-marked, "and to spread your feeding among many. I sip only from strong young men. I happen to like strong young men, and the current fashion for cravats hides all. But we all have our proclivities."

"Such a violation!" The words were torn from him. "We . . . we're evil."

"Come, Rufford. That is not what you have told yourself, is it?"

Ian laughed a wretched, painful laugh that bordered on hysteria. "Oh no. I have compared myself to a banker who lives on interest. Self-delusion! It's all a damned lie!"

"Is it?" she asked, almost gently. "Is the lion evil when it feeds on the gazelle? And we need not even kill. Taking blood is the nature of things. It is our nature."

"Asharti . . ." he choked, and then could not continue. He could not speak of Asharti's depravity to one he did not even know.

Beatrix Lisse did an unthinkable thing in a drawing room in Regency England. She came to sit beside him and em-braced his shoulders with one arm while she put her hand over his clasped hands. He tightened against her pity. "Every race has its evil ones," she whispered. "Must we all be judged by the worst of us?"

He turned an anguished gaze on her. She did not recoil. A tiny smile she meant to be encouraging played over her lips before she grew serious. "You think Asharti's cruelty is our destiny. There *are* those of us so bored with living, so inured to cupidity and violence, that we have lost touch with emo-tion. I was once nearly one of them. But it does not have to be. I came back from the brink. And we all use compulsion, but not like Asharti. She is sick, not you. Have you not felt the joy of your strength sing in your veins?"

"Oh, that I have," he said, his throat full. "I am sure she feels the same."

"It is not a sin to take joy in what you are. Each must ac-cept our own darkness, human and vampire alike, in order to be whole. But you, you must accept that you can be good, too. You are not a monster." Her voice was a soothing whisper. She straightened. "Now, ask again."

Ian's head hung between his shoulders. He could not master his voice enough to speak.

"You should be asking about the legends," she said for him. "You must know them. They are used to frighten children everywhere. But they are not all true. We have never been dead. We are not burned by symbols of religion, only by the sun, and that we can learn to tolerate with time, a little. We are not repelled by garlic *per se*, though I certainly draw the line at sipping from any peasant who has garlic breath. Humans sense the energy of the Companion, which is why we seem so vital to them. Those vibrations are, by the way, how I knew you when I saw you, along with the scent of course. We don't turn into bats. That was a myth invented to explain translocation by drawing the darkness."

Ian raised his head, recognition in his eyes.

The Countess lifted her brows. "Did Asharti draw the darkness?"

He shook his head. "No. Never that I saw. I saw you do it. And . . . I did it once."

"Did you?" she asked, curiosity piqued. "How did you know . . . ?"

"A . . . friend was reading an old scroll. It seemed to talk of us. It said. . . . it said that when our blood sang, we could disappear. I tried letting my blood sing on a ship out of Tripoli."

"Dear me! This is interesting on several fronts. You called on the Companion without coaching. A ship, you say? Dangerous."

"I had no idea what I was doing. I nearly drowned."

"No, you wouldn't have drowned. What happens is that the power concentrates in a vortex so intense even light cannot escape. Reflections in mirrors disappear. In the end the energy becomes so dense it forces us out of the space our body occupies. With practice, we can control where we reappear with fair accuracy. Quite a handy skill, really."

"I am sure it is," Ian said bitterly. Then he raised his head. "So we are invincible, except if we are decapitated?"

"Not entirely. There is one way to subdue the Companion. . . ." She paused and put a finger to her lips as she stared at him. "But I think I will not tell you that. Best to keep a secret or two."

Ian shrugged, but inside he shuddered. "Caution? But I cannot harm one such as you."

She examined him thoughtfully. "And what of this scroll? Where is it?"

"My friend has it."

Her brows drew together. "That is the other interesting front. This . . . friend seems to know a lot about you."

Ian felt a thrill of fear around his spine. Had he betrayed Miss Rochewell? To what lengths would this woman go to preserve her secrets? "Only I recognized what she had found."

"It is really so hard to lie to one as old as I," the Countess remarked. "Did she run screaming from the room when she realized what you were? Did she faint? They do, you know."

"She did neither, my lady," Ian said, stung into defense of Miss Rochewell's courage.

Lady Lente shrugged. "Perhaps she is stupid."

Ian gritted his teeth. If he could not lie, then he would tell the truth and defend Miss Rochewell with his life if need be. "She knew. She saw my strength when we were attacked by pirates. Afterward she saw the healing when she tended to me. I . . . I even fed from her, wretch that I am. In the end, she knew nearly everything. And she did *not* run screaming from the room. Even now I can hardly credit it."

"Well. I see." She peered at him. "And is she in London?"

"You will not harm her or compel her. She is no threat to you."

"You presume to order me about? It is too dangerous for humans to know what we are." Beatrix Lisse sipped her wine, insouciant. "I must protect our kind."

"You will *not* harm her." In two strides he stood over the redheaded woman.

"You are a fledgling," she sneered. "Do not presume to set yourself against me."

Somewhere along his veins he felt the power of his Companion thrill, growing with the anger that suffused him. This woman must be shown that she dare not harm a hair on Miss Rochewell's head. *Companion!* he thought, as he had on the ship. Power surged up instantly. It burned along his limbs, its flames leaping into a glowing ball in his heart. Life! He was alive!

Beatrix Lisse stood, her eyes going red. "Stand down," she whispered.

Ian saw her darken at the edges as she, too, drew her power. Let her. She was most likely stronger than he was. He did not care. *Come to me, Companion! Together we are more than one.* He could give her something to make her think twice. He could feel her trying to use compulsion on him. The anger ratcheted up a notch. He would never allow a woman to rule him again! The power coiled in his belly, ready to burst forth. He craved the power he called, rejoiced in it.

"Look at me," the vampire woman hissed. And he did. Not because she commanded but because he knew he must if he would prove his strength.

Silently she poured her will over him. It cascaded in a torrent that left him breathless with the power of her age. He stood, trembling with fury before her, willing his own new power out through his eyes. A symphony in his veins came to some crashing crescendo.

Abruptly the light in her eyes died. She gasped and clasped her white throat. "Oh, dear me, but you are strong," she laughed, falling into the wing chair.

Ian stood there, startled. The power shushed back down along his veins. He reached out blindly to clutch the back of the other wing chair as the song of the Companion ebbed and left him weak in his knees and trembling. "What . . . what are you about?"

"I wanted to test you. Sit down before you fall down, Rufford." The bubbling laughter faded only slowly.

"Test me?" Anger began to boil again. "You will not hurt her."

"No, no, I will not hurt her. One can't leave corpses littering the landscape. That would draw attention to us far faster than your little friend could. If necessary I will just erase her memory." She was laughing at him again.

He was not sure he wanted Miss Rochewell's memory of him erased, but he couldn't take time to examine that feeling just now. "What did you mean, you were testing me?"

"I had to make you angry enough to really set yourself against me. Your little friend gave me a perfect avenue." She looked up at him wryly. "Are you going to sit?"

Ian sat stiffly. "Why? Why did you do it?"

Lady Lente grew serious. "You *are* strong. Perhaps the strongest I have ever seen. For one so new it is astounding. I had to use all the power I had just to stand against you." She looked at him speculatively. "Rubius thought it might be so. Which is why he asked me to return to London. Your strength makes you important."

"You haven't answered." He asked again, growling the question, "Why?"

"You can be so boring, Rufford." She sat forward. "You know why. There is something which must be done. You may be able to do it."

"I am doing nothing but going to White's for some deep play," he said, still angry. He would indulge no more of her games. He rose and stood over her.

"You must find Asharti." Her contralto voice throbbed with emotion, not compulsion. "You must kill her. We should have done it years ago."

"I could not kill her. And I will not put myself in her power again. I'll go to America."

"She will find you. She has guessed you may be a threat to her."

"Then after America, China and after China, India."

"A life on the run? And it is a very long life. She has eternity to find you, you know."

Ian sagged as the truth of her statement penetrated his anger.

The Countess turned deadly serious. "I said you would

have a choice and you will. Normally we would kill a made vampire like you without thinking. But Asharti cannot be allowed to start a cult of new vampires. She cannot bring down governments so blatantly. Rubius needs you. We need you. And when it comes to the sticking point, you will choose to help us." She examined him. "There is something more important at stake for you even than her threat to your life."

"What are you talking about?"

Her eyes were hard. She was about to tell him something he would not like. "Your soul is not your own. Your experience at her hands has scarred you. I have seen her wound that way before." Her eyes flicked over some painful memory before she turned her face up to him again. "She may have dealt a killing blow to all you were, all you are capable of being. You must get over Asharti, somehow. You cannot run from her, because you will take her with you."

Ian breathed out slowly. He could not answer. He stared in accusation.

The Countess met his eyes. "Only one with the blood of the Old One in his veins has a chance against her. *You* must stop her. For your new kind. For the world. For yourself."

"I am no match for her. I have a drop of her blood after she had a drop of his blood. Who knows how much she has taken since I saw her take it from his finger?"

"You saw the Old One yourself?" The woman's delicate brows drew together.

"I saw him." Ian remembered the cold, dead air of the temple, the otherness that had sat there in the dark. "She called him He Who Waits."

Lady Lente looked stunned. "None of us has seen him. For us, he is only a legend."

"So, tell me the legend."

She gathered herself. "There was a race from. . . . somewhere else, so long ago that only Rubius remembered them living among humans. Normally, they dwelt in the lands around the Fertile Crescent. Our people were hunters dressed in skins and gatherers of grain and berries in the high valleys of the Carpathians north of the strangers and their monuments. But One among them came north. The Companion in his blood infected a fountain; no one knows how. We call it the Source. The legend has it that he wanted to make humankind over in his own image. He did, at least in part. At first all who drank there died. But one or two survived. We discovered that blood from the survivors could save others. That was how our race was born."

"Immunity," Ian muttered. "And what of the Ancient Ones?" Ian felt he was listening to a story told around a campfire with beasts roaring behind him and sparks flying into the darkness.

"They left," she said simply. "The One who infected our fountain remained behind; either as punishment for his hubris or because he missed his time of going. No one knows which."

"So he waits."

She nodded. "He waits for their return." They thought about how long he had waited.

Ian came to himself. "But I still do have a choice?"

"Yes." The dark eyes looked at him calmly.

"Well then, you'd better send to this Rubius and tell him to deal with Asharti, because I am not up to the task. My only choice, even if it is a bad one, is to keep one step ahead of her. If he wants to kill me for refusing, let him."

The Countess pursed her lips and lifted her chin, then sighed. "Very well. In the meantime, we will take care of loose ends in preparation for your journey to America."

Ian glared at her. Had she given up on getting him to go after Asharti so easily? And there was another thing. "I do not care to have Miss Rochewell's memory tampered with."

Her eyes narrowed. She almost spoke. Finally she said, "I reserve judgment until I have seen her. From your reaction I surmise she is in London. Who else knows about you?"

"No one," Ian said emphatically. Then he was struck by a thought. Blundell!

"What? You cannot hide from me." She must have seen his mulish look, for she said, "I will hurt no one. Can you not accept that? But we cannot have everyone knowing what we are."

"I went to a doctor, looking for a cure. A specialist in blood."

"Does he have a sample?" she asked sharply.

Ian nodded.

"Well, then that shall be our first exercise in translocation. We will retrieve this sample, and induce the good doctor to forget about you." She stood and looked down at him. "You fear me, even despise me. But I am your kin. You can learn to find joy in your condition, even as I do. But to be at peace you must get beyond your time with Asharti."

She held out her hand. "Come. I will teach you to control the darkness. It is unlikely he can discover our true nature by studying the Companion under one of those modern devices—what are they called? Microscopes? But we can take no chances."

She beckoned. Ian stood. There was so much to learn from this woman. He would deal with the consequences at some later date. And he would prevent her from violating Miss Rochewell's memory, by some means. For now, she took his hand in hers. She smiled, and the glow of strength from within her was almost blinding.

Ian stripped off his waistcoat and tugged his shirt over his head in his rooms at Albany House as dawn began to light the sky. He rubbed the stubble on his chin as though that could banish the confused feelings in his breast. He had seen wonders tonight—the wonders of what he was and some glimpse of what he could become. Beatrix Lisse had taught him, in that accent he had decided was Dutch laid over some other accent, even older, how to direct the power of his Companion. He had felt it cycle up until he could hardly think and he blinked out of space and time to reappear in Blundell's study. Materializing in the midst of all that glass in the dark when one was trying to keep the household from awaking—such a risk! They had taken Ian's blood sample back and the Countess—Beatrix, as she insisted he call her—compelled the doctor's mind into a pleasing blank when it came to vampires.

The shudder that coursed through Ian now had nothing to do with the adventure, nor with the draft against his bare chest from the window he threw open. He breathed in the predawn foggy air to clean his lungs. He had reveled in his power tonight. He had fed with Beatrix and she had not tried to compel him. Beatrix! He was still afraid of her. But she was of his kind.

His mind came again to what she had said about Asharti: *"You cannot run from her, because you will take her with you."* Beatrix was right on two levels. She had posted a letter to Rubius. The leader of his new kind lived in some monastery in the craggy Transylvanian Mountains. Beatrix said he would gather the others. But if Beatrix was right and they could not stop her, Asharti would hunt him across the world. Why would she not? She intended to conquer it anyway. He would leave a trail of grisly death and servitude to Asharti behind him in his travels. And his leaving would not protect Henry's family or Miss Rochewell. Could he abandon them to the fate that tortured him?

But Beatrix was right on a spiritual level, too. The shame and the self-loathing that constantly washed over him were rooted at least in part in the time he had been Asharti's slave. Flashes of degradation from his months in the desert raced through his mind until he was breathing fast and shallowly. She would haunt his soul as well.

He leaned out into the dark of a London night, sweat beading his forehead. A crier told the hour somewhere. Lamps burned in Albany Court, haloed with mist. A late carriage clattered on the stones of Piccadilly past the entrance to the Court. God, but he just wanted to be what he was before this whole nightmare had begun!

But he couldn't. He stood and shut the window. He could not cure his new condition. He could not outrun it. Damn her! A flare of anger burned in his breast. Asharti was going to destroy, not just him and all hope he had of a meaningful

life, but everything, for everyone. Beatrix may have given
him a choice, but Asharti had not, bitch goddess that she was.

He had to face her.

He was not enough. But who else was there? He would
need more strength if there was to be any hope at all of winning against her. He knew where to get that strength; from
blood—the blood of the Old One. It was his only hope.
Then, when he was stronger, he would accept Asharti's invitation to meet her in Tripoli.

Though he had been to Kivala in person, he did not know
its location. But he knew someone who could help him find
it, someone who could read the tablature that told how to
gain entrance to the inner sanctum of the Old One. His mind
raced. His heart thumped against his ribs as the plans
slipped into place. It was not fair to ask her. She would be
shackled to a monster. What could he give her in return? She
had mourned for Africa on the ship. Perhaps he could give
her something she loved and escape from a life she *must* find
as empty as he found his. He would endanger her by taking
her to that temple. Was she not already in danger? It was too
horrible, too perfect, that it was she who held the key. But
there was no choice.

It was time to strike a bargain.

Beth and Miss Fairfield sat with Major Ware at Lady Jersey's evening of cards and dancing. In the lull of a musicians' break, the swirl of conversation, laughter, the clink of
glasses, all receded. Beth pressed the Major to return to the
subject he had raised the other night.

"I understand the fall of Morocco is serious for British
interests in the region." She noticed that Emma Fairfield
took her attention from the Major's handsome, very English
face with some difficulty. "But we mere mortals are interested in more thrilling fare. When did these killings start?
Do they continue even now?" What she wanted to know was
whether Ian Rufford was responsible for the killings. If so,
they would have ended with his departure.

The Major glanced between the ladies. "You will find the details distasteful, I'm afraid."

"You underestimate us, Major. Doesn't he, Miss Fairfield?"

"Of course he does. Men always underestimate us."

Beth knew she could count on Miss Fairfield.

The Major sighed. "Well, the leader of the cult is a woman."

Beth felt a shudder of anticipation. "Her name?"

"She is called Asharti."

Beth kept her face still and hoped that her shock did not shine from her eyes. Asharti!

"The nomadic tribes serve her with a zeal they never showed for their own leaders," Ware continued. "It is said she can be in two places at once, that she has a black nimbus of pure energy around her and she cannot be killed. That is what they say, at any rate."

Mr. Rufford's persecutor was real, and only Beth knew that all those rumors were most dreadfully true. The independent confirmation of Asharti's existence made the pain she had seen in Rufford's eyes take on a new resonance. "So, the drained bodies, they are hers?"

"Hers and her followers'. Who knows how many there are now?" Rufford was not to blame for those at any rate. Beth peered at the Major. He was hiding something. His eyes contained a pale echo of the pain she had seen in Rufford's eyes. Had he met Asharti?

Miss Fairfield chuckled. "The power of a pretty face."

"Perhaps. But I have seen things in Africa . . ." Major Ware's attention drifted, remembering something horrible, something that struck him to his soul.

The quartet in the back of Lady Jersey's long ballroom struck up a waltz. Mr. Blakely, whose offer of marriage she had refused two days ago, came up and pointedly claimed the hand of a reluctant Miss Campton to Beth's left. The major's light blue, protuberant eyes shifted to Miss Fairfield, almost unconsciously, as though she were a counterweight to the thoughts that circled so like vultures behind his eyes. He set down his delicate china cup on a side table. "Miss Fairfield," he bowed formally, "may I ask you for this dance?"

Emma Fairfield blushed, cast down her eyes, and stood. Somewhere Beth was conscious that the attention of the room had turned to the doors. She watched Miss Campton and Miss Fairfield place their hands on their partners' arms and circle into the dance. She realized she was standing alone and looked around for some acquaintance. Miss Belchersand turned a deliberate shoulder to talk to a young man. Beth felt the prickle of a blush creep up her throat.

Slowly her gaze rose as if commanded, though she wanted to conceal her embarrassment with downcast eyes. There, across the room, stood Ian Rufford, bowing to his hostess. He was dressed in a perfectly cut black coat, the evening breeches demanded by Lady Jersey clinging to his muscled thighs. His snowy cravat was impeccably tied, his softly curling hair confined imperfectly in a ribbon. His cuffs were tailored a shade too long to conceal his scars. Beth felt a stab of something she could not name shudder down her spine. To see him after nearly two months . . . she had almost forgotten how magnetic he was.

As he rose from kissing his hostess's hand, he turned. His blue eyes searched the room and caught hers. She meant to look away, but she was trapped, staring into those familiar blue eyes. The pain she was accustomed to seeing there was shielded somehow—not gone but set behind a hard glass wall. He seemed . . . resolute. He straightened, murmured something to Lady Jersey, bowed his excuses to the woman on his right—the wonderful redheaded woman who had recognized the marks of his feeding the other night. He made his way through the crowd straight toward Beth. The throng melted in front of him. He looked so alive he fairly glowed. Mothers whispered in their daughters' ears; daughters curtsied as he passed. He did not notice. One bold mama accosted him. He nodded briefly and then bore down on Beth again.

"Miss Rochewell," he said, standing awkwardly in front of her, if any man so handsome could ever be called awkward. He nodded. She made her bow in confusion.

"Mr. Rufford. I . . . I hope you are well." She could feel the eyes of the room upon them.

He cleared his throat and looked around as if he were on some foreign terrain. "Would you . . . would you do me the honor of dancing with me?"

She shot him an astonished look. "Dance?"

He raised his brows and smiled, shrugging. "It is the custom in England. Do you waltz?"

She felt the blush rise farther. "Yes." Her aunt had considered the waltz indispensable.

He held out his hand. She placed her brown fingers over his pale ones. He led her to the edge of the whirling sea of couples. Swallowing, she placed her left hand on his shoulder. He encircled her waist with his arm. She seemed to watch herself place her right hand in his outstretched one. The touch of his bare palm shivered up her arm. She was very glad she had eschewed gloves this evening. They stood, poised on the brink of the music. Then he stepped out, flowing away on the strings, and she floated with him, conscious of his hand on her waist, her palm in his, the bulk of muscle in his shoulder under her hand. Her brain was suddenly overloaded, and only her senses remained. They whirled in circles, drifting past other couples as though they were standing still. No one blocked their flow as the music carried them through the crowd. Beth found she was breathing hard, not from exertion but from exhilaration.

"You give me much credit with the world by dancing with me," she said in her blunt fashion, so that she would not have to say anything important. "Was it your purpose to be kind?"

"I . . . I wanted to see an old acquaintance."

She could practically feel the rumble of his voice in his chest. She was closer to him than she had been since the night of the pirates, before the battle, when he had brushed her lips with his, and after, when she had bandaged his naked body. She could not think of that now.

"How do you go on, Mr. Rufford?" she managed, looking up into blue eyes.

"Better, thank you. And you? Your . . . your aunt is well?"

"Yes, quite well," she answered the easier of the two questions. She did not say she had no money and was about to be put out of her aunt's house, or that she was afraid of being locked up until she ran mad with some irritable old lady on a remote estate.

"Good." He cleared his throat. "That is good. And . . . and how do you find England?"

Oh, this was asking too much of her! She had done her share of banal civilities, even if she had not yet gotten to the weather. "Stifling." She glanced up again, this time defiant.

The rigid muscles in his shoulders relaxed under her hand. "I expect so," he said. "I am finding it moderately difficult myself."

"Have you found your cure?" she ventured.

"No." His voice was bleak, contained. "But I have found one who can help me."

They whirled past the Countess of Lente. All thunked into place with a dreadful finality. Both Rufford and the redhead glowed with vitality. With a start, Beth realized that the Countess's perfume was cinnamon, a feminine version of Ian's seductive scent. The Countess had recognized the signs of his feeding, too. Beth jerked back to Rufford's face and saw him grow uncomfortable under her gaze. Of course! He had found another like himself. She drew a long breath and ventured a smile she knew would be weak. "Ah. I am glad." He had found his society, his destiny. She wished she could say the same.

The music ended. "I wish you the best," she murmured as he led her from the floor.

"And I, you." He returned her to her chair. "May . . . may I have leave to call upon you?"

Beth blinked at him in astonishment. "Uh . . . yes. Yes, certainly."

Major Ware returned with Miss Fairfield. Beth woke to her responsibility. "Mr. Rufford—may I present Miss Fairfield and Major Ware?" She saw at a glance that Rufford and Ware knew each other and that there existed some constraint between them.

"Rufford." Major Ware frowned, holding himself in check. "We meet again."

"Major."

Beth looked from one to the other. Rufford was deprecating. The Major showed a kind of reserve bordering on fear. Of course! Ware had been in North Africa. He knew about Asharti, Rufford's nemesis. It was clear. The Major knew about Mr. Rufford. She was sure of it.

Rufford cleared his throat. "I am indebted to your kindness, sir."

"A fellow Briton . . . it was nothing." Ware made a dismissive motion with his hand.

Rufford looked down at Beth. "Major Ware took me in when I was ill in El Golea."

"Bit under the weather. Soon put to rights." Major Ware cleared his throat. Beth noticed that Miss Fairfield blushed as she thought about Major Ware's kindness. And Major Ware did not believe that Rufford had been "put to rights." "Are we on for Wednesday?"

"By all means. I assume you mean to make a party of it?"

"A few Whitehall acquaintances. Shall we say tennish, at Brooks'? You are a member, I believe."

Rufford growled assent. Behind him the magnetic Countess of Lente glided up.

"Rufford, you desert me. I am disconsolate. Look, the musicians strike up again."

Rufford bowed to the party. "I am called. Pray excuse me."

Beth watched him lead his equal into the dance. The light of the candles in the chandeliers blinded her. Realization washed over her like cold water. When had she fallen in love with him? Poring over scrolls that spoke of mysteries? Touching his naked, wounded body? Playing chess? Or was it the first time she had seen the pain and self-awareness in his eyes?

"Well, your credit is raised," Miss Fairfield remarked. "See all the jealous looks? The very eligible Mr. Rufford ignores everyone to the point of rudeness to ask you to dance. . . ."

Beth could not concentrate on her friend's words. She loved him and he was lost to her. She was not like him or

Lady Lente. Not that she had ever had a chance to win his favor. She watched the Countess throw back her head and laugh, beautiful and intensely alive. Who could love someone like plain Beth Rochewell when creatures such as Beatrix Lisse, Countess of Lente, existed? "Excuse me," she said, her voice thick. "I believe I have the headache."

"Shall I call your carriage?" Major Ware asked, solicitous.

"I shall just find my aunt, thank you." Blinded by her filling eyes, she stumbled away.

Sixteen

Ian absently lifted Beatrix's evening cloak from her shoulders in the foyer of the house at number 46 Berkeley Square. He pushed down the currents swirling in his breast.

Tomorrow he would propose the unthinkable. But just seeing Miss Rochewell tonight shook him. Her knowledge of his secrets had been disconcerting. What he had accepted on a ship in midocean seemed absurd in the middle of Lady Jersey's great hall. Did it seem that way to her as well? Was she sorry she knew so much about so vile a monster? Still, she had danced with him. The feel of her waist beneath the horrid lavender muslin she was wearing still seemed to burn his palm. He could still feel her small fingers in his other hand. Why could he think of nothing else? Was he afraid of her? She could further his plans or refuse to fall in with them. That was it. She would not reveal him. On the contrary, it was the fact that she would keep his secret to her grave that made her dangerous.

"Lord, Rufford," Beatrix was saying as she undid the buttons of her long white gloves. "You are the catch of the town. You could have your pick of any female in the room tonight." She looked sideways at him, under her lashes, as they strolled into the drawing room. "I was surprised you favored that little brown girl with your notice." She lounged over to the decanters on the sideboard, left for them by the servants, long retired. "Do you know her?"

"I met her aboard ship on my way to England."

"Brandy?"

"Yes."

"So. She is the 'friend' who read the ancient scrolls and helped you draw the darkness."

"Yes." He took the cut glass filled with a double dose of brandy and met her eyes, defiant. He saw a small smile play across her fulsome mouth.

"Interesting. She knows about you, yet she showed no distaste. On the contrary." She raised her glass to her lips, waiting for him to speak, but he turned and gazed out into the night through her tall drawing room windows. "Well, we have covered your traces with the doctor," she continued. "I can take care of the Major. Whitehall is a different matter. You may well be arrested as a traitor if you refuse to go in league with them against Asharti. Of course, no prison can hold you, but it will make England impossible. Not that you care, of course. When will you start for America?"

He did not answer her question. "What will you do?" he asked, without turning. She had not named Miss Rochewell as one of his "traces," but he knew one as old and wily as Beatrix would not have forgotten.

She seemed not to notice that he had not answered her question. "Harder to say. I would like nothing better than to return to Amsterdam." She sounded wistful. "But I must do what I can about Asharti first. I will to Rome. Ulberno is there. Perhaps Dumesnev will meet us, in case."

"In case of what?"

She studied him. "In case we are called on to clean up Asharti's leavings. In other words, in case you decide to help us and are successful."

"Doubtful you should be needed, but by all means proceed there." He bowed and turned to leave. At the door he paused. "I would not tamper with Miss Rochewell's memory," he threw over his shoulder. "Her memory may be your only chance to get you what you want."

· · ·

"I think I have located just the situation for you, dear Lizzy." Beth felt her stomach tighten for two reasons. Her aunt would never give up that hated name, though by now Beth had asked her not to use it. Beth looked up from her book. A cozy fire burned in the grate. Lady Rangle was flipping idly through the *Ladies Journal,* looking at the fashion plates. She was dressed in pale gray gauze. They had spent one of their rare dinners at home and now only waited so they could be fashionably late to the Fairfields' ball. "You hardly seem excited at my news. Of course, if you are expecting a marriage proposal from Mr. Rufford after he danced with you last night, my work will have been unnecessary."

That was gratuitous, even for her aunt. Lady Rangle had been wondering aloud what on earth Rufford had been at dancing with "Lizzy" all evening. "I met him on the ship, Aunt. He was only being civil." She had said those words or close enough to her aunt a dozen times today.

"Then you might show a little interest in your future. I must have spoken to a score of people. I really quite extended myself." Languidness stretched into petulance.

"I apologize, Aunt. I am most grateful, and agog to hear the results of your labor." Beth knew her features were at odds with her words. But what could her aunt expect? Beth thought her spirits could not sink further than they had as she watched Ian Rufford dance with the dashing Countess. She loved him and he would never know that. But she was wrong.

"Well, Chively has a great-aunt or something who lives in the Yorkshire West Riding—quite remote. He says she takes a deal of entertaining, likes to have all the papers and magazines read to her several times over, and requires help with her needlework, sorting yarns and such. Nothing you cannot do. You read a great deal anyway."

Beth glanced to her book, *The Language of the Gods, a Discourse on the Writing of the Ancients*. Hardly the same kind of reading. "I expect I can fill the requirements."

"Now, she is often quite cross. She has the gout, you know. But you will not care for that. And you will not have to look after much of a household, even though the house is large, since there are only three or four old servants left, plus the cook of course."

"I am to be the housekeeper as well?"

"Well, it isn't a fashionable establishment, so you should be able to manage it. You must earn your keep, and they are offering twenty-five pounds the year—remarkable, since the old lady is quite the economist. Never has a fire, even in the main rooms, until Christmas. Handsome rates, since you will not have to put out for your board unless you want to eat your own food. The old lady is on a bland diet, of course."

What could be more bland than English food after the rich diet of the Mediterranean? The prospect of a cold house on the bleak Riding with five sour people in it who ate bland food was almost too much for Beth. But she was in no position to refuse. "Thank you, Aunt. I am most grateful. When may I begin?"

"I took the liberty of telling Chively you could take the stage to York day after tomorrow," Lady Rangle said airily, "since I am promised to post to Bath to see dear Rangle's cousin's funeral. She had quite a fine collection of jewelry, or it would be if it were reset in the modern style." She was obviously relieved to be rid of Beth.

"Well. That gives me tomorrow to pack." Beth could not help that her voice was flat.

The knocker sounded in the hall.

"How inconvenient. A caller so late? Who could it be?" Lady Rangle frowned.

Beth fluttered, knowing one who could visit only at night. He had only meant to achieve a civil escape from a social dilemma when he promised to call, and yet . . .

"The Honorable Mr. Ian Rufford, my lady," Edwards intoned behind her.

Beth saw her aunt's amazed expression change to one of avarice as she glanced to Beth, speculating. "Do show him in, Edwards."

He entered and immediately the room seemed smaller. He was dressed for some event, perhaps Miss Fairfield's ball. His coat was black, his neck cloth white perfection. She was so glad he refused to cut his hair into that awful style brushed up from the nape. He bowed. "Lady Rangle, Miss Rochewell." But his eyes were only for Beth. The wonderful puckered lips pressed themselves together resolutely.

"Mr. Rufford," Lady Rangle cooed, holding out one languid hand that dripped a pearl gray bit of gauze masquerading as a handkerchief. "How very nice to see you."

Rufford stepped forward and kissed the knuckles offered as required, but he looked exceedingly uncomfortable. "A pleasure," he mumbled, glancing at Beth, who flushed.

Lady Rangle's sharp eyes missed nothing. "If only I was feeling more the thing," she mourned. "My indifferent health—I am afraid I worry my many friends exceedingly."

Disappointment and chagrin chased each other over Rufford's face before he schooled it to blank civility again. "I see my visit was untimely. I should not like to tax your strength."

"Alas, I shall have to leave Lizzy with the burden of carrying my part of the conversation." In astonishment Beth watched her rise. She could feel Rufford's relief and embarrassment, though she could not bring herself to look at him. Lady Rangle tottered toward the door. "Do ring for tea, my dear . . ." she murmured. "Or perhaps Mr. Rufford would like brandy?" She did not wait for an answer but drifted out the door, leaving Beth to stare after her. Rufford stood in the center of the drawing room as though rooted to the spot.

"Shall I procure . . . ?" She trailed off.

"I do not care for anything."

Beth noted with alarm that he began pacing in distraction up and down. Electric energy spun off him and flung itself about the room. Suddenly Beth had never longed more for her aunt's company.

"I hardly know how to begin," he growled, whirling on her. She chanced a glance up at his face. He was very flushed.

Even as she watched, the color drained away and he went quite pale. *Dear me,* she thought, *he looks as though he were about to faint.* "I have always believed in being straightforward. You could try that."

To her surprise, he smiled, and she saw his color come back even as his shoulders relaxed a bit. "Yes. How very practical."

She smiled wryly in return, remembering how he once had disparaged practicality, and gestured to the chaise vacated by her aunt next to the fire.

He sat, ramrod-straight, and cleared his throat. "Very well. I have a proposition for you. You want to get back to Africa. You are obviously a fish out of water among all these insipid, ignorant, parochial people. You cannot live in Africa without being . . . married."

Beth stared at him in amazement. At the mention of Africa, her heart had given a familiar skip of longing, but now she could not believe what she suddenly thought might happen here. *Silly girl,* she told herself. *How dare you imagine such things?*

Rufford met her eyes briefly, then cleared his throat again and got to his feet. "I, on the other hand, require arcane knowledge which I know you possess."

"What knowledge?"

He sat again abruptly. There was a pause. "I need to know the location of Kivala."

"You have been there."

"I wandered in the desert half-dead for weeks until I happened upon El Golea. I could not find Kivala again. But you can. You have the texts that show the way. I can tell you the general area where 'the spine of the earth' must be. Together, we can find the city."

"Why?" she asked. He had wanted directness. . . . "I thought you wanted no part of Africa."

He spoke with difficulty. "I . . . I don't. But I cannot escape it. Asharti knows where I am. She threatens to hunt me down. She is making vampires, many vampires. That's what we are, you know, vampires." His voice tried to be hard and cracked on the word. He took a breath and continued. "Asharti is a danger to the fabric of our world, vampire and human . . ." he trailed off.

Vampire! She had not said the word to him. He must have gotten it from somewhere else. The Countess! Of course. "And . . . ? You have not told me why you must go to Kivala."

"I think I can stop Asharti. The answer lies at Kivala, behind two tablets I cannot translate. I can't run away while she destroys . . . everything."

Beth nodded slowly and gazed at him. What did she see? Confusion, courage, the pain she knew so well. The resolution had almost disappeared. What happened if he asked? Dared she imagine it? What if she was wrong?

"So," he said, looking down at his hands, "I . . . I have come to ask you to marry me." But he could not leave it at that. "I know . . . I know that a creature such as I am has no right to ask such a thing. But it would be a marriage in name only. You would be able to conduct your researches, mount expeditions. I would fund everything. You could have the life you want, unencumbered by a husband who made demands of you, but with all the advantages of the married state. Unless, of course, you wished to marry another rather than . . . well, rather than have liaisons. Then I should disappear and let you have your freedom."

Beth had never heard such a daunting speech. Her heart closed for a moment as the world shifted around her. Had she ever imagined the pain a proposal of marriage by a vampire could cause? And all because he did not even pretend to love her. She was astounded to realize that if he had said he loved her, she would have said yes in an instant. She looked down at her hands.

"I . . . I will disclose everything about my state, though you know most already." He cleared his throat. "Apparently, I will not age. I can disappear, and exert my will over others. A parasite in my system requires that I feed on human blood, and there is no way around that. But I will never violate your person. That once was only because . . . because I was taken

unawares. You will be entirely safe with me. The more so
since I have become very . . . strong."

He was immortal? The consequences of that statement
almost overwhelmed her. "I will age." It was the one difference that mattered, somehow.

He blinked. "I will always provide for you, but if my
presence becomes . . . unwelcome, I will not burden you
with it." An image formed in her mind of a cracked and lined
old woman living alone in some palatial house while the vibrant man who looked thirty careered around the capitals of
Europe having liaisons with beautiful women like Beatrix
Lisse, Countess of Lente.

"I would help you find Kivala even without your kind offer." The revelation cost her something, but in her confusion
she could not tell exactly what.

He chewed his lip and got up to pace again. "I know. I
know you would. That is a testament to your character and
your sympathy, undeserved as sympathy is in this case. But
there are texts at the tomb that must be translated in order to
enter, which means you must go with me. I trust no one else.
If you go in my company without the protection of a wedding band, your reputation will be ruined, your life made . . .
difficult. I could not bear to harm you in such a way. You deserve only the highest consideration, and distasteful as this
must be . . ." He whirled on her, his face aghast. "Of course,
you probably have other offers. I am forgetting myself."

"I . . . have no other offers," she murmured.

Rufford raced on, as though he were afraid to stop. "If
you marry someone else, still you should not return to Africa
with anyone but me. With Asharti on the loose, who else
could protect you?" He stumbled to a stop. "But perhaps you
don't wish to go to Africa. . . ."

"I do want to go to Africa." Beth was surprised her voice
was calm. Indeed, Mr. Rufford's chaotic speech had created
some small island of hope inside her. Still, she had to know
a little more. "I simply hate to saddle you with an unpleasant
burden, for who knows how many years. I am still young,
you know. You will tire of me even on this trip, I imagine."

"Burden?" He looked blank. "I could not imagine a more congenial traveling companion. You never complain. You are interested in everything. Your observations are always penetrating. And you play a very decent game of chess." He smiled a rather touching, secret smile. "Just at my level. What more could one ask?"

"Or a little beyond your level." She tried to keep her eyes serious.

"That I do not concede." His gaze rested on her with an expression that contained wonder and almost tenderness.

Beth felt the door of hope open a little wider. Now was the moment. She either threw herself through that door or closed it forever.

"I should be happy to accept your offer of marriage." The words, once uttered, almost shattered her. What had she done? She felt her eyes grow large. She could not get enough air in this stifling room. Why ever did Lady Rangle always set these chairs so close to the fire?

They stared at each other as though a chasm had opened up right here in the drawing room and they tottered on the edges. "Right," Rufford said, recollecting himself. "Ahhh, when would be convenient? I had thought tomorrow? There is some urgency, you know."

"Tomorrow!" This was becoming altogether too real. "One can't get married upon a moment's notice. There are the banns, the arrangements . . ."

He fished a heavy paper from the breast of his coat awkwardly. "I have a special license. Just in case, you know, you agreed. A ship leaves Portsmouth for Casablanca before dawn Saturday. I think we should start there. Kivala is somewhere east of the Atlas Mountains and west of El Golea."

Beth drew her brows together. "However did you get a special license?"

He glanced away, then deliberately back. "It's very hard to resist a vampire's request."

"Oh." Beth's mind darted over the possibilities inherent in that statement. Had he compelled her to accept him? She hadn't felt compelled . . . but tomorrow? Who would she get to stand up for her? And she had nothing to wear, an objection she could never voice to Rufford. She was becoming positively missish. *The pink will do,* she thought. "Could we settle upon day after tomorrow? That would give me time to pack, and yet we could still make the sailing on Saturday." Rufford nodded. But he must pass a final test. "One thing I must know."

His eyes opened in apprehension.

"What is behind the doors you want me to unlock that will allow you to defeat Asharti?"

He swallowed. "You are ever practical." He took a breath, and she could see him resolve to tell her the truth and let her make her own choice. "It is a temple. In it, a strange being waits whom Asharti calls the Old One, He Who Waits. His blood made the first vampires. It makes Asharti strong. If I can get him to give me his blood, perhaps I can defeat Asharti." He shook his head, embarrassed. "It's not much of a chance." He shrugged. "It's the best I have."

He had passed the test. She squared her shoulders. "You deserve your chance. I will do what I can."

He peered into her eyes, searching her soul. He did not seem to see what he had anticipated. He shook himself. "I expect I must ask your aunt for permission. I don't suppose she is equal to it now, but there is so little time. . . ." He fidgeted with the license.

"Up to it? She is probably waiting for it." Beth rang for Edwards.

"Do you think . . . ? I mean it is sudden."

Beth raised her brows. "You will find her grateful for taking me off her hands."

Beth was not wrong. Lady Rangle cared nothing for propriety when so great a catch as the very rich brother of a Viscount was involved. She cooed and clucked, "Oh, Mr. Rufford, how satisfying it is to see a man so carried away by love!" Both Beth and Rufford were discomfited. "Thursday, you say? But how will I recruit a respectable attendance?"

Beth glanced at Rufford. "Mr. Rufford and I were thinking of a private ceremony."

"Yes, Lady Rangle. We are beginning our wedding trip from Portsmouth on Saturday. I thought we would visit Miss Rochewell's beloved Africa."

"Oh! Oh, dear. No reception after the ceremony?" She looked from one shaking head to another. "No." She sighed, obviously mourning a chance to show off her niece's catch to jealous matrons. "That will look so havy-cavy. Well," she acquiesced.

"I . . . I will send round with all the details. Whom should I see about the marriage settlements?" Beth could see he had not thought this far. A sheen of perspiration broke out upon his forehead. Her own thoughts were already spinning ahead to the wedding night and on to all the arrangements to be made for an expedition and then back to the wedding night.

"My man of business, Edgely at Drummond's, will see to it. Do you go to the Fairfields' ball?" Lady Rangle asked with slightly more animation. "We were just about to leave." Ahh, Lady Rangle saw an opportunity for an informal announcement of her triumph. Beth was wrung with conflicting anticipation of dances in Mr. Rufford's arms and society's astonishment that someone like Mr. Rufford could have offered for someone like her.

Rufford bowed punctiliously. "May I escort you, ladies? My carriage waits."

All the way to Fairfield House, through streets crowded with carriages, Beth responded incoherently to her aunt's chatter. Not that she wasn't grateful for the distraction—Mr. Rufford was as silent as she was. But doubt assailed her. Why ever had she agreed to this mad plan? Because he needed help? Of course, but marriage? And the fact that he was right about it ruining her reputation was only an excuse. She wanted Ian Rufford as a husband, mystery, painful past, even vampire and all. He did not love her. He had admitted that. She had vowed she would never marry without love on both sides. Yet he liked to be with her. He wanted to protect her. And there was that mysterious expression when he looked at her. . . . Were these together something on which she could build? She was not the Countess of Lente. She might endure a lifetime of the pain of his constant association with creatures more ravishing than she. But in the moment she accepted him, she realized she could not imagine her future without him. The months until she saw him again had been a desert more bleak than any in North Africa. There would be danger at Kivala, if they could even find the place. That was nothing to the danger she faced on the interior landscape of her heart. He had it in his power to make her pay a horrifying price for her love. But better she pay it in his presence for however long she could induce him to stay with her than suffer the huge rip in her life made by his absence.

As they alighted from the carriage, Lady Rangle was claimed instantly by the ancient Earl of Silchester and began whispering to him. Beth placed her hand on Rufford's arm and felt the electric warmth shoot through her. He looked down at her with eyes full—of what? She could not read them. He had not said six words to her since informing her aunt of his intentions. But he filled her present with his presence and that was enough. She indulged in a tiny pang of regret that she would be seen on his arm tonight in a light blue dress of figured muslin that was her aunt's idea of maidenly propriety. There was nothing wrong with light blue, of course, on Miss Fairfield, but it was a disaster with Beth's coloring.

As they entered the house, blazing with light, and ascended the stairs, Beth had a terrible thought. What if Mr. Rufford was embarrassed by being seen with her in public with her odd looks and odd manners? Would he regret his offer? She resolved to be as circumspect as possible. Inside the great ballroom of Fairfield House, they came first to Miss Fairfield and her brother, greeting guests near the door.

Miss Fairfield glanced from Rufford to Beth and smiled a knowing smile. "Miss Rochewell, how good of you to come. You are looking well." Her brother shook Rufford's hand.

"I am not, Miss Fairfield, and you know it," Beth said. "Why my aunt insists on pastel colors I have no idea, unless it is the same impulse which drives her to call me Lizzy no matter how many times I protest."

Miss Fairfield laughed. "Then you must order your own dresses. You have no choice."

"No choice indeed. You have no idea." She caught Rufford looking strangely at her, even as, behind her, she heard an old woman say in the loud voice of the deaf, "What an odd girl!"

So much for circumspection.

They made their way into the hall, trailing stares. Lady Rangle talked in excited tones to Lady Jersey and several other matrons. Beth saw the astonished glances, Lady Rangle's self-satisfied look. She could practically hear her aunt saying, "He is so eager that it is to be a quiet, immediate affair. The ardor of the young!" She flushed with the imagined conversation.

"May I get you some refreshment?" The rumbling voice above her startled her into the present. "It is quite warm in this room."

She spared him a glance and looked quickly away. "I am fine, thank you."

"Rufford!" The musical voice was unmistakable. The Countess of Lente sailed into view in all her glory. It was emerald green tonight. Beth shrank inside. "I wondered where you had got to." There was a sharp edge to the beautiful woman's voice. "Have you decided to go abroad?"

"We have, but to North Africa, rather than America." Beth saw relief bloom in the radiant face, followed closely by puzzlement. "Countess," Rufford continued, "will you permit me to introduce Miss Rochewell, my future bride? Beatrix Lisse, Countess of Lente."

The Countess raised a single brow. "I am charmed to meet you." She looked quizzically to Rufford.

It was Beth who found a need to explain. "I hope to be useful to his . . . quest, Lady Lente. I can read the ancient texts and—"

Rufford interrupted. "We leave on Saturday. I trust that is sufficiently urgent?"

"It is." The woman looked at Beth curiously. "I hope you know what you are doing."

Beth gathered herself. "I do." But it sounded frail even in her own ears.

The Countess sailed away, saying only, "We will talk, Rufford." In her wake, Beth could clearly hear the surrounding chatter.

"Whatever could he see in her? Such a brown girl."

"And that dress! Dreadful."

"Well, I know what he might see in her. One does in those kinds of girls."

"Her manners are so free—"

"All those foreign climes. You know what the Equator does to one."

"All well and good, but why *marry* her?"

"A few hundred pounds a year could keep one like that."

Beth stiffened. So did Rufford. He had heard as well. Beth was mortified.

"Refreshment is in order, no matter what you think," he said sternly, and guided her over to the table with a champagne fountain. Of course the Countess of Lente would provide the latest fashion in refreshment. "Punch or champagne? Never mind. Champagne." He took the crystal dipper and filled a glass. "Drink this."

She took a sip.

"Miss Rochewell?"

She turned to see a man nearing sixty, dressed not only in a bottle green coat but one that actually sported skirts. "Yes?" Was her reputation so free that anyone could accost her?

"I am Bernard Chively." Beth's stomach sank. "Your aunt arranged for you to care for my own dear aunt. You can take the Mail Coach on Friday. The place is in quite a state, of course. We haven't had a housekeeper for months. Now, you won't mind my aunt's crotchets, will you?" Here he pinched her cheek. "We pay extra just to compensate."

Beth found herself trembling. "Mr. . . . Mr. Chively. I—"

"Miss Rochewell will not be going to wherever it is your aunt resides," Mr. Rufford said decisively. "We start our wedding trip on Saturday." Mr. Chively's mouth dropped. "I am afraid you must find another victim for your aunt's ill will. You will excuse us." He took Beth by both elbows from behind and guided her away. Just as well, since she felt somewhat unsteady.

"Drink your champagne," Rufford ordered roughly.

Beth was so embarrassed she could not speak. He must be so chagrined to find that he had offered for one who was on the brink of hiring herself out as a housekeeper and companion. How could he ever respect her? How could he . . . ? No, she would not think of that. She sipped the champagne, her eyes averted. She began to breathe again.

"More. Drink the whole glass."

She did.

"Your father spent your portion?"

"On his last expedition."

"Your aunt would not . . . ?"

"I refused two offers. She was at her wits' end. I couldn't hang on her. I could find no position, no recommendation, without her help. Finally I asked, and she did help me."

"I see."

"I am sorry to embarrass you. Perhaps he will not tell anyone."

"We will be long gone in any case."

He took her empty glass and set it on a passing servant's tray. "Dance with me." She looked up at him. The blue eyes were serious, the bowed lips sensuous. Then a glint of humor twinkled in the eyes. "Make them stare," he commanded.

Her smile was tenuous. He turned her. It was a waltz. She had not noticed. Again she felt his hand on her waist. Again she placed her palm in his, feeling the warmth of his skin in places down somewhere unfamiliar. Her hand on his black coat sensed the muscled shoulder beneath. She had touched that naked flesh once. She heaved a breath as the music swept them away.

The room whirled around her. She could see the bent heads whispering. Miss Belchersand and Miss Campton were looking daggers. Her aunt buzzed from group to group.

Mr. Chively was descending upon her aunt, grievance writ loud on his features. She did not care. She wanted to remain here, just so, with Mr. Rufford's arms around her, swirling on the music. She let her head fall back as she spun, giddy, and let him guide the dance. The chandeliers above twinkled like the bubbles in champagne.

The music stopped. Mr. Rufford bowed. "You have fulfilled your social obligation. Let us go." He took her hand and led her toward her aunt. Before they could reach their destination, however, Rufford caught sight of Major Ware and bore down upon him. "Ware, just the man I wanted to see," Rufford said.

Ware looked startled at his vehemence. "What? What is afoot?"

"I am going abroad on a mission of which you would approve. I will not be accosted by your confidants at Whitehall, however. You'll keep them at bay until Saturday?"

"I . . . I shall certainly try."

"You are a diplomat, Ware. I count on you. We have booked a packet. But if you could arrange a cutter, we could reach our destination faster. As you know, time is of the essence."

Ware cleared his throat. "Do you have a chance of succeeding?"

Ian glanced down for a moment, then met the Major's eyes. "A chance." He almost turned to go. "And Ware . . . one more favor I might beg?"

Ware nodded, his eyes still wide. "Whatever you wish."

Rufford looked stern. "St. James's Church at five Thursday. I have need of a best man."

Ware looked in astonishment from Rufford to Beth. "Congratulations, old man!" he sputtered, shaking Rufford's hand. Then his face went gray and he looked back to Beth.

Beth wanted so to reassure him. "You should be congratulating me, Major Ware, in spite of convention. Am I not blessed with a most extraordinary fiancé? Be assured, I think so."

"Do you?" Ware examined her.

"Yes, and you may have known him longer, but I know more of his secrets than you do."

Ware practically stepped back a pace.

"Can you bring yourself to serve us?" Rufford asked, his voice harsh.

Ware looked from one to the other and said, "Yes. I think I can."

Rufford nodded brusquely and drew Beth into an alcove.

"There is much to do," he said. "Do you have someone to stand up with you?"

"My aunt . . . though she is promised to a funeral in Bath for some cousin of her husband. I am not sure she will forgo it since the ceremony is to be so private—"

"Not your aunt. Let her go to her funeral." It was as if he pronounced a verdict.

"Well . . ." Beth hesitated. "I might ask Miss Fairfield."

"Yes. She will do. Send word if you come to a stand. I am at Albany House, number five." He paused. "I will be quite engaged tomorrow. But I shall meet you and Miss Fairfield at the church Thursday." Something struck him. "Will St. James's do? Or would you prefer to choose another?"

He would never be able to get the Reverend at St. James's to marry them on a moment's notice. It was the most stylish church in London. All the *ton* displayed their acquaintance and their tailor's or their dressmaker's finest work there each week. She raised her brows. "Whatever you think." That would give him an out when he couldn't arrange for St. James's.

"All will be in order; do not fear."

"I do not fear you," she said simply.

He leaned forward and took her hands. "You will never have cause. Now let us get you home." He led her protectively out toward her aunt.

"Lady Rangle," he announced, "your niece has the headache. You will take her home." His tone brooked no contradiction, but Beth saw her aunt's expression turn mulish. Lady Rangle turned to Lady Jersey to find an ally for her complaint. "You will take her home or I shall." Rufford's voice was all soft threat.

The very thought of such a scandal left Lady Rangle outraged.

"Oh, go, Cecilia. Let the young people have their way." Lady Jersey laughed and pushed her aunt toward the door. "It is exhausting to be affianced."

Before she knew it, the carriage had been called. Rufford handed her into the darkness. A touch of his hand, no more, a salute, and the carriage clattered away.

Once inside, snug in her pelisse, the lap rug securely tucked about her, Beth sighed and collapsed into the upholstery. The emotional drain of her private uncertainty that Rufford even wanted to marry her, and the public's certainty that she was not worthy of him, were almost more than she could bear. She stared out the window at the passing streets. It had rained, and now a damp fog settled over the city.

It was not far to Curzon Street. Beth entered her aunt's house feeling that the entire evening had been unreal, dream and nightmare in one.

Seventeen

The next day was a blur for Beth. She slept hardly at all. She alternately resolved to write a note to Rufford crying off and fluttered with hope that she could bring him ultimately to care for her. And then there was the fact of his nature, the terrible mission he was bent on, the danger to him, to her for that matter, in finding Kivala and what might wait there, the fearful conflict with Asharti he was resolved on—at times she felt faint.

She wrote to Miss Fairfield in a much revised missive asking for her help, fully expecting a civil snub. But Miss Fairfield's reply was enthusiastic. In the morning, Beth packed her few things in a small trunk. In the afternoon, she steadied herself by going over the scrolls again and consulting her book on navigational mathematics to calculate the seasonal differences that would reposition the moon from the time the scrolls mentioned to the time they were likely to arrive in the area east of Casablanca. They would need good sextants and chronometers. Portsmouth was the place to acquire those, a town full of sailors. She made a list of supplies for the projected caravan and a list of tasks and arrangements to be made when they reached Casablanca. She was good at this. She could be useful to him. He might come to depend upon her.

It should not have surprised her that Lady Rangle made no protest that it would be Miss Fairfield who supported Beth. A ceremony not seen by more than four people could not compete with a chance at Rangle's cousin's jewelry. She accepted with complaisance that Beth would be gone by the time she returned. Beth had never felt more estranged from her only living relative or from England. The prospect of getting back to Africa grew more and more enticing.

Living with or apart from a vampire who never grew old was a thing so beyond her experience, it would not profit her sanity to speculate on it. She was having trouble thinking beyond her wedding night. All possibilities there seemed horrid. Would he? Would it be like Gibraltar? What if he did not? What if he sucked at her neck and she never wanted it to stop?

Her aunt was engaged to dinner with Lady Wolverton, but Beth begged off. She could not endure another scene like last night's gauntlet of disparagement. So it was a lonely evening home with her thoughts and an early bed, if not early sleep, for Beth.

Ian had no leisure at all. His first call was to a dressmaker of the first water in Piccadilly, slipping from his curtained carriage into the shop of Madame d'Arette. She recognized his name from some of the bills she had presented to him in former times for his companions. His reputation for having made his fortune induced her to put off her other clients. There ensued a somewhat exhausting round for Ian of choosing fabrics, explaining what he wanted, and estimating sizes. Madame could be heard screeching at her seamstresses as he put on his blue glasses, pulled up his cloak collar around his cheeks, left the shop, and strode the three steps to where his carriage waited. Thank God it was a dim, grim day in London.

Next was a milliner's shop, whose mistress was shown

scraps of the fabrics and who promised to take care of everything, then a shop that sold things he had too much knowledge of for the comfort of the shopgirl. The avaricious old jeweler rubbed his hands in delight as Ian left his shop pocketing several small boxes. He engaged a post chaise and four to Portsmouth for Friday evening, being sure it would arrive before Saturday's early-morning tide. That would allow them to spend the day together. If she wanted to spend the day with him. He ordered a lap rug and hot bricks for her on the journey. Finally, he spent most of the afternoon in the dim confines of Mr. Edgely's office, making sure she would be taken care of no matter what happened to him.

Then he went to Beatrix.

"What brings you out in the stark afternoon?" she said, disapproving, her wrapper revealing almost everything in its dramatic décolleté. "It must be an hour to sunset."

"Don't be supercilious with me," he ordered in the face of that one raised brow. "You will get what you want, you and Ware both. But I need the help of Miss Rochewell."

"How can she help you? She will be only a liability."

"I don't care to tell you. Suffice it that she is indispensable. And my debt will be paid with my name and my support for her natural life."

"You needn't marry the chit!" Beatrix's keen glance darted over his face even as she put on a pout. He knew that pout was meant to distract him from her eyes, which wanted answers.

"Should she not get something out of the bargain?" he asked.

"Why will she do this? She did not seem the avaricious type." Beatrix lounged back into the sofa in her boudoir, her auburn hair in delightful disarray.

"No, she is not." He frowned. "She wants to return to Africa."

"That cannot be enough to marry one like you. There must be something more at work." Beatrix observed him narrowly. She was not to be denied.

"Perhaps," he said shortly.

Beatrix waited.

"She . . . she may think me a better man than I am." It was as much as he could say.

Beatrix cocked her head. She smiled a very tiny smile. "Everyone should have someone who thinks they are better than they are, Rufford. In that case, I support your decision. What do you want of me? You do want something."

"Yes," Rufford said, wary. He handed her a paper with a very long list of names on it.

After a second sleepless night, Beth saw Lady Rangle off to Bath at the crack of one in the afternoon. The house seemed big and empty. She sat on her bed, thinking that it was less than three hours until she should have to call a hackney carriage, since one could not really walk to one's own wedding. She harbored some secret fear that no one would be there when she arrived, that it was all some horrible mistake, that she wasn't to go to back to Africa or marry a man who had wormed his way into her every thought.

Of course, he did not care for her. Every time her fancy got the better of her, she returned to that one stark fact. *"A marriage in name only . . . unencumbered . . ."* The words echoed in her mind. He had been embarrassed by her poverty on Tuesday night and the fact that she was despised socially for her dress, her manners . . . Dear God! Of course he couldn't love her.

She thought about her father for the first time in days. Guilt stabbed at her. She used to think about him a dozen times a day. What an ungrateful child to forget him so! She longed for the acceptance she had taken for granted in the life he had built for her. As she was alone in the house except for the servants, alone in London except for the bare acquaintance she had asked to stand up with her and the man most women would run screaming from . . . the longing for the comfort of her father's gruff tut-tutting, telling her to keep her chin up, overwhelmed her. Perhaps for the first time since her father's death, she cried, cried for him, cried

for herself, cried for the life she would never know again.
And they weren't just those attractive tears that run down
one's cheeks. Sobs racked her and she wrapped her arms
around her body for comfort. There was none.

Lying on her bed, hiccupping from the tears, she slept at
last, exhausted by grief held in too long, unhappiness suppressed during her sojourn in her aunt's house, and her most
recent unrealistic hopes now doused by her sense of practical reality.

She was wakened by a tapping at the door. Shadows of
late afternoon in February stretched across the floor.
"What . . . what is it?"

"Packages for you, miss," came the footman's voice.

"I shall be with you in a moment!" she called. She
glanced at the clock. Half past three! She struggled up and
glanced in the mirror. Her eyes were only a little swollen.
She splashed water on her face from her basin, smoothed her
gray cambric gown, and presented herself in the downstairs
hall. Servants hovered around stacks of boxes, big and
small, wrapped with brown paper and twine.

"They are all addressed to you, miss," the upstairs girl
said, her eyes round.

"To me?" She peered at them. True! Who could have sent
them? A footman, James, silently passed her a card. The servants were suffused with excitement.

Beth flushed. *"The Right Honorable Ian Rufford,"* the
card said, then handwritten: "With the compliments of the
groom."

"Could you take them upstairs, James, if you please?"
She turned, then asked shyly, "Polly, do you think you could
help me dress? I am so pressed for time."

Polly gave a huge smile, glanced at the others with a su-
perior air, and said, "O' course, miss. I am quite a hand with
hair, I am."

They trailed James and his huge precarious burden up the
stairs. "I'll have a carriage at the door at ha' past four sharp,"
James promised as he laid the parcels on the bed.

"Thank you." Beth smiled, a little wavery but a smile

nonetheless. She turned to the packages. "I suppose I should open these. Polly, can you get out my pink dress?" She took a small scissors from her needlework bag and cut the string of the largest package. The tissue paper inside revealed a satin not white and not quite golden but a rich color like buttery cream. Polly gasped. Beth held her breath as she pulled the shoulders of the dress up and let the heavy fabric fall. It was edged with Brussels lace and quite shockingly décolleté. The waist was the new lowered style, halfway between breasts and true waist, with an overskirt of more lace in that rich creamy color. The sleeves were lace alone, long and tight in the latest fashion.

"Beautiful," Polly whispered, tossing the pink one onto a chair. "I didn't never see a wedding dress in just that shade, but Lord it will be perfect for you."

Beth's throat was full. She laid the dress out on the bed. Wordless, they set about the other packages. Delicate kid slippers in supple leather of the same rare color, stockings, gloves, exquisite silk underthings, a tiny beaded reticule, a long cloak in creamy wool lined with sable that came with a huge sable muff, and the hat! Frothy cream perfection, it looked as though its lace and feathers and shining ribbons might melt at any moment.

At last there were only tiny boxes left. Polly was still giggling in delight, but Beth could hardly breathe. One small box held a string of pearls. Not just any pearls but large, lustrous cream-colored pearls that matched the dress perfectly. They were accompanied by pearl and diamond drop earrings and pearls and diamonds on the ends of golden hairpins to wear in her hair. They were far too expensive. Her debt suddenly oppressed her. He had offered for her without loving her and felt obligated to make sure she did not embarrass him. It was almost too much.

"Well, lordy, miss. Ain't you going to put them on? It's nearly four o'clock."

She managed a smile. "Of course."

The silk chemise caressed her skin. The dress was heavy. It pressed her breasts up until they swelled into the neckline.

Polly laid the pearls around her neck. Beth hooked the earrings on her ears. Polly sat her down, unbraided and brushed her hair, then wound it in a knot that dripped ringlets, fastened with the jeweled pins. She pulled curls out to the side and rolled them into tidy ringlets to frame Beth's face. She looked at her reflection, round-eyed. The color of the dress made her skin glow. Her green-gold eyes seemed huge in her face, her dark hair heavy and rich. Polly carefully set the frothy hat at a rakish angle and tied the satin ribbons under Beth's chin.

Beth stood. How had he ordered a dress that fit so exactly? Had he used the dressmaker her aunt frequented? How had he known? Beth stopped halfway to the bed. He *could* not know from the time when he had undressed her in Gibraltar! Oh, dear! She flushed. "The cloak, Polly."

"You aren't never going to hide that dress before the boys gets to see you looking like Cinderella, are you?" Polly accused. "I'll just take it down for you."

A soft rap sounded on the door. "Carriage, miss."

Beth felt pressed on every side. She was marrying a vampire, for God's sake, a man every woman in her right mind would call evil, and she was going off to Africa on some insane chase that might well end in death. And anyway, a man who could order women's underthings and knew how dresses would fit her was not respectable enough to marry. Even worse, her marriage to that man would be a bargain only. She wanted to burst into tears again.

Beth realized her brows were knit and her shoulders tight. She let out a chuckle under her breath. She was turning into the kind of woman who had vapors and went into a decline. Silly cow! She was marrying a man who had a parasite in his blood—a disease, albeit a strange one. She was going to Africa to explore new mysteries, just as she had always done, as she longed to do again. And if her husband was not like to love her, well, that was a fate no worse than thousands of women embraced wholeheartedly every day. This was an eminently practical arrangement, and she intended to make the most of what it gave her: a chance to return to the land

and the occupation she loved, a chance to finally find her father's lost city. She would not dream of love from Ian Rufford. Nor would she have the vapors.

"Thank you, Polly. I swear I could never have arranged my hair so charmingly myself. You have a real talent." She smiled at the girl as plain, she noticed, as she was herself.

Polly preened and blushed. "I hopes someday to be a dresser, miss."

"If I am ever in a position to make a recommendation for you, I shall certainly do so."

Beth went down the stairs carefully, smiled wryly, and shrugged under the stares and murmurs from the help gathered in the hall. Even the cook peered round the door casing to the kitchen stairs. Edwards opened the door into the twilight as the servants broke into discreet applause. Polly lifted the cloak around Beth's shoulders. James stood grinning at the open door of a carriage provided with fine black-liveried drivers. It was by no means a hired hackney coach.

"What, what carriage is this?" she sputtered, looking about her.

"It came a quarter hour ago. Sent by Mr. Rufford."

The driver touched his high-crowned beaver hat. "St. James's Church it is, miss."

Beth stepped up into the carriage. No musty squabs for her but rich red upholstery that one sank into. The stairs were lifted in, the door closed, and they were off. Alone in the closed carriage, Beth put her fear aside. She had made her choice. There was no going back. Life had already changed irrevocably, just as it had changed the moment her father died. One must make the best of things. It was very nice to know that at least one looked as well as one could, being dreadfully short, with brown skin and oddly colored eyes.

It was not far to the church, but the streets were crowded, as it was the hour when members of the fashionable set were coming home from their rides in Hyde Park. Several young men peered into the carriage quite rudely to get a better look at her. She was too busy being nervous about arriving at the church too early to mind them. What if Mr. Rufford was not there? She suddenly realized that she had no one to give her away. So be it. She faced her future alone.

Christopher Wren's church came into view on Jermyn Street, its plain brown bricks and arched windows framed in pale Portland stone looking too ordinary to be such *haute ton*. The carriage door was opened. And there he was in stark black coat and trousers, a white cravat, moderate in height but perfectly tied. She hardly noticed. She had eyes only for the dear face, the blue eyes, the softly curling hair too long for fashion, tied back with a ribbon. His eyes went dark. She reached for his hand with her own gloved one. Events began to move quite slowly. Inside the porch of the church, he took her cloak, saying nothing. She could hear him breathing.

"Thank you for your kind gifts," she murmured. "The pearls . . . You should not have—"

"They were little enough," he said roughly. "I am repaid by seeing you in them."

There was Miss Fairfield, shushing him away. "The groom should not be consorting with his bride before the ceremony, sir. What are you thinking?" She turned to Beth. "My dear Miss Rochewell, I . . . I hardly know what to say except that you are widely thought to be the luckiest woman in town. And . . . and that dress is quite lovely on you. No one deserves this more."

Beth smiled. "You are probably the only one that thinks I deserve it, then, including myself. How much I thank you for your support today!"

The church proper was not as large as a cathedral, but the round arches of plain plaster and the windows set with clear glass still dwarfed the tiny party gathered near the altar. Major Ware, a man and a woman Beth did not know, and Mr. Rufford stood in front of a clergyman in his vestments who was thumbing through a Bible. All looked up as she walked into the dim candlelit glow.

Major Ware hurried forward. "Miss Rochewell, would you think it presumptuous if I asked to have the honor of giving you away?"

"Who will support Mr. Rufford, sir? I should not like to rob him of you."

"His brother the Viscount has arrived with his Lady and is happy to fill that role."

She nodded her grateful acceptance. Miss Fairfield hurried to her place, and Beth placed her arm on Major Ware's sleeve. He was dressed in full regimentals, with several stars and ribbons holding medals in evidence.

The next minutes passed in a blur. Miss Fairfield and the man who was Mr. Rufford's brother stood at their sides. The clergyman introduced himself as Reverend Jessop and smiled benevolently upon them as he spoke. Beth could not quite focus on the words, but she answered "yes" when called upon by name and "I do" when it seemed apropos. She wondered what the Reverend might think if he knew he was marrying her to a vampire. Mr. Rufford stood over her, saying that he did, and then she looked up at him, and his eyes were such deep pools of indigo she thought she might lose herself in them. He bent. Those wonderful lips brushed hers for the second time. They were so soft, so tender. A throbbing started somewhere between her legs. The Reverend Mr. Jessop pronounced them man and wife. Then Miss Fairfield was hugging her and Major Ware and Lord Stanbridge were pumping Mr. Rufford's hands, congratulating him on having such a beautiful wife. No one ever meant such silly platitudes. She felt all in a whirl.

"Our carriages await us," Mr. Rufford declared. He turned to Beth, almost shyly, and offered his arm. "Mrs. Rufford?"

The name came as a shock. She stared at him, but it was too late to protest that he must be talking about someone else. She had done this thing. She could hardly get her breath. Still, she placed her hand on his arm and felt the shock of his flesh under the fabric. He had never seemed so . . . physical. Not even when she had probed his bare flesh with these very fingers? Tonight loomed ever larger. She was no simpering miss. She knew about maids and men. She had seen him naked even. He had seen her naked, too. She flushed. But not with . . . intent in either heart, surely. Tonight might be different—if he intended to be a husband to her at all. But he did not. *A marriage of convenience only.* That was all he wanted. But would it not be convenient and practical for a man to have a woman to hand in all senses? What did that mean about tonight?

The small wedding party had dinner in a private room at Rules Restaurant just off The Strand, featuring ducks, partridge, and venison, all taken from the owner's estates in Scotland, as well as lobsters and endless side dishes in no fewer than five removes. Beth's mind whirled while she picked at her food. A thought had occurred. If Ian did mean to be a husband to her in the bare essentials of that word, then she might run the risk of . . . She hardly dared think the word—offspring. Would a child bear the terrible consequences of her infatuation with a vampire? The room was warm. She was having trouble getting her breath. Should she beg the company's pardon and excuse herself?

Before she could make the room stop pulsing long enough to decide, the tall, fair woman next to her began to speak. "I am so glad we could attend your wedding, dear . . . Mrs. Rufford."

Beth smiled wanly. "Did you come up to London only for the wedding?"

The blue-eyed woman was Rufford's sister-in-law, Lady Stanbridge. "I am ashamed to say we did not know. We came to thank Ian. He did a great kindness to us, and to our children."

Beth nodded, coming to herself a bit. "I do not doubt it. He is very unselfish."

Lady Stanbridge chuckled. "I think you may be right. It was not always so. He has changed a great deal since he has been away."

"That is understandable, with what he went through."

Lady Stanbridge grew serious. "He would tell us only

that pirates sold him into slavery. We can only guess what horrors he endured." She raised her eyebrows. "Perhaps you know the whole."

"No." Beth shook her head. And it was not a lie. It could not be her place to tell what little she did know.

"We thought him dead for more than two years." Lady Stanbridge sighed and looked at Beth from under her lashes. "After the first joy of his return, I could not help but note how bereft he looked. Henry and I were exceedingly worried about him. He seemed so . . . distant, unable to take pleasure in even simple things." She gazed down the table at her brother-in-law, and Beth followed her look. Rufford felt their eyes on him and glanced their way. His face softened and he raised his glass silently. Beth smiled in return. Lady Stanbridge glanced between them. "Perhaps marriage will agree with him," she said. "He deserves happiness."

"I hope it will." Beth was not sure it would. But she knew at that moment that she wanted it to agree with him, that she wanted to soothe his doubts about himself and make him happy.

"Once more into the breach, my friends." Rufford rose from the tables and bundled the party away, refusing to answer any questions.

But as Beth sat opposite the gentlemen and between Lady Stanbridge and Miss Fairfield in the crisp air of London February, their destination soon became apparent. They joined a long line of carriages depositing their cargoes in front of number 46 Berkeley Square. It struck Beth that Miss Fairfield and Lady Stanbridge were both dressed well enough for a ball, as was she herself, if it came to that. But surely the entire town would have been buzzing for weeks at the prospect of the Countess giving a ball. Beth had heard nothing about it.

After shedding their cloaks, Beth and Rufford climbed the great staircase to the first floor. The footman announced the Honorable Ian Rufford and Mrs. Rufford. To Beth's amazement, all around the crowded room people turned and applauded.

"The married couple!"

"Lucky dog, Rufford!"

"Cut me out, sure!"

The cries of the men and looks of either astonishment or jealousy from the women shocked Beth. The Countess stepped out of the crowd, wearing lustrous midnight blue. "The guests of honor! I had almost given you up." She kissed Beth's cheek. "Stunning, child." She presented her own cheek to Rufford, who obliged her.

"I could not have wished for better, Beatrix," Rufford said, looking around the room.

Lady Jersey, Lady Sefton, and the Countess Lieven represented the Patronesses of Almack's. Two royal Dukes lumbered ponderously forward. Two Diamonds of the First Water had brought out all the fashionable young men. The Countess smiled complacently. "I have been busy, have I not? No one else's credit could have brought this off, you know."

"I know. Thank you."

"Well." She shushed them into the room. "Go display your trophy, Rufford. Every man will be green. The world is at your bride's feet tonight, just as you wished."

Beth found herself receiving compliments from a hundred people as though it were a dream. The very people who had cut her dead or dismissed her now openly fawned. She danced with Rufford time after time without breaking any social rules, since on one's wedding night it was far too early to be fashionably bored with one's husband. Several people remarked on her aunt's absence, but Beth played up the funeral without mentioning it was for a second cousin.

Still, the specter of a child vampire who needed blood instead of mother's milk lurked in the back of her mind. What was her duty here? Rufford was so attentive she began to wonder if it was for show only. She sent him off to dance with Miss Fairfield, who had danced all three of her allowed dances with Ware and was now finding the evening insipid. In the ensuing moment of calm Beth saw the Countess float by.

An idea flashed into her brain. Here was a woman who

could banish or confirm her image of conceiving a vampire child. Before she could hesitate, she rose, murmured an apology to the Stanbridges, and stepped after the red-haired woman. "My lady . . ." The woman turned, surprised. "Could I have a word with you, uh, privately?"

The Countess's head cocked, ever so slightly. "Of course, my dear." She led Beth to an alcove and sat on the delicate settee inside the embrasure. "What is it?"

Beth chewed a lip. How did one ask what she wanted to ask? There was no way. So one just asked. "I wanted to know something I think you can tell me."

"Why do you think I can answer?" The woman's dark eyes examined her.

"He told me nothing about you," Beth said hastily. "Do not blame him. I knew the moment I heard you ask that girl about why she wore the scarf. And because of your perfume."

Realization dawned in the woman's dark eyes. She sat back. "What, then?"

"It is about . . . children."

"Whether you can have them with him, or what they will be?"

Beth nodded, grateful. A woman after her own heart. "Both."

"Children may be possible. He is new to the Companion. Among those born with the blood, a child is a rare thing, between two of us almost unheard of. Between human and vampire, a little more likely. But only a vampire mother produces a vampire child, because the babe is smeared with the mother's blood as it is born."

Beth was relieved. If she did have a child, it could not be vampire. But the concept of a vampire child still bothered her. "How . . . ?" What question could she ask without betraying a horror the Countess obviously would not feel?

"The Companion is quiescent until they reach puberty. They cannot draw the power, for instance. But it must be fed, and we must help them to their blood. It is up to the parents to instill proper values about the taking."

"Yes . . . a challenge. Children always are, are they not?"

"But rewarding. The blood is the life." She said it as though it was a mantra. "But you do not understand that, do you? Rufford knows, though I have never said it to him. He has felt the difference between his existence now and how he was when he was merely human. We are more alive than you are. It is a thing devoutly to be wished for, though the likes of you would never credit it. I only hope that he can accept it in himself."

Beth lifted her chin. "You seem very sure of what I would think." But in one way the Countess was right. Rufford must make peace with his state.

Lady Lente cocked her head, considering Beth. "I told him he must get over Asharti. She damaged him in many ways. I hope his expedition to Africa will help him escape her influence. Perhaps you have a role as well." She paused. "Do not fail him."

"What do you mean?" Beth asked, startled. Then more seriously, "What should I do?"

"Have courage. You will know when the time comes." She stood. The interview was at an end. "I like him. I am sorry he has this burden. But I am glad he can be useful to our kind. He is exempted from the death sentence imposed on those made by wantons like Asharti. I wish you both success." She nodded once and glided out into the room, leaving Beth wondering.

Ian searched the room for his bride but did not see her. His bride! How strange that she had accepted him, knowing what she did. He would never give her cause to regret it. Once he had found Kivala, he would remove her safely to Gibraltar while he went after Asharti. He would protect her with his strength, his life, for all of hers. A pang shot through him. She would grow old as he did not. He renewed again the private vows he had made along with the public ones today: he would never take her blood, he would protect her from infection by his own blood and the evil it brought, and he would never force her to accept the physical intimacy of marriage with such as he was. He had thought at the time that the vow to resist taking her blood might be the hardest to keep, if the need was on him, but after dancing with her tonight he was not sure.

Even he had not anticipated her transformation, though he knew the colors chosen for her by her aunt had never shown her to advantage. Her exotic beauty had always been there. Yet when people thought her a boring eccentric, they had been unable to see beyond the fact that she was different. But tonight her marriage to a man desired by other mamas and the cachet of being feted by none other than the Countess of Lente ripped the blinders from all eyes.

Ian might need blinders in order to avoid the effect Beth had on him. The heave of her breasts in that dress, the feel of her small, erect form in his arms as they whirled around the floor, the softness in those luminous green-gold eyes as she looked up at him, had made him long for a complete relationship, even as they stirred memories of undressing her in Gibraltar. But he also remembered his temptation to compel her acquiescence to his desires. That was a temptation he would *never* indulge. He must not become like Asharti, whatever the cost. Beth had acceded to his bargain because she was destitute, but she could not want a true union with a creature such as he was. *Let that fact suppress my unruly desires.* It had been long since he had allowed himself release in a physical sense. Celibacy was really the only choice. He would get used to it.

Beatrix emerged from an alcove, surveyed the room, and bore down on him. "Remarkable achievement, is it not? If only I did not find myself overheated and in need of a sojourn on the balcony, life would be perfect."

Ian shook his head in mock despair. "Are you never subtle? A wrap?"

"Hardly." She led the way to the French windows that gave out onto a balcony overlooking the square. In the brisk air she turned and cleared her throat. "Close the doors, Rufford." Then, as he did so, "I find myself in an awkward position."

He raised his brows. "How so? Does she not justify your sponsorship?"

"Of course she does," Beatrix snapped. "She is lovely, intelligent, and disarmingly candid. No, I am afraid I must put myself forward in a role I find uncomfortable." She took a breath. "As a bridegroom, you should know that it is not possible to pass your condition to any offspring. Only if her blood contains the Companion is it passed to a child she produces."

Ian had not considered that possibility. His thoughts leaped ahead to the idea of Miss Rochewell producing his child and what that entailed. A vision of a family of his own like Henry's, full of love and mutual respect, wavered in his mind. He felt himself flushing. "There is no danger of that," he said dampingly. "Why do you take this upon yourself?"

"Because you are ignorant of your condition and . . . because she asked me."

"She asked *you* if a child would be vampire?"

"She is not, as I said, unintelligent. She heard me question a woman who bore your puncture wounds, smelled my 'perfume,' and concluded that I would know your circumstances."

Ian drew himself up. "You need not worry. The situation will not arise."

Beatrix turned to look out over the dark trees, their bare, clacking branches glistening with droplets from a rain shower that had moved through the city while they were engaged inside. "She seemed to think it might, and was preparing as best she could."

Ian wanted to know a thousand things; whether she looked as though the event would be distasteful to her, exactly what she had said . . . But he could ask nothing. "Our bargain was for a marriage of convenience only."

"Who knows what she thinks that might entail?" Beatrix asked the night. Her words drifted back over her shoulder.

"I never meant her virgin state to be a part of the cost to her," Ian said stiffly.

Beatrix turned. "Perhaps you need more advice about females than vampires. I suggest you take your time with her. You are right about her being a virgin, in spite of what everyone thinks about her life in foreign climes. Thank goodness you have been dallying with every woman in town. You can afford to go slowly."

Ian's face hardened. "Don't believe every rumor about me."

"Lord, you fought a duel over one silly cow." Beatrix laughed.

"That does not mean I was guilty, only accused."

Beatrix's eyes narrowed. "And exactly how long has it been, Rufford?"

"A lady would never ask that question." He opened the doors and gestured her inside.

She did not go. "Not since Asharti?" She examined him, her eyes concerned.

She had no right to be concerned. "Not your business."

To his annoyance she smiled with some secret knowledge. "Then I shall be forced to let nature take its course, I suppose." She shot a glance at him. "But go slowly."

Eighteen

Beth found that the Countess had made arrangements for the newly wedded couple to stay in her best bedroom that night. At midnight, as the other guests went down to supper, married couples had pushed the two across the room to each other and begun calling for them to retire. Lewd comments and applause propelled them upstairs. Rufford seemed as nervous as a rat where cats are on the prowl. Her own back was ramrod-straight in apprehension. The great blue bedroom to which they were led had a fire crackling in the grate and candles set about the room. A man's nightshirt and some soft silk sleeping gear were laid out upon the bed, which was turned back in what was meant to be an inviting fashion. It only felt like a threat. Brandy and Madeira were set out on the sideboard along with a tray of sweetmeats.

Rufford cleared his throat. "That will be all," he said to the ancient servant with the knowing look in his eyes. Beth drifted to the fire, where she stood warming her hands with her back to the room. The door closed behind the servant with a finality she found chilling.

Beth chanced a glance behind her. The tension in the room was palpable. Rufford stood rooted in the center of the carpet. "I will sleep in this chair," he volunteered, pointing to one of a set in the corner. "It looks as though the dressing room is through those doors."

She did not speak but nodded silently and scooped up the silken pile from the bed and closed the door behind her. A young girl waited to help her undress. The dressing room contained a trunk half-packed and filled with clothes. Pomona green and old gold, deep russet and mink brown, they spilled out in profusion. He had bought all these for her.

For the past two days she had anticipated this moment, dreaded it, and now it was upon her. Everything would happen or not happen in the next minutes. What did she want to happen? The girl unhooked her dress and Beth slipped out of it. He had already told her his choice. He said he would sleep in the chair. Yet if they did not consummate their marriage tonight, the tension would grow until it was a great thunderous storm between them, so crashing loud they would not be able to hear each other even if they shouted. The girl folded the dress carefully in tissue and laid it on the trunk. Beth unwound the pearls from her neck. But to tell herself the truth, that was not the only reason she wanted consummation. She wanted to make love to Ian Rufford, had wanted it for a long time. It was a mystery to her, this physical act. But some part of her knew that she would never be whole unless that mystery was solved. Perhaps the solutions would be another piece in the puzzle that was Rufford, too. She resolved to do what she could to bring about exactly what was making her tremble inside even now.

Would he do it? He could not be attracted to a mere brown dab of a girl with odd-colored eyes. Yet he was a man. Men had carnal unions with women they did not care for all the time. And perhaps, if he came to depend on her, he would grow used to how she looked. They would become comfortable together and retrieve the friendship they had shared, spoiled now by his fear of his condition and the prospect of being man and wife. They *were* friends. That buoyed her. She dismissed the girl and slipped out of her underthings.

He might lose control. She had heard men did. Perhaps he would take her blood. She did not find that so horrible. In

Gibraltar when he sucked at her neck, she'd been transported away from the everyday, from practicality, to some place where magic happened.

She slipped the soft silken gown over her head. It brushed her nipples and hardened them. She was frightened. But not of what most people would think she should fear.

When Miss Rochewell retired, Ian paced to the fire and wondered how far he should undress. Certainly he could not sleep in his coat. He removed it with difficulty, it was so snug, as well as his cravat, his shoes and waistcoat, leaving him in shirt and breeches. That would do. He poured himself a brandy. He had not drunk much tonight. Now he was in need of liquid fortitude. He glanced into the mirror and saw that his open shirt revealed the scars at his throat. He stiffened, pushed down the memory of rope against his neck, and fastened the button at his collar.

She returned, her hair unbound, in the off-white nightgown he had purchased. It was modest, unlike the public garments he had given her, its neckline high, its long sleeves demure. She looked lovely. "Would you like some Madeira?" he asked, then remembered earlier conversations. "Or . . . or brandy?" He took his eyes from her by force.

She shook her head.

He sat with jerky movements in the chair, but she did not climb into the high bed. She stood, wavering there before him. He could see her unbound breasts move beneath the loose silk fabric, so fine it was almost sheer. Her dark nipples were taut. His throat grew tight. "Shall I put out the candles, or shall you?" he asked stupidly.

"It is a shocking waste," she said, "but I like the light. Let us leave them lit a while."

"As you wish." He threw back the brandy and turned to reach for the decanter. He must turn away or she might see a very obvious sign of the effect she was having on him. How, in God's name, was he going to sleep in a chair in her bedroom tonight or other nights? He repeated his vows in his

mind. "Well, I shall just take this extra quilt. . . ." He kept his
back turned as he sidled over to grab the white embroidered
coverlet laid across the foot of the bed. He turned to make a
dash to the chair, and she was there, close, looking up at him
with those luminous eyes. The weight of her breasts beneath
the silk made his loins tighten further.

"Must you sleep in the chair?" She flushed.

"Our bargain did not include. . . . any obligation on you
of a more . . . intimate nature." His throat was so full he
could hardly speak. He cleared it, then wished he had not.

"Oh. I was not sure." She looked daunted. He saw her
gather herself. "I was hoping we could discuss that bargain a
little more fully."

"Of course." He pulled the quilt between them. What
would she think if she saw his erection? He was not a
slightly built man. It would be distasteful to her. He would
give anything he could name to suppress it. But that was not
likely. "What did you wish to . . . discuss?"

She took his brandy glass, sipped, and made a small face.
She took a breath. "It is just that if you are to be my husband
and you will live a very long time, then, if I am true to the
vows I have made today and they do not include a . . . consummation . . . well, then I shall never know the joys of the
marriage bed." She flushed. "I find that hard."

"Fidelity was not included in your obligation." He did not
like that thought.

"Oh, you mean I should take lovers?" she asked, her eyes
searching his face.

He started to answer, thought better of it, and took the
brandy glass back. He gulped and felt the liquid warm his
belly. Why not? The rest of him seemed to be on fire.

"But . . ." she mused, and took the brandy glass. She
sipped. Her lips were right where his had been. She had
turned the glass to be sure of it. Was that on purpose? "If I
take lovers, would they not expect me to be an experienced
woman? How will I get experience if not from you?"

"Blast their expectations, Miss . . ." He colored. "Elizabeth." The sound of her name in his mouth was intimate.

"I prefer Beth . . . Ian." Her voice was husky.

He managed a lopsided grin. "At least I know not to call you Lizzy."

She smiled. Her eyes crinkled when she smiled. "That is wise."

"Beth, then." It was like breathing. Beth. Where was he? What had he been saying?

"So, it isn't possible to renegotiate the bargain?"

"You want to include . . . carnal . . . experience then?" He was not sure he sounded calm.

"I have nothing left to sweeten the pot. I have already said I would help you, whatever you need." She sipped the brandy and stepped even closer. Thank God for the quilt.

He cleared his throat again. She was bargaining to give up something precious to a woman. "I am not sure you understand what you would be relinquishing."

"I am a married woman. What need have I to be a virgin? Who would expect it of me? No, if I am to be of the married state, I think I had better have it all." Her color suddenly drained away and all her boldness with it. "Of course, it would need be just the once, just to show me how one goes on." She looked down at her bare feet. "If you found you could not bring yourself to it, why a bargain is a bargain nonetheless, and you have already fulfilled your part."

The silly chit thought he could not bring himself to lie with her when he was burning for her to the point of pain even as they sat here talking so inanely? God, he had vowed he would never thrust himself on her, but he had counted on her never volunteering. He had no right . . . with what he was.

But she knew what he was. She must know what she wanted. She had even asked Beatrix about children. He found that the quilt had dropped between them, and he was gripping her upper arms through the silk and searching her green-gold eyes for guile or for demanding. She had demanded once. She had said, "Love me," when she was half out of her mind with fever and loss of blood. Now she asked, and with so little self-confidence it was endearing to a fault. She tried to be casual—certainly she spoke as no woman he had ever heard before. He thought he would burst, and whether his heart or his cock would burst first he could not be sure.

He leaned down and brought her so close her breasts pressed against his ribs. He should not. . . . She would feel his need. She lifted her mouth, that fulsome mouth.

Beth felt the urgency in him and the hardness at his loins as he drew her in toward his body. Her breasts brushed his ribs. The scent of cinnamon and ambergris was both familiar and exciting. Her own breathing alternately stopped and came so fast and shallowly she thought she might faint. He wanted her. Of that there could be no doubt. He might not love her, but he would lie with her tonight. Her own body was almost in pain between her legs. Was that desire doing that? She certainly wanted him. She lifted her mouth to his. He bent above her. His lips trembled against hers as his grip on her arms grew harder. He would leave bruises. She did not care.

Then his tongue was searching her mouth. She had never felt the strange intimacy of a wet tongue inside her mouth. It was not unpleasant. She touched his tongue with hers, and with that encouragement he probed deeper. He took her into his arms and held her, pressed against the length of his body. She could actually feel his loins throbbing against her belly, and between her own legs the ache was becoming almost unbearable. She ran her hands over his back and felt the muscles beneath his shirt.

Suddenly he tore his lips away from hers, gasping, and held her head against his chest. "We must go slowly, so that you will have enjoyment of this night."

"I was enjoying that," she said, trying not to complain. She heard his deep chuckle rumble in his chest. He had never felt so male, so fundamentally different than she was. He let her go and stepped quickly to dim the lamps on the far side of the room, leaving only the candlesticks on the bedside tables and the branch near the door. This last he took and put by the bed. The flickering light was soft.

He took her hand and drew her to the bed. Her fear was drowned in the passion of his kisses. "I will show you more enjoyment," he murmured. "After all, it is a husband's duty." He smiled when he said it, and the dark pools of his eyes looked deep and deeply into her. Was it only duty that drove him? He slipped the shift over her head, leaving her naked in the warm room. She wondered if she looked like the female Egyptian figures painted on the walls of tombs who always attended kings on their way to the underworld. She would like that.

He could not seem to breathe. She felt self-conscious and, in order to be busy, she tugged at the ribbon at his nape. His hair cascaded over his shoulders and she ran her fingers through it. How she loved that hair! Then she pulled his shirt from his breeches and unbuttoned the neck. He stayed her hands in his large one. "I am not a pretty sight, I'm afraid," he said, his voice hoarse.

She looked up at him. "Your scars?" She smiled. "I have seen them, you know." She gently freed her hands. "Even touched them." She ran her hands up under his shirt, over his welted back, and pulled his shirt off over his head with one smooth movement. He hastily unfastened his cuffs and drew it off. He was still a little embarrassed, she could see. She lifted her mouth for more kisses as she reached for the buttons of his breeches. She could hear the breath rasping in his throat.

He took her hands away and lifted her onto the bed. "Let me." He looked down at his breeches. His hands were clumsy. "You're sure you would not prefer that I wear the nightshirt?"

"Do you think I will be shocked?" she asked, amused. "I have seen men naked, bathing in the Nile, the Tigris. I have seen statues with full erections."

"Yes, well, perhaps you will be disappointed then," he said roughly as he finally freed the last button and slid the trousers over his hips.

"No," she said, looking her fill and then opening her arms to him. "Not at all."

He smiled wryly, then, and some of the nervousness left

him. His body was as powerful as she remembered it but
paler now. The scars did not stand out so much. And his most
male parts, which she had seen only quiescent, now
throbbed erect, better than any stone statue, since they promised heat as well as adamantine hardness. Her only doubt
was that he was so large and she felt so small. She had never
regretted her size more. Was it even possible?

He seemed to be having similar thoughts. He looked at
her with such—what was it, wonder?—in his eyes. He laid
her back upon the pillows. Nervously she spread her knees.
That was what one did, she knew. He slid in beside her.
"Time enough for that later," he said. "First let me introduce
you to some other pleasures."

He slid one arm under her neck and lifted her, even as he
bent to kiss her. His other hand cupped her buttocks, pressing her against him. She realized she was wet between her
thighs. He kissed her deeply, even as he stroked her back. At
last, when she could hardly breathe, he pulled away, only to
bend his lips to her nipple. He sucked and pulled at her until
she moaned a little; then he turned his attention to her other
breast. She had never believed so much feeling could be
concentrated in such a little mound of flesh. As she arched
against his mouth, he slid his hand between her thighs. He
seemed to control all of her body between his hands and his
mouth. His fingers slid up and down her slit, and some point
of feeling there wakened. Her hips began to move of their
own accord, willing him to continue. Back and forth he
rubbed, slick wetness sliding across pure feeling, until she
was panting and gasping in his arms. He stopped. The feeling ebbed. She wanted to protest. Was there to be no more?
Then he began again, faster, harder, and the feeling came
back tenfold. Somewhere she realized that she was clutching
at his back. The feeling in her nipples as he suckled there
was sent down to the point between her legs and back again,
redoubled, until she crashed through some final barrier and
the feeling shot up through unbearable to ecstatic and she
bucked and rocked against his hand, crying out in some
gasping breath she did not recognize.

As she collapsed he moved his mouth's attention back to hers and pressed his palm against her mound. With one wet finger, he searched inside her.

"Ohhhh," she managed, into his kisses. "I had no idea." She opened one eye. "You did not tell me." An echo rippled through her, forcing a little gasp of pleasure.

"What would I have said?" he whispered, holding her against his muscled chest.

"How about, 'This is wonderful and women who say it is only a duty are very wrong'?"

"I . . . I don't think some women like it very much."

She put herself up on one elbow. "How strange! I wonder why not."

"Perhaps you have to be a little . . . open to the world to allow yourself to enjoy it." His eyes were not serious, though his mouth managed serious quite nicely.

"I expect you are right." She looked at him shyly and smiled. "Thank you."

He nodded. "The least I could do," he murmured.

"Now, it is your turn, Ian." His given name was still so strange to her. She had a thought. "Is men's enjoyment the same?"

He looked surprised. "How would we ever know? The . . . result is similar. Though not quite as long lasting, I think."

"Interesting," she declared. "Now, what must I do to give you the maximum enjoyment and length?" She snuggled into his chest. Cinnamon and ambergris washed over her. She ran her hand down his belly and touched his erect member tentatively, running her hand along it. A drop of moisture quivered at its tip and she slicked it down his length.

"You have good instincts," he gasped.

She ran her hand downward and cupped his testicles. *Yes,* she thought as she felt them tighten. She wanted nothing more than to give him the pleasure he had given her. If she could, even in her inexperience, come anywhere near sharing that pleasure, then surely he would want to do it again and again, as she did even now, and their marriage would be very convenient. Then maybe he would begin to feel for her what she felt for him.

Ian lay beside her and wondered how he would restrain himself from coming the moment he entered her, if indeed he could last that long. He had never known a woman so open to the sexual experience, so innocent and yet so wonderfully eager to be pleased and to please in return. Especially as it was her first time. He had half-hoped that all that riding about on camels might have broken her virginity, but it was intact, which meant that it was his job to break it—gently, if he could. He had made sure she had her pleasure before the deed was done, in case it proved so painful she drew back. He had never had a virgin before. His early experiences were with village women glad to oblige him, and later he had graduated to fair cyprians and married women with as much experience as he had and more.

The ache in his loins was such that he knew he had better prepare her as best he could before he tried to enter her. It was like to be over fairly quickly after that. He wished he had time to take Beatrix's advice and find a willing partner or two before he came to Beth, all pulsing male need.

He cradled her and kissed her hair. Her small hand stole to his cock and her thumb took the semen seeping at its tip and rubbed it along the length. He gasped. God, let him find strength! She cupped his balls and they tightened even more, though the pain from holding himself in had already done its share of tightening. Her hips began to move unconsciously against his, and he thought she might not need much more preparation. He eased his hand into her moist folds and found that her nub was already swollen with passion again. He kissed her and murmured, "Don't be afraid," as he touched the inside of her knee.

She opened to him instantly, a soft look in her eyes. "I'm not."

He took his cock in his own hand, the better to control its entry. She was so very small! Still, he found her passage. His cock felt the barrier. Hanging above her, his weight carefully supported on one elbow, he bent and kissed her, deeply, thoroughly, to focus her attention on her mouth. Then he pushed against the barrier, once and out, again and out. She arched against him, and he pushed through. She gasped once. He slid almost out. Then she opened her knees flat and gripped his buttocks, pushing him back into her with a sigh.

She was so tight around him. He slid in and out. She pulled him down, demanding kisses. Then she kissed his neck across the scars made by Asharti, his breast where Asharti had opened him and sucked his blood. "Deeper," she moaned.

It is not a command, he told himself.

She pulled him down against her breasts, her mouth searching for his. Her teeth scraped across his lips and down, down toward his neck.

Memories flooded him. He could smell his own blood in the stale, hot air inside the tent.

He knelt on all fours in front of her, head hanging, his knees spread wide, just as she liked them. His cock was throbbing, demanding, erect, as it hung down, vulnerable to her. She stalked around him, naked, occasionally striking him with a supple switch to make him flinch. She was haranguing him in a language he did not understand, but her tone was derogatory. He knew she was reviling him. She put her hands on the welts across his buttocks and slid one down to slap his cock sharply from behind. Then she sank her sharp canine teeth into his left buttock and began to suck. He groaned. She both kept him filled with lust and bottled up his release, or he might have come with the very rhythm of her sucking. When had he come to find it . . . stimulating as well as disgusting?

After a moment she withdrew her canines, allowed the blood to seep a little, and rubbed it across his buttocks. Then she sat astride him, her own wet slit sliding over his buttocks to the small of his back. Her juices mingled with his blood. She pulled up his chin, so that his back arched and pressed

*her breasts against his shoulders. Then she raked her teeth
over the places in his neck where she had fed before, tantalizing him with the promise of attack. She rocked her open
female membranes against his back as she finally struck and
sucked and sucked.*

Ian rolled away with a guttural cry and pressed his hands to
his temples.

"What is it?" The girl's voice was worried. "What have I
done?"

"Nothing," he croaked. "Not your fault. It's mine." He
rolled over to hide his softening cock and shut his eyes tight.
Asharti had won again tonight. In some ways he was still her
slave. His refusal to make love to a woman for all this time
was because he was afraid of this, though he had not admitted it. Maybe he would never be able to come again unless
the woman he was with whipped him and sucked his blood.
Or maybe he would never enjoy a woman at all, because *she*
would stand between them with her demanding and her humiliation and the fact that she had made lust into something
shameful.

Beth sat up in bed, the sheets clutched to her breast, aghast.
What had happened? One minute he was kissing her thoroughly while his member claimed her virginity, and the
next he was clenched up tight, his delightful man-part
shrunk.

"I . . . I failed you. Tell me how."

He opened the eye she could see, and it was fierce with
hatred. "*I* failed."

"But I don't think so," Beth persisted. "I am definitely not
a virgin anymore."

At that, he chewed his lip and sat up, his wavy hair cascad-
ing to his shoulders once again. "Are . . . are you all right?"

"Yes." Beth did not quite know what to say. She was
fairly sure he had not experienced the pleasure that she had

known tonight. Unless she had missed it altogether. But then he would not be so miserable, would he?

"Did, did it hurt?" he asked.

"A little. But the rest of it was nice," she said earnestly. "*Very* nice. Did you . . . ?"

He shook his head.

"We could try again." She hated sounding tentative, but she knew so little.

"The result would be the same," he growled. "I'm afraid you have married a eunuch, my dear." His face was so closed and hard she hardly recognized it. "My apologies."

He did not give her time to reply but pushed out of bed, grabbed his clothing from the floor, and disappeared into the dressing room. He did not come out again.

Nineteen

Beth endured a long and sleepless night, wondering what was best to do about what had happened and wishing she had someone to advise her. He had called himself a eunuch. But she had met many eunuchs in Africa, usually black slaves of Muslim owners, and she knew that eunuchs had all or parts of their male equipment removed by a blade. They did not get erections, even if they were lucky enough to retain the part that got erections, which most of them weren't. White slaves had only their testicles cut off. But she had felt his sac last night and it seemed full to bursting. So he was not a eunuch, and he must know that, too.

Was it a figure of speech? He meant he could not do it anymore, but not necessarily due to a physical condition. It wasn't that he found her so unattractive that he could not bear to consummate their marriage. He had wanted to lie with her at first. She was sure of it.

In the deep of the night with the house quiet, she remembered what he had implied about his experience with Asharti. Even then, Beth had guessed that the vampire woman forced him somehow to sexual acts he found distasteful. Were the scars of that experience preventing him from taking his pleasure now? Beth grew more certain as the sky promised dawn. It was Asharti and what she had done to Ian that stood between them. The Countess said that Asharti had damaged Ian. She thought Beth could help. But how? The mere fact that she had seen his failure might prevent him caring for her. She would give up that part of married life wholly, even though it had been wonderful to lie in his arms, if only it would not poison all their friendship.

A servant roused her quite early in the morning with a cup of chocolate and a scone and the news that the carriage was waiting and that the maids had packed her trunks for the journey to Portsmouth. She must have slept in the hour before dawn.

Beth gulped her chocolate, washed herself from the basin, and dressed hastily in the Pomona green sarcenet traveling costume left out for her. It was decorated with darker green braid, with hunter half boots and a matching pelisse. He had even provided a matching knit reticule, as well as a fetching military-style beaver hat with a dashing pheasant's feather.

She hurried down, regretting she was late, though it was so early. Why hadn't the servants woken her earlier? She might have had a breakfast with him. She might have been able to say . . . what? What was there to say?

There was no time to have a word with the Countess, either, for her hostess was not yet risen, though what Beth would have dared reveal she did not know. She dashed into the breakfast room for tea and toast, to find Major Ware pacing there.

"Major!" she exclaimed, startled.

The Major bowed. "Mrs. Rufford, a word if you please."

"Of course," Beth murmured, and forced herself to quiet. What could the Major want?

The man's pale blue eyes blinked repeatedly. His shoulders were stiff with disapproval. "Rufford has engaged his brother Stanbridge and me to . . . to ensure that the settlements he drew up are executed in your favor in case . . . in case his task does not go . . . well."

"He contacted you? Last night?"

"Send us word and one of us will hasten to your side and provide you escort home. He has provided handsomely for you."

"You don't think he's coming back, do you?"

"As he said, there is a chance. There is always a chance." Ware's eyes did not agree. He gathered himself. "I cannot persuade him to leave you in England. How can he be so selfish? I ask you now to stay behind."

Beth was shaken, but she dared not show it. "He wants to take me no more than you want him to do so. But he cannot do it without me. You have too little faith in him. He will prevail."

"I have faith in his courage," the Major said, going pale. "He knows what he faces and yet he goes. He will not run shy."

"No, he will not. Neither will I. I thank you for your kindness, Major. I must go now." The carriage drew into the graveled drive just visible outside the breakfast parlor.

The Major sighed and followed as she rose. Her boot heels clicked on the marble of the foyer. He handed her into the carriage laden with trunks. She had hoped Ian would unburden himself to her during the long journey to Portsmouth, but she found she was to go alone and he to follow after the sun had set. That meant they could have spent the day together inside a darkened room if he had wished it. He did not. Major Ware saluted and the carriage pulled away.

The drivers and outriders took the greatest care of her. But the journey was most miserable. She was installed at an inn, knowing she would not see her husband until near dawn.

He came. His face had not softened. They were whisked to the ship by a small launch in the hour before sunrise with hardly a word between them. This time the boat was a cutter in the service of His Majesty, arranged, apparently, by Major Ware's friends at Whitehall.

"Weather's like to be foul this time of year, so it should give us some ripping good wind once we make it out of the Channel. I'll wager we make more than two hundred miles a day." The Captain, whose name was, regrettably, Stilton, was a lanky youth who had taken a cutter as command rather than be put ashore now that the Royal Navy was standing down with Bonaparte's defeat. The ship was ever so much tidier than the merchantman they had last sailed in. The bright red coats of the marines and the navy blue of the officers' uniforms made a pretty show. "You will find your cabins aft with mine," the Captain added. "We have moved the bulkhead a bit. There ain't much room in a cutter," he apologized, "but room is what you sacrifice for speed."

"A welcome sacrifice," Ian remarked.

Beth for her part could not but focus on the plural of the word *cabin*. Sure enough, when a Lieutenant showed them to their berths, there were two, and it became clear that they were not to share a bed. She stole a glance to Ian's face, but it was as closed as ever.

"What?" she asked, realizing she had missed some question. "Oh, just the small one and the little valise. The others can be stowed in the hold."

She unpacked, used to the cramped quarters. Even she had to bend her head. She sat on her bed in the growing light, alone. When she finally went on deck, the sailors were very courteous. She made excuses for her husband's sun sickness and promised she would not be a bother, even as the cutter rolled out into the open Channel and set to sea.

She spent the blustery day in her cabin, working out just which scrolls would be useful and storing the rest, waiting for sunset. She heard him go on deck. He did not stop at her cabin.

She came up behind him in the fading light on the leeward rail opposite the Captain's private territory at the windward side and touched his arm. Ian straightened at her touch as though she had slapped him. Beth was hurt, but she said in a low voice, "The Captain promises ten days to Casablanca."

"I could wish for less."

"I will need your help to fix the likely location of Kivala."

He nodded again and turned away. "Let us hope we can find it."

"Surely we can go back in time," she said, trying not to plead, "to when we were just friends. We might even find time for a game of chess."

He glanced back at her. The pain in his eyes was the equal of any she had ever seen there.

"Is that so much to ask?" She knew her voice did not have the confidence she wanted.

"No. It is little enough. That may be why it is so difficult." He pushed himself off the rail. "Let us ask the Captain to use his dining table for our calculations until supper."

They pored over maps. Beth questioned Ian most particularly. After Kivala, Asharti had gone south and west to Marrakech. He had staggered east to El Golea. "The spine of the earth must be in the Atlas Mountains," she said, sitting back. "It is the only range between the two."

Ian leaned over the chart. "So the sandstone washes are in this diagonal." He sighed. "It must run for hundreds of miles."

"Do you remember how long you traveled northeast?"

He chewed those lovely lips. "Weeks." He shook his head, despairing. "I wasn't in great shape at that point."

Beth thought for a moment. "You said there was an oasis two days out from Kivala."

He nodded. "It was the only one for many miles, according to Fedeyah."

She pulled the chart close and got out the Captain's magnifier. "Did you hear the name?"

He hung his head and rubbed his temples. "Maybe . . . I don't know."

She bent over the chart, muttering. "The two peaks would have to be the tallest. That means the Middle Atlas Range. Atlas el Kebir. Stop me if these sound familiar . . . Haasi Zegdou . . . Haasi Chafaia . . . Haasi Ghemiles . . ." She raised her eyebrows at him.

He shook his head. "It's no use. There were so many. . . ." He looked guilty and ashamed.

"And you were weak and in pain," she said with some aspersion, "so you might just want to forgive yourself a little. Now just a few more. You never know. Haasi Fokra . . . Haasi—"

"Wait. Haasi Fokra!"

"Is that it?" She watched him stare into space.

A grin grew on those lips. "Yes. Yes! I remember. She and Fedeyah . . ." He trailed off.

"Very well then." She smiled, cutting off his other memories. "Haasi Fokra. Our first destination." They exchanged their first open look since the Countess's blue bedroom. Beth found it electrifying.

"We are on our way," he said. Suddenly he bent over the chart. "Show me."

She pointed. He marked El Golea and then Algiers with a finger and studied the distance. "It seemed so much farther. We wandered in the desert looking for it for almost two years."

"You must have tried here, in the desert under these mountains. See how far south?"

" 'Mouydir,' " he read. "Perhaps. I do remember an oasis called In Salah." He pointed to other mountains in the middle of the great desert. "And here—Bir al-Kasib."

"It looks like she was exploring washes at the base of mountains. She must have known to look for terrain similar to that around Petra. The sandstone washes lie between mountains and the desert, cut by spring runoff."

He sat back, staring at the map. "It makes it all seem so real, seeing it on a map like this."

"It must have seemed too real at the time, I should think." She was in dangerous territory.

"Perhaps it is better to think it a nightmare than to believe such things can really happen, that such evil lives in the world unchecked."

"Not unchecked . . ." she whispered.

They disembarked at Casablanca, only a week out of Portsmouth. They planned to press straight through the mountains into the desert by camel caravan as soon as they were provisioned, traveling by night. Ian knew they would have to be discreet in Casablanca. It was now controlled by Berbers in Asharti's service. The first night there, Ian saw two of her made vampires. Actually, he smelled them first—that distinctive, almost cinnamon smell, made more pronounced by the fact that these particular two did not see the value of frequent baths. Ian melted into the darkness of the streets and began bathing twice a day if he could manage it. The servants at their lodgings thought him mad. But better their attention than Asharti's followers.

The days in Casablanca were frantic ones. Ian spent nights practicing his new skills of mind control and relocation. He worked for hours on end with the heavy cutlass given him by Captain Stilton, very different from the foils he had practiced with some lifetime ago. He fed frequently in little sips, lest his hunger draw him into indiscretions. He kept himself as remote as Beth would let him. His failure on his wedding night should have made all sexual activity repellent, but it did not. He found Beth's presence continually disturbing. Several times he had had to turn away from her lest she see his erection. That was the torment of it all. He wanted her more than ever. Her soft voice was torture. Seeing the swell of her breasts brought almost physical pain, and any touch had an instant and disastrous effect. It was only the consummation of his carnal need that was impossible. His failure did not quench the fire at all.

His worst regret was that he failed Beth. A woman who wanted so much from life should not be denied this most elemental aspect of it. It tortured him that he caused her to suffer. Not only was she shackled to a monster, but one who could not fill her womanly needs. She could never love a man like that. He saw that clearly, now that he knew how much she reveled in relations between men and women. The fact that she tried to bridge his distance with her friendship only made him regret the more. He had, somewhere down deep, wanted her to love him. She had accepted what he was.

He had thought that perhaps . . . but all that was gone. She offered friendship. He would try to provide it.

He had been thinking about his failure incessantly, of course. He was amazed and touched by her giving nature, how much she enjoyed the lovemaking on their wedding night. It occurred to him that Beth's dawning sensuality had been part of his problem. Asharti defined herself through sexuality and power over others. When Beth grew even a little more confident in her sexuality, Asharti had come washing over him and ruined all. Didn't every man dream of a wife who enjoyed the act of love? If he could only share that with her, might she not love him?

Damn Asharti! It was his slavery to her that had unmanned him! The fear he had always felt of her turned to anger and boiled in his belly. It was a larger version of the flame that had blossomed in his heart when he decided he must face her. Her casual evil had done this thing to him, to Beth, to the world. The insouciance was what angered him most. Everyone in the world was there to be used by her. She had no conscience.

The anger continued to burn in him even through his growing doubt that he would be able to best her. She had probably taken blood of the Old One many times by now. And how would he convince the Old One to share blood, even once, with him? Ian's only hope was that what the Old One had gotten of Asharti was not what he had counted on—a thin hope at best.

Beth seemed to have unlimited faith in him. He could not share his doubts. What he could tell her was how amazed he was at her competence. In Casablanca, Ian could only marvel at his new wife. He had given her carte blanche with his bankers and she used it. Each evening she would account for her daylight hours with casual references to contacts made with her father's old suppliers, contracts sealed, list items completed. And what lists! She had thought of everything. She spoke Arabic and the Berber dialects. She drove a daunting bargain. And she hardly counted these skills at any worth. Beth controlled their success now. Ian wished that control did not make him feel uneasy. She was an odd combination of innocence and practical confidence. He was comfortable with neither. He watched her sometimes as she slept. He wanted so to protect her from all ugliness in the world, including his own. She was his responsibility, no matter that she led their expedition.

"I have news, Ian," she said, coming into their simple rooms as dusk fell ten days after their arrival in Casablanca. She was swathed in russet-colored fabric with a tiny gold geometric border. Across her forehead lay the gold chain hung with tiny moons and stars he had bought her last night at the bazaar after they finished an exotic dinner of a dozen courses one ate with one's hands. Ian had been grateful for the napkin over his lap as she fed him succulent bits of an aubergine paste with her fingers. Her skin had fairly glowed in the candlelight. "The caravan awaits us on the outskirts of the city. We can be off."

"Tonight?" he asked, surprised. He was oiling the mechanisms on his two pistols.

"As you like." She opened the door and motioned to a servant who carried a large soft package and a long wrapped tube and dragged a crate across the doorsill. "I'm afraid I may not be quite as good at sizes as you were." She dismissed the servant.

He ripped the soft package and found several striped burnooses, some soft leather boots, and a hip-length leather jacket lined with fleece. "For the mountain passes," she murmured.

He grinned. "Excellent!" Then he laid back the paper of the long package to reveal a metal scabbard from which a finely wrought hilt protruded. He looked up at her.

"I hope this one is better than the cutlass Captain Stilton gave you," she deprecated.

The slither of metal on metal filled the room as he took the sword from its sheath. The blade gleamed silver in the light of the lamps. The hilt balanced in his hand. It was a wonder of craftsmanship. "Thank you," he said simply. "You are a marvel."

"Nonsense," she said, dismissing his praise. "Pistols carry only two shots. You need something substantial to defend yourself when they are empty. Open the crate."

Ian pulled open the crate with his bare hands almost without effort. That always surprised him, even still. He glanced to Beth expecting dismay, but she only said, "Thank goodness. I forgot to tell the boy we needed a crowbar."

Inside, cold emanated from cloth bundles pressed into the crate. He unwrapped one. Ice clattered to the floor revealing a jar of claret liquid. He caught his breath.

"I have been paying for donations. The ice should last across the mountains. You must get through the last two hundred miles yourself."

"You really have thought of everything."

"Tosh. We will find a hundred things I have forgotten. But this *is* what I know how to do. I have been doing it since I was fifteen, you know."

He managed a smile. It could be comfortable to have her in charge. "Thank you, then."

She bobbed her head and turned from the room. He pulled her back, on impulse. It was the first time he had initiated a touch since London. The sear of her flesh on his must surely require bandages. Then, there he was, looking at her with nothing to say. His loins began their familiar burn. "As soon as you have read the transcriptions on the tablets at the doorways, you will leave the temple and start immediately back to Casablanca with the bearers. Once I have the Old One's blood, I will push on to Algiers alone. You understand?"

"Yes. But first, don't we have to get started?"

He let out a half smile and nodded. "To the caravan, then."

They slipped into the night. The bazaars were doing brisk business. It was almost March and still warm this far south. Women entirely covered in brown and black fabrics bloomed in groups like dark flowers. Men in burnooses and others in the wonderful embroidered vests of the Berbers, Nigerians in colored turbans above their black faces, milled together in the streets along with goats and sheep and pigs.

Life of a thousand varieties fought for room. The smell of exotic fruits and spice drifted in the air. Perhaps that was how Ian missed him.

He came out of an alleyway, pushed through the crowds, and jerked Ian into the darkness. Ian fell to his knees on the hard-packed sand. His adversary was Berber, and now that they were alone in the cool damp of the close earthen walls, Ian could smell the cinnamon.

"Christian bloodsucker!" he growled in English. "You are not one of Asharti's."

"I want only to leave your city in peace." Ian picked himself up off the sand.

"There is no peace unless you swear allegiance to Asharti." Ian saw his adversary's teeth gleam in the dark. "They have sent others against her. To no avail."

Ian drew himself up. "I'll wager *you* did not kill those sent against her. You are a weak imitation of her. She does not allow you her own blood, does she?"

The man swelled with rage. Ian could feel him call on his Companion, and the power answer. In a second, he would strike. Ian opened up the connection to his own partner. *Companion, come to me. Bring strength and life.*

The man's eyes went red. "For Allah and Asharti!" He charged.

Ian pushed him away, but not before the butt of his head had broken several ribs. "Give way. You cannot kill me," he panted. The singing in his veins throbbed and flowed. His own eyes would be red now, he knew. The fool charged again, trying to get hold of Ian's arm, no doubt to rip it from the socket. He latched on to the wrist, but Ian lifted him bodily in the air and dashed him against the wall. "Give over! You do not need to do this."

The man shook his head. Ian saw the red eyes pulse, his lips draw back over fangs. "Swear to Asharti, or die," the man hissed. He looked like an animal, just as Ian must himself. The vampire drove in low. He got Ian's forearm and wrenched it. Ian felt the bones go, but it was not off. He picked the man up by the scruff of the neck and pushed him flat against the sandstone wall with his body. This fool would never give up! He was a beast under Asharti's control. And the blood singing in Ian's veins whispered that in some ways this creature *was* Asharti. He would tell Asharti they were here. Asharti would come after them. After Beth. Ian raised both hands to the man's head. Even with bones protruding from his arm, when he twisted, the neck snapped. Ian backed away. The vampire slid down the wall, still staring, still red eyed. *God help me. It isn't enough.* The beast began to rise. *No. God damn your eyes!* With a growl fueled by his Companion, Ian lunged in and twisted with all his might. The head came off in his hands.

In shock, Ian stood staring at it. Blood dripped from the neck. He dropped it as though it burned. It bounced once in a muted thud. The body toppled. He turned in some kind of nightmare slowness to the entry of the alley. Several people looked on, shock and horror writ large on their faces, before they vanished into the crowd.

Beth! Ian felt time move again. He dashed to her side, grabbed her hand, and pulled her through the milling throng. They stopped running as the houses began to thin.

"What happened?" Beth panted. She was staring at his clothes.

Ian glanced down. He was covered in spattered blood. "Vampire. I had to kill him. Someone may know we have been here."

She looked up at him. He could see she understood the implications. "Then let us go."

Twenty

They made good time over the mountain pass through the cold of snow and wind at almost four thousand feet. They pushed on relentlessly with a guide Beth had hired in Casablanca. Ian felt all the dread of heading back into the land he had sworn to leave behind. Kivala, if he was lucky enough to find it, the Old One, and even Asharti herself lay somewhere ahead in the desert that spread more than a thousand miles across the shoulders of the African continent like a sandy shawl. He must go back there, where all his fear and horrible memories waited, if he was ever to reclaim his life.

Ian's ribs healed that first night. He tugged on his hand until the bones slipped back beneath the skin. Beth did not know he was hurt and he did not want her to know. She would be upset and feel she had to help. There were some things he wanted to do himself. The bones in his arm knit. As he and Beth went higher, it grew too cold to travel by night, so Ian pulled up the hood of his burnoose and donned his spectacles and they traveled by day, with him ensconced upon his camel. Beth directed everything now. He was just a passenger on her caravan. But his time would come. Soon it would all be up to him.

• • •

Beth watched the last of their ice melt as they reached
Zagora on the other side of the pass that snaked between the
Southern Atlas Range and Atlas el Kebir. Beth knew the
blood Ian needed would be gone soon. Their days in
Casablanca had been torture. She wanted so to touch him.
The night of their wedding had opened some vista of sensuality that made being around Ian a physical trial. The movement of his shoulders under his coat, the way he pressed his
lovely lips together so severely, everything attracted her to
him and raised her blood. But she was only too aware that
she could not speak of what had happened. She could not be
the one to bridge the gulf between them. He made that plain.
The most frustrating part was that she knew he would never
speak of it willingly. They talked of their plans and the
everyday events. But she wanted more.

The village of Zagora consisted of a few hovels and some
sheep and goat pens. Beth had resolved to buy more blood,
rather than make Ian forage. The hardened and debauched
residents of Casablanca had not blinked at trading money
for their blood. Here the story might be different. She
dressed in a woman's robes rather than the trousers and
boots she favored for riding camels, and left Ian asleep in the
tent. With a clean lancet and a sack of dinars she strode into
the village. The largest hut seemed to be a public gathering
place, whether mosque or tavern she could not tell, since all
the buildings looked equally dusty, their sandstone corners
rounded by wind. She entered alone. She dared not let the
camel keepers or their guide see her purchase.

Her eyes adjusted to the darkness slowly. A young
woman, dressed in a shift only partly covered by a shawl
wrapped over her shoulders and around her head, came forward and asked what Beth wanted. It was a tavern. She asked
for water and then, after a hesitation, asked in careful Arabic
if she could buy something else. Beth set her bag of dinars
on the table and let the clink draw the girl's attention.

"What can I get for you, great lady?" the girl asked, her eyes never leaving the bag.

"I want to fill this water sack with blood, a little from several people," Beth said, watching for her reaction. She did not have long to wait.

The girl's eyes went big. She backed away. "Allah, not another one!" She put one hand to her throat. Several men got up, menacing. Now that Beth's eyes were used to the dim light, she saw that several had marks at their necks.

"Filth of Asharti!" a man growled.

"A thousand pardons!" she said hastily, bowing and backing out of the room. One of the men grabbed for her. She turned and dashed for the door, leaving the water sack behind.

"Ian, Ian," she said, scrambling into the tent. "We have to go."

He was up in an instant. "What?"

She dragged him out as he pulled up his hood. The camp was already being struck. The tent came down as he exited. "I asked to buy blood," she whispered. "They had already given."

He put on his blue spectacles, squinting painfully. Camels dragged to their feet by the drivers protested with honking cries. Packs were settled, tents folded. "They have not the courage to attack," he observed. A line of men stopped uncertainly at the edge of the village. "But it is time to go."

They headed east, under the looming Atlas el Kebir. The air was warmer now. The caravan members shed their cloaks and traded boots for sandals. The caravan began to move at night again. Ian and Beth took their lunars for position in the stark desert sky. The days stretched on. Haasi Zegdou, Zagamira, they went from water hole to water hole. They came to Haasi Fokra more than two weeks after they had left Zagora.

As they approached the shallow pool among the date palms all Beth's doubts assailed her. She had been so busy worrying about Ian she had not had time to doubt her ability to help him if they actually found Kivala. Who knew if she would be able to translate the texts that told how to open the door into the temple? She dreaded thinking she might fail him in the thing that mattered most to him. And to the world. The attack of the vampire in Casablanca shook her. From the blood that covered Ian she knew what he must have had to do to it. No, to him. If Ian was human, so were the others. The poor village that had been victimized by Asharti's army—what better evidence of what a world ruled by Asharti might be like? Ian depended upon her. . . .

He stood looking at the pool in which he had washed before being brought to Asharti. Behind him the caravan unpacked and prepared to rest. Dawn was not far away now. Beth was directing the pitching of tents. He could hear her talking with the camel master and the guide. But those things were of now, and he was back there, then. Over there was where Asharti's litter had been placed. She was so anxious to proceed she had not even let them pitch her tent. Just there, Fedeyah had handed him the oil he rubbed on his body. He could practically smell the myrrh of the oil and the cinnamon scent of Fedeyah that matched *her* scent.

He looked up and saw Fedeyah crossing to him. It seemed so natural.

"So, English, you have returned." The spectrally thin face was flat and blank, framed by the hood of his burnoose.

"Yes," he said to the man who had given him, nightly, to the woman that man had loved for what, a thousand years? The man had also saved his life but, in doing so, condemned him.

"This is perhaps a long way to reach Tripoli. You were to meet her in Tripoli, yes?"

There were several possibilities here, none of them good. Fedeyah was old and powerful. More powerful than a secondhand drop of blood from Asharti after she had drunk from the Old One? He would not like to find out. Then, too, though this man was part of his nightmare, he was also the only one who had treated Ian as a human being. Did that not count for something? Alive, Fedeyah would go to Asharti. If he was dead, she might come looking for him. But only if Fedeyah had told her where he was going. "You know I am not going to Tripoli. Not yet."

Fedeyah nodded. "I guessed as much. When we heard of the death in Casablanca, the tales in Zagora . . ."

"She knows?"

"She knows all." Fedeyah's voice was sad. "Including that I will not kill you now."

"Why did you leave me the water sack of your blood?"

"Only Allah knows that. I do not. I have paid. I will pay again after this day."

"How can she make *you* pay? You are vampire, Fedeyah."

"But she is stronger. She can hold me with her will. I have a body that heals wounds. That does not mean I do not feel pain. It only means that each day I am fresh for punishment."

The horror implied by Fedeyah's flat voice made Ian want to shudder. "You could leave."

Fedeyah shrugged. "Once, perhaps. Only then I did not. Now, there is no fighting back, no leaving." He paused. "She comes back to Kivala regularly, you know. She brings the Old One slaves and drinks of him. She will come back again and again until she is as powerful as the Old One himself. Then Allah help us all."

They thought about that. "Where is she now?"

Fedeyah went flat-eyed. "Wherever she wishes to be."

Ian would not get him to betray her. "If you will not kill me, why are you here?"

"Perhaps to see the fruits of my labor. Perhaps to see you once before you die."

Ian studied the Arab. He shook his head slowly. "You come to see if I am strong enough to be the one to set you free."

Fedeyah said nothing.

"Ah, Fedeyah. . . . We are none of us free of her. Perhaps we never will be."

"She can be killed. Do you know that?"

"Yes. Beatrix Lisse told me. But don't think Asharti's death would set you free." Ian watched the Arab's brown eyes widen slightly. "Only you can do that." He clapped the Arab on the shoulder once and turned toward the camp. Let the man kill him now, if he would.

But nothing happened.

Beth waved at him. "Ian, come inside. It's almost dawn!" she called.

Ian walked deliberately across the sands, past the nestled camels and the drivers settling in to sleep against their sides. At the entrance to the tent he turned.

Fedeyah was gone.

"Who was the Arab man? Was he out here all alone?" Beth asked, lighting a lamp inside the tent. "You must ask him to join us, if only for protection."

"There is only one from whom he needs protection."

Beth froze and stared at him. "Asharti?"

"He has loved her for six hundred years, though he is a eunuch."

"How dreadful," she murmured. "Does he know what she is?"

"Yes. But that does not free him." Ian took a breath. "She knows I am here."

Beth's green-gold eyes were big. She turned and tossed some pillows on the thick sleeping pads set on the sand with a carpet between them. "Then you will need your rest," she said matter-of-factly. "Do you think she can intercept us before we reach Kivala?"

"It depends on whether Fedeyah tells her immediately and where she is now."

"Is he a . . . ?"

Ian nodded. "He was kind to me sometimes, in small ways. And he left his own blood to give me immunity to the parasite. He saved my life. I suppose I should not love him for that."

"I thought you had gotten over thinking about suicide." She put her hands on her hips and cocked her head at him.

"Perhaps this whole expedition is suicide." He grinned, though the expression was lopsided. "So I guess I win either way."

Beth's eyes flashed. She stalked over to him. "This is not a suicide mission, Ian Rufford! If we die, we die seeking a new life, not giving in to some death wish." Her anger startled him.

"I stand corrected," he said raising his brows. He reached out a hand. "We seek new life."

Her anger dissipated as quickly as it rose. She shook his hand, shyly. Her touch had its accustomed effect. He should pull back. But this might be the last night they had together, or the last but one. And he did so want to feel her breasts against him. He gathered her into his chest, feeling her small straight body, tight because it was not sure it should trust his embrace. *Beth, Beth. I so want to be the man you need.* He brushed her hair with his lips and felt the almost pain in his genitals. He was rock-hard in an instant. But for how long? She was right to distrust his embrace. It would break its promise to her. That was part of what he thought he might retrieve from Asharti. He would die at Kivala or begin his return to the world. He let Beth go. She smiled up at him, uncertain. He swallowed and turned away, ashamed of what he had been about to do and the appalling failure to which it would lead. Was there hope for him? He believed the advice he had given Fedeyah, at least. Only he could free himself from Asharti. . . .

They took their readings from the sextant and the chronometer for position at about eleven o'clock the next night, then calculated the seasonal difference between where it would be on the full moon of the half solstice and where it was now. That differential would put it almost exactly between the twin peaks of the tallest mountains in Atlas el Kabhir, the spine of the earth. Beth pored over the scrolls and checked the reference once again by lamplight.

"We are very close now." Beth rolled the papers on which she had recorded their position each night and tied them with a ribbon. Her breeches and boots had become as familiar as the sand and wind to Ian. Indeed, her small form seemed even more feminine in shirt and waistcoat and breeches than in her woman's robes. Ian heard a camel bray behind them. "Watch each ravine opening for one that looks familiar," Beth said.

"They all look familiar," he muttered, dubious.

"We'll take our position frequently," she assured him.

"Let's hope we made the proper conversion for the difference in seasons."

"You confirmed our mathematics with the sailing master of the cutter. I think we're fine."

"Do we have enough water to hold out if it takes some time to search?" Ian asked.

She turned and gazed in the bright light of a moon nearly full to the waiting camels and the men. "I think we can make it back to Haasi Fokra if we find Kivala tonight or tomorrow. It will not be pleasant, but it can be done." She chewed her lip. "I would send one or two back now, but it would be a death sentence if they were set upon by roaming Bedouin or Berbers. There is safety in numbers." She turned and smiled at him. A warm breeze ruffled her disobedient strands of hair. It occurred to him that Beth belonged here, in the desert, as Asharti could never belong with her white skin, no matter that the vampire made herself up to look like an Egyptian goddess. Once he had hated the desert. But one could not hate Beth's place.

He returned Beth's smile and took her arm as they trudged back to the caravan. He found himself seeking her touch, even with its consequences. "We move," he ordered in Arabic.

Beth climbed up to her camel's back, one foot on the beast's knee, turned onto the saddle, her own knee hooked over the horn. Ian mounted his beast in a bound. The camels lurched to their feet, protesting with honking brays all along the line. The men ululated and flicked their sticks. The caravan wound into the desert once again.

For Ian time seemed to have stopped. Day had followed day in such monotony that they were like insects suspended in amber, caught between the need that drove them on and the fear of what lay ahead in a blue-black night above a gray sand. It was almost morning when Ian's new night vision saw a black spot appear along a dune to the east, and then another. He stared. The spots elongated as they rose over the dune and were joined by others. Raiders!

"Run!" he yelled in Arabic. "We're under attack!" He laid his crop across his camel's flank. Cries echoed along the line. He saw Beth glance to the horizon and kick her camel forward. The caravan lumbered out toward the northeast along the sandstone cliffs they had been following, but the animals soon outstripped the men who ran beside them.

They would not outrun their attackers. There were a dozen of them, Berbers by their dress. The swift, small horses skidded recklessly down the dune and galloped out. Ian thumped his heels against his camel and wielded his crop without compunction to catch up to Beth, who had the lead. "We'll never outrun them. Head for that ravine!" He pointed ahead and to the left.

She spotted it and turned her camel's head, yelling in Arabic, "Drivers! The ravine!"

Ian pulled his mount around and saw a straggler lose his head to a curved sword. Ian pulled his pistol from the belt fastened around his burnoose and felled the lead rider. A dozen would be enough to decimate their little caravan. Another driver fell. Camels skittered away. The Berbers yelled in triumph. Ian let fly his second shot. One of the riders jerked back; his horse rocked on its haunches and fell, dumping the rider. Ian threw away the pistol and reached for his other. Two more shots. His blood began to hum.

The remaining four camel drivers and the guide had turned and were trying to make some defense with short swords. But they were no match for the thundering black-robed horsemen.

Ian missed with his next shot or the man just kept coming. Two drivers were down. He shot the leader of the raiders in the head at almost point-blank range. Already dead, the rider jerked at his horse, who stumbled into Ian's camel. Ian went down, scrambling to reach his sword before the others could overtake him. He glanced away to see Beth disappearing toward the sandstone walls. They would not protect her if the Berbers got by him.

Sword out, he scrambled up in time to slash at a rider. The returning slash cut his shoulder. It did not matter. He had to keep these barbarians from Beth. The song in his blood ramped up. He spared only a glance to the falling man, who clutched his side. They might be Asharti's, but they were not vampire, or they would be stronger. Six leaped from their horses, swords drawn. Ian hefted the sword Beth had given him. The black robes and turbans circled him in the waxing light. Six? Only six? He grinned as his Companion surged along his veins. Two more Berbers joined the circle. Very well, eight. He let his eyes go red.

The next moments were a blur. Slashing on both sides. A head rolled and another. His sword found a belly and withdrew. He felt a stabbing pain in his groin. Another stroke he parried. He switched his sword to his left hand and struck out, while his right hand squeezed a throat until his fingers found bone. There were three now. He could see the fear in their eyes. A growl in his throat grew into a roar. He lunged at one and put his sword clear through the man's chest. One of the remaining men shrieked. Both turned and ran. Ian did not run after them. His Companion rose in him. The pain shot through him. Then he was in front of them, turning to face them. They trembled, gibbering. Two strokes and it was done.

He stood in a circle of bloody sand and body parts as the power eased back down his veins. The singing sank to a hum and was gone. Ian blinked.

What had he done? Of twelve, not one was left alive. Most were not whole. He breathed out slowly and dropped the sword. The sound as it hit the sand was loud in the silence of death around him. Twelve Berbers, six drivers . . . Beth!

He looked around him and started for the black slash of the ravine at a run. But again his Companion rushed up through his veins. His surroundings blurred. The pain slashed for a single instant. He was at the ravine. It loomed above him. Beth stepped out of the shadows.

"Ian!" She stumbled to meet him. "Ian, are you hurt?" She touched him, examining him in the dim predawn that she could not see in as well as he could.

He looked down at his own body, realizing his wounds for the first time. His burnoose was splashed with blood, his hands covered in gore to the elbows, but only his shoulder and his groin shrieked and told him he was hurt. "I'll be fine. It won't last long, you know."

"Sit," she ordered. "I'll gather up the camels."

He started to protest. "We need you whole," she said, annoyed. "Be sensible."

He sighed. "Yes, O Sensible One." He slid down against the rock wall as he watched her stand still and cluck to the frightened beasts. To his amazement, not only the camels but also several horses came slowly up to her outstretched hand. She tethered the camels to one another and led one horse. Two others followed meekly. Her air of calm acceptance attracted them. Was that acceptance born of her practical connection to the world? He wished he felt connected. Ever since he had become . . . say it, a vampire, connection to the world of men and animals and living had been growing more tenuous. Now he felt most alive when the Companion was surging through his veins. He didn't like to think about that.

As he watched Beth approach, he could feel his sinews knitting themselves. He was healing faster than he had before. If he concentrated, he could feel the split ligaments in his groin reaching for each other, the blood vessels reuniting. His body was making itself whole—a useful talent, to be sure. His soul wanted wholeness, too. Would that that were as easy.

He leaned back against the rock wall of the ravine, cool now with night. He rolled his head and stared into the darkness as the narrow rift disappeared into the high rock walls. Then he sat straight and looked at the opposite wall, the sand floor, the view out across the desert. A premonition cascaded over him. Uncertainty warred with recognition. He peered into the dark cleft again with sight that now penetrated where human eyes could not have seen. There! He pushed himself erect and took a few steps into the darkness.

A giant's stair was cut into the rock wall with steps impossibly high. The night he had been here with Asharti came flooding back: his exhaustion, despair. His only glimmer of hope had been that he would die, no matter how horrible the death.

The hand on his shoulder made him jump. He swung around and only just stopped himself from striking out at Beth. "For God's sake!" he swore. "You almost got yourself killed."

"Sorry," she said sheepishly. "I called. You did not hear."

He glanced behind her to where she had hobbled one camel and one horse and tied the rest together. His senses sifted the air. Just faintly, he smelled cinnamon and the coming dawn.

Beth studied his face. "Is this . . . ?"

He nodded and strode to the pack animals. "If we hurry, we can make it, if not to the temple itself, then to shelter in one of the tombs before the sun rises very far." He untied two leather water bags, slung them both upon his shoulder, and strode past Beth. He did not wait to see if she followed. Beth would not falter now.

She did not, though she sometimes had to run to keep up. But she did not complain. They passed the great pillars of the entrance to the city. Beth craned to see their capitals as they hurried by. The ornately carved doors to the occasional tombs made her hesitate, but he called her on. He knew how much she wanted to study these most wonderful proofs of her father's dream. But somewhere the sun was already over the horizon.

Once she touched his arm. "What were Berbers doing this far south?" she asked.

"I have no idea," he said shortly, intent on gaining shelter.

She nodded thoughtfully. "Just wondering."

They had walked for more than an hour before they came

to the ruined square, with its toppled columns and desecrated statues. Ian paused to get his bearings. Which way?

Beth wandered over to one huge stone head, chipped and shattered by its fall, and stood staring at it. Ian was drawn to her side. "What is it?"

"You tell me," she said softly.

Ian cocked his head to examine the face. The eyes slanted; the lips were tiny and straight, the nose inhumanly long, the diminutive chin pointed. "A likeness of the Old One? He Who Waits."

Beth gave a shudder, as well she might. Ian wondered for the thousandth time if there was some way he could have avoided bringing her to this godforsaken place. She glanced to another statue, still standing. This one clearly had the head of a sphinx, like the one in Cairo, even down to the fact that the head was a little too small for the body. But the two statues had originally matched, being two sides of an arch. She chewed her lip, speculating. "If they had finished revising both figures, their presence might have been hidden forever." She glanced up at Ian and managed a smile. "Now we know who built the Sphinx so long ago that it could erode from rainfall. Whatever happens, I shall be grateful for that knowledge."

A breath of dawn brought a stronger scent of cinnamon, now tinged with ambergris. Ian shook himself. "Over there." He led the way among the ruins as he felt the sun peek over the wall behind him. He was taking her into a place of unthinkable danger. He must send her back to the surface once she had decoded the entry to the chamber of the Old One. But the camel drivers were dead. What if the Old One killed him? It was not only a possible but also a likely outcome. She had water enough to get back to Haasi Fokra, but she would be alone in a desert that had Berber raiders in it. That had never been the plan.

Berbers. What had Beth said? "What were Berbers doing this far south?" Air hissed in through Ian's teeth. Because they were part of an army that belonged to Asharti? Asharti had every reason to be here in the place that was the source

of her strength. The attackers were not vampires. But only a
hundred or so of her vast hordes would be vampires.

It could be. Suddenly the scent of cinnamon hanging in
the air might have two meanings. Ian grabbed Beth's hand
and broke into a run.

They slid through the archway into the rift on the far side
of the great square just as the rays of the sun stabbed over
the far walls. Ian felt a wash of burning discomfort on the
back of his bare head, and then he reached the protective
shadows of the rift. It was not long before they stood before
the great temple facade. The rosy limestone cut into a thousand fanciful gargoyles and a parade of scenes in bas-relief
all brought back the horrid night when he had lost his humanity. The enormous columns rising to support the wonderful pediment framed a gaping black doorway four men
high that led to the inner chambers where the Old One
waited. Inside lay death, perhaps. Ian stood, the stillness of
the dead city seeping into his soul. Once death was all he
had wanted. That was no longer true. He glanced to Beth. He
wanted life, and he must conquer Asharti to get it.

Beth held her breath in front of the temple. It was beautiful,
just like Petra, and menacing when she remembered what
must lay within. She shuddered, not because she was afraid
of the temple, though she should be, but because she might
be about to fail Ian. Ian looked back at her, his eyes filled
with determination rather than that old helpless pain. No
matter what the obstacles, he must prevail here if he was
ever to be whole in spirit. She *had* to do her part.

She swallowed and followed him into the darkness. They
were weaponless, but no human weapons could best what
lay inside this temple. What would happen if she did open
the door? What would the Old One, whose broken image she
had seen in the square, do when Ian confronted him? But she
had faith in Ian. He would know what to do.

The first room came into view only slowly as her eyes adjusted to the gloom. Dust hung in rays of light emitted by the

open doors. Shadows loomed. Slowly they resolved themselves into giant statues guarding another door. The statues'
heads were ibis, their elaborate collars of gold and lapis
lazuli dimmed by dust. Fantastic! How different from the
empty rooms at Petra. Had those at Petra been looted?

Ian stood looking down at the floor. What? What was that
thrumming in her feet? She wanted to leap back, but it would
do no good. The temple itself seemed to throb. It . . . it felt
like the rhythm of a . . . heartbeat, only faster.

Ian stared up at her. "The blood has changed him. He
lives in our time." Ian looked, well, excited. He held out his
hand for her. "Come. Your part will soon be done."

She hoped to God it would be done successfully. She had
never felt so ignorant and so inconsequential in her life. It
was only the dry warmth and the strength of Ian's hand that
kept her determination up. The clatter of their feet on the
stones threw back echoes as they ran for the black opening
of the passageway between its immense guardians. *Lord,* she
thought, *how much gold and lapis went to make those immense collars?* The passageway led down.

"You will be able to find your way back easily," Ian whispered as they slowed to a walk on the increasing grade. "The
passage leads to only one place."

Beth thought they would descend forever. She could
smell a stronger version of Ian's cinnamon and ambergris
scent, stronger than the Countess's delicate perfume. She
knew what that meant. The throbbing heartbeat of the temple was getting stronger as well. After a time, she could also
see a pulsing glow that matched the throbbing in the floor.
Ian slowed further and pressed himself against one of the
passage walls. She followed his lead as he edged into a room
that took her breath away.

Light! It was filled with pulsing light in a hundred colors.
Light streamed from a central swirling column and corus-
cated across ceiling and walls and a pool of water at its base.
She gasped. "What is it?" The column appeared to be made
entirely of gigantic jewels constantly laved by water from
the fountain. They gleamed bright with every flash.

"I think it is his signal," Ian said slowly. "To the ones who left him here."

She approached, fascinated.

He jerked her back. "Don't look at the individual jewels, Beth. They can drive you mad."

She almost laughed at him. "I'm not that avaricious!"

"Asharti warned me," he said simply.

She stared at him, suddenly serious. There were more things here than she could imagine, so why not jewels that could drive one mad? They circled the fountain warily and entered another downward passage.

"It's not much farther now." Ian had to raise his voice over the thrumming sound, which seemed to be all around them.

He was right. They came to another great set of doors. But these were closed by a rectangular tablet carved with small figures. Beth's moment of truth had come. She squared her shoulders and marched forward into the dim light cast by two great emeralds the size of grapefruits winking in niches nearby.

The thrumming faded from her mind as her eyes raced across the tablature. Her fingers traced the carved stone as though they might see what her eyes could not. The writing was like the Egyptian symbol language unlocked twenty years ago by the Rosetta Stone, and yet not like. Her heart sank to her feet. She could not read it! Failure nipped at her heels and distracted her. She glanced to Ian and shook her head. He smiled, as though he had no doubt of her.

"Look again," he whispered. The heartbeat of the temple receded. Oh, let him not believe in her so implicitly! Her heart seemed to have taken up permanent residence in her throat. She turned back to the stone tablet. Very well. Some symbols were the same. She recognized the symbol for life. What was this? Yes, ancient Arabic; no, Aramaic! Both! And Coptic. Yes, yes, yes! She had been expecting it to be only one language, but it was many. She began again, this time speaking slowly as she translated.

" 'The song swells across the world' . . . no. Larger than the world. The universe?" She nodded to herself. " 'The song swells across the universe. Blood calls to blood. Come for me! Is there no' . . . atonement? Yes—'atonement possible in the length of a life?' " She turned to Ian. "Then this part is set off, you see? Like a quotation. 'That is not . . . dead which can eternal lie. And with strange aeons even death may die.' Then it ends with: 'Forgive me.' "

She turned big eyes on Ian. "How unutterably sad! He has waited here for thousands of years! Do you think his fellows will ever come for him?"

"I do not care to be here when they do," Ian said, his mouth grim.

"Perhaps they were benevolent rulers. Maybe they set us on the path to civilization." Thousands of questions bubbled inside her. Behind this wall was one who could answer them all.

"And perhaps you have forgotten the slaves who must have given their miserable lives to build their pyramids and cut this city out of the stone?"

"Who says slaves built these?" she asked. "Maybe they built them themselves."

They looked at each other, thinking about that. Ian came to himself first. "Slaves shed blood one way or another," he growled. "Now, which symbols make the doors open?"

Beth felt as though she had been slapped. "I . . . I don't know." She looked again to the great tablet. Nothing leaped to mind. She touched each symbol in turn. Nothing happened. She touched every other symbol. Nothing. "Did you see what she touched?" She glanced to Ian and saw his face fall. So much for his blind confidence. Panic rose. She would fail him here. . . .

"I was kneeling behind her and not . . . not well." Even in the green light cast by the emeralds she saw him flush with shame at admitting the extent of his slavery.

But his memory might be the only hope she had. "Think back," she ordered, knowing it would cause him pain. "Can you remember even a single symbol?"

He shook his head in frustration.

"You remember the green light, don't you?" She could not let it go.

He frowned in concentration. "Yes. The thrumming in the floor was slower then, before the blood. My feet were cut, so I was glad to kneel. I was weak, even though she hadn't taken my blood for several days. She meant to offer me to the Old One."

"Where were the other slaves?"

"Behind us, gibbering." Ian's eyes flickered over the lettering. "She turned to the tablet. She jerked my rope. My neck was raw. I crawled behind her."

Beth wanted to take him in her arms and comfort him, but she could not. "And then . . ."

"She read the tablet. She touched various places on it. . . ."

"Any pattern you could see?"

"It seemed random." He peered over her shoulder at the stone. "But . . ."

"But what?" Beth pushed down the frantic beat of her heart.

"I think she touched that symbol, that one there. I remember because the rope cut my neck when she had to reach for it." He pointed to the symbol for blood.

"Do you remember any others?" she asked, a thrill coursing through her.

He shook his head, ashamed of his failure. "No."

The end, then. She had failed. But no . . . wait! There must be some inner sense to the pattern chosen to open the door; a cryptogram within the words themselves. Her eyes darted over the symbols, seeing the words come alive now.

THE SONG SWELLS ACROSS THE UNIVERSE. BLOOD CALLS TO BLOOD. COME FOR ME! IS THERE NO ATONEMENT POSSIBLE IN THE LENGTH OF A LIFE?

FORGIVE ME.

A flutter in her heart sped to her brain. What had the Countess said, like a mantra? Her hands moved over the symbols. Yes, it was here. She pushed at the first symbol. *The.* She could not reach the next. "There," she commanded

Ian. "Touch the one you saw her touch. He reached up and pushed at it. *Blood.* She was sure of herself now. *Is. The. Life.*

The great doors swung open silently, one bearing the huge tablet with the hieroglyphs. Beyond was a black vortex of some swirling viscous substance, like a great unseeing eye ready to suck one into the unknown. She jerked back, aghast.

"Your part is played, Beth," Ian whispered as he stared at the whirling current. He glanced at her and smiled in what he must think was reassurance. The smile was only a little crooked. "Wait for me at the main door to the temple. If I am not out in an hour, leave this place. You can make it to Haasi Fokra. Send word to my brother. He will come for you."

She shook her head. Everything within her protested. "I will not leave you. . . ."

He took her hands. His grip was strong, full of life. He smiled at her, tenderly. "I am so sorry to have dragged you into this. But who else could have opened the doorway?" He squeezed her hands. "Now it is my time upon the stage." He folded her in an embrace. His arms tightened around her as though it was their last contact. He was preparing to sacrifice himself.

This was the embrace she had longed for. Her thoughts raced. Once he had wanted to die. Now he was going into that vortex so desperate to live he would risk what lay beyond. He had purpose. He might have found enough of himself to love her. His embrace said he was willing to build the bridge between them. Why did it come only now, when it might be too late? She couldn't lose him now. "I'm coming with you. I can help . . ." she whispered into his shoulder.

"Too dangerous," he said. "I have seen what he can do. And now he has been roused by blood." She started to protest. He held her away from him and touched her lips with two fingers to still her. "Remember, don't look at the jewels in the signal, my love." She saw the muscles in his jaw clench. "You are brave and resourceful. You can make it back."

He pushed her up the ramp. How could she let him do this alone? She turned to see the vortex bow out at his touch, like bubbling pitch. He thrust himself into it and was swallowed. She ran to the black whorl and pushed at it. Her arm disappeared to the elbow and she leaned into it but couldn't break through. It would not let her in! She threw herself at the center only to bounce back. She stood, appalled. Her chest heaved. Something meant to get Ian alone. There was nothing for it now but to obey him. She forced herself to turn and run up the ramp.

Twenty-one

Ian pushed into the black vortex of whirling viscous fluid, trying to focus on what must be done. He had no idea what might wait for him on the other side of the dark veil. What had been impossible and horrific might have become something even worse with the application of blood. He popped through the blackness and stumbled to the side of the entrance, senses reeling.

The echoing chamber he remembered was still dim and blue. It took a moment for the confusion of the vortex to abate enough for Ian to realize what he was seeing. The huge throne still stood at the far end of the room, but it was empty now. The smell of rotting flesh underlay the heavy cinnamon scent. A pile of putrid corpses lay against the far wall. Movement in the shadows caught his eye. A larger, more attenuated shadow shifted behind the throne.

The Old One paced relentlessly, his form impossibly tall, his steps agitated. Even as Ian watched, he stopped abruptly, turned, and peered at the vortex. He stalked forward into better light. Ian was shocked. His eyes, once so lazy, so eternal, now snapped around the room. His countenance was stretched and . . . raw-looking.

"Where are you, intruder?" he croaked in Arabic Ian could barely comprehend, and his voice was like a wound.

Ian took a breath. This was what he had hoped for. His heart beat in his throat. He knew what he would say. He had no idea if it would work. But there was hope.

"Old One!" he called in university Latin, standing, still, in what light there was from a thousand sapphires, glowing from within. "I have returned."

The head, a parody of human, snapped around. The flat black eyes fixed on him. The Old One went still. "Ah. The one who knows suffering, yet chooses to live," he answered in Latin. How did he know? When he was last here Ian had only wanted to die. Or did the Old One see somehow that Ian had now changed? "You have the Companion. I can smell it."

"Yes. To my cost," Ian admitted, hoarse.

"For that I admitted you. Why do you come to your death when you have stolen eternal life?"

Ian stepped forward as anger took him. "I did not want your parasite. I do not want your life. *She* infected me. Asharti."

"Ah, the one who brings blood." The eyes closed, the vibrations increased in intensity. The forehead creased. "She should not have shared the Companion."

Ian's certainty grew. "The blood is always a mixed blessing, is it not? Life and pain."

"Yes."

Ian could not help but notice that the Old One did not sit, still, upon his throne as he had the last time. Perhaps he could not. Perhaps all stillness had been lost to him. Ian had to take a chance now. He swallowed. All depended upon the next moments.

In the entrance hall, Beth paced under the immense guardian statues of Thoth in their jeweled collars. She could only imagine what might be going on below her, but her imagination was not lacking. Was Ian being torn limb from limb by the Old One? He needed the Old One's blood to

match his strength with Asharti. How could the being
whose likeness she had seen in a broken statue ever give Ian
precedence over Asharti when Asharti brought the blood he
craved?

Each moment was an agony of waiting. The Countess had
told her to have courage in order to help Ian. But Ian
wouldn't let her help. She wanted to scream in frustration! A
pulsing darkness whirled in the entrance. She froze. She
knew what that was. A second pool began to coalesce behind
it. The room was suffused by the scent of cinnamon and ambergris.

The first darkness dissipated and a beautiful woman
stood there, black eyes, black hair, a perfect creamy complexion, and a perfect body, revealed by the gauzy fabric
draped over her shoulder and caught with a golden girdle at
her waist. In that belt, a curved sword swung, its hilt set
with jewels. The swell of her breasts was capped by clearly
visible nipples, and her long fingernails and shorter toenails
were painted metallic gold. She was almost a deity. This
woman could enslave men without using the compulsion of
a vampire.

Beth trembled. Who else could it be? Asharti.

The second pool evaporated, and the tall Arab she had
seen at Haasi Fokra appeared.

Asharti looked around and fixed her gaze on Beth. She
cocked her head. "Was it you who tore my Berbers limb
from limb?" Her aristocratic nose sifted the air. "No. You are
not our kind. Fedeyah!" She turned to the Arab behind her.
"You said you saw my slave."

"Yes, my goddess. It was he who killed the Berbers, not
this human child."

Asharti turned toward the passage, sniffing again. "He is
here. . . . He has defied me! He is with the Old One even
now! I must call him to heel." She stalked toward the dark
portal.

Beth's mind raced. This woman was lethal. But she must
not be allowed to interrupt Ian. He must get what strength he
could before he faced her.

"You think because he was your slave he is still your slave?" she called.

Asharti turned, glanced once over Beth, and said, "Kill her, Fedeyah."

Beth's heart skipped. "He is not. I have set him free." She had no idea what she was saying. She only knew she had to make them listen to her.

"You?" both Asharti and Fedeyah asked, one in derision, one with long-suppressed hope.

"Yes. Which makes me stronger than you are, Asharti."

Asharti sneered. "A human?"

Beth managed a slow smile and nod.

"How?" the Arab asked. His voice was flat, but underneath some emotion surged and was checked. He was concealing his interest in the answer from Asharti.

"The . . . the power of love." Would this woman believe that? Belief washed over Beth. Her voice grew stronger, as she remembered Ian's embrace. "Enough love to erase the scars you left."

"Set him before us," Asharti smirked, "and see whose call he answers." She looked at Beth curiously. "Do you know what he is capable of—the pleasures he can provide a woman?"

Beth flushed. "Yes, but for me he does it willingly."

Asharti growled and it spiraled up until it was a bark of anger. Her fingers formed claws and she advanced upon Beth. Beth tried to stand her ground, wishing she had not gone so far so fast. What could she say to delay the evil goddess now?

"My queen," Fedeyah called. "My queen, why not save her? If he loves her . . ."

Asharti stopped. Her claws relaxed and she tapped one grotesquely long nail on her chin. "You are right, Fedeyah." She grabbed Beth's wrist. "Come, girl. You will see the end."

"Asharti stole peace from both of us when she gave us blood," Ian said to the Old One. "Is the waiting easier when you feel every moment of the passing hours?" Back in England he had imagined the Old One's existence becoming a hell once the blood brought him back to time and need. Had it been mere wishful thinking or was he right? All depended on the answer.

The Old One stopped his incessant pacing. He fixed his basilisk stare upon Ian and lifted his tiny chin. "I refused the blood once," he said, in that echoing rumble that never came from a human chest. "So long ago. I had the courage once to slow time. I no longer have the courage."

"She created your need. Now only she can fulfill it. She exacts a price. She always does."

"That which we long for becomes our curse." The words rumbled from the hanging tapestries to the great throne. "A self-inflicted curse." The Old One began his pacing again. The very air vibrated with a restless power.

"Let me lift the curse." Ian pushed all his hope for the future into this one plea.

The creature stopped and turned. "You?"

"You cannot refuse blood when she brings it. If I kill her, there is no more blood."

"Pain," the Old One mused. "Denial."

"For a while—short in the scheme of things. Then time slows. You can bear the waiting."

"Ahhhh," the creature sighed, and the longing Ian heard in that sigh made all human suffering seem transitory by comparison. The eyes fixed on him again. "You want my blood."

"No, with all my heart. Would I could get rid of the damned Companion altogether. But it is the only way I can best Asharti."

"Why?" The voice vibrated with the very stones of the temple.

"She is creating vampires everywhere. She will destroy the human race, the ones I love, me, unless you give me the strength to stop her."

"You? You are but newly made."

"But I am all there is." He knew he was not adequate to

the task. She was still his master. He hated her for that more, for the first time, than he hated himself for succumbing.

The Old One lifted his stick-thin arms into the dim blue light. "Brothers!" he cried. "I stand at a crossroads. I crave the blood. Yet feeding makes the waiting torture and Asharti uses my strength against the very flock you shepherded for so long. She shares the Companion. What would you have of me?" He waited. The temple vibrated with his essence. No voices answered him. Slowly his arms lowered. His head bowed. "I am so alone. . . . When will you forgive?"

Silence stretched. Ian held his breath.

"It may be aeons until I can go home," came the strange voice—a breath, no more, in the blue dark. "I must suffer the deprivation. How else can I endure the waiting?"

He stalked over to Ian. Ian stood his ground in the face of the overpowering vibrations. The being stretched above him, dwarfing his six feet. Those stick arms held the threat of fantastic strength. Ian had seen it. "You promise you will not bring me blood?"

Ian nodded. "I cannot prevent you from seeking it in the outside world." There could be no lies in this bargain.

"I can prevent that." The Old One held his own wrist to his needlelike canines and ripped a wound there. "Drink," he commanded, and extended his wrist. Blood seeped into Ian's upturned mouth, thicker than any human blood. Its intense taste was sour metal on his tongue. Like rich copper pudding, it slid down his throat, burning. The taste combined with the putrid rotting smell underlying the reek of cinnamon and ambergris. Ian almost gagged and turned away, but the Old One's long, attenuated fingers snaked around his neck and held him there. Ian had made his choice. Now the Old One would hold him to it. He gulped convulsively.

Behind him, the vortex burbled. The Old One was letting someone through. Beth? The Old One might want no witnesses to his gift. He tried to look, but still the Old One held him. Still he was forced to drink the metallic blood.

"Betrayer!"

Ian's heart sank. Asharti! The Old One loosed his hold on Ian, and Ian dropped to his knees and hung his head. The Old One's blood coursed through his veins, burning.

"You give your power to another? It is I who bring you blood! We made a bargain."

Ian raised his head. Asharti stood in front of the vortex, Fedeyah by her side. Her fist was wrapped in Beth's hair as Beth fell to her knees. *No,* he thought, through the fire in his body. *Not Beth.* He struggled to his feet. Why had the Old One let Asharti through the vortex? Ian knew he could control the entrance. One thing was clear. Whatever happened, Ian could not let Asharti hurt Beth. "A bad bargain," he choked. "It's been renegotiated."

"You challenge me?" Asharti spat. "A drop of his blood is not enough."

Ian straightened. Asharti had been given but a drop. He had just gulped more than a cup. Even if she had been back again and again . . . But perhaps volume didn't matter. The burning in his veins and the weakness he felt said that the effect, even of so great a dose, was not immediate. It might actually weaken him to begin with. Yet Asharti was here, now, spoiling for a fight, and she was strong enough to kill Beth with a single blow. Could he keep her at bay until his body could assimilate the blood? He was about to find out. "I challenge you," he managed.

Asharti looked at the Old One, wary. "What outcome do you favor?"

"What will be is now and ever shall be." He sat on his throne. "It is not for me to decide."

A dreadful smile spread across Asharti's face, even as her eyes went red. The Old One would not take sides. She cast Beth aside and pulled out her gleaming sword. With a cry she sprang forward, slashing at Ian.

Ian stepped to the side and her slice hit only air. He would have to sustain some damage to hold her off. First, deprive her of her weapon. She whirled in rage and came after him again. This time he stepped into her swing. The blade sliced his shoulder, but he caught her wrist. She was incredibly strong. He could not win a straight-out contest of strength, so he brought her fist down and jerked his knee up. The blow caught her off-guard. The sword clattered to the stones.

Asharti threw herself against him. Ian braced himself for her weight and got his forearms up even as he kicked at the sword. She would try for his head. The sword went spinning away. She clawed at him, reaching around his defense, leaving bloody tracks on his face and neck. She ripped his burnoose, baring his bloody shoulder. Using all his weight, he crashed his body into hers. She fell back. The fire in him was shooting pain throughout his body. He could hardly see for the veil of black gauze that seemed to fill his head. Asharti threw herself on him again. He lashed out in an uppercut that had his hip behind it. Gentleman Jackson would be proud. Now was not the time for half measures. She staggered back again, but his blow had little effect. Dazed, he stumbled forward to pursue his momentary advantage, but she was up. She hit him a stunning blow to his head. He staggered. She followed with a kick to his ribs. He could feel them break. He fell to his knees. Somewhere he heard Beth crying his name.

Beth! If he succumbed to Asharti, Beth would bear the brunt of her vengeance. He staggered up and turned. The burning in his veins subsided into something bearable. His vision cleared. He could feel his ribs knit, almost instantaneously. His shoulder tingled with healing capillaries. And he felt strong. Maybe not as strong as Asharti, but he was not an easy kill.

He straightened and looked at Asharti, filling his gaze with derision. Asharti made a sound in her throat like some wild animal and threw herself on him once again. She held her fingers with their long nails like a scoop and went for his belly. Disembowelment might not kill him, but it would weaken him. He hit her hand aside and stepped to the left, trapping her other wrist in a grip that was growing stronger. But she twisted away.

"You think you can best me?" she panted as they circled each other. "You who serviced me as many times a day as I demanded it? You who came only when I let you come?"

The old feelings of shame welled from his center. To have Beth hear it said, so bluntly . . .

"Ancient blood makes no difference. I am a master, you my slave," Asharti snarled. Ian felt her will wash over him. She was right! He was nothing. How could he stand against a goddess? He staggered and recovered. But he knew he could not win this day.

"Ian, don't listen!" Beth cried. "She's afraid of you. You aren't the man she could compel anymore. You are vampire."

Ian glanced over to Beth. A trickle of blood from her temple coursed its way down her cheek. In the bluish light the blood was black and her eyes glowed with . . . faith. Faith in him.

"Don't you feel that strength?" Beth asked. "You have ancient blood."

Ian looked back at Asharti. Yes. He did feel strong. The song in his blood was rising.

"The blood is the life," Beth said, dragging herself up to stand against the wall. "That's what Beatrix said. It's not wrong to feel that strength."

"The blood is the life," Fedeyah whispered beside Beth.

"The blood is the life," the Old One breathed.

"She can't compel you," Beth insisted, her voice urgent. "No one can."

Ian felt the breath whistle in and out of his lungs. Blood flowed in him, through him. The Companion hummed in a vibration that ramped up some scale he could not hear. He turned to Asharti. The fire flickering through his veins flapped up into anger. How dare she!

Asharti must have seen his eyes harden, for she threw herself at him with renewed fury, clawing at his body. "You are nothing!" she shrieked. He felt her nails stab into his belly and he thrust her away from him before she could push her whole hand up under his ribs, grabbing for his heart. She slid over the floor just in front of Beth. Ian felt the power shushing through the muscles in his arms. He knew his eyes were red, his canines sharp. The bloody hole in his abdomen was knitting. He was vampire, and he was strong with ancient blood and with his own determination. He would finish it.

Asharti did not attack him. She whirled and grabbed for Beth.

No! Ian lunged forward, but it was too late. Asharti had Beth by the neck from behind. Her other arm embraced Beth's waist, almost like a lover.

Ian went still. He willed the blood song back down the scale. "Kill her and it solves nothing," he said. To his surprise the words seemed to boom inside the stone room. Asharti and Fedeyah both started at the sound. "I will kill you anyway."

"Perhaps I'll take her with me. I enjoy being serviced by a woman once in a while."

"If you escape, I hunt you. You will pay, now or later. Think of it as being written."

Ian saw the speculation in her eyes. Then they flared red. "What have I to lose?" She tore through fabric and through flesh. Blood bloomed across Beth's abdomen. She shrieked in pain. Ian yelled his protest and the temple tolled with it. Asharti leaped for the black vortex. Ian sprang to catch Beth as she fell.

"No, God no, what have I done?" Ian cried, eyes only for Beth and the blood, blood everywhere. An inhuman shriek behind him brought his head around. He saw Asharti stumble back from the vortex. The Old One had closed it.

Asharti turned, her eyes big. The Old One rose from his throne, a grotesque shadow in the dim blue light. A rumble ground out from the narrow chest and turned into a roar. Ian hunched over Beth as if he could protect her. If the Old One was going to kill them, there was nothing Ian could do and he knew it. A feeling of helplessness washed over him as the Old One stalked forward.

"Beth," he whispered, though it was lost in the roar above him. "Beth, I'm sorry."

The Old One loomed above them now. Asharti began to laugh, that throaty laugh. But it had never before sounded so insane. Ian held Beth close and turned his back like a shield as the Old One strode . . . by them. Ian looked up in astonishment. He was closing on Asharti. He had spared Ian and Beth. Asharti wailed, then looked behind her. She was caught between the vortex that wouldn't open and the ancient horror that now hung over her, roaring. Ian saw it all. He knew what would happen here with dreadful inevitability. The Old One had decided he couldn't risk Asharti surviving to bring the blood that made his waiting torture. Ian bowed his head over Beth as Asharti's wail cycled up the scale, along with the roar. The noise was deafening in the stone room.

Then the shrieking stopped, though the roar continued. Ian chanced a look. Pieces of Asharti were being flung in all directions. The Old One was ripping her limb from limb. Blood fountained up and spattered the walls. Fedeyah keened. It was over in seconds. What once had been Asharti was gone. The roaring ceased. In the silence, Asharti's head rolled into the heap of bodies in the corner.

Fedeyah clapped a hand over his mouth to prevent his screaming. Ian felt his gorge rise. The Old One straightened and licked the blood from one long finger with a slender, supple dark tongue. The silence stretched. The Old One's flat black eyes flicked up to Ian.

"I . . . I thought you would not make a choice." Ian's voice shook, all trace of power gone.

"Perhaps it was written that I would choose; thus the end that was written was achieved."

"What will you do with us?" Ian asked. Fedeyah looked incapable of speaking.

"Do with you?" The Old One looked at the three of them. "I will do what is written."

Ian nodded and rose slowly, shifting Beth to carry her. He could feel her blood, warm against his flesh where the

burnoose was torn away. He clutched her to him and made
for the vortex. "Come on, Fedeyah," he muttered. He must
get Beth to safety before he could tend her wound, before the
Old One decided that they, too, were a menace.

He could feel the power of the Old One throbbing at his
back. Would he let them through the vortex? Ian stumbled
ahead. The voice boomed out once more. He stopped in his
tracks.

"She will die."

Ian looked down at Beth. She lay limp in his arms, her
head lolling back, baring her lovely neck. Blood soaked her
clothing and there in her midriff was a horrible gaping hole
through which tissue could be seen pulsing. He let out a
whimpering sound that didn't seem human. He turned to the
Old One, inarticulate with pain, unable even to protest.

The Old One sat, deliberately, on his throne. He went still
and watched Ian for an excruciating moment. "You have the
ancient blood," he said deliberately. "There is life for both of
you in it. Go. I do not wish to know what you will do. You
will do what is written."

Ian stared at him, trying to understand. Did he mean . . . ?

"Stay . . . ahead . . . of the vortex," he said. His voice had
slowed.

Ian whirled and saw the black whorl that was the door to
this fantastic chamber begin to pulse and grow. "Come on,
Fedeyah, we're getting out of here." He shoved the Arab into
the spinning blackness with his hip and plunged after him,
clutching Beth.

The gelatinous liquid of the vortex sucked at him. He
held his breath and thrust ahead, finally popping out into the
corridor into the dim green light from the two emeralds. He
stumbled. Fedeyah was just scrambling up. The vortex
tugged at Ian's foot. It was expanding. "Let's *go*!" Ian
shouted, and ran up the incline. The sound of rumbling, like
grinding stones, followed them. Ian glanced back and saw
the giant stone doors crumble into dust as the black goo of
the vortex whirled out. God! The Old One was going to
bring the roof down.

Ian concentrated all his strength on running, trying not to think of the thunder behind him or to remember Beth's wound. The fountain of jeweled light glowed through the doorway. He dashed past. He glanced back to see if Fedeyah followed or had been ground to dust. The Arab lunged just ahead of a boiling blackness that was gaining momentum. The fountain of jewels glowed through the blackness. The room around the pool did not collapse, but as the vortex passed into the passage beyond, the grinding sound resumed and grew in intensity.

Ian put his head down and concentrated on covering ground. His lungs ached. His legs throbbed as the passage grew steeper. He shot through the doorway under the guardian statues as blackness rolled out behind him. It seeped forward as he plunged for the temple doors.

He was out, into the sun. The blinding light seared his eyes as well as his skin. His burnoose hung off one shoulder, exposing his flesh to sunlight. He made a dash to shelter in the shade at the far side of the ravine, slowing to catch his breath. He hung, panting, clinging to Beth as the red and gold stonework of the temple began to crumble. Blackness whirled in the doorway.

The Old One was burying himself under tons of rock, leaving only the pulsing signal to his faraway compatriots and the throne room where he would wait for them. He would not need will power to refuse the blood. It was done.

Ian glanced to Fedeyah. Pain was writ plain in the man's face. "So, she is gone."

The Arab's chest heaved as though there were not enough air in the whole of Africa to sustain him. "Am I free?" Who he asked, no one could tell, least of all Fedeyah. "Gods!"

Ian followed Fedeyah's gaze. The blackness rolled out across the sand, reaching for them. "It isn't finished!" Ian yelled. Clutching Beth, he ran along the ravine wall. The grumble of collapsing stone grew louder. Then it was out into the searing afternoon sun that lit the open square. He would never make it before passing out from the pain, he thought, remembering another time he had exposed himself to open sunlight. His flesh blistered. He would not die from sunlight, but Beth would die if he didn't keep ahead of the vortex. He pumped his legs, covering yards at a stride. The vortex gained. He looked for Fedeyah but didn't see him. Around him, darkness rolled up like a sandstorm. Pillars crumbled and crashed. The great steps of the amphitheater tumbled. Pain coursed through him. He would not make it.

Wait! There was an answer. It was so risky he wanted to scream. Could he take Beth with him? But there was no choice. He stopped. The rumbling overtook him. *Companion. Come to me. Come fast.* Power whooshed along his veins in one smooth swell. Dimly he was aware of dust clogging his lungs, stones under his boots caving in. It did not matter. He was still. And the blackness that whirled around him and Beth for a single instant held them in time and space until . . .

Sun hit the crown of his head like a blow. He stood in front of the opening to the ravine, holding Beth. Darkness dissipated around them. The mouth of the ravine was silent, but he could hear the grinding sound and the wall of dust approaching. Ignoring the pain of the sun on his body, he strode out into the open desert, away from whatever might emerge from the ravine, before he turned.

Black liquid was flung into the sky above for two hundred feet. The vortex raced toward them. A smaller darkness circled beside them and Fedeyah shrieked as he popped through into the calm. He stumbled to his knees in front of Ian and Beth. As the vortex approached the open desert, the impenetrable black began to collapse in on itself. In seconds, it was gone, leaving only scrubbed stone walls and eddies of sand that slowly stilled. The giant's stair had disappeared.

Ian knew that if they went back along the ravine, they would find no trace of Kivala.

He looked down at Beth, ignoring his flesh searing in the sunlight. Her face was gray. Sticky blood covered her clothes and his blistered skin. Was she dead? Lord, he should not have jostled her so! He set her gently down and touched her throat. A tiny, erratic pulse still beat there. It was not too late.

Ian knew what he had to do here. The Old One had told him he could save her, but only by damning her to his own hell. Did he have the right to make her into the monster that he was? He took a breath. Right or no, he could not let her die because she had helped him. And he could not live without her. So simple—so horribly complex. There was no time for Hamlet's hesitation. He knew he would do this, so he might as well get on with it.

Kneeling, he called to his Companion. He put his hand over his blistered chest. A smile came unbidden to his lips. *Companion mine, come to me. Sing in my veins with the power of ancient blood.* He did not have to ask twice. He felt his eyes go red and power hum along his arteries. His canines lengthened. The pain of the sun receded. He glanced back at Fedeyah, who stood gazing at the ravine with haunted eyes and heaving chest. Fedeyah would not interfere.

Cradling Beth, he opened her jaw, slashed his wrist with a single sharp tooth, and concentrated on pushing his blood down his veins and into her mouth. "Drink, my love," he encouraged softly, even as the power sang in him. "The blood is the life."

She couldn't swallow, but he held her up so the blood slid down her throat. *Now let's see what the blood of an Old One can do.* Could it heal her before she got immunity to the Companion? Would she be as sick and fevered as he was for so long when Asharti had infected him? He refused to think about the worst and instead remembered that the Old One thought she could be saved. If it took the last drop of his blood, he would do it.

Beth swallowed convulsively, coming to consciousness. He held his wrist to her lips. She looked up at him, questioning. Then, with faith in him gleaming in her eyes, she suckled at his wrist, drawing at his wound. Her hands snaked up to hold his wrist at her mouth. She smiled at him as she sucked and licked his wrist tenderly. He cra-

"I hope so," Ian said. "His signal still pulses and he has suffered enough for remaking us in his image. Even gods should be forgiven."

Fedeyah bowed. "I must leave you. With your permission, I will take a horse."

"Of course." Ian's brows were drawn together in concern. "Where will you go?"

Fedeyah snorted derisively. "Who cares? What purpose has my life now?"

"Give yourself time, Fedeyah," Beth whispered. She could feel his pain. He was glad Asharti was dead, and devastated.

"Time is what I have."

Ian held out a hand, but he did not stand. Fedeyah took Ian's hand, shook it once, and strode toward the camels.

"Fedeyah!" Ian called. The Arab turned. "If you can't find worth in yourself, perhaps one day someone will find it for you."

The Arab chuffed out a breath, and a small smile touched his mouth. "Worth is earned, English, and I have done nothing to earn it."

Dim horsemen appeared at the crest of a dune. "Asharti's followers," Ian said. The resolution in his voice said he was ready to fight against any odds.

"I'll give them the bad news. They will not trouble you." Fedeyah glanced up at the late-afternoon sky. "Perhaps I'll go to Casablanca. Asharti left some rubbish that requires removal."

"Others of our kind will join you. Beatrix will bring them. Don't risk too much."

Fedeyah touched his forehead. "Good-bye, English."

They watched him stride away.

"Much as I hated her, I think he loved her that much." Ian's voice was distant, reflective.

"I suppose that means there's hope for him," Beth said. Ian turned his gaze on her. It was hesitant, questioning. "If someone can love her, they can certainly love him." Beth tried a smile. Dared she admit how much she loved Ian?

Now that he had given her his blood, what had happened to their bargain? Now he didn't need her anymore.

They watched the sun set and twilight set in, Beth's head against Ian's shoulder. It was as if they could not move. Whether it was shock or just the demand of their new blood for time to settle in, Beth could not tell, but the time of quiet steadied her. She listened to Ian's flesh repairing the burns. She thought about the life ahead with new blood in her veins. She wasn't frightened of being vampire, as long as she had Ian.

Why not? Why wasn't she afraid? It would be a strange life. She was now strange herself. But had she not always been an outsider? In Africa they thought her white; in England she was the strange Egyptian girl. And she had always been a mystery to herself, uncomfortable with her mother's blood in her veins. But it was her mother's blood that drew her to Africa and to love the mysterious. Like Ian. Like herself? She had wanted to solve Ian's mystery, but it was the answer to her own riddle she had been seeking all along. In some ways the mystery now was solved. She was vampire. She loved Africa. She loved Ian.

As true night fell, the singing in her veins turned to irritation. She shifted in Ian's arms.

"What is it, Beth?" His voice was anxious.

"Nothing."

"You need blood." She saw his eyes go red. His canines lengthened and he opened the inside of his elbow this time. "Drink," he commanded.

She leaned into his arm and drew at the wound. The wonderful warm liquid flowed through her, calming the irritation, softening the song even as it strengthened into some chorus that made her feel whole. Life! The blood is the life. She throbbed with it as she raised her head.

"Better?" he asked.

She nodded and smiled at him. "Better perhaps than I have ever been."

Ian cleared his throat. "I am so sorry for burdening you with this horrible condition. If there had been any other

choice . . ." He searched for words. "It was my fault you
were injured in the first place. I brought you here." His eyes
locked with hers, regret shining in them.

"I have no regrets." His gaze turned, wondering. Then
he held her tighter and his eyes went indigo dark, a fact that
she could never have seen in this light before she took his
blood. The air around them seemed to vibrate. That vibration touched places that made her shudder. His head
dipped toward hers. She waited breathless, his scent wafting over her. Then he shook his head as though to clear it
and set her gently against the wall of rock. He got to his
knees and offered a hand to help her up. "We should go, if
you feel up to it."

Beth felt the loss of his electric touch. He still
wouldn't, couldn't, build a bridge across the gulf that had
opened between them on their wedding night. But everything had changed. She had felt his love when he embraced her and sent her to the surface. He had done
something abhorrent to him when he made her like him,
just to save her life. If there was to be a bridge across their
gulf, it must be built now, before it opened wider. If he
could not do it, she must.

This was the moment the Countess had been talking
about. Now was when she must have courage if she wanted
to help Ian, help them both. She took her future into her own
hands. She must try for what she wanted. And what she
wanted was clear with her new sight. "May I use some water
to clean up and change my clothes? We have plenty now
there are only two of us. And have you had time to fully
heal?"

Ian's mouth was mobile. Was it a smile? His eyes were
soft. "You are always so practical." He looked down at his
chest and fingered his shoulder. "I think so."

"I'll need some lessons, you know. You don't intend to
abandon me, do you?" She could hardly credit her boldness.
But she had no choice. Or maybe she had choices for the first
time.

"Like Asharti abandoned me? I should think not!" he

sputtered. He made a wry mouth. "Though the news will not be good." He reached to take her hand, then thought better of it and gestured to the camels, now nestled for the night.

"News? I know most everything." She walked into the open desert. The night was warm. The moon was rising in the east. It would be almost full. Already it silvered the sand and made Ian glow. Or perhaps it was the Old One's blood that shone from him. "I know about the immortality, the sensitivity to sun, your ability to compel, the blood, the disappearing. If there are other things, you will tell me and I will know them, too. It isn't bad. It just is."

He stared at her for a long moment, then wrenched himself away. "I'll lay out the bedrolls and pitch a tent," he growled. "You must be tired." He stalked away.

She had never been so far from tired. She was strong and alive and knew what she wanted. Unstrapping a water pouch, she mentally counted those remaining. Yes. They could easily spare this one. She could feel him moving behind her.

Now she must go carefully. She must let him come to her and trust that the resolution she had seen in him, the fact that Asharti was dead, and the sureness brought by the Old One's strength would counteract the shame and horror that had come between them. But to let him come to her, she would have to be bolder than she had ever thought possible. She must forget that she was short and brown, with odd-colored eyes. She must trust the singing in her blood and be what she was, who she was, without regret. She and Ian were kind to kind now.

Remember the embrace in the temple, she told herself. *Remember that Father always said your mother was the most beautiful woman in the world.* How much did she want Ian?

Enough to be bold. She took off her boots.

He finished pitching the tent. She could feel him standing behind her. His vibrations rolled over her. She might always know where he was, now. Half-turning, she said, "Can you hold the water bag and pour it over me?" She kept her back turned as she unbraided her hair and shook it out. She found the strength somewhere to just let him wait. His breathing grew uneven.

She turned and cupped her hands. He stepped forward (dear God—the nearness of him!) and squirted water into her hands. She splashed her face. And then she did the bravest thing she'd ever done. She looked him right in the face, smiled, and pulled her shirt over her head and tossed it aside. "Can you pour, please?" she asked.

He looked stunned, gulped, and held the water bag over her head. His reaction gave her courage. Water cascaded on her upturned face. She splashed it over her neck, smoothed it over her bare breasts, and rinsed the half-dried blood from her abdomen. "Oh, that feels good," she murmured. The water stopped. She paid no attention but busied herself with her belt and her buttons and slid her wet trousers down. Her breasts hung as she bent to free her feet.

When she straightened, she held out her hands for more water. "This blood is very sticky," she remarked as she splashed her belly and rubbed. His breathing was a series of ragged gasps. The muscles in his jaw and his strong throat worked. She was having trouble controlling her own breathing. Her nipples were tight. Her breasts felt almost as swollen as the mound at her groin. There was no mystery about what her body wanted. It wanted to finish what they'd started on their wedding night. He wanted that, too. Needed it, she wagered, in many ways. She must give him a chance to prove to himself that Asharti was really dead and her power over him gone.

"Beth," he said, as though it were torn from him against his will. She looked up and tried to feign surprise. His eyes were dark with desire. There was no mistaking the tension in his body. His hands were clenched at his sides, one clutching the water bag.

Only the certainty that he did not want to resist, that he was only unsure he could build the bridge, allowed her to reach out and cup his jaw with her hand.

"Ian . . ." She stepped into him, brushing her breasts

against the burnoose and his bare chest. Now she could feel his swollen member. She smiled. "I love you."

"I can't," he said through clenched teeth.

"She's dead and we're alive, so very alive. Of course you can," she whispered. Doubt lingered in his eyes. Somehow she had to push him, yet let him come to her. "If you don't love me, I understand." But she did not pull back. She looked up and watched him struggle.

"Of course I love you. You know that. Don't pretend you don't," he said crossly. "I've loved you since the *Beltrane*."

She ran her palm over his chest. The skin was smooth again, except for the scars. He had healed. But he was hot to the touch. She pressed herself into him and felt the throb of his erection and heard his sharp intake of breath. The vibrations humming at the edge of her consciousness ramped up another notch. "Then there is only one thing to do, isn't there? The blood is the life."

His embrace was sudden and strong. He held her head against his chest. "Beth . . . Beth. After what I've done to you? You don't know what it means yet, but you will."

"I think neither of us really knows what it means. Already I feel the flush of life the Countess spoke of." She looked up at him. "Is it not wonderful?"

His eyes scanned the horizon, seeing nothing. "Yes. Too wonderful. Asharti felt this."

"We are not Asharti."

He looked down at her, his eyes alive with emotion. "No."

For the second time that day he lifted her effortlessly into his arms. He ducked under the tent flap and laid her on the blankets carpeting the sand. He kissed her and she kissed back, their tongues searching each other's mouths. He held her against him and pressed his loins to hers, letting her feel the full extent of his erection. She held his head, kissing him, moving her hips against him. The blood beating in her body began to sing. A silly word, but the only description she could think of. She was wet and ready. She had been ready for more than a month.

His burnoose was in the way of pressing more of her flesh

against his. She grabbed it, meaning only to pull it away to bare more of his body, but it ripped to the hem. She was stronger than she thought. It didn't matter. He was naked now. That was what she wanted. He moaned into her mouth and moved his knee between her thighs. She rubbed her moist flesh up and down his leg. His vibrations cycled up again.

He pulled his mouth away, panting, and swallowed. Beth knew he was going to try to delay his own pleasure again for hers. Not this time. This time she wanted his ecstasy more than she wanted her own release. His hand slid down between her thighs.

"Time enough for that," she breathed. "We have unfinished business."

He looked startled. Was he hurt by the reference to his failure? She would not give him time to be hurt. She smiled at him tenderly and pushed her fingers through that lovely long hair. "Let me feel you inside me, please?" She brushed her nipples across the light hairs covering his chest. At least he wasn't thinking about his scars. She licked his throat, producing another moan.

"She-devil," he murmured.

"Yes." She moved one thigh up over his. "And no. Only your Beth."

He rolled her on her back with something like a growl. She lifted her hips instinctively. His cock pressed at her opening. He entered slowly, pushing and withdrawing, thrusting inside her a little farther each time until he pressed fully home. She felt the exquisite sensation of opening to him, almost discomfort, almost ecstasy. She rocked against him, moaning, cupping his buttocks as they bunched and released. She wanted more! He pushed in and out faster. Yet she could feel he was trying to hold himself back, trying to prolong the experience. Her blood was shouting at her now, a chorus with his, their vibrations intertwining and humming up some scale she'd never heard before. She wanted more of him. She rocked against him, faster. He slid inside her and out, the muscles in his arms rock-hard as he braced himself above her. Her legs coiled around his waist and her hips bumped against him in counterpoint to his thrusting. She heard the panting and the small sounds that escaped their throats as though from far away.

Then she heard nothing but the blood screaming in her veins and saw nothing but light bursting. She felt him still against her, except where his cock jerked rhythmically. She herself spilled over into vibrating white light, contracting in her turn again and again as he thrust in and out again. At last they froze, locked in receding rapture, for what seemed an age. Was this like dying? Did he feel this way, too?

It was over. Beth clenched her eyes shut and felt the buzz in her head. God in heaven! Well, she would not have to ask Ian whether he had found his pleasure. She opened her eyes.

He kissed her softly. "Beth," he murmured. "Beth. Your name is like breathing."

She liked that. He lowered himself gently and rolled with her to the side, embracing her, still inside her. She liked that, too.

They stayed that way for a long time, shuddering with aftershocks. Finally he eased out of her. She ran her hands over his body, saying nothing. He cupped her neck and kissed her, gently. Her blood hummed faintly now. But she could feel that she would want him again. Soon.

"I think I will find this marriage very convenient," she remarked, brushing her lips across the damp skin at his throat.

"Ever practical Beth," he murmured.

Had she said something wrong? He must have felt her stiffen. "Shuush," he said. "It is only one of the things I love best about you."

She relaxed into his arms, running her hands across his burly shoulders. The whip scars were still there. They always would be. Perhaps they would not matter so much to him anymore. "Men are lucky," she said. "They have so much more experience of loving than women."

"Not like this they don't. Take my word for it." He was kissing her ear. Another thing she liked. "Maybe it's the

Companion." He looked down at her. "That is what shares our blood."

She sighed. "Companion. Well, it has its good points then. I'm glad we will have a very long time to do more of this."

He lifted up his head, so he could look at her. He would be able to see her in the darkness as well as she could see him. "You . . . you accept it so much better than I ever did."

"Your only experience was of Asharti. My only experience is of you."

"People will call us monsters." His anxiety was ramping up again. "Are we damned?"

She smiled. "Could the Companion not be a gift from God instead of a curse?"

"I don't think God contemplated vampires."

"No? I'm not sure what God contemplates. Maybe he contemplates everything."

"We are an aberration." His voice was bitter.

"Wherever the Old One comes from, he is not an aberration. Is God not there? There are others of our kind, like the Countess, even here. I liked her." She lifted herself up on one elbow. "I don't pretend to know much about God. But I feel in my heart that he counts on us to make choices. And if I'm wrong, if there is no God, then we must make choices on our own. Either way, we can but try to make good choices, even with his most mysterious gifts."

"It's going to be difficult, Beth," Ian said, a note of sternness in his voice.

"Maybe good and easy don't go together. But I feel alive. I love you. Isn't that good?"

He kissed her and crushed her to him. She could feel the growing effect her body was having on his, just as she felt her humming blood begin to sing again. "I love you, Beth. I want to be with you in Africa, where you are most at home, or wandering the world, or in a drawing room in England, or in Casablanca fighting the remainder of Asharti's army. It doesn't matter. I guess I'm glad to be alive." He seemed in awe of that fact.

"The blood is the life." She believed it. He might come to believe it, too. The future beckoned. She ran her hand over his hip. His vibrations hummed up the scale. He bent to kiss her. His breath smelt like cinnamon. Cinnamon and ambergris.

Don't miss

The
Hunger

by

Susan Squires

Beatrix Lisse is the toast of London society. But no one knows the secrets behind this mysterious beauty. And no one knows that Beatrix has a sworn enemy named Asharti—an enemy who is about to destroy the one man who can save Beatrix's tormented heart...

Coming in October 2005

From

ST. MARTIN'S PAPERBACKS

H 01/05